Praise for *Ransomed Dreams* and other novels by Sally John

"*Ransomed Dreams* is another wonderful weave of compelling characters, poignant pacing, and the twin truths that forgiveness is costly but love can meet the expense head-on. Sally John is an insightful, inspiring storyteller."
SUSAN MEISSNER, author of *The Shape of Mercy*

"Sally John has done it again—interesting characters, exotic locations, and a compelling storyline. The unexpected twists in the protagonist's life left me evaluating the sources of my own sense of security. Thought provoking."
KATHRYN CUSHMAN, author of *Leaving Yesterday*

"*Ransomed Dreams* is another inspiring story from Sally John that profoundly touches the heart. This novel will captivate readers with its characters, intrigue, and twists and turns. A must-read for anyone who has lost their way and their dreams to discover hope!"
SUSAN WALES, author and producer

"Sally John delivers an intense and emotionally satisfying reminder that our lives can change in a heartbeat."
ROMANTIC TIMES on *In a Heartbeat*

"Talented author Sally John weaves a web around her readers, drawing them into her characters' world. . . . Oh what a satisfying read—one of the best of the year."
NOVEL JOURNEY on *The Beach House*

"[Sally John] writes an enthralling story with fully developed characters that are experiencing problems that many women of faith face daily. And she does it with warmth, realism, and sensitivity."
ARMCHAIRINTERVIEWS.COM on *The Beach House*

"Once in a very long time, a book comes along that has the ability to touch hearts, change lives, and inspire hope. *Castles in the Sand* is one such book. . . . A profound, inspiring read of a family torn apart and the longed-for home."
READERVIEWS.COM

Praise for *Borrowed Dreams* and other novels by Sally John

RANSOMED DREAMS

RANSOMED
dreams

SALLY JOHN

Tyndale House Publishers, Inc.
Carol Stream, Illinois

Visit Tyndale's exciting Web site at www.tyndale.com.

Check out the latest about Sally John at www.sally-john.com.

Ransomed Dreams

Designed by Jennifer Ghionzoli

Edited by Kathryn S. Olson

Published in association with the literary agency of Alive Communications, Inc., 7680 Goddard Street, Suite 200, Colorado Springs, CO 80920, www.alivecommunications.com.

Library of Congress Cataloging-in-Publication Data

John, Sally, date.
Ransomed dreams / Sally John.
p. cm. — (Side roads ; 1)
ISBN 978-1-4143-2785-3 (pbk.)
1. Married people—Fiction. 2. Life change events—Fiction. 3. Victims of violent crimes—Fiction. 4. Invalids—Care—Fiction. 5. Americans—Mexico—Fiction. I. Title.

PS3560.O323R36 2010
813'.54—dc22 2009054157

Printed in the United States of America

16 15 14 13 12 11 10

7 6 5 4 3 2 1

In memory of

Kyle John,

1981–2008

Your own ears will hear him.
Right behind you a voice will say,
"This is the way you should go,"
whether to the right or to the left.

ISAIAH 30:21

Acknowledgments

The characters in this book know much more than I do about the Spanish language, art, Chicago, Mexican food, Catholicism, cartoons, Scriptures, words in general, and phrases in particular. For help in these areas and more, I am hugely indebted to Sue Laue, Karlie Garcia, Kelly Paige Standard, Yolanda Larez, Troy Johnson, Joe and Laura Irrera, Carrie Younce, and the John ladies—Aliah, Kaiya, Tracy, and Elizabeth. Thank you all!

Thank you to those who make possible my dream of turning a story idea into a book with pages, cover, and a place on a bookshelf so that others might read it: Lee Hough, Alive Communications, and the entire Tyndale family.

Thank you to the gifted editors who refined the work and cared as much as I did for it: Karen Watson, Stephanie Broene, Lorie Popp, and Kathy Olson.

And as always, for their unfailing support and prayers, thank you to friends at Church of the Advent; my son, Christopher; and my husband, Tim.

Prologue

CARACAS, VENEZUELA

At precisely twelve minutes, thirty-five seconds past ten o'clock in the morning Venezuelan time, Sheridan Montgomery's world ceased to exist.

She lay on a sidewalk, not quite facedown, not quite on her side. A crushing weight pinned her against the flagstones. A hand gripped her head viselike, pressing her cheek into the cool, rough surface. Her left arm protruded from beneath her at an awkward slant, aligning her wrist mere centimeters from her eyes.

She gazed at her watch. Its crystal was a web of fine veins. The second hand did not move.

Twelve minutes, thirty-five seconds after ten.

Eliot had given her the watch four years before, on their fifth anniversary. She had protested at the sapphires that ringed its face, at the twenty-four-carat-gold and silver band. It was too beautiful, she said. Too elegant.

"Elegant?" He had laughed. "With numbers big enough for Big Ben?"

"Still," she had said. "Sapphires?"

"Small ones. For a touch of sparkle."

A touch of sparkle. It was how he described her. The nickname began when they got engaged. She didn't want a diamond ring, just a simple gold band. He honored her choice, saying she was the only touch of sparkle needed.

She had kept the watch for his sake. Eventually she grew to appreciate its large numbers that helped her notice the time. She was still late to everything, but not *as* late. The graceful sweep of the second hand became a reminder to slow down and savor the moments.

She blinked again. The watch still read twelve minutes, thirty-five seconds past ten.

Pain ripped through her, an excruciating wrench from stomach to chest to throat. She opened her mouth, but the scream would not come. She had no breath.

"Let's go!" a voice above her roared.

Air slammed into her lungs, searing her throat. She gagged.

"Sher!" The voice again, softer, a rush of hot air at her ear. "Sher!" It was Luke. The grip on her head loosened. The weight shifted.

Chaos bombarded her senses. Loud shouts. Shrieks. People a blur of motion. A pungent scent. A dryness like a mouthful of cotton. Arms encircling her, roughly jerking her upright.

And then she saw it.

The scream still would not come, only a mewling, its sound lost in the raging clamor.

Luke held her tightly to himself, moving them as one, her feet scarcely touching the ground. He rushed them away.

Away from the pandemonium.

Away from *it*.

Away from the sight of her husband sprawled facedown, the back of his ivory linen suit coat turning to a brilliant shade of scarlet in the morning sun.

PART
one

CHAPTER 1

TOPALA, MEXICO
EIGHTEEN MONTHS LATER

Like everything about the small village tucked into the foothills of the Sierra Madres in central Mexico, sunrise was a leisurely event.

Sheridan waited for it, tea mug in hand, shawl over her cotton nightgown, bare feet chilled against the tile floor of the second-story balcony. Alone, she listened in the dark to the squawk of roosters and clung to their promise that the world would once again know light.

"Oh, good grief," she murmured to herself with a groan. "That is so maudlin. Truly and hopelessly maudlin. You might try something more chipper. Something like . . . Something like . . ." Her foggy brain offered nothing.

She scrunched her nose in defeat. The morning had shuffled in on the heels of a sleepless night. *Chipper* was not going to happen, no matter how hard she tried to talk herself into it.

If she could turn the calendar back eighteen months, she would not be talking to herself. No. Eliot would be right next to her, responding, most likely pointing out a dozen chipper thoughts in that funny way of his.

Nostalgia and regret hit her, a powerful one-two punch that still took her breath away. She clenched her teeth, waiting for it to pass, mentally spewing forth a verbal attack at the counselor who had promised her that time healed all wounds, that month by month they would see improvement.

What drivel that was! Eighteen months—or to be more precise, seventeen months, three weeks, and two days; but who was counting? All that time had passed and only one thing was healed: Eliot's gunshot wound. His other wounds, the invisible ones, still oozed like toxins from a waste dump site. He was not the same man she had married.

Sheridan took a deep breath and let the bitter argument go. Nostalgia and regret settled back down into whatever corner of her heart they'd found to hide out in. Their impact, though, lingered.

Would time ever erase her longing for the Eliot she had married? The animated one, the one others adored, the one who was *engaged* in every detail of life, whether simple or complex, with every person who crossed his path. The one from B.C.E., Before the Caracas Episode. Now, in their A.C.E. days, he might as well be a deaf-mute for all the interest he showed in the world around him.

Sleep deprived, she totally blamed him. She didn't mean to. It wasn't like he had much of a choice. The bullet that shattered his nerves shattered their life. Everything about it was over. Health, career, home, friends. All gone. Kaput. Some days she barely recognized herself and Eliot. Where were the Mr. and Mrs. Montgomery she once knew? These routines, hometown, health, acquaintances, and even personalities seemed lifted from the pages of some stranger's biography.

"Oh, honestly. Get over it already, Sher." She forced a swallow of tea and focused on the scene before her.

A lone sunbeam pierced between two mountain peaks and sliced into the distant mists. Another followed. And another and another until finally pure light broke free. Valleys and canyons burst into sight. Loud birdsong erupted. Then, as if God had uncurled His fist, long fingers of sunlight shot forth and touched the wrought-iron railing where she stood.

It was achingly gorgeous.

Sheridan flicked at a tear seeping from the corner of her eye. "You should have stayed in bed, you foolish, stubborn woman."

Sunrises were the worst because they represented the best of what had been.

Most days she could ignore that thought. Evidently not today. She and Eliot were morning people. *Had been* morning people. Their daily ritual of tea and conversation at an east-facing view, awaiting dawn, was seldom missed. With crazy-full schedules, they needed such a time to relate on the deepest levels. Some days their hearts positively danced and sang in union. Naturally, through the years the tune changed now and then, the tempo sped up and slowed down, but the music never stopped. It never stopped. They always talked. They always connected.

Until that day in Caracas.

Now she watched sunrises by herself.

"You really should've stayed in bed."

But it was so beautiful. And it went on and on like a slow waltz. At the bottom of her street now, purple haze still shrouded the town square. The sky brightened in slow motion above it, the fiery ball itself still hiding behind a peak.

Something moved in the semidarkness below. A person. Early risers were not uncommon, but she was startled. Something felt off about this one.

Or was that just her hypervigilance? Compliments of the incident in Caracas, it kicked into gear at times without warning, filling her with anxiety and suspicion.

Now she could see that it was a man. He passed the bandstand, his strides too deliberate for a villager, too American. He headed straight for the steep incline that led up to her house. In city terms, the distance was perhaps a block. In Topala terms, it was simply up beyond the sculptor's shop.

The sun overtook the peaks and the man came into view.

"No way." Her heartbeat slowed, but not quite to normal.

Even with his face concealed by a ball cap, his body clothed in a generic khaki jacket and blue jeans, a city block separating them, she recognized him. She recognized him simply because the air vibrated with him.

Luke Traynor owned whatever space he occupied.

Sheridan set the mug on the table beside her, tightened the shawl around her shoulders, and massaged her left arm. She felt no surprise at his unannounced arrival nor at the early hour. It was as if she had always expected him to show up sooner or later.

But as he climbed the narrow street, an uneasiness rose within her. Her muscles tensed. Why was he here? He had promised not to come. Sixteen months ago he promised. Not that she was keeping track. . . .

The sound of a soft whistle drew her attention back toward the square. Javier, the young sculptor, stood on the porch steps outside his shop. Behind him, the handicraft shop owner emerged from his door.

Javier raised his chin in question.

Sheridan gave a half nod. They needn't be concerned. The stranger was, so to speak, a known quantity. Not that she felt the least bit glad to see Luke. Eliot would most likely be severely distressed at his arrival.

Wishing Luke were an apparition did not make it so. He continued his steady pace, arms swinging gently, head down as if he studied the cobblestones, making his way to her house.

Since that day in Caracas—the day her husband died in every sense except physically, the day this man saved her life—Sheridan had understood intuitively that Luke would always be a part of her life. And there he was, out of the blue, ascending her street in the middle of nowhere on a spring day as if he visited all the time.

She suddenly remembered the date. "Good grief."

It was Annunciation Day, a day of remembrance, of celebration for when the angel Gabriel visited Mary and announced her future. How apropos. Luke appeared without warning. He would not have come unless he had something to tell her, some message that would irreversibly change her future.

Was this his joke or God's?

Luke neared and looked up, straight at her.

She saw not the man whose presence had always triggered apprehension in her, but rather the guardian angel who had saved her life.

Sheridan turned and made her way inside, down the stairs, and through the house.

❧

Sheridan opened the front door and stopped.

Luke Traynor stood less than six feet away, at the low gate in the stone wall where her front terrace met the steep hill.

She returned his steady gaze, knowing full well her own expression did not mirror the one before her. While dread, relief, and excessive gratitude rearranged every muscle on her face, his remained perfectly composed. The sharp nose, thin lips, and deep-set eyes could have been made of the same cobblestone he stood on.

He flashed a rakish grin. "I was in the neighborhood."

"That's the most ridiculous thing I've ever heard."

He cocked his head, somber again. Always the gentleman, he waited for her to make the first move.

Sheridan clutched her shawl more closely and resigned herself to riding out the emotional disarray rumbling through her. She both loathed and loved this man. Of course he knew that, so it didn't matter how she reacted to him except that she'd like herself better if she were polite.

With a quiet sigh, she walked to him, planted a kiss on his scruffy, unshaven cheek, and eased into his embrace. Nestled against the rough collar of his jacket, she smelled the familiar scent of him, an indescribable mix of earth, sun-drenched air, and confidence that bordered on lunacy. She felt the hardness of his body, always unexpected given his average height and build.

"Sheridan. How are you?"

"Fine." She backed away, crossing her arms.

"And Eliot?" he said. "How is he?"

"Fine."

Luke blinked, a slow movement of lids indicating he could take the truth.

She wanted to shriek obscenities at him. The disconcerting thing about angels, though, was that it was impossible to keep up any sort of pretense. Like an angel, Luke had stayed close beside her for long weeks after the shooting. He had gone with her to the edge of hell, holding on to her until she came back. He knew her better than she knew herself. Glossing over answers was a waste of time with him.

She tried another phrase. "We're doing about as well as could be expected."

He nodded.

"Eliot is still asleep."

"It's early. Perhaps I can greet him later."

The resistance drained from her. Yes, Gabriel had come to deliver a message, and he would not leave until he'd done so.

She had no inkling how to shield Eliot and herself from this unexpected source of distress but gave a lame attempt. "I don't suppose you're passing through town and simply must be on your way right now, this very minute?"

"Sorry."

She inhaled, her shoulders lifting with the effort, and blew the breath out with force. "Coffee?"

"Love some."

CHAPTER 2

CHICAGO, ILLINOIS

Her forehead against the cold windowpane and her arms crossed, Calissa Cole seriously pondered taking up smoking again.

It might be worth it.

On the one hand, there was stigma, expense, bad breath, the risk of dread disease, the squander of time and energy trying to find a smoke-friendly spot on the sidewalk protected from rain, snow, sleet, wind, heat, and humidity.

On the other hand was sheer, unadulterated stress release.

Yes, it might be worth it.

"Ms. Cole?"

She turned to see a nurse, the young one with the bouncy ponytail. "Yes?"

"You can come in now."

"Thank you. By the way, do you smoke?"

"Uh, no."

"Good for you."

"Do you want me to ask someone—?"

"Nah. I quit eight years ago."

With a curious smile, the nurse left, her white shoes squish-squishing on the linoleum, her ponytail swaying.

Calissa pivoted back to the window.

It was monsoon season in Chicago. Spring showers on steroids. Pewter had colored the entire city for an entire week. No wonder she wanted a cigarette.

She shut her eyes and hummed. *Chicago is my kind of town.*

It was. Calissa loved Chi-town. She was beautiful no matter what color she wore, no matter how many days in a row she adorned herself in the same one.

A typical early spring day in her city was not why Calissa considered smoking a good thing to do.

With a sigh, she jerked at the collar of her blouse to straighten it. She smoothed her gray pin-striped jacket and skirt. A glance at the muted cell phone in her hand revealed no messages. She dropped it into her handbag. The nurses fussed at her whenever she checked for messages on it in the ICU.

Calissa strode down the hall toward the double doors, her pumps clicking as if she had a purpose in mind other than to sit at her father's bedside and urge the unconscious man to hang on for just a while longer. *Hang in there. You can do it.*

If she was lucky, maybe Nurse Ponytail would say the same thing to her.

Or tell her who might have an extra cigarette on hand.

CHAPTER 3

TOPALA

Sheridan glared at Luke, seated across from her at a small wrought-iron table in the front courtyard. Her emotions still ran high. She was happy to see him. She didn't want to be happy to see him, therefore she wasn't really happy to see him. She wasn't supposed to see him ever again. He'd said he wouldn't come. She and Eliot had made sure no one could even find them. He would be so upset that Luke had found them. That was the heart of the matter. How had he found them?

"How did you find us?"

A tiny smile twitched the corner of his mouth. "How? Not *why* did you find us?'"

"I don't really care to know *why*."

"Actually I prefer to wait until Eliot joins us before I explain the why. When do you think he'll be available?"

"Don't change the subject." She tapped her finger on the table. "No one—and I mean *no one*—knows where we are."

Amusement shone in his gray-green eyes.

"Don't laugh at me."

"I'm not."

"Yes, you are and for good reason. It was a stupid question."

"Perhaps *unnecessary* is a better adjective."

"I can't believe I asked it. People like you can find anybody they want, whenever they want. It doesn't matter if those people don't want to be found."

"Sheridan, I'm not the bad guy."

"No? You're here, and you're not supposed to be, first off because you promised and second because we want to be left alone. You ignored both of those. That adds up to a bad guy of the worst sort."

"There are extenuating circumstances."

"As Eliot would say, tommyrot."

"Well, yeah. Most of life is."

"Oh!" She should be quiet. Her ears hurt from the pounding in her chest.

She averted her face and tried to focus on the courtyard. The small enclosure at the front of the house usually calmed her. Bougainvillea vines teemed with crimson blossoms and ran riot over the high walls. Plants overflowed in dozens of terra-cotta pots scattered about the colorful tiles—bright red geraniums, emerald green succulents, fragrant white alyssum, and jasmine.

It was a losing battle. Luke, the angel–slash–bad guy, had brought darkness with him. Shadows from the past loomed over her, obliterating the peaceful beauty.

And he hadn't even gotten to his message yet.

She looked at him. He waited quietly for her to say whatever it was she had to say. The sheer familiarity of him struck her again. There really was no reason to hold back.

"Ambassadors should be allowed to retire in peace." She nearly hissed the words.

"Yes, they should." He took off his ball cap and ran a hand through his hair, medium brown and too short for a hat to indent. "After what happened in Caracas, I understand your and Eliot's need to create a safety zone far away from the world you knew. I apologize. I've disrupted your safety zone—"

"Disrupted? You've violated it, Luke!"

"I am truly sorry."

"Who else can I expect to show up on my doorstep?"

"No one. I promise." His tone conveyed security. It always had, even when circumstances blatantly denied it.

But obviously some faction in Venezuela hated the U.S. ambassador. Did they still? Enough to finish the job they'd begun? "If you found us, then that means our location is no longer secret."

"This is only me here. I wasn't followed."

"Extenuating circumstances." "This is only me here." Then . . . why? She avoided his gaze, fearing what she might see. Fearing what she might convey.

"Sheridan, I didn't come for what you're thinking." He hadn't lost his uncanny ability to sense what was on her mind. "This is not between you and me."

Relief gave way to a twinge of disappointment. There was nothing between them. Good. She wouldn't want that complication. "All—all right. Th-then . . ." Now she stuttered. She really should have stayed in bed that morning.

"As I said, we'll wait for Eliot before getting into why I came."

A new fear took hold. Something had happened. Something beyond her control would hit her. Again. She wasn't ready. She just wasn't ready. Handling surprises was another of those unhealed areas.

Luke looked beyond her shoulder. *"Hola, señorita."*

Sheridan turned to see Mercedes, the young woman who worked for her, and struggled to compose herself.

Luke stood and reached for the coffee tray Mercedes carried, speaking easily in his fluent Spanish. "Let me take that."

"Gracias, señor."

"Luke," Sheridan said, "this is Mercedes Rodriguez. She lives with us." She caught the eighteen-year-old's playful smile. "What do I call you?"

Mercedes turned to Luke. "I am . . . ," she said in English and then paused, jutting her chin, stretching to her full height, which at the most was four-eleven. "I am Señora Montgomery's backup."

Luke chuckled. "Pleased to meet you. I'm Luke Traynor, business associate."

Business associate. That was generic enough. It blended, like his appearance, into any situation. It was, like his appearance, easily *not* recalled.

He held the tray while Mercedes transferred the coffee carafe and other items to the table. True to both their friendly demeanors, they exchanged pleasantries.

A flush of gratitude surprised Sheridan. In all honesty, where would she be without these people? They were both her "backups." Without Luke, she'd be dead. Without Mercedes, she'd be curled on the floor in a fetal position, unable to take another step in the perplexing maze that defined this new life.

Even now Mercedes was covering for her. Twenty minutes ago, the girl had found Sheridan in the kitchen, fussing over coffee beans scattered from one end of the room to the other. With soft, shushing coos, Mercedes had held Sheridan's hands and walked her out the door. Sheridan knew that the humble teen would prepare and deliver the best coffee in the village along with a basket of pastries.

True, it was a less-dramatic rescue than Luke's, but a rescue all the same and of the sort that was performed over and over again.

Sheridan wondered, though, who was going to rescue her from whatever surprise awaited her.

CHAPTER 4

Eliot awoke totally alert, every brain cell at attention and ready to respond.

Which startled him.

He never woke up totally alert, at least not since before that business in Caracas. How was it Sheridan put it? B.C.E. At least not since then.

Since then, he experienced two approaches to waking. Either he swam through an opiate-induced fog or he thrashed about until some limb thwacked the wall. Neither of those had happened. He just opened his eyes, his body at rest. No pain, no grogginess from painkillers.

The bedroom was dark and quiet. Thanks to thick adobe walls, shutters on the east window, and heavy curtains on the north French doors, it could be noon or midnight for all he knew. He glanced sideways. The clock was facedown on the nightstand, but he made no effort to right it. He lay still, not moving a muscle for fear of setting off alarms to wake up the monsters that wrenched and gouged every inch of his body day in and day out.

Today should have been the fog wake-up call. There was no rhyme or reason to his nights, but last night was one of the unbearable sort when the pain seared, emanating from a place so deep it seemed to exist outside of himself, a place where drugs could not go.

In lucid moments, like now, he realized how odd that sounded.

Nonetheless, he would take the maximum doses, as he had last night, in hopes of even a small bit of relief. Sheridan sat with him, as she always did on such nights, and massaged his hip and lower back and neck. She would have turned the clock upside down, not wanting to be aware of the number of passing hours.

All right, God. You've got my attention. Why the reprieve?

The unbidden prayer startled him less than the alertness. He had been silently talking to God since A.C.E. Who else could undo what had been done? His life had been taken from him, his world not only turned upside down but cut open and shaken empty of everything but pain.

He didn't blame God. Evil existed. Eliot did not have the wherewithal to figure out why he had brushed up against it and God hadn't protected him. He did not have the stamina to recall the prayers of his childhood or even the stories about Jesus. His strength accommodated only one prayer: for God to remove the pain that the doctors said would never go away.

Is it gone?

He continued to lie perfectly still, curious but too frightened to move in order to find out whether it was gone or not.

His new world was a painful and scary place.

The fog rolled in, no doubt leftovers from last night's medication. He swam toward it, grateful for the escape.

CHAPTER 5

AFTER MERCEDES WENT BACK inside the house, Sheridan poured coffee and handed a mug to Luke.

"Thanks." He took a sip and his eyes widened. "Mm."

"Mm-hmm. Wait until you try her *bolillos*."

He lifted the napkin on the basket and took out a bread roll. "She's delightful."

"She's a godsend." Sheridan rested her head against the back of the chair and closed her eyes against the sun. "Eliot had a bad night. I don't know when he'll be available to see you."

"Not a problem." He spoke around a mouthful of bread. "How is he?"

"I told you."

"You said 'about as well as could be expected.' That's a synonym for *fine*. It doesn't say much."

"Why don't you ask whoever told you how to find us how he is?"

Luke didn't reply.

There was no need for him to ask anybody how Eliot was or how she was. The answer was written plainly all over her. It was in the road map etched around her eyes. It showed in the lack of cosmetics to brighten the brown eyes or sallow skin, in the shaggy hair left to its own wavy tendencies, its auburn silvering unchecked. It showed in the hint of accumulated tortillas beneath the elastic waistband of her gypsy skirt. It was in the echo of her angry tone.

She wanted to cry. The arrival of Luke Traynor was like ripping off a scab, exposing raw nerve ends.

She whispered, "They were just beginning to leave me alone."

"They?"

The images swamped her, their horror as intense as ever. A blood-spattered sidewalk. Her husband sprawled facedown, scarcely alive. Her coworker Reina on her back, already horribly, obviously dead. The storefront windows shattered like her watch crystal. The end of the world as she knew it at twelve minutes, thirty-five seconds past ten. Luke whisking her away, window-glass slivers, the shards of her life's work, crunching under his feet.

Luke's chair scraped across the tiles. She sensed him moving close to her.

"Sher."

She opened her eyes. He sat hunched over in his chair, elbows on his knees, the closeness of him forcing eye contact. It was how he would get her attention in the hospital or the hotel. At times when she flailed on the edge of insanity's pit, he'd pulled her back through the sheer power of his presence.

She didn't want to depend on him again. She did not want to grow accustomed to his face again.

"Go away, Luke."

"I know I've violated your safety zone. I've invaded and most likely destroyed your carefully constructed cocoon, not just the Topala one but your emotional one. You know I would not have come if it weren't necessary. I told you sixteen months ago that, all things being equal, you would never see me again. I am so sorry. Things just got unequal."

She didn't want to hear what things got unequal. Things were always unequal when Luke Traynor was in the vicinity.

She had first met him in Honduras, where Eliot served as an assistant to the ambassador. Luke arrived, a foreign service officer on a temporary assignment. Despite his affable demeanor, something about him unsettled her. Later he joined them again, that time in Venezuela, and her reaction to him remained the same.

In Honduras, her husband had been on the fast track to an ambassadorship, which he was awarded in Venezuela. Like his father and grandfather before him, he was a political appointee. As his wife, Sheridan was privileged to live a lifestyle that sometimes embarrassingly bordered on royalty. When she wasn't attending an elegant dinner party with heads of state, she immersed herself in her passion of social work. As if those ingredients didn't create the yummiest of cakes, there was the icing on top it all: she loved and adored Eliot, who loved and adored her in return. Joy and satisfaction filled their days.

Naturally, all was not perfect. They trafficked in politics and poverty and the darkness that accompanied those realities. While Eliot negotiated in the limelight, others were involved in undercover shenanigans. Others like Luke.

It was never acknowledged that Luke was a spy. On the surface he was a public diplomacy officer. He was the voice of the U.S. when it came to explaining American policies and values to the citizens of his host country.

But both times he'd worked in her husband's embassies, political unrest had ensued. He might not have been directly responsible, but Sheridan thought he fit the bill. The bottom line was that if not for their silly games of intrigue, Eliot would still be the ambassador. She would still be engaged in real work, not nursing an invalid.

In the past, whenever she voiced concerns to Eliot about fomenters and turmoil, he would smile and say, "Welcome to life in the diplomatic lane. We'll just keep our heads down and pretend they're not here, all right?" His chipper spin was unflagging.

Then came the shooting. It took little effort for her to connect the presence of Luke Traynor with her husband's being chosen as a target. If

Luke perpetrated the unrest, the backlash could naturally strike out at the ambassador. It was her personal theory, one she never bothered sharing.

The irony of it all was that the man responsible for the violence was the one who saved her from it. Perpetrator and rescuer. Bad guy, guardian angel. The man she fell in love with when she wasn't looking.

She blamed it on how he went above and beyond angel duty. In the chaos of that awful day and in subsequent weeks, he stayed with her like stickiness on glue. She was whisked with her injured husband from one hospital to another, from Venezuela to the States. Friends and embassy staff could not get to her. Luke, though, never left her side.

He guided her through her own medical care for a broken arm and cracked ribs. He deciphered needs she could not articulate and arranged to have them met. Through doctors' pronouncements that Eliot was not going to make it, Luke held her tightly and would not let her imagine the funeral.

She figured he did it all out of a guilty conscience.

And yet she would not have survived the ordeal without him.

Whatever. It was over.

Luke broke into her thoughts. "I'm sorry, but I did have to come."

"You bring the past with you, and I just can't go there."

"I don't want you to. Tell me about now."

"I don't talk about now either, about how Eliot and I are now. We just are. Okay? I say we're fine, and that keeps me moving forward."

"You passed the one-year anniversary. Did you celebrate it in some way?"

She stared at him, struck as always by his understanding. "We had champagne and lobster. Caviar, too."

"Cake?"

"Sure. An entire sheet cake. One candle, U.S. and Venezuelan flags outlined in full color on vanilla icing. Invited the whole village."

He smiled in a gentle way. "Seriously, Sher. You've lived with this for over a year now. Through birthdays and holidays. Your wedding anniversary. You made it. That is a huge deal."

She had hoped so. She had hoped it would mark a turning point, that Eliot would finally just buck up and be *present* despite everything. That he would lose the deaf-mute persona. That their ordeal with post-trauma symptoms would fade into oblivion.

But when she had told Eliot the date and hinted at new days ahead, he'd moved a bony shoulder, the closest semblance to a shrug that he could muster. The anniversary was far from a huge deal. Another six months had passed with no hint of change.

"What's life like here in Topala? What do you do for fun? Any volleyball teams around?"

She clenched her hands into fists on her lap. Luke was coercing her to talk about herself. It both repelled and comforted her that he could still do that.

"Yeah, right. Volleyball." She winced. The lack of physical exercise was bad enough, but even worse was the lack of camaraderie she'd always enjoyed through team sports. "I walk."

"Great vertical climbs here."

"Yeah. And I paint."

"Really?"

"No, not really. It's about as artistic as a paint-by-numbers kit. It's a tool, a way to work out anxiety. A counselor suggested it."

"What exactly do you paint?"

She exhaled in frustration. "Local scenes. Acrylics on four-by-six pieces of Masonite. The sculptor sells them in his shop to tourists. Can you believe it? People actually pay money for my trauma-induced hobby."

"They must be attractive if people buy them."

"They're mediocre souvenirs."

A seam appeared between his eyes. The gray-green darkened to all gray.

Her breath caught. "You knew about them, didn't you?"

Before his eyes went blank again, she saw his answer. *Yes.*

Yes?

"Sheridan, I needed help tracking you down—"

"Don't patronize me! What else do you know about me? about Eliot?"

"It doesn't matter. I want to hear it from you. How you are. How you really are."

"Tell me!"

He gazed at her, expressionless.

"Luke Traynor, you owe me that much for coming here and tearing apart my so-called cocoon."

"All right." Still hunched forward, he spoke in a low tone as if that would cushion the emotional blows he was delivering. "I know that you regularly attend the village church. You give impromptu English lessons to local kids. You sign your paintings 'SC'—I take it for your first and maiden names, Sheridan Cole. When Javier, the sculptor, is asked about the painter whose work he sells in his shop, he shrugs like he doesn't understand English and says, '*El artista*, he live Las Trojes.' You have caring friends, like Mercedes, like that posse who watched me walk up here earlier."

Sheridan felt a warmth for those villagers who had begun to trust her in recent months. What would happen to that now that her past had caught up?

Luke went on. "Eliot is a recluse. You spend most of your time with him. You're his nurse, secretary, chauffeur. He only comes out when you drive him down to Mesa Aguamiel once every four weeks or so. You go to the bank, shops, Internet café. You pick up mail at the post office." He paused. "Mail that's forwarded from a Chicago PO box number." He stopped talking.

She pressed her lips together. They wouldn't stay put. "You lousy scumbag."

She shoved his knees aside and brushed past him, her wrought-iron chair clattering against the tiles.

CHAPTER 6

"TRAYNOR'S HERE?" Seated on the edge of his bed, Eliot slid his arm through the shirtsleeve Sheridan held for him. "I can hardly believe that."

"Well, you may as well believe it." She eyed his back, the visible ribs on his gaunt six-four frame, the nubby scar below his left shoulder blade. "He's right outside in the courtyard, eating one of Mercedes's egg burritos."

Eliot placed his other arm into the short sleeve of the guayabera, an oversize white linen shirt with pockets at the hem. He worked on the top button.

"It means," she said, "we'll have to schedule exercise later."

Nothing about him indicated that he'd heard her comment. He disliked physical therapy so much he wouldn't even talk about it. She suspected his pride ached more than the legs she moved about in patterns doctors had designed for him.

Eliot said, "No surprise that he found us, though." He was still on Luke.

"No. No surprise." She clipped her words and squashed a complaint about being discovered. Like the exercise comment, it would fall on deaf ears. At least Eliot was handling the news with a trace of his old equanimity. Maybe it would carry them through the meeting.

He fastened the button and fumbled with the second.

Sheridan sat in an armchair and tried not to remember how she used to snuggle within the confines of his well-toned muscles. She tried not to recall the strong hands that gestured confidently and elegantly as he conferred with presidents and prime ministers.

Eliot said, "It would be easy enough to track us down."

"I thought we made it difficult."

"Any tourist could stop in at Davy's cantina and learn, for the price of a luncheon special, something about the Americans living in the area."

"But why does this hypothetical tourist choose Topala in the first place?" She spoke more loudly. It sometimes got his attention. "How does he get that close to us?"

"Perhaps through the banks." He finished the third button, rested his hands on the bed, and twitched a shoulder. "Or they follow the mail from Chicago to Mesa Aguamiel."

Luke had mentioned the mail. But— "No!" she exclaimed. "Malcolm would never tell! Would he?"

Eliot ignored the question, her second stupid one of the day.

She answered it herself. No, Malcolm Holladay, an old friend of Eliot's father, would never tell. Ages ago Eliot Sr. convinced a district attorney to drop drug charges against Malcolm's son. Later he pulled strings and the son was admitted to the Naval Academy. The boy was now a retired admiral.

Malcolm, a rich and powerful man, reminded Sheridan of a loyal bulldog. Short and thickset, he held an undying allegiance to the Montgomery family and still treated Eliot like a son. The legendary tales she had heard suggested he would endure torture before telling anyone that he arranged for her and Eliot's mail to be picked up at a Chicago post office box, packaged, and sent on to another post office box in Mesa Aguamiel, Mexico.

The Chicago address was not secret. They had made far too many acquaintances over the years to not keep in touch, however superficial their communication might be via e-mail or on paper. There were the foundations and charities with which they remained involved monetarily. But no one received their true address in return. How, then, had Luke found them?

Third stupid question of the day. If Luke was involved, then the vast resources of the federal government were involved. Anything was possible. Find a needle in a haystack? No problem. Find a man with no forwarding house address or phone number? Easy.

Eliot's eyes, the solid blue of a Mexican summer sky, shone with creative energy. He was lost in his make-believe scenario.

"You know," he said, "not that many viable roads lead from Mesa Aguamiel. A question here, a question there. Money changes hands. 'When do Señor and Señora Montgomery pick up their mail?'" He paused. "Maybe we were followed from there to here."

She shuddered. The last couple of times they'd gone to town, she had felt distinctly less jittery. Driving thirty minutes from home on the old highway, sharing it with several tourist buses, had seemed almost routine. She had taken it as a hopeful sign that she was making progress in the emotional department. Maybe she owed an apology to that counselor after all.

"No matter." Eliot reached for the next shirt button. "The fact is, we just hoped they would leave us in peace. We never expected them not to be able to find us, not if the need arose."

"I expected the need to never arise."

His rare smile creased his cheeks. "The naive princess reigns."

The old nickname surprised her. It felt like a butterfly wing brushing the tip of her ear. A tickle played down her spine. He used to have a whole litany of playful endearments. *Naive princess. My touch of sparkle. Sher the sure thing. Miracle whiz woman. Miss Why Not?*

Those were B.C.E., though. Past tense.

Eliot said, "Is he in the front or back courtyard?"

"What? Oh, uh, the back."

"He probably flew into Mazatlán." The coastal city was about a ninety-minute drive from them. "Did he drive up from there this morning?"

"I don't know."

"But you talked to him?"

"Yes, we talked."

"About?"

"Coffee. Mercedes. Acrylics on Masonite."

"Ah."

Sheridan's jaw went rigid. She made a conscious effort to loosen it by reminding herself that Eliot was alive. His peculiar mannerisms should not be sources of irritation.

But they were. They drove her up the wall. His personality quirks had lost their endearing quality. Like now. Instead of being simply thorough about Luke's visit, he obsessed over inane details and pulled her along with him down rabbit trails that would whirl them into tail-chasing circles.

Eliot took his horn-rimmed glasses from the nightstand. With both hands he carefully put them on, their dark frames a contrast to the gray-blond thatch of curls. Then he grasped the sides of his walker and struggled to his feet, huffing softly with the effort.

"All right." He exhaled the words. "Let's go see what old Traynor has to say and get this over with."

CHAPTER 7

Sheridan and Eliot went out through the French doors of his first-floor bedroom and followed the walkway toward the center of the courtyard. Like in the front, bougainvillea cascaded down rock walls that enclosed the back patio. The house bordered the fourth side. Orange, lemon, and lime trees grew in the dirt yard, fruit burgeoning on their limbs. Other flowering plants thrived in pots.

Eliot clunked his walker in a steady rhythm along tiles designed with intricate swirls of bright reds and blues. The squares of concrete provided a fairly smooth surface, an important plus in a flood-prone town.

Luke stood as they approached. His jacket hung on the back of his chair. His long shirtsleeves were rolled up.

Since calling him a scumbag earlier, Sheridan had avoided him, staying indoors and helping Eliot with his morning routine. Mercedes had seen to Luke's needs, giving him food and drink, old newspapers, and a tour of the kitchen.

"Mr. Ambassador."

Smiling, Eliot let go of his walker and shook Luke's outstretched hand. "You always were a charmer, Traynor. I'm just Eliot now. Welcome to casa de Montgomery."

As they talked, Sheridan watched Luke's face closely. She discerned no overt reaction to the radical changes in Eliot that he must certainly be noticing.

Except for deepened crow's-feet, her husband's face at fifty-two remained as youthful in appearance as ever. She'd always been enamored of the attractive blend of teen and maturity in his fresh face. But his body carried the trauma in shuffling feet and hunched shoulders. From a side angle one might guess he was eighty. Even his voice weakened after too much use. He was putting up a strong front at the moment, but he would most likely tire soon. Sometimes his thoughts wandered off and never came back.

The doctor said it was all to be expected, of course. Eliot's body had sustained an incredible amount of damage, most of it irreversible. His mind had to make adjustments. The chronic pain and the loss of his work took a toll on his personality, once the most pleasant she had ever met and, unlike Luke's, genuinely gracious.

Luke said, "I must say you are looking fit, sir."

Eliot chuckled. "Now you've crossed that vague line between charming and outright lying."

"I disagree. The last time I saw you, you were in a hospital bed, bruised from head to toe, all but buried under tubes, IV lines, and beeping machines."

"Ah, I stand corrected, then. It's all relative." He gestured toward the chairs at the table, and the two of them sat. "I can't recall much from those foggy days of morphine. Did I ever thank you for rescuing my wife?"

"Yes, you did most definitely. And I said, 'You're welcome,' and then I believe you fell asleep."

"Passed out, more likely." He shook his head. His ghosts were of physical agony and a brain fogged with drugs, not images on a sidewalk. "I'll ring Mercedes for some iced tea."

Sheridan took a step toward the house. "I'll go in and tell her."

"I'll ring. Please, join us."

"No thank you. I need to take a walk. You two can discuss business while—"

"Sheridan." Luke's charming tone turned solemn. "I wanted Eliot in on this because it will impact him. However, the 'business' concerns you more directly than it does him."

Her husband removed a tiny pewter bell from his shirt pocket and gave it a quick shake. "I feel ridiculous using this thing. At least they don't make me carry around the cowbell. The house isn't large enough for either, but I suppose that's relative too. It seems enormous to me because I can't easily move through it. I've been upstairs only once since we moved in, to take in the view. These few meters between here and that kitchen door seem absolutely insurmountable."

As Eliot rambled on, Sheridan saw Luke aim a questioning glance at her. She imagined that he wondered if Eliot had heard him or if Eliot was still lost in a medicated haze.

Yes and no. No and yes. It depended on the day.

She merely blinked in reply. *Welcome to my world, Luke. Casa de not what I signed up for.*

❧

After Mercedes had served them tea and gone back into the house, Eliot ended his polite chitchat. "Well, Traynor, what brings you all this way? What news do you have for my wife?"

Luke eyed both of them from across the table before replying. "I want you to know, Eliot, that I would not have come if it weren't necessary."

"I presumed that, of course."

"But it's personal. The fact is, I'm not here as an employee of the government."

Sheridan flinched. Luke was all about government. He worked as a diplomat in foreign embassies. He most likely did all sorts of dirty work for the government. If the government hadn't sent him, then who?

He was watching her closely. "Calissa."

"My sister?"

"She asked me to find you. Your father suffered a stroke."

"When?"

"Ten days ago."

"I was in Mesa Aguamiel a week ago yesterday. There was no e-mail from her."

"She didn't want you to read it in an e-mail."

"Ask me if I care."

"That's what she said you would say."

"Ask me if I care if he's even dead. Go ahead. Ask me." Sheridan put a hand to her mouth and shut her eyes. When had it become so easy for her to spew out such filth?

That was an easy one. The seed was planted just before moving to Topala, the last time she spoke with Harrison Cole, her so-called dad. Hidden away inside of her, the seed grew, nourished by a constant diet of stress. Now she was giving birth to a vileness she never would have imagined possible.

She looked at the men and lowered her hand. "The last thing he said to me was that I'd gotten exactly what I deserved. That if I hadn't insisted on doing my own thing in Caracas, if I had just stayed put and stuck to the wifely script, Eliot never would have been shot."

Her husband's mouth was a grim line. "You cannot, absolutely cannot, give any credence whatsoever to his words. I've told you that time and time again."

She nodded. Still, she and Eliot had been at *her* place of business when the attack occurred. How could she ignore that fact? They weren't anywhere near the embassy. They weren't at some state affair. They weren't at the airport. They weren't doing any sort of government business whatsoever. The United States ambassador to Venezuela was with his wife in a seedy neighborhood, doing what *she* wanted to do.

"Sheridan—" Luke leaned across the table—"he will probably die within days if he hasn't already. Calissa said he's left a raft of unfinished details, that she's in over her head."

"She's one of his assistants and has a dozen of her own assistants to take care of details."

"She said that what she most desperately needs right now is her sister."

"Calissa has never needed me in her entire life. . . ." Her voice trailed off. Calissa was seven years older and had seemed to Sheridan to be a strong, independent woman for almost as long as Sheridan could remember. Growing up together with a mother who adored them and a father who apparently didn't had forged a special bond between the sisters, but it had been severed years ago. When their mother died, Sheridan was thirteen; Calissa stepped effortlessly into the matriarchal shoes. Sheridan lost her sister as surely as she'd lost her mother.

It was too much to take in. Luke, her father, her sister had all violated her safety zone. She jerked as if a long bandage had been ripped from her flesh.

Luke slid a small white envelope across the table. Nothing was written on it. "It's for you, from her."

She hesitated. Calissa was shrewd. A personal note hand-delivered by Luke? This wasn't simply about Harrison suffering a stroke. Her sister wanted her attention.

"Traynor," Eliot said, "why you?"

"Excuse me?"

"Why you? Why did Calissa send you?"

Luke blinked slowly.

Sheridan felt a stab of annoyance at Luke's diplomatic two-step. Since his injury, Eliot had lost his own diplomatic knack for weighing words and couching them in ambiguity. It was almost an even trade. Instead of the two-step dance, they took jaunts down rabbit trails.

At last Luke spoke. "I met Calissa at the hospital, in Houston." He referred to her sister's visit during Eliot's stay there.

"I wasn't aware your paths had crossed."

Sheridan opened her mouth to speak but closed it. Reminding Eliot that she had told him of Calissa's meeting Luke would only annoy him.

Besides, he spoke the truth. He was unaware of it as he was unaware of many things. Pain and meds occupied too much memory space.

Luke said, "I gave her my card. She contacted me a week ago. She figured that with my State Department connections, I had the means to find you."

"Which of course you did." Eliot's eyes narrowed behind his thick lenses. "And why, pray tell, did you agree to do it?"

Luke smiled briefly. "Your welfare concerns me. We almost died together. That tends to quicken one's relationship. Why wouldn't I say yes to Calissa's request? I couldn't let someone else deliver this difficult family news."

"How convenient you were available. In between assignments, are you?"

"In a manner of speaking."

Sheridan tuned out Eliot's inquisition and Luke's bunk. She fingered the linen envelope. It was sealed. Not that sealed meant unopened. Luke had single-handedly extracted her from the scene of an assassination attempt. Surely a little glue would not be an issue for him.

She broke the seal, pulled out a folded blank card, and opened it. At the sight of her sister's handwriting, she ached for the relationship they didn't have.

Sheri -

Even Isaac and Ishmael came together to bury their father. The older brother probably told the younger surprising tales about their father, things the younger would not know or remember. Please come.

With love,
Lissy

"Well?" Eliot's tone was harsh. "What's in it?"

She looked at him, shutting the card and tracing her thumb along its fold. He was getting tired. Tact went the way of the diplomatic two-step when he was tired. "Calissa says that Isaac and Ishmael came together to bury their father."

"Hm. Harrison Cole is not exactly an Abraham."

"I don't think that's her point."

"No. That would be a stretch even for your sister." Eliot pushed back his chair and slowly rose. "Traynor, my wife owes her family nothing. Please convey our condolences to Calissa, but I'm afraid we are not able to travel at this time. It was good of you to stop by." He reached across the table and shook Luke's hand.

"A pleasure to see you up and about, sir."

Eliot glanced at Sheridan. "I think it's time we got to work. I'll be in the study."

She stared at his receding back, her own shoulders slouching like his, the weight of the world pressing in. The rhythmic ping of aluminum against concrete blotted out all thought.

"Sher."

She turned to Luke.

The seam between his brows was scrunched again. This time it stayed there. "What do *you* think?"

"That I can't think about it right now." The words popped out of her mouth and she recognized what she was saying. If she'd learned one thing through the past year, it was to know when to quit, when to step back from life. "I have to shut down."

"And how do you do that?"

"Church. I go to the church." She anticipated the peace and safety that surrounded her as she sat in the pew. It would be like pressing back into place the bandage that Luke's news had forcefully removed.

"Is the church open?"

"Yes, it's always—oh!" She glanced at her watch and stood. "There's a service at noon. I can make it."

"A service?"

"It's Annunciation Day." She recalled her earlier comparison. "You know, kind of like what we've just had, *Gabe*?"

"Gabe." His smile was unfeigned, the first real one since his arrival. "As in Gabriel the angel?"

"You came and you announced."

"And it's thrown your world off-kilter, as Mary's must have been." He tilted his head slightly, accepting responsibility but not apologizing for it. "Mind if I join you?"

"Yes."

"Understood. Not a problem."

The familiarity of him took hold of her once more. How many times had he joined her in a hospital chapel simply to keep her company?

The truth was, no matter how much she wanted to deny it, she had needed him then and she needed him now.

She said, "But it's okay."

He gave a slight nod.

CHAPTER 8

Sheridan entered the living room that served as their study. They'd furnished it with a large desk and several bookcases. Eliot was in his recliner, his feet on the raised footrest. A book lay open on his lap, his glasses on top of it.

"Eliot."

He looked up. "Is Traynor gone?"

"No. He's going down to the church with me." She sat on the ottoman beside his chair. "Mercedes is already there. Did you remember it's a holy day?"

He sighed, a loud exhale of frustration. "And you can't miss a service."

She tamped down her own frustration. She missed services all the time. There was no space in her schedule to attend the daily Mass or even every Sunday. But the ancient liturgy grounded her like nothing else, and sometimes, like now, she absolutely craved it.

She said as she always did, "Do you want to go?"

And like always, he replied, "I don't care to, no. When will you be back?"

"An hour. An hour and a half at the most. Why don't you rest? When I get home, we'll eat lunch and then work."

"We are not obligated to entertain him, you know." Obviously Luke was at the forefront of his thoughts. "I don't think I was rude to him, but we can't welcome this sort of intrusion into our lives. I am no longer in service to the United States."

"It wasn't exactly national business that brought him here."

"You don't think so? Sheridan, the man is a CIA operative. He doesn't have a personal bone in his body. No matter what Calissa told him or what he told us, he came because he has something to gain. You're not actually considering going to Chicago?"

"I haven't thought about going anywhere beyond church." A shudder went through her. She could not imagine leaving Topala, traveling back into the chaos of the real world, into a huge city. How she had survived five months in Houston during Eliot's recuperation remained a mystery. Getting them on the plane to Mexico thirteen months ago used up every last ounce of stamina she had. The counselor told her it would be restored. Of course, she didn't believe that woman's word about anything.

Eliot said, "Is there any hint at all in Calissa's note about why Traynor's interested?"

She thought of the note she'd slid into a drawer between the folds of a camisole. It was a banal hiding place, but at least the thing was out of sight. "There was the reference to Isaac and Ishmael."

"Two brothers who probably lived in the equivalent of different countries, at odds over family business. A significant age difference between them. A dead, or nearly dead, father. There are similarities to you and Calissa, but beyond those things?"

She heard the question in his voice.

And she chose not to answer it.

There was more "beyond those things," but what exactly she didn't understand. Something, though, kept her from wondering aloud with him. Something inside of her curled up protectively around this peculiar message from her sister.

Calissa had written a cryptic note that might just as well have been stamped "For Your Eyes Only." She had contacted a spy who had a connection like none other with Sheridan. Calissa had probably paid a lot of money for his spur-of-the-moment travel expenses.

Surprising tales, the note said, *about their father, things the younger would not know.*

Sheridan looked at her husband of ten years, her best friend and confidant. His eyes were shut. Out of weariness? pain? anger that their location was known? or just plain indifference? More and more it had taken on shades of indifference, of detachment from her, and really, of life in general.

Things were changing between them. Since moving to Topala, they had lived in what felt like physical safety, that centerpiece around which they'd made every decision since the shooting. Luke had it right. She was Eliot's nurse, cook, housekeeper, secretary, chauffeur, companion. She wasn't sure where *best friend* and *confidant* fit anymore.

Calissa's note was personal. It didn't involve Luke or the government. It declared a sister's love. No. She was not going to answer his question about "beyond those things."

Instead she said, "It was signed, 'With love, Lissy.'"

"And you believe that? that she cares?"

She stood, covered his legs with a light blanket, and kissed his forehead. "Yes, oddly enough, I think I do."

CHAPTER 9

As LUKE WALKED beside Sheridan down the steep hill, he said, "How does Eliot get around town?"

"Mostly he doesn't. We have a car. It's parked at the cantina."

"You don't use it much, then?"

"Only when we go into Mesa Aguamiel. Here in the village we all walk or ride a burro everywhere. Neither of which he can do, of course. Too many hills."

"Topala, the place where time stopped. This can't be a walk in the park, no matter how idyllic it appears. How do you get food and stuff?"

"It's delivered by truck, weekly or daily, usually to the square. I hire the boys to lug propane and drinking water up the hill." She gave him a sidelong glance. "Don't you know these particulars?"

"No."

"Little blip in the research, eh?"

He ignored her smart remark.

She noted how he strode with athletic ease over the uneven cobblestones, his eyes hidden behind sunglasses under the bill of his cap. She had always been impressed with the way he moved and spoke. He epitomized the quality of being at ease no matter what. There was absolutely nothing awkward about him, either physically or socially. It always disconcerted her.

She said, "Do you know what's in Calissa's note?"

"I have no idea. She didn't tell me, and I didn't open it."

"How did she convince you to come? And please don't give me that line about being concerned about our welfare."

"That is true, though."

At some deep level his words resonated. What he had done for them in the aftermath of the shooting spoke volumes of care and concern. Ludicrous as it sounded, the guy probably did sense a connection with her and Eliot because of that day. But . . .

"But it's not enough, Luke. Not enough to disrupt your life and bring you all this way."

"Yeah." He hesitated, no doubt taking time to choose just the right words. "I half expected a 'tommyrot' out of Eliot. You're right. There is more to it."

So. That was that, then. Eliot had been right. Luke came because he himself had something to gain. Her tiny flicker of hope that he might have come purely because of altruism was snuffed out. Poof.

She took a deep breath. "Okay. Thank you for being honest anyway."

"Sure."

They fell silent and continued their walk downhill. Below them lay the town center, now awash in sunlight and tourists.

Until Luke's arrival that morning, this daily influx of visitors did not disturb her. Most of them came up from cruise ships docked in Mazatlán. They came, they went, all in short order. They purchased trinkets and handicrafts. They ate the luncheon special, complete with a slice of banana cream pie at Davy's restaurant. They climbed back on the bus, perhaps wondering how five hundred residents survived in a town founded by silver miners in 1565, where pigs freely roamed the streets and electricity was a fairly recent addition.

Yes, tourists were as much a part of the landscape as the whitewashed adobe buildings, as common as the red-tiled roofs. Not a threat.

Until now.

She scanned the strangers dressed in trendy cruise wear, crisscrossing the square, going in and out of the shops. She wondered which ones were studying her.

As usual, village boys dogged the tourists, holding out palm-size wooden replicas of Topala buildings that they'd carved. The kids were born salesmen, aggressive, smiling affably as they eased into the bargaining process without batting an eyelash.

On the far side of the square, where the church steeple rose far above everything, she noticed a handful of tourists heading through the massive doors, cameras in hand. Her heart sank even further. Of course they were always drawn to Iglesia de San José, a baroque beauty finished in 1775, a jewel in the middle of nowhere. But she had so hoped for a respite during the service. How could that happen with a bunch of goggle-eyed, photo-snapping intruders?

"Sheridan." Luke stepped in front of her, causing her to halt, and removed his sunglasses.

She returned his gaze and sensed he wanted to tell her more. "Don't," she said. "Just don't go there."

"I'm sorry. I can't have this between us."

"It's not. I know you came for other reasons that have nothing to do personally with Eliot or me. And you know I know. It's who you are. Leave it at that." She took a side step, but he blocked her again.

"Calissa said I would be interested in what she wants to tell you. For professional reasons."

"Fine." She swept past him and this time he let her go. Her only thought was to get inside the church, tourists or no tourists, Luke or no Luke.

They reached the bottom of her hill, went by the sculptor's shop, rounded the wrought-iron bandstand, and entered the square. Despite traces of her mother's Spanish bloodline in her eyes and complexion, she could never be taken for anything other than American. Her dress labeled her as a local. She most likely appeared to be an American villager. It was an odd combination that invited strangers to speak to her, and so she averted her eyes from them. Most days she totally avoided going down the hill during the busy times.

Some of the boys approached, their sights on Luke as they loudly greeted her. *"Señora maestra!"* It usually made her smile, their "teacher" nickname for the woman who took every opportunity to shove an English lesson in their faces.

Not today. She held up a finger at them in warning. They got the message and went another direction.

The church bells began ringing. As often happened, the insistent clang set off memories of her mother.

Ysabel Cole had loved the sound. She would grasp her daughters' hands and run with them toward the large cathedral in their Chicago suburb. Laughing, her eyes dancing beneath dark wavy hair, she would call out excitedly above the loud peal in her mishmash of English and Spanish. "*Vamos!* Hurry! Jesús is calling us, *mis niñas*! He is calling us!"

Sheridan had known her mother for only thirteen years. Not nearly long enough, but it was thirteen solid years of Jesús calling to them in bells, in the bread, in song, in a hug, in beauty.

After Ysabel's death, Sheridan gradually lost the ability to sense Jesús calling her. She still found inexplicable solace, though, in the old liturgy. Sometimes she wondered if it was God Himself or if it was simply the memory of a mother's love.

Not that it mattered what it was exactly. All that mattered was the promise of a momentary escape from fears that gathered like thunderclouds over her, threatening once more to drench her with the inconceivable.

She made a beeline for the front doors, hoping Luke would stay outside and keep all the camera toters with him.

❧

"Why so downcast, my child?" Padre Miguel greeted Sheridan after the service outside the church.

The old man's soft voice, compassionate smile, and velvet eyes were a magnet to her. They almost hinted at times that Jesús still knew her name.

She bent to hug the short priest and sighed. It was as if he drew thoughts straight from her heart and off her tongue before she could censor them. "My father is ill. The doctor said he will not last long."

He clasped both her hands between his. "You will go to see him." It wasn't a question.

"I don't know."

He stared at her, his eyes like laser beams.

"Padre Miguel, it's a long story."

"No, not so long a story. Refusing to forgive is a short, uncomplicated story." He smiled again and squeezed her hands. "Go and make your peace."

Then there were times when his magnetic personality absolutely repulsed her. "I—"

"Oh! You worry about señor. Of course! He does not want to travel. We will watch over him. You can depend on us." He gestured broadly as if to include the entire town.

Eliot considered the priest a meddlesome fool and escaped to his bedroom if he heard his voice anywhere near their house. The image of her husband's response to seeing villagers and Padre Miguel on their doorstep made her cringe.

"I-I'll think about it."

"And I, señora, will pray." He squeezed her hands one more time and let go, turning to greet someone else. "Bless you."

Sheridan moved away and spotted Luke. He leaned against a low wall that bordered a sidewalk around the old building. Ignoring the gorgeous vista behind him, eyes hidden by sunglasses, he appeared to be watching her.

During the service, he had sat in a back corner, giving her space. It hadn't helped all that much. Tourists had disrupted her quiet time, moving in and out of the church, clicking cameras even during the serving of the Eucharist. There was no getting lost in the ancient words of love and hope or in the texture of unleavened bread dissolving slowly on her tongue.

Nor was there comfort in Padre Miguel's compassion. On the contrary, he had saddled her with the charge that making peace with the loathsome man she called Dad was *her* responsibility. Hers. Why would she care about making peace with Harrison Cole?

It wasn't about making peace with him. It wasn't even about him. It was about that note. That note for her eyes only. That note that she could not show or explain to Eliot.

Could not explain because she didn't understand it herself. It was about her father's past, something Calissa thought she should know, something that would take her into emotional tunnels she'd left behind when she was seventeen.

"Sher?"

She blinked, surprised to see Luke standing in front of her at the edge of the square, across the street from the church.

"You okay?"

She glanced around, unable to remember walking there, unable to collect her bearings.

Her left arm ached, the one broken when it hit the sidewalk as her husband and coworker were shot. Her chest felt as if a thick rope cinched it. Her throat went dry. She could not swallow, could scarcely breathe. Colors spun before her eyes.

It was over. Her security in Topala, her solace in the old church, her comfort in the simplicity of watching the sunrise or teaching the kids or relating to Mercedes like a daughter. Over. All of it.

Luke pulled her to himself and held her tightly.

At that moment she knew of only two things for certain. He would hold her until she stopped shaking. And then . . . then she would go to the house and pack her bags because her sister asked.

CHAPTER 10

CHICAGO

"Is she coming?" Calissa paced back and forth as far as the phone cord stretched, all of half a step in every direction.

Nearby a nurse harrumphed for the umpteenth time. Nurse Harrumph-umph. She must have used up all of her good graces in allowing Calissa to take a call at the nurses' station outside the intensive care unit. Evidently moving about the small space pushed the phone privilege too far.

Calissa turned her back and did her best rendition of a soggy patch of moss. Knees locked in place, she pressed a tissue against tear ducts which had lost any ability to stem the flow. Her father lying on his deathbed had nothing to do with the crying jag. Nope. This untidy, damp situation was due to sheer anger.

"Luke, are you there?" She snapped the words.

"Yeah."

She wanted to reach through the line to wherever in the world he was and squeeze his Adam's apple. The guy could speed-talk faster than an auctioneer when he wanted to. "Well?"

"I can't say yet." The words came slow as honey squeezed from that plastic bear's fat little paunch. "She's not exactly confiding in me."

"Surprise, surprise." Calissa bit her lip. Luke was her best shot at getting her sister to town. *Best* shot? Try *only*. "Look, I'm sorry. So what *has* she said?"

"'Ask me if I care.'"

"That one was predicted. Anything else?"

"Not really. The church service affected her. Put a crack in her defenses."

"Church service? What church service? What is today? What month is it? March—it's not Easter, is it?"

Luke chuckled. "That usually falls on a Sunday."

"I knew that."

"You just don't know what today is."

Calissa concentrated on bringing herself under control. Ten days ago she had confronted her father—vertical and breathing on his own at that time—with information she had found by accident. In quick succession he turned beet red, sputtered incoherent statements, blanched, and collapsed in a heap on the Persian rug in his living room. Since calling 911, she'd had no idea of the date, let alone any religious holiday.

"Calissa, she needs a little time. Things are complicated. I don't think Eliot would travel. She'll have to arrange care for him."

"Where are they?"

"Mexico. A small village that appears lucky to have running water."

She had expected as much. Mexico had always been Sheridan and Eliot's favorite vacation spot, especially the remote areas. It was his birthplace. The language would pose no problem for either of them.

But why, oh why, couldn't they have just stayed in Chicago? Or at least in the States? Why was it her baby sister had to flit all over the hemisphere in pursuit of whatever it was she pursued?

Her throat felt thick. It wasn't from anger. "Is she all right?"

"She's . . . she's like a porcelain vase sitting on the edge of a very high, unstable shelf."

"What a crock. It's been a year and a half."

"Meaning recovery time has maxed out?"

Calissa kneaded her forehead. Sheridan was falling apart south of the border and with a man she never should have trusted in the first place ten or whatever years ago. Hadn't she warned her? Hadn't she said, "You don't really know him, Sher"? Hadn't she told her to wait? to not hotfoot it down the aisle and off to some dangerous foreign capital city with a virtual stranger? Where had it gotten them? Almost killed. Not working.

Luke said, "You want her home."

"Yes, I want her home."

"I'll do what I can."

She knew he would do all he could, because that's who he was.

Talk about trusting a virtual stranger. Calissa had met Luke Traynor once and intuitively understood—even before he handed her a State Department business card—that he moved in dark circles. Despite his carefree personality and what some women would consider boyish good looks, he was at home in an underworld nobody wanted to talk about.

And besides that, he loved her sister.

Stranger or not, what better combination could she hope for? If anybody could bring Sheridan home, it was this guy.

CHAPTER 11

TOPALA

"Señora!" Mercedes beckoned from the doorway of the sculptor's shop.

Already past due getting home after the midday church service, Sheridan shook her head and kept walking. She had no time to stop. Eliot's agitation would be in full swing, not the best scenario for discussing travel plans.

"Please!" Mercedes mouthed in English.

The girl's efforts to speak the language always sparked a response in Sheridan. There was a swell in her pride as a teacher. There was even a nudge to her old passion to fight the status quo of underprivileged women.

There was, too, another response—that peculiar twinge in her heart that had nothing to do with any role she'd ever played in her life. Simply put, she felt toward Mercedes what she imagined a mother might feel toward her child.

Sheridan turned from the street, sidestepped some tourists, and climbed the stairs to the covered walkway that ran in front of handicraft shops. She followed Mercedes into Javier's display room, a small, rectangular space of shelves and tables. At the moment he was showing one of his beautiful dolphin figurines to a couple. He ignored his friends passing through into the private courtyard behind the store.

Mercedes sat on a bench beneath a tree and pulled Sheridan down beside her. Her brown-black eyes were large pools of fear. "What is happening?" She switched to her native tongue. "What did that man want?"

Sheridan assumed "that man" was Luke, although she hadn't seemed disturbed earlier by him. What had changed? "You mean Señor Traynor?"

"Yes! Oh, my! I went home and Señor Montgomery was so upset. He threw a book onto the floor. He called Señor Traynor very bad names. He spoke too fast in English. I couldn't follow most of what he said, but I understood those words."

The scene she described was almost too bizarre to believe of Eliot. But then, Luke Traynor had not shown up on their doorstep before. She tried to downplay it. "Honey, you've seen both of us upset often enough." They'd never win an award for Emotionally Stable Couple of the Year.

"He threw a book and cursed! He never throws things. He never, ever curses. Even when he is in the worst of pain, he is polite. He is a true gentleman."

The girl's take on Eliot amazed Sheridan. True gentleman? She wondered why she herself did not see him through such eyes anymore.

"And you—" Mercedes clamped her mouth shut and made the sign of the cross.

"I what?"

Mercedes glanced nervously around the yard. She leaned over and whispered, "You hugged that man, that Señor Traynor, *in the square*!"

Hugged? Sheridan thought of Luke's embrace and how it must have looked to others. What to her was a life preserver could appear like anything but to an observer.

"Señora, are you leaving Señor Montgomery?"

"Oh, honey, no!" She paused and, like any good amby's wife, mentally parsed her words.

Yes, she had been attracted to Luke. It was ancient history, a fleeting misstep during a time of turmoil. Anyone would be attracted to such a man given the circumstances. It was over. Whatever "it" was. A silly crush.

But how much was proper to reveal to the young woman, a live-in employee who never commented on her employers' strained relationship and separate bedrooms? With each passing day, though, she seemed more and more like a daughter in whom Sheridan could confide personal details.

Like any good diplomat, she chose a middle ground. "Mercedes, this is not a marital issue. You remember what I told you about the time when Eliot was shot?"

The girl nodded. "It was an attack at the grand opening of your women's job-training center. You got hurt, your arm and ribs. Your close friend Reina, your coworker, died. Señor was struck. The assassin got away."

"Right. Well, Luke—Señor Traynor—protected me that day. He shielded me so that I did not get hit. And then he got me to safety." *And then he took care of me for weeks and weeks.*

"He was your bodyguard?"

"No, just a . . . a diplomat. He worked at the embassy too."

Mercedes's eyes were still large, but curiosity had replaced the fear. "So he is a hero?"

Sheridan couldn't help but smile. At this point she'd go with whatever helped the girl understand. "Something like that."

"You owe him your life!"

"Yes, I do. I will always be grateful to him." She paused and parsed again. "About the hug. Unfortunately he came to report that my father had a stroke and is most likely dying. Therefore, I was upset." Inwardly she flinched at the half truth of what had caused her distress, but she didn't want to get into familial dysfunctions. "Señor Traynor knew that, and so he hugged me—"

"Oh, señora! I am so sorry! You must go to your father!" Mercedes's resemblance to Padre Miguel could be uncanny.

"Yes, I think I must, but I don't believe that Eliot is up for travel. I'll contact the nurses who helped us out when we first came here. They can work shifts at the house—"

"No! No! I can do it. I can take care of señor. Please, señora, please! Let me do this for you."

"But you do so much already, Mercedes. I wouldn't want you to shoulder the entire burden yourself." Even as she spoke the words, she thought of the girl's history. The eldest of a brood raised by a widowed mother, Mercedes had matured early in life. She was totally capable of caring for Eliot and their household. In reality, she probably already did more than Sheridan.

"Señora, you know Javier will help. He can sleep there, and I can sleep here so nothing looks inappropriate. And in the daytime he'll drink coffee with him and play chess and drive us places. You agree that señor likes having him around." She smiled knowingly. "Right?"

Sheridan caught her meaning. Eliot did not easily welcome visitors, nor did he particularly care for interacting with the locals, even the nearest neighbors. He avoided going out beyond the enclosed courtyards. On Saturday evenings, when villagers gathered on the square and music filled the air, he never joined Sheridan as she watched from the balcony, basking in the merriment floating up from a block away. Whenever she suggested they might go down the hill and join in, he rebuffed the idea.

But he enjoyed the company of Javier, the gentle artist who adored Mercedes and was an above-average chess player. On particularly bad days, it was only the sight of the flirting couple that calmed Eliot.

It might work. It just might work. All she had to do was convince herself that Luke's hug did not awaken old feelings and that she could leave the cocoon without falling apart at the seams. And then all she had to do was convince her husband that he could get along without her for a few days.

Which was probably tantamount to persuading both of them that the sun rose in the west, pulled by six oxen with purple bows on their tails.

CHAPTER 12

"You can't be serious." Eliot squinted at his wife. She had just breezed into the house, at least half an hour later than promised, and announced she was going to Chicago after all. "Why on earth?"

"Eliot." Sheridan slid into the armchair across from him at the desk. "She's my sister."

At least his wife had invoked the name of Calissa and not the smutty-mouthed coot known as her father. *Bottom-feeder* did not begin to depict the man. Harrison Cole crept through life at a level lower than slime. It always had and still baffled Eliot that Sheridan was connected to him, biologically or otherwise.

She waited, that look on her face, the one she'd acquired over the past year, the one that snarled his insides. It pinched her mouth, her eyes, her forehead and reminded him that their life had been irrevocably changed by circumstances nowhere near their control. And there wasn't a thing he could do about it.

Twelve years his junior and his second wife, Sheridan had been called his "trophy wife." She was without question attractive, but not in the showy way that phrase indicated. When she first heard the reference, she had laughed until tears ran down her face. She insisted that the only times her appearance had turned heads was when she was a towheaded two-year-old. Athletic and taller than average, she embodied the healthy glow of a Midwestern girl. The hint of Spain in her fine complexion and dark eyes blended into oblivion unless one studied her closely.

Neither could her personality support the "trophy" label. She was far too devoted to good works, far too intelligent and real. A good thing it was for him. A flibbertigibbet would have hightailed it from the hospital long before the morphine dissipated from his pathetic body.

But there were moments when, like now, that look came over her face and he felt a stab of fear. Was there an end to her rope?

She had said something.

"Pardon?" he asked.

"I said, do you want to go with me?"

"Good heavens. Why would I want to go all the way to Chicago in order to watch Harrison Cole die?" He heard the peevish tone in his voice. It was another recent development. Like the incessant pain, it had become part of the warp and woof of his existence.

"Well, Eliot, that's probably not exactly the question, is it? I believe the question is, are you up for a trip in order to accompany me to a funeral because that's what husbands and wives do for each other?"

He smiled grimly. At least in all the recent upheaval, Sheridan had not lost her candor. It was one of the characteristics that had first piqued his interest in her, the one he could trust the most.

The one that promised she would warn him of any rope ending.

"Eliot?"

"Touché. We both know I have not been up for husbandly duties for quite some time. I am certainly not up for a trip to accompany you to a funeral."

"I know, and I'm sorry. But that's just the way it is."

That's just the way it is. How often she summed up their life with that pointless phrase.

"I'm sorry too," he said. "But do you honestly think you're up for it? You still look over your shoulder when we go into Mesa Aguamiel."

She shrugged. "I have to try."

"Right now?" Struggling against the anxiety thrumming in his head, he grasped at straws to keep her at home. "We have quite a bit of work to do over the next few weeks." Sheridan played an integral role in his work. With her help, he was writing a book, a mix of U.S. history in Latin America, his experiences growing up an ambassador's son, and his own diplomatic career. His agent expected to see a large section of it soon.

"Mercedes can help."

"Mercedes?" He nearly barked the name. "Her English is progressing, yes, but I doubt she's literate enough to write or to proofread."

"She's not bad. And so much of what you and I do together is dialogue about what and how you want to write. If you converse in Spanish, she can take notes."

"Meaning that, on top everything, I'd have to translate!"

"You've been translating since the midwife placed you in your mother's arms in Mexico City. Language is not your issue."

True enough. He'd spent most of his life not speaking English. His parents did not settle in their home state of Connecticut until both were in their seventies. Eliot had grown up in Latin American countries. Except for a brief time with his parents in D.C., his stateside stints added up to a grand total of two: Harvard and a hospital in Houston.

Sheridan leaned across the desk. "Your issue is health, Eliot, and Mercedes is perfectly capable of administering your meds. She knows how to exercise your legs. She's a better cook than I am and already takes care of most of the housekeeping details. Javier will do whatever you need him to do." She paused. "I only want ten days."

The stab of fear escalated into a tidal wave of terror. Clenching his fists on his lap, he rode it out, avoiding her eyes and silently cursing the shooter and his choice of bullet that fragmented upon impact with his shoulder blade. It damaged nearly every organ, bone, and nerve in his body. It should have killed him. Why hadn't it killed him? Death would have been preferred to the incessant pain, the unending weariness. The need—for crying out loud, at his age!—for a walker.

Eliot felt the compress of a cool, damp cloth on the back of his neck.

"Take some deep breaths," Sheridan said.

He did so and tried not to think of depending on Mercedes and Javier to intuit his needs. Even worse was the uncertainty of Sheridan in Chicago with her father. If he remained in a coma, then he wasn't talking. A good thing. Sheridan didn't need to hear any tommyrot from the old man.

She said, "I don't want to go, but I have to. It's just the way it is. Luke is staying down at the inn on the square. We can get a flight out late tomorrow morning."

Sheridan had to be the only woman on the face of the earth who could pack on a moment's notice. She never wondered what to wear. She probably still followed her lifetime practice of keeping her passport and other essentials in a bag, ready to go. No doubt she would be gone by morning.

He was out of arguments.

"Luke gave me a cell phone," she said. "Mercedes can call me from Mesa Aguamiel whenever you need to. I'll leave messages with Mercedes's aunt. She can call me too. Her family and friends are always coming and going between towns. We will stay in touch fairly easily, considering Topala still hasn't quite made it into the twentieth century, let alone the twenty-first."

She had it all planned out. He had nothing to say.

"Ten days, Eliot. That's all I need."

"And if he doesn't die within the designated time frame?"

"Then Calissa can handle things by herself. I'm in and out of there." She paused. "You are going to be just fine for ten days."

He doubted that. With his entire being he doubted that.

CHAPTER 13

ON THE HIGHWAY TO MAZATLÁN, MEXICO

Sheridan gazed out the side window of Luke's rental car. The passing brush melded into a fuzzy streak of browns and greens. What she saw more distinctly was Eliot's blank face as he expressed a civil good-bye. No amount of hand-holding or promises to bring back pizza packed in dry ice from Gino's East coaxed even a "safe travels" from him. An "I love you"? Forget it.

Maybe it was more fear than the anger she assumed he hid. Despite hints of improvement, the post-trauma debris still cluttered their reactions to even the smallest of daily challenges. A change of routine? A major ordeal. She was nowhere near being completely free of fears, and it was harder for him.

Luke cleared his throat, breaking the silence that had ridden with them for the forty minutes since they'd left Topala. "He'll be all right."

Luke's ability to read her mind did not lower her blood pressure. "Give it a rest, Gabe. I'll deal with this myself."

"It was that bad?"

"It was horrible. You know, nothing ever used to rattle him. He was the quintessential peacemaker. So collected, so in control. Now he obsesses over how papers and books are positioned on his desk."

"That's the thing: his desktop is a big deal because he's no longer in control of other things. Not of an embassy, not even of his own ability to walk from the courtyard to the kitchen. Your leaving forces him to face the issue, to face what he's lost."

"Tell me, what would you do under the circumstances?"

"If I were physically disabled and not able to engage in the only work I'd ever known? No contest. I'm thinking beach scenes with a bevy of beautiful nurses and flowing tequila."

"Good grief. Save your flippancy for the boys. I'm not buying that scene. It's not you in the least."

He braked behind a slow-moving pickup truck, waited for several oncoming vehicles in the two-lane highway to go by, and pulled out to pass the truck. He eased the car back into their lane and finally spoke, his voice whispery. "No, it's not me. I'd probably want to crawl into a hole and not talk to anyone."

"Like Eliot."

"Yep."

"And if you were married, what would you want from your wife?"

They sped another distance down the highway before he replied. "I'd want her to stay right beside me." Again he put words to Eliot's attitude.

"But why?"

"Because she would be my only link with sanity." He rasped as if the words strangled him.

His rare display of emotion dismayed her. She protested. "But you said he'd be all right."

"He will be. He just won't have an easy time of it."

"No way. You can't lay that responsibility on me, that I'm his only link with sanity."

"I'm not. It just is."

She sank back against the seat and looked again out the side window. *Men.* She should have been a nun.

For a time she had pondered the option. It was her mother's influence, of course. Ysabel's impassioned voice had echoed after her death, a rhythmic throb in Sheridan's teenage heart. *"Jesús is calling."* Ba-boom. *"Jesús is calling."* Ba-boom.

But there was another theme that Ysabel had instilled into the life of her youngest. Time and again, through her actions and words, she reminded Sheridan, *Remember to help the helpless women who live in poverty. Give them tools; give them hope.*

Ysabel had never shared details from her own experiences growing up in poverty in Venezuela, scraping by as a young adult by working in a café in Caracas because there was no other option. In what was left unsaid, though, Sheridan understood that for her mother, being poor and without education led to unspeakable horrors. It was a common story repeated in every language, in every nation.

Sheridan went to college in Chicago and lost herself in the field of social work and volunteerism. The voice of Jesús and the convent idea faded, replaced by the flesh-and-blood reality of helping others.

It was easy to follow in her mother's footsteps of social activism. Ysabel had loved the Hull House museum and its association's outreach programs. Founded in the late 1800s as a settlement to serve the needs of immigrants in Chicago, it remained a viable force in the city. As a child, Sheridan accompanied her mother, a model volunteer. As a college student, Sheridan plugged into the House located on the campus where she earned degrees. As a graduate, she taught at the university and created job-training skills programs for women.

She'd taken on her mother's dream and made it her own.

Then she met Eliot Logan Montgomery III, and suddenly she wanted more. She wanted a partner in every sense of the word.

Eliot was nothing like the men her own age, those self-absorbed, narcissistic thirty-year-old dullards. In two minutes flat, he had tuned into her heartbeat, connecting with her passion to make a difference in the world because it was his own. On their second dinner date, he offered her all of Latin America in which to live out her dream.

Not to mention . . . She smiled to herself and murmured, "He did look good in a tux."

"Hm?" Luke said.

"Nothing."

He glanced at her, brows rising above his sunglasses.

She really needed to lose the verbal self-talk. "I was reminiscing about how I got here. It was like I was Fed Ex'd overnight from single in Chicago to married in Latin America."

"If I remember correctly, you met Eliot in Chicago and married not too long after. Right?"

"Yes. We met at a fund-raiser. He was in town on business; a friend told him about the event. Eliot was all about giving to worthy causes, so he came."

"Love at first sight, then?"

"Not exactly. Maybe love at about third sight. First sight was more of a gelling. I was a serious thirty-year-old, teaching and trying to save the city single-handedly. Eliot shook my hand and made me laugh. Then we talked poverty and he made me imagine the possibilities. When he proposed, it was as if he'd handed me my dream life on a silver-plated platter. Married to him, I would have the entire world at my fingertips along with endless resources to attack poverty." She smiled. "Well, almost endless. My friends thought he was haughty because of that uppity East Coast dialect, but I was intrigued with the way he talked. And then there was the tuxedo. He looked really good in it. Really, really good."

"I assume he owned it."

"Naturally. *And*, on the third date, I saw him in his very own white tie and tails."

He chuckled. "When did you first see him in sweats?"

"Still waiting for that occasion."

"That's what I figured. So what warranted white tie and tails?"

"Oh, he flew me to New York to attend a gala at the United Nations."

"Is that all?"

"Yeah. I was sort of impressed, though."

He smiled. "And how did you end up here exactly? I mean, after all you two have done and the places you've been, why move to Topala?"

His questions jarred her back to the present. She glared at him and didn't bother to subdue her snide tone. "Oh, come on. Surely you have a clue as to why we chose Topala."

"No, actually I don't."

"Which means that 'they' don't have a clue either? Honestly?"

"Okay." He exhaled an audible breath and held up a hand, Boy Scout style. "I promise from here on out, I will not ask you for information which I believe I already have."

"That's a little wormy."

"Best I can do, Sher."

"Don't call me that."

He looked at her briefly. "I often call you . . . I thought it was your name."

"It's a nickname!" Her voice rose into the female range of emotional shrill that she so detested. "And it's for personal friends only!"

She flounced within the confines of the seat belt, turned her back to him, and pressed her forehead against the window. The streak of browns and greens blurred into a puddle of watercolors.

Sheridan glanced at her watch, a cheap replacement for the one with the broken crystal, necessary only because Eliot's medications required she be aware of the hour at any given moment. The second hand did not sweep. It chopped along.

She wished she didn't know the hour right now. The Mazatlán airport still lay at least thirty minutes away. By factoring in the preboarding wait time, a flight to Los Angeles, a layover, and a red-eye to O'Hare, she totaled up a minimum of eighteen hours spent with Luke Traynor up close and personal.

Did she really have enough energy to maintain an eighteen-hour snit?

On the other hand, if she didn't keep up a snit, what was she going to do with the other stuff? That stuff that felt like the absence of loneliness? Like the sun had risen after eighteen months of rain and everything looked different? Bright and shiny and new, full of promise, full of hope. Did she bask in it or deny it?

She pressed her sleeve against her damp cheeks and shifted upright in the seat. "You don't have to escort me the whole way."

"Sorry. Calissa hired me as tracker, messenger, and bodyguard for the whole way."

"Oh, good grief."

"Keep in mind, she remembers you with a cast on your arm. Last time she saw you, you couldn't move without saying ouch and holding your side. You've answered her e-mails, but since you left Houston thirteen months ago, she has had no clue of your whereabouts."

"I am not a little kid anymore."

"A big sister is a big sister for life."

Which explained why Calissa had flown down to stay with her in Houston while Eliot played his game of tag with life and death. It wasn't like she and her sister were even semiclose.

Luke said, "Did I ever tell you about my mother and my aunt, her older sister? They live in the same nursing home. Aunt Cindi actually punched another resident, some ninety-year-old guy who cheated at Monopoly with Mom."

Sheridan stared at his profile for a long moment. Not a muscle moved. It was the telltale sign. "You made that up."

"I do have an Aunt Cindi."

Sheridan's quick smile turned upside down. Why fight it? Luke Traynor was watching over her. Again. He would be whatever she needed at the moment, be it comedian, stoic, or bodyguard. He would swallow up the darkness.

Just like before.

For weeks, he was her shadow, day in and day out. At first she didn't notice him. He was a faceless voice who said, "Sign here; sign there; eat this; drink that." He was a touch on her elbow, directing her into a car, a hospital, a plane. He was a stabilizing presence that held her when her body would not stop trembling.

Gradually he, the man, came into focus. She saw an inexplicable friend who made the phone calls, asked the doctors pertinent questions beyond her grasp, and produced her luggage fully packed with her clothes, cosmetics, other personal items, and laptop.

Later, as she grew aware of life beyond Eliot's hospital room, she connected events and drew a straight line from Luke's arrival in Caracas, to a breakdown in political relationships, to Eliot bleeding to death on a sidewalk.

It tore her apart. She loved the man she believed was responsible for the attack on her husband. How could that be?

At last Eliot woke up and stayed awake for longer periods of time. He was more alert than he had been, which wasn't much, but it was enough. Sheridan realized she was slipping on a dangerous slope. She told Luke to leave.

He'd said, "Not yet." He'd said things weren't finished. She put up an angry front. It seemed safer than telling him how she really felt.

But he knew of course. She saw it in his eyes that smoldered green and in how he avoided physical touch. No longer did he offer a shoulder for her weary head or a hand on her arm to steer her through the maze of corridors.

Calissa arrived and hired a personal assistant for her. Eliot began to discuss the future as if he might have one. Sheridan slept through a night without calling hotel security or Luke.

Things were finished.

In hindsight she saw how Luke had orchestrated their good-bye. She hadn't known he planned to leave. It was morning when he told her at the hospital's main entrance, not night at the hotel when she was at her most vulnerable. He promised that, all things being equal, their paths would never cross again.

"What does that mean? What sort of 'things'?" she had asked.

"Business. Government. Politics. National security." He flashed a smile. "Impersonal." As if to emphasize the last word, he put out his hand to shake hers.

Countless times the man had held her close, sometimes through the night, and now he was shaking her hand. She could not recall if she had told him where to get off or thanked him.

So. He had not found her in Topala for his own personal reasons. It must be a doozy of a payoff from her sister to get him to break a promise.

Sheridan wondered, if she drew a straight line from him this time, where would it lead? From Luke, to already on the road to Mazatlán, to a plane going to Chicago, to . . . what? Losing herself in the hope again that he would stay?

She rubbed her forehead. For now it led right to a headache.

CHAPTER 14

CHICAGO

Calissa grabbed the ringing cell phone off her desk and, flipping it open, spotted a name beginning with *T*. "Traynor! Where are you?"

"The Mazatlán airport."

"Sheridan?"

"Yeah, she's here."

"Thank goodness!"

"We should be in Chicago early tomorrow morning."

"Should be? *Should* be? Tell me it's my hypersensitive mode. Tell me I did not hear *doubt* in your voice."

One of his insufferable conversational lulls ensued.

She nearly bit through an acrylic nail and winced at the pull on her real fingernail.

Finally Luke said, "She's afraid. She's way out of her safety zone here."

"Safety zone? The world is her playground. She's traveled carefree as a bird since she was a kid. She made her first missions trip to the Caribbean at fourteen!"

"That was B.C.E., as she refers to it. Before the Caracas Episode. The minute we entered the city, she got that deer-in-headlights expression. It hasn't gone away yet. She's white as a sheet and stumbling over her own feet."

Calissa paced her private office—not all that large, but at least it was bigger than the nurses' station and no eagle eye watched her hemorrhage anxiety all over the place.

"Okay," she said. "Okay. But you're familiar to her. She once told me she felt safe with you. Of course, that was in Houston before she came to her senses and told you to get lost." She halted. "You are with her, right?"

"She's in the ladies' room."

"Is there only one exit?"

"Calissa, I've got things under control."

"Except for that niggling doubt. Don't you have handcuffs? a rope? something to tie her to yourself?"

He chuckled. "You hired a friend with connections, not a bounty hunter."

"I'll pay you more. Name the price."

"I'm changing the subject. How is your dad?"

She stepped in front of her sixth-floor window and looked down on a crowded, wet Michigan Avenue enveloped in mist. It vied with the ICU for the Most Dismal Scene in Chi-town award. "No change. He seems to be in an inexplicable holding pattern."

"How are you?"

"I'm about ready to eliminate hairstylist costs. No need to color roots if they're all yanked out, is there?" She paused. "I'm in a holding pattern too. I can't move forward without Sheridan. We both need her here. Isn't she out of the bathroom yet?"

"Maybe you ought to hop a plane and meet us in L.A. Do this yourself."

Calissa tugged a fistful of short hair. "Sorry. Call me from there?"

"Yeah. If we make it. I mean, maybe she had a wig in her handbag, a change of clothes. Different sunglasses. Just a scarf might fool me. I should have been watching for a tall, nervous woman running toward the car rentals."

"Shut up."

He laughed, and the line went dead.

Calissa closed her phone and draped herself over the couch that didn't quite accommodate her long frame. It was a love seat of worn leather that she'd purchased ages ago when her father gave her the office space and officially promoted her to assistant.

An assistant. One of his assistants.

The esteemed congressman from the state of Illinois had many assistants in Chicago and D.C.

But only one of them was his daughter, who had access to the attic in his house and who uncovered a history of deceit and who shouted it at his seventy-four-year-old face until it was time to call 911.

And Sheridan thought *she* was out of her safety zone.

CHAPTER 15

MAZATLÁN AIRPORT

Sheridan held her palms under the faucet, catching the trickle of cold water. She splashed it onto her face and moaned quietly. In days past, being sick in a crowded public restroom might have upset her, but at the moment she really didn't care. Self-consciousness was the least of her problems.

The dike had broken. Back in Topala, she'd been able to hold things in place. Peace and safety leaked out through the holes punctured by Luke and her sister, but she had ignored the seepage. She focused on bolstering Eliot, packing clothes, writing lists for Mercedes, and pretending Luke did not tug a heartstring. She had made a successful exit, emotions intact, dike intact.

But then, with each passing mile in the car, the pressure built. As they neared Mazatlán and the traffic and crowds grew to hordes, the wall gave way. In one gushing flood, all sense of security left her.

The old fear invaded. For some moments she thought she was back in Caracas, in a car speeding crazily away from bloodstained sidewalks and shattered windows. Even her arm ached, and every breath pierced her ribs.

Luke took over. Again. She couldn't remember saying a word. She couldn't remember walking inside the airport. She only remembered breakfast moving upward and him steering her toward a restroom door.

She looked in the mirror now, holding a paper towel against her mouth. The eyes that gazed back were scarcely recognizable. Shot through with red, irises dark and blending with pupils, they belonged to a stranger.

No, not a stranger. Rather to a woman ripped from her cocoon in a safety zone called Topala.

❧

Sheridan found Luke not far from the restroom, his knapsack and her luggage at his feet. Weaving her way through scurrying throngs, she approached him.

"Luke, I can't do this."

"I know."

Sheridan blinked back tears that had begun stinging in the restroom.

"I'll do it for you."

She shook her head. Good grief, that was the last thing she needed. "I have to go back."

"To what?"

"My cocoon." The more she thought about the image, the more she liked it. Soft, warm, cozy. Safe. No man to remind her how lonely she was. "My Topala cocoon."

"It's not there anymore."

His words hit her like a physical blow to her chest. "I don't like you."

"Understood. But, Sheridan, the hardest part is over. It really is." He cocked his head, his forehead creased. "Think of what you've just accomplished. After all these months hidden away, you've taken your first step back into a crowded city, back into the real world. You're over the big hump. The next step will be a breeze. LAX? Not a problem. Now, it's time to go."

In one swift motion he picked up his knapsack, slung it over a shoulder, and scooped her bag into his hand. He touched her elbow, pointed to a sign, and began to walk, long strides that moved him quickly away from her.

The whole scene reeked of déjà vu. . . .

❧

It was ten days or so after the shooting. Sheridan and Luke were at the airport in Miami, in some sort of private VIP room. They waited to board a flight to Houston, where they would meet up with Eliot. He had stabilized at the hospital in Caracas, and now the United States government wanted him closer to home.

"Why can't I go with him?" she blabbered at a feverish pitch, the cast on her arm a constant weight that added to her distress. With each breath she could have sworn a bone sliver from a rib punctured her insides. "I don't understand. I just don't understand."

Luke said something, but she couldn't make out the words.

It had been impossible to focus since the nightmare erupted. Her own screaming from that day still echoed in her ears, drowning out others' speech. Adrenaline pounded throughout her body, unabated bursts of energy that kept her awake and frenetic around the clock. She was truly aware of only two things: her proximity to Eliot and an incessant *God, wake him up! Wake him up!*

And now *they*—those powers that stood hidden like the wizard of Oz behind a curtain, pulling the strings that directed their lives—*they* decided that she would not travel with him.

Luke spoke again. At times when the words were lost, his tone got through to her. Its quiet, calming insistence centered her momentarily.

She stopped yammering and turned her energy to clawing at the heavy, wrist-to-shoulder cast as if she could remove it. Two bones were broken, snapped when she landed forcefully on them on the flagstones.

Luke pointed toward a door and leaned in, his nose nearly touching hers. "It's time to go." He touched her good wrist. *"Now."*

She watched his retreating back as he opened the door and walked through it. He strode into a crowded hallway. The door swished shut.

A terror seized her, a primal fear that obliterated the nightmare of the shooting. This was something far worse, too awful for words.

Sheridan raced out the door. "Luke! Luke!" She screamed his name again and again at the passing throng that had swallowed him from sight. "Luke!"

And then he was beside her. She trembled, violent spasms that shook her from his embrace. He drew her back in, tightening his hold.

"Don't leave me! Don't leave me!"

"I won't, Sher. I promise I won't. . . ."

&

Sheridan shook her head, flinging off the memory of that day in the Miami airport. It was a unique moment in time that would never be repeated. And yet . . .

That nameless, debilitating panic pounced again, its tendrils encircling her throat as Luke walked away in the Mazatlán airport. She had no choice. She raced after him.

"Luke! Luke!"

He turned.

What was she doing? What was going on? What was *wrong* with her?

She hurried down the corridor, by now hyperventilating. The crowd swirled around her. Blackness crept along the edges of her vision.

"Sher, what is it?"

She grabbed his free hand with both of hers. The touch of another human being eased the panic.

"What is it?" he asked again.

"Just don't leave me," she said. "Please."

He gently squeezed her hand. "I won't. I promise I won't."

CHAPTER 16

CHICAGO

"Aargh." Calissa closed her cell phone and resisted the urge to smash it against her desktop.

A deep chuckle resounded from behind her.

She turned. "Shut up."

Bram Carter let loose with a guffaw, his mouth a perfect oval in the middle of a full, pearl-white beard. "'Aargh'? From the silver-tongued pixie herself?"

She spread her arms in a gesture of defeat. "I am completely out of words."

"Come here, darling."

Calissa wondered if she let Bram get away with *pixie* because her heart thrummed whenever *darling* resonated in his rich baritone.

Moving around the desk, she carefully laid the phone on it and stepped into his waiting embrace. She sighed. His chest always reminded her of an extra-firm, king-size pillow. If she could replicate it, somehow encase the rhythmic beating of a strong metronome in soft broadcloth and silky lapels, and get the patent, she could buy a Caribbean island and retire.

"So." His voice rumbled in her ear. "What did your spy have to say?"

"They're at LAX. Oh, I wish we'd found them a direct flight to Chicago. Sheridan is an absolute basket case."

"Define *basket case*."

"Blubbery. Clingy."

"Sounds like a surefire guarantee she's not going anywhere by herself. A clingy Sheridan will get here, as long as the one she adheres to stays on task."

"He will. But, my golly! She's forty years old. She's worth a fortune in Montgomery money. She's not tied down to work. Her husband almost died a *year and a half* ago. How long does PTSD last, anyway?" Calissa leaned back and looked up at Bram.

The light reflected in his bottomless eyes the color of burnt coffee. "You think that's it? Post-trauma symptoms from the shooting?"

"My sister is not a flake. What else could it be?"

"You said she had professional help."

"At the hospital. Since then, I don't know what she's been up to. Traynor said they've been living in a tiny Mexican village. It didn't sound like the sort of place where therapists make a living."

"We can't imagine how much Sheridan has going on still, even after all this time."

Calissa studied his face. It was handsome in its mature lines, surrounded by a halo of neatly trimmed thick hair the same color as his beard, both prematurely white. She said, "What do you mean, how much she has going on?"

"Darling, in case you haven't noticed, you sisters grew up in a most unconventional environment. She must sense from your note that the past is about to turn a deeper shade of bizarre."

"Meaning, *of course* she's a basket case at this time."

Bram kissed the tip of her nose. "Of course."

"And where am I on the loony scale? One to ten. She's a twelve. I'm a what?"

"A woman who can't commit to marriage."

She groaned and buried her face in his tie, anticipating his question, the one he asked at least once a month.

"Calissa, will you marry me after the funeral?"

After the funeral? She tensed, willing herself not to whip back a few steps. *After the funeral* was a twist on the proposal that never included a time frame. Was this an ultimatum? Was he finally getting tired of asking?

Abram Carter was everything she could wish for in a husband. He was her best friend, had been for eons. He was in no way threatened by an independent woman. Not that money was all that important, but he had plenty and then some. He was unattached; his ex hadn't bothered him in over a decade. There were no children. He had meaningful work, which he never allowed to consume him. He was tall enough that she could add three-inch heels to her five-nine frame and not see the crown of his head. And with her, he had the patience of Job.

Would that continue?

She smoothed his tie, a splash of pastels that only he could get away with wearing at serious board meetings with Chicago's muckety-mucks. "Um." She cleared her throat. "I don't know."

She didn't know? *She didn't know?* Where had that come from? Her monthly reply was never *"I don't know!"* It was always, always *"Not now."*

"Hm," he said.

Evidently he noticed her different answer too.

She waited. The moments ticked by, and he said no more.

Smart man.

CHAPTER 17

LOS ANGELES AIRPORT

Luke stuffed his knapsack in an overhead compartment and lowered himself into the luxurious first-class seat next to Sheridan's. "You okay?"

She moved sideways until her upper arm rested against his. "Yes."

His tiny smile conveyed empathy. "I am sorry it's so hard."

"If you hadn't come . . ." Oh, why bother? He was there. She was a mess. End of story.

"If I hadn't come," he said, "then your sister would have contacted the State Department and all sorts of people would be involved. NPR would do a blurb on the curious life of Mr. and Mrs. Montgomery. *Newsweek* would send a photographer. Late-night hosts would make jokes."

"I thought Calissa *did* contact the State Department."

"No. I wrote my cell phone number on my State Department card." He paused. "Just in case of a situation exactly like this one, when you needed to be contacted quickly and discreetly."

"If you hadn't come, I'd be at home."

The lights dimmed in the cabin. He said, "You need to buckle up."

She did so, managing to keep her shoulder against his arm through the process, loathing her need to touch him, to reassure herself that the angel had not deserted her.

The sense of déjà vu washed over her yet again. She was right back where she'd been a year and a half ago, scared absolutely witless. Or was it fear? Maybe it was simply the abruptness of it all. She hadn't been away from Eliot's side in so long. Suddenly he was gone and it was Luke beside her.

She said, "You know, I've been within shouting distance of Eliot for a long time now, 24-7. If he whistles, I can hear him from anywhere in Topala. If he could whistle, that is. Which he can't. He can't shout either, for that matter. We have a cowbell."

"He'll be fine. He's a strong man, inside if not outside. You've left him in good hands."

"I'm talking about me." She shivered. "He's the fixed point in my life. My universe revolves around him, measured in yards, by an hour or two at a time. I'm not just there for him. He's there for me. We have nothing else, no one else."

"Sounds like an ingrown toenail." Luke reached above her and turned a knob until the flow of stale air stopped hitting her in the face. "You were going to have to cut it out sooner or later. Think of this trip as necessary surgery. It's painful now, but you'll both recover and be healthier for it in the end."

"We were fine."

"Sher—Sheridan, you were not fine." His exasperated voice was too low for other passengers to hear. "If you were missionaries, maybe you'd be fine. I mean, who lives like you two do, in the middle of the Dark Ages where you can't even get phone service?"

She shut her eyes as if that would tune him out.

"But you're not missionaries, are you? You're not even ambassadors spreading goodwill. You're just two scared ostriches with your heads buried in the sand. You think you can avoid more pain. Believe it or not, you are inflicting it upon yourselves because you can't keep inhaling that sand and stay alive for long."

She felt movement, heard the unclick of his seat belt, and looked up to see him spring to his feet. He yanked open an overhead bin and rummaged in it.

"Sir!" a flight attendant shouted from her own seat at the end of the aisle. "Sir! You have to stay seated!"

Sheridan realized the plane was gaining speed. People craned their necks to see what Luke was doing.

"Sir!" she screamed now.

He waved a blanket for all to see, slammed the bin shut, and plopped back down, all in one swift motion. "You look cold."

"Thanks." She took the blanket from him and spread it on her lap.

"I'm sorry. It's really none of my business."

She met his eyes, lit by the reading light above him. They were more green than gray.

She remembered the first time she had noticed a change in their color. It was in Houston, at the hospital. He had come into the waiting area and handed her a small paper bag. She reached inside and pulled out the old red cobbled leather Bible with onionskin, gilt-edged pages, its language Spanish. In the bottom right corner in fading gold letters was *Ysabel Maria Cole*.

"It got shipped to the storage unit," he had said.

After the shooting, she never returned to her beautiful home in Caracas. Security said it was too dangerous. It didn't matter. She wasn't going to leave Eliot's side anyway.

One of the perks of being an amby's wife was having a large staff. Luke contacted those people she'd grown to love over the five years many of them had spent with her. They packed her and Eliot's things, shipping most of them to a storage unit in Virginia where, again, *they* took care of it all. One trusted assistant, a native Venezuelan, had chosen personal items that Sheridan needed. Those were in the bags sent immediately to the Caracas hospital. More of her things arrived later in Houston. With such upheaval, it was easy to see how one Bible had been missed.

She remembered how she had held the book, staring at Luke,

astonished at what he had produced. He explained how he once heard her talking about the cherished possession. When he didn't notice it among her things, he had it tracked down.

Until that moment, Luke had been a mere shadow performing his duty. Whether out of guilt or because the government paid him to do it, he protected her and Eliot and saw to their needs. As she held the Bible, though, the result of his act of kindness, he took on color. Green twinkled in his irises.

Like now.

She turned away from it. But the truth she saw in them flashed in neon lights before her: Luke cared. He really did.

Was that really why he broke his promise and came?

❧

Once they were airborne, the flight attendant served them drinks. Obviously still rattled by Luke's earlier behavior, the woman ignored his apology and spilled hot water on Sheridan's tray.

Accepting a wad of napkins from her, Sheridan wanted to commiserate with her. "He's always like this—just one big disruptive force."

The woman grunted in reply. Sheridan half expected a federal marshal to appear in the aisle.

But he cared. Somewhere deep in his black heart he cared.

"Luke, I want to explain about me and Eliot."

"Save it. You need to rest."

"Inhaling sand isn't all that bad, not once you get used to it. Topala isn't in the Dark Ages. It's been good for us to live there. It was exactly what we needed."

"Needed. Maybe that time is over?"

"I'm talking. It's none of your business."

He smiled. "Sorry."

She pulled the blanket up to her elbows. In the dark cabin, most passengers were settled in for the middle-of-the-night flight, but she needed to talk. Sleeping was out of the question. Luke didn't need it himself. He could function for days on little or none.

She took a sip of tea and set the cup back on the tray. "Thirty years ago, Eliot and Noelle honeymooned in Topala."

His brows rose. Noelle was Eliot's first wife, a fact he knew. "Really?"

Ha! He did not know about the honeymoon. She gave in and smirked at him. "Really. They were booked into a Mazatlán resort. On their second day, they drove up to the village to sightsee and ended up staying there for something like ten days. Which probably explains that little lapse in your goody bag of information."

He ignored the jab. "Did you and Eliot ever visit there?"

"Don't you know that either?"

"Uncle!"

She couldn't help but smile. "I win?"

"It's yours."

"All right."

It was a game they used to play, after his eyes changed color. Whenever she pestered hospital staff for things for her husband, at times totally obnoxious, Luke would whisper, "Inside, they're crying uncle. You win." It diffused her anxiety, gave her breathing space.

"No," she said now. "I never went to Topala with Eliot before. It was their place."

"Weird choice for you to move there?"

She shrugged. "Not exactly. It's not like I knew Noelle. When she was killed in a car accident, they had been married for ten years. I didn't meet him until years later."

He nodded. Of course he would have known that tidbit.

"We wanted a home that was not overtly connected with our past. Eliot thought Topala fit our needs. It was obscure and quiet. We stayed awhile in Mesa Aguamiel and met Mercedes there. Then we found the house, bought furnishings, added things to accommodate Eliot's, uh, situation." She heard the quotation marks around the word *situation* and felt a stab of guilt. Her pride was ridiculous, especially with Gabe the angel who could see right through her. "Handicapped. He's handicapped. I can't seem to say the word."

"It's got to take some getting used to."

"Yeah. Anyway, you probably know that he was born in Mexico?"

"Sure. The Montgomery family is legendary in some circles. They've made history with him, his father, and his grandfather being ambassadors."

"As you can imagine, he always felt at home in foreign countries, especially Mexico. Language and culture were not issues. Compared to the U.S., living expenses are cheap. Not that money was a major concern, but given his medical expenses, it weighed in on our decision."

"He's old blue-blood money, right?"

"The Montgomery pockets run deep."

Eliot's family money seemed almost freakish in its supply. Great-grandfathers on both sides had invested wisely and taught their children, who taught their children well. Eliot was the only child and the only grandchild. His family—grandparents, parents, aunts, and uncles—had been deceased for some time.

"When I first learned how much money I was marrying into," Sheridan said, "I was stunned. I figured Queen Elizabeth must be a distant relative. He's never flaunted his wealth. He's always been generous. I bet you would never know he was obnoxiously rich if you hadn't been told."

"Probably not. So you chose Topala."

"Y-yeah."

Luke did his slow blink.

"We did." She paused, remembering how her protests made no impact on Eliot. In truth, Topala felt too remote, too much like a closet that had no back door.

"It took me a while," she admitted. "I thought we should stay in Mesa Aguamiel. It was bigger, offered more amenities. I should say it offered amenities, period. But Eliot was like a crazy man insisting on getting us as far off the map as possible. It was only about three months after the shooting when we started discussing. We were both still living out of the nightmare. Topala was the best choice at the time."

"Understandable. The smaller the city, the safer it would feel."

"Yes." She felt suddenly exposed. Why had she told him all that personal information? The government knew where they lived, but they could not know the emotions that went into their choice. "I shouldn't have said all that."

"Sheridan, I will not repeat any of it."

She swallowed, hoping he told the truth.

"I promise."

Could she trust him?

It was too much to ponder. Exhaustion finally hit her. She transferred her cup to his serving tray and locked her own in place. Curling her legs beneath herself, she tilted the seat, faced the window, and leaned back against Luke's arm. The touch settled her.

In the past it had helped her sleep, on airplanes, on hospital waiting room couches, in limos. Maybe it would again.

CHAPTER 18

CHICAGO

After their mother died, when Sheridan was thirteen, Calissa had changed from sisterly ally to authoritarian. Trying to fill the hole in their family, she set absolutes for the young teen about clothing, schedule, activities, and friends. Sheridan battled her at every turn but, in reality, had little say in the matter. Their father saw to that. He backed whatever Calissa said, sometimes with violent tongue-lashings. Sheridan figured she had both of them to thank for honing her strong will.

Those bitter memories pounced the moment the plane landed at O'Hare. She had shoved them from her mind long enough to call Mercedes's aunt in Mesa Aguamiel; she promised to get the message to Eliot that Sheridan had reached Chicago. Not being able to talk directly with him agitated her as well.

By the time she and Luke got their bags and met the limo driver, her headache neared migraine proportions. Finally the interminable trip ended . . . at the hospital.

The hospital? Not exactly where she wanted to be.

She watched the limo pull away from the curb, their baggage in its trunk. "Tell me he's coming back."

"He's coming back." Luke pointed a thumb at the entrance. "Ready?"

"No. Why are we here? Why not Calissa's office or condo? or a hotel? I need a shower." She had slept on the plane, but not all that well.

"Calissa thought it best that you see Harrison first."

"Calissa thought. Calissa thought. When I was fourteen, she thought debate club sufficed for extracurricular activities. When I was fifteen, she thought I was still too young to date. When I was seventeen, she thought 10 p.m. should be my curfew."

"Your point being . . . ?" His lips twitched.

"When I was thirty, she thought Eliot was the worst possible choice for a husband."

His smile faded.

She heard his unspoken question loud and clear. "No, that is not why I married him. I had quit listening to Calissa long before that. Being back here just brings it all up again. All her control. All her . . . Oh!" She exhaled in frustration and disgust.

"Okay," he said evenly, giving her space to calm down.

She pressed her lips together. Spouting off was not helpful. Her head pounded. She wasn't ready. She needed more coffee, a change of clothes. She needed to fill her lungs with fresh air down by Lake Michigan.

She needed to stop listening to the old tapes in her head. She was a grown woman, no longer accountable to her sister's directions or responsible for her well-being. And she was certainly not accountable to a dying man's opinion.

"All done?" Luke said, as if reading her mind.

She glared at him.

"Okay, then. Shall we go inside?"

"Like I have a choice?"

"You always have a choice."

It was a conspiracy. She was convinced of that. God or the government or her father or her sister had forced her to this moment, this place in time.

Forty-eight hours ago she was content. Consumed by her husband's needs, yes, but content to exist within the status quo. Then her sister spoke, and now Sheridan stood outside a Chicago hospital, bone weary, dependent upon Luke Traynor, and questioning, out of the blue, her marriage.

"No, Luke, I don't have a choice. Calissa will not give up until I hear whatever it is she thinks I need to hear."

His eyes softened. "Think of it as taking a vitamin."

"More like a nasty antibiotic that'll make me nauseous." She turned away. "Let's get it over with."

"One more thing."

The automatic doors swished open. She waited to move through them but did not look at him.

He said, "I just want you to know that I'm here for you. For as long as you need. For whatever you need."

"You're working for Calissa."

"The job ends today, right after I escort you inside."

For a moment, she could not breathe. If he had said that sixteen months ago, she would have lashed out in anger, the perfect cover for her fear that she wanted him to stay. And now?

Now there was no fear. She felt only intense loneliness. She felt her life was pointless, without purpose. She felt flattered and feminine because Luke Traynor had gone to a whole lot of trouble to find her.

She shook her head and walked inside the hospital. She should be afraid. She should run for the hills.

Well, she would do just that. Once she got through the family reunion and Luke got his payoff information, she would find her way back home to Mexico all by herself and as soon as possible.

Sheridan walked through the long corridors, Luke wordlessly at her side. The standard hospital odors comforted her. If she couldn't breathe in a Lake Michigan breeze, she'd take instead the pungent mix of clean and filth. To her it had always meant hope for the hurting people who crossed her path. As a social worker, she often watched those folks trade sickness and disease for help and healing in hospital settings.

That perspective probably saved her during Eliot's long hospital stay when she all but lived at his bedside. Even now she drew an odd strength from it. She was on familiar turf, despite what waited at the end of the hall.

Calissa paced there, arms folded across her midsection, a cell phone clasped in one hand. The phone's power would be on, against ICU rules.

Larger boned and an inch or two taller than Sheridan, Calissa Cristina Cole cut an imposing figure. Public persona in place, she wore a black pantsuit and pumps, a white blouse, no doubt silk. Diamond stud earrings, probably a gift from her longtime friend Bram, sparkled even at this distance. Her hair was short and spiky, its symmetry akin to the needles on a cactus. The style with its blonde frosts on the naturally blonde hair added youth to her forty-seven years and yet did not detract from a mature confidence.

"Sher!" Calissa strode down the hall, her arms outstretched.

Sheridan stepped into her fierce hug. She sensed the strings attached to it and cringed inside. How soon before Calissa would tell her what she wanted?

"Let me look at you." Calissa held her at arm's length, peacock blue eyes sharp as laser beams focused as if they could pry into Sheridan's brain. "You're exhausted. I am so sorry to have dragged you all this way. Thank you for coming, hon."

In the time it took her sister to reel off the comments in her distinct, articulate voice, Sheridan rehearsed a number of replies, none of them appropriate. How was it Calissa could make her feel thirteen again? "You know, you have the ability to persuade a zebra to give up its stripes."

Calissa's chuckle was forced. She stretched her hand toward Luke. "Old sister joke. Hi."

"Hello, Calissa."

"Thank you for, uh . . . for escorting Sheridan."

"Not a problem."

Sheridan eyed her sister closely. She never faltered over words. There were new lines etched around her mouth, a new sadness.

"Well." Calissa rubbed her hands together and took a deep breath. "Are you ready?"

"For what?"

"To tell him good-bye."

"Liss," Sheridan said, her tone stuck in a teenage whine. She held out her hands, palms up. "Can I have a little more information here?"

"About what? This is why you came. Our father is dying. You need to tell him good-bye."

"I don't need to, and that is not why I came. I came because of your note. Because you have something to tell me."

Calissa opened her mouth as if to speak, but no sound happened. Her face folded in on itself, creases appearing first in her forehead and on down until her mouth closed around a whimper.

Stupefied at the sight, Sheridan could not move. Her sister, the epitome of self-control, breaking down?

Against all reason, in spite of his rash temper, Calissa adored their dad. She always had. Where Sheridan had only memories of conflict and harshness, Calissa carried remembrances of a congressman who welcomed his oldest daughter's input on political issues even when she was a kid. Adding to that all the years of working alongside him and impacting the government meant her sister must be hurting deeply.

Sheridan wrapped her in a hug. Whatever else was going on would have to wait. There was no choice but to submit to Calissa's agenda.

❧

Gangplank came to mind, that thing mutineers were forced to march along just before plunging themselves into murky ocean depths.

Sheridan had often considered herself a mutineer in the Cole family. Long before she met Eliot and moved physically from Chicago, she moved away from her father and sister in every other sense. At seventeen she moved in with a friend's family for the summer, that autumn to a college dorm, and she never looked back except when holidays rolled around and the coercion overwhelmed her. Congressmen had to keep up appearances. The least she could do was stop by for turkey with important constituents.

Now, walking beside Calissa toward the ICU, she felt a familiar adolescent pressure to conform to her family's lead even if it meant certain . . . death?

She rolled her eyes at the high drama and reminded herself that she was not a child.

Calissa, her composure regained, kept a steady pace through the corridors. Her pumps clicked smartly against the linoleum. With nods and gestures, she directed Luke to a waiting area and Sheridan through a set of double doors. The sisters breezed past the ICU nurses' station.

"They know you're family," Calissa murmured and stopped outside a room.

Large windows afforded a view into the room. Sheridan didn't look inside.

Calissa said, "He looks so awful."

Sheridan nodded, familiar enough with the results of physical trauma. "The stroke."

"More than that. His entire person is . . . gone. I don't know how to prepare you."

Again Sheridan nodded, puzzled at her sister's hesitancy.

"I really believe he's held on just for you."

"Meaning when he stops holding on, it'll be my fault? Give me a break, Liss."

"Oh, Sher. You don't believe that's what I mean. The thing is, he needs to make his peace with you."

"Now that he can't speak? Whoop-de-do." Too late, Sheridan bit the inside of her cheek. "I'm sorry."

"You don't have to do a thing." Calissa squeezed Sheridan's shoulder and smiled gently. "Except come all the way from Mexico."

They stepped into the dimly lit room. Machines hissed; monitors blipped. Tubes all but buried the figure in the bed.

Sheridan halted at the foot of the bed, unwilling to move closer. A wave of nausea rolled through her at the sight of him.

Gone was the handsome, magnetic Mr. Cole who wooed thousands of voters and served for decades in the United States House of Representatives. As Calissa had said, the change in him wasn't simply physical. It went beyond his inability to speak or open his eyes or breathe on his own. It was as if he'd been turned inside out and his inner self exposed in an indescribable aura of vileness.

Sheridan nearly gagged.

"Dad," Calissa said a little too loudly, smoothing the blanket at his shoulder. "Sher's here. Remember I told you she was coming?"

Sheridan stared at her sister. Was she oblivious to it?

"We couldn't get a direct flight for her from, um . . . She looks good, Dad. Healthy. I think she's even gained a few pounds." Calissa looked at Sheridan and mouthed, *Talk to him.*

Only a small cry came out of Sheridan. She spun on her heels and raced from the room.

CHAPTER 19

TOPALA

Eliot eyed the array of pill bottles on the tiled kitchen countertop. Every system and organ and gland of his body was coddled, corrected, or anesthetized by the chemicals encased in gelatin or chalky tablet. Because of them he ate, slept, felt a heartbeat, and rarely considered throwing himself onto the street in hopes a burro would trample him to death.

Mercedes nimbly picked up one bottle after another, opened and shut them, shook pills into a tiny yellow bowl. Sheridan should have been doing it. Sheridan never used the yellow crockery. He preferred the dull brown one to hold these incessant reminders of his prison sentence.

In an infantile attempt to nettle Mercedes, he spoke quickly and in English. "If you laid these containers end to end, they would stretch from here to the moon."

"Or to Chicago." She responded without hesitation in English. "And back."

"I prefer one way to the moon."

She shook her head once, placed hands on her hips, and squinted.

Eliot thought he was looking at a squatty Aztec version of his wife. "We are not going to do this."

"Do what, señor?"

He switched to her native tongue to ensure she understood. "We are not going to pretend that you are taking the place of my wife."

She widened her eyes in surprise. "Oh, I would never pretend that! Señora is irreplaceable. That's why we need seven of us to fill in for her. Javier and my aunt and cousins and our neighbors here and Padre Miguel and—"

"The padre!"

"Why, yes, of course. He fills in the prayer gaps."

"Prayer gaps?"

"The ones left by señora. She will be busy traveling and praying for her dying father and not so much for us." She smiled. "So padre does his part and we all do ours. Javier drives. My family brings us messages from señora. I cook and give you the pills." She slid the bowl toward him. "But you have to swallow them all by yourself, señor."

Eliot Logan Montgomery III, former United States ambassador, had lived and breathed diplomacy since childhood. The son of an ambassador, he grew up overseas. He had a front-row seat watching others serve the needs of humanity. It developed in him a deep respect for all peoples regardless of race, creed, age, or gender. It served him well in his life's work.

But negotiating with an eighteen-year-old, uneducated Nahua squaw about taking his meds was absolutely preposterous.

"I'll take them in the study." He tightened his grip on the walker, whipped it into position, and spun on his heel.

The next moment he was on the floor, arms and legs entangled with the walker.

"Señor!" Mercedes knelt beside him and attempted to set limbs and aluminum aright. "Señor!"

He jerked away from her grasp.

"Are you hurt?"

"No." Fiery darts ripped through every inch of his body. Pinpricks of light exploded in his head. That idiotic little bell cut into his side. His eyes stung.

The bloody bullet should have killed him.

CHAPTER 20

CHICAGO

"And there she goes." Calissa watched Sheridan flee and patted the tiny space on her dad's shoulder that was not covered by a tube. "Maybe it wasn't such a good idea to bring her so soon to see you. Sorry about that, Dad. I should have thought about her all-night flight. She's exhausted. Not to mention you don't quite look like yourself with all this paraphernalia around you. It was too much for her to take in. The hospital smells probably got to her too."

Fighting every urge to race after her sister and ream her out, Calissa forced calm into her voice and sat in a chair, close enough to keep one hand on Harrison's arm.

"She'll be back." Full of doubt, she pumped conviction into her tone.

Or maybe it was just a bunch of hot air.

Whatever. She was determined to do all that it took to foster hope in her father and in herself. Certain things had to happen before he checked out, and as usual, it fell to her to make sure they happened.

While Sheridan scampered away like some scared rabbit, Calissa held down the fort. Again, *as usual.*

But fort holding came with the territory of being the eldest child. She understood that. She accepted that as her lot in life. No, it wasn't fair. It just was, period. Bitterness didn't help. Harboring resentment was a dead end.

But still . . .

How long had she been doing it?

She hit the speed dial for Bram's number.

"Darling?" he answered.

Instantly her shoulders lowered several inches, the tight muscles released at the sound of his rumbling voice. "Hi."

"Hi. Let me guess. According to my watch, not enough time has passed for things to have gone according to schedule."

"Mm." She glanced at the monitors on the other side of the bed. Her dad's heart rate had escalated soon after she said, "Sher's here." It had not yet come down to anywhere near what they told her was necessary. She avoided looking at the blood pressure number. *Don't die. Don't die.*

Bram said, "And you can't talk." He knew how she measured her words in Harrison's room, being extra careful not to upset him or the nurses, who had forbidden her to use her cell in his room.

"Mm," she replied.

"Plan B?"

"Okay."

"Say, one hour?"

"Okay."

"Love you."

"Love you too. And, uh, thank you for not saying, 'I told you so.'"

"I'm saving it for in person." He chuckled. "You're adorable when you're flustered. I wouldn't miss seeing your face for the world when I say it."

Calissa closed up the phone on his laughter.

But, listening to its echo, she smiled. Unlike any other sound, it soothed and bolstered her. Why was it she kept telling this man no?

She gazed at her father and saw the answer.

Her smile disappeared.

CHAPTER 21

TOPALA

"Señor!" Mercedes's anxious voice came through the closed bathroom door. "Are you all right?"

"Yes," Eliot snapped, dripping wet beside the shower stall. He toed the bath towel hopelessly tangled under the legs of his walker. Why he had even dragged the blasted thing into the small space was beyond him. If Sheridan were there, he would not have bothered with it.

"Señor!"

"I'm fine!"

"You don't sound fine." She spoke, as he did, in English, her rhythm an annoying singsong.

"I am fine! I can manage a simple shower by myself." He could. He did so most days. The bathroom screamed *handicap accessible*. They'd had all the special effects installed. He didn't have to climb into a tub or even over a threshold. He simply walked into the shower, holding on to strategically placed handrails.

It was the idiotic towel that posed problems. Given his defective sense of balance, he could not bend to the floor and retrieve it. He glanced around. Surely there were other bath towels available, not just the one laid out by Mercedes.

"Señor, what—"

"Mercedes, please, please stop hovering and just tell me where the bloody towels are!"

He took a deep breath. He simply must settle down. Why did he continue to fight it? Bottom line, he was not the man he had been and he never would be again. Kicking a towel and yelling at the help was not going to change that fact. It was not going to bring back his career. It was not going to bring his wife home any sooner than ten days.

Sheridan's absence loomed before him—a long, dark, airless tomb. How was he supposed to survive in such an environment? It was too soon, far too soon for him to be without her. She held him together, kept him from fraying apart at the edges. And the thought of her in Chicago, where memories would be unearthed, threatened to send him right back to bed.

The door clicked open and bumped against the walker.

"Mercedes!" He'd endured untold humiliations due to his physical limitations. He was not about to add helpless and naked before an eighteen-year-old girl.

"It's me, señor." An aged face appeared in the opening. Padre Miguel smiled and pushed the door wider. "Forgive me for barging in. Mercedes heard you say 'bloody towel' and became quite upset. I was in the kitchen." He shrugged. "Are you hurt?"

Bloody towel? The priest's Spanish rendition of his English phrase missed the point. "Good heavens." He switched to Spanish, where he should probably stay put. "No, I am not hurt. I simply wanted a towel."

Padre Miguel swept a glance over the room. "There."

Eliot followed his nod to a wicker shelving unit and saw a stack of neatly folded towels on the top shelf. About waist height. In plain view.

He grabbed one and wrapped it around himself. "Thank you."

Grinning, the short man resembled an ancient friar in his brown priestly frock with knotted rope belt. He wriggled through the small opening. "Funny how often answers stare us in the face and we don't see them, isn't it?" He righted the walker and pushed the door completely open. "It is a puzzle. Do you think our subconscious refuses to let them in? Like some sort of self-inflicted blindness?"

Eliot gaped at him. He was one bizarre little man and vexing to the core. "Padre, do you mind?"

"Oh." He let go of the walker and stepped back. "You'll want to get dressed. Let's continue this discussion in the courtyard, shall we? Mercedes has prepared a marvelous lunch for us. See you there." With a wave and a smile, he turned and strode away.

Eliot cursed under his breath. He began with the day he was born and didn't stop until he reached the point yesterday when he watched Sheridan walk down the hill, her luggage in Luke Traynor's strong, capable hands.

CHAPTER 22

WILMETTE, ILLINOIS

"Nice house." Luke climbed the wide, open staircase with Sheridan, her bag in his hand. "Did you grow up here?"

She cocked her eyebrows at him.

He shrugged, the image of innocence.

So, okay, maybe he didn't know everything about her.

"Yes, I grew up here. My parents bought it before I was born. I can't understand why my father has kept it all these years just for himself. It's too big for one person to need or to take care of."

She touched the wallpaper. The large floral print had a tired appearance. It was the same with the old-fashioned draperies on the floor-to-ceiling front windows below.

They reached the landing with its turn in the stairway and a window.

Luke stopped, gazed outside, and whistled softly. "Lake Michigan meets your backyard?"

She glanced at the scene. The sloping expanse of grass hinted at a greening spring, but there was no horizon. Only whitecaps differentiated the pewter sky from the pewter water. "Yes, that's the lake."

"In your backyard." He smiled at her. "Funny. I never saw you as a spoiled brat."

She let his teasing remark go and continued up the steps. Hers was a story so typical it bored. Poor little white girl has everything she could ever want except an emotionally healthy, loving family.

"What about you?" She changed the subject. "I never imagined you as being a kid, period. Where did you grow up?"

"Here and there."

She eyed him now beside her. "Can we dispense with the tight-lipped rigmarole? We're practically living together again, except this time I'm not preoccupied with assassins and whether or not my husband will live through the night." She attempted a snippy tone. "Apparently your job is not over yet."

"Calissa wants to talk to me here. It may take a while."

"Whatever. I really hope I never see you again, Luke Traynor, but for now a regular conversation might help pass the time. For instance, you had to grow up somewhere."

He narrowed his eyes in a somber expression. "Okay, but you must swear not to tell a single living soul."

The angry facade didn't hold. She burst into laughter. "I can't believe you said that."

"It's good to hear you laugh." He smiled.

"Oh, I give up. You're not going to answer. Forget I asked."

They had reached the top of the staircase. He set down the bag and clicked the handle into its raised position. "My dad was in the Navy."

"For real?"

"Yes."

"A straight answer. Will wonders never cease?"

He tilted the bag onto its wheels. "Where to?"

"I'll take it from here." She accepted the handle from him. "So I guess you were a military brat, not a spoiled one."

"My mother would debate you on that one. I always wondered what it would be like to stay put for years on end. My parents retired to a city where I never lived. There is no house for me to visit where the walls breathe out memories."

She glanced down the long, wide hallway with its several doors and framed prints of foxhunting scenes on the walls. If she held her breath, maybe she could avoid inhaling whatever it was the old place exhaled.

"Sheridan, are you okay?"

"Sure."

"It's been a crazy morning."

"And I'm still walking and talking. At last count, we're at two down, two to go."

"Meaning?"

She held up a finger at a time, numbering as she spoke. "I have survived one, a reunion with Liss; two, a reunion with Harrison."

"And the two to go?"

"Hear my sister's message and, if Harrison dies on schedule, attend the funeral." She shut her eyes briefly. What an ugly thing to say. *I'm sorry.*

"What about being in this house? A lifetime of memories must be coming at you. You're okay here?"

Well, obviously not.

Earlier she had assumed she would stay in a hotel or at Calissa's condo in the city. When they left the hospital, though, Calissa informed her otherwise. Her place was a mess. The kitchen was being remodeled; the guest room had become her office away from the office. Calissa rounded off her excuses with the opinion that the house was the best place to talk privately, and of course, it was spacious enough for them to stay, Luke included.

Sheridan sighed to herself. Luke perceived what she was feeling, but what could he do? Whisk her off to the Drake? He was being paid to whisk her off to exactly where she was.

She said, "Sure."

"'Sure,' you're okay?"

"Sure."

"All right." His tone indicated he did not believe her.

"All right. So stop hovering." She started down the hall toward her old bedroom, pulling the suitcase along the worn runner, and thought about a hot shower. She would wash away travel grime and maybe even a memory or two while she was at it.

❧

A short time later, Sheridan emerged from her old bedroom's bath wrapped in a terry-cloth robe and towel drying her shampooed hair. Some equilibrium had returned.

On her desk was a large silver tray. Calissa must have put it there while she was in the shower. Except for the bone china place setting, the display looked like something from a hotel with its covered dish and a white thermos carafe.

Sheridan lifted the cover from the silver-rimmed plate. An omelet sat there, a beautifully formed fluffy oval covered with hollandaise, surrounded by strawberries and grapes and sprigs of parsley.

"Bram." She smiled. Her sister's significant other had to be responsible for this edible work of art. If the coffee in the carafe was his as well, she just might be able to function through the remainder of this hellacious day.

Even in the years before his hair and beard turned snow-white, Abram Carter had reminded her of a Santa Claus without dimples, a cherry nose, or a belly that jiggled like a bowlful of jelly. He was jovial, giving, carefree, and yet one of the most hardworking people she'd ever met. Time and again he had used his connections to help her in some aspect of her work. As the owner of a Chicago newspaper and magazine, Bram moved within a vast network of business associates. The only chink in his delightful character was his relationship with Calissa. It never made sense to Sheridan what the man saw in her sister.

She poured herself coffee and carried the tray to the double bed. With thoughts of procrastinating over a quiet meal, she climbed atop the old-fashioned, off-white chenille spread and sat cross-legged.

"Mmm." She swallowed her first bite. "Spinach, lemony, a touch of nutmeg. He has not lost his touch. He's almost as good as Mercedes. Thank You, God." *God. Thank You. Yes.*

She smiled again. Of course God would show up in her room. It was the only place in the house that might exhale His presence.

"Thank You for this food and for this cozy spot. This safe spot."

Despite the tears shed throughout the years in her bedroom, she felt surrounded by good memories. For thirteen years her mother tucked her into bed every night with prayers and hugs and whispers of love. That was what the walls breathed out around her now.

She thought about the crucifix her mother had given her when she was twelve. Within days after Ysabel's death, Sheridan had flung it hard and high. It bounced off the wall and landed atop the tall bookcase. Out of sight, out of mind did not happen. She never forgot it was up there.

Not much was changed in the room. It still had the white furniture with gold trim, pale blue shag carpet with matching frilly curtains, and three framed posters of Latin American scenes. Knickknacks, books, papers, and pens still sat on shelves and in drawers. Old clothes, mostly volleyball team T-shirts and sweats, hung in the closet.

It was kind of pathetic how her dad never had the place cleared out. After twenty-some years she figured he'd have believed her declaration, when she left for college, that she was never coming back.

Sheridan pulled the desk chair over to the bookcase and climbed on it. Stretching on tiptoes, she swept her hand around the dusty top until she felt the cross.

She carried it to the bed, sat back down, and brushed the dust from it with the napkin. It was about five inches long, made of wood. The body of Christ on it was a simply carved figure without detail.

What was it Ysabel used to say? She would caress the piece and speak in a reverent tone. *"Jesús is not dead on the cross, but we cannot forget how He suffered there for us. It is only through His suffering that we are healed."*

Sheridan rubbed her thumb over the crucifix and let the memories of her mother's voice come.

"Sheri, He is alive and right here with us. He lives in us. Don't ever forget Him. This life is a journey of suffering, but it will pass, and then we shall see Him face-to-face."

Whenever her mother said such things, a painful expression had scrunched her pretty face. Most often joy spilled from her, but Sheridan understood that Ysabel's life was one of perpetual suffering, compliments of Harrison. Even as a youngster Sheridan comprehended his disdain for Ysabel. It was continually in his facial expression and tone if not his words.

Sheridan slipped the cross into the nightstand drawer beside the bed.

Eliot suffered something awful. Her mother would have been able to talk to him about that, not so much about the physical aspect of pain but about how it hurt to be cut off from relationships and work. It was her mother's story.

Good grief, it was Sheridan's own story.

Suddenly overcome with a desire to talk to Eliot, she scooped her handbag from the foot of the bed and pulled out the cell phone. She had left him two messages from the airports, but that came nowhere close to being in touch. Even with daylight saving time, there was only a two-hour time difference, so calling Eliot was no problem.

Except that he wasn't at the other end of the phone to answer.

"Oh! You are such a fool, Sheridan." *You drop off the face of the earth and now expect your stupid can't-find-us system not to work? You can't call him, just like no one has been able to call you all these months. And you know he is not going to go to Mesa Aguamiel. First of all, he doesn't trust Javier to lead a mule, let alone drive the car. Even if he did manage to go, he's not going to wait at some stranger's house in case her phone rings.*

What had she been thinking? She had willingly cut herself off from the only true relationship she had left. No, their life was not what she signed up for, and yes, it was a hiding from reality. But at least it was predictable. Out of the limelight and out of politics, she and Eliot did live in peace. There were no surprises more serious than leaks in the roof during monsoon season.

There was no Luke messing with her emotions.

She missed everyone. Eliot. Mercedes, Javier, Padre Miguel, the village children. Her mother. The voice of Jesús calling her. She even missed the father she never had.

She turned the phone off, yanked open the drawer, and tossed it in with the crucifix.

CHAPTER 23

TOPALA

The promise of a scrumptious meal outdoors was Eliot's sole incentive to leave his room and join the padre at the patio table for lunch.

All of Mercedes's dishes were scrumptious. In honest moments, Eliot admitted to himself that her cooking ability was her saving grace, else he would have dismissed her long ago.

As he slid the spoon from his mouth, he shut his eyes. Cumin, cilantro, tomato, garlic, chicken, a hint of black beans—not his favorite but she made them work—and a delicate broth.

Padre Miguel chuckled. "It is lovely, isn't it?"

He swallowed and looked at him. "Yes, it is."

"I imagine you must have been exposed to the very best. Your embassies probably employed highly trained chefs."

Eliot bristled and pursed his lips.

The little old man with big brown eyes reached across the table and touched Eliot's arm. "Señor Montgomery. Some of us backward locals know how to use the Internet. Neither Mercedes nor your wife needed to tell me that you were once an ambassador. And rest assured, friend,

I do not pass along personal information." He smiled and removed his hand.

The spot on Eliot's arm burned as if a branding iron in the shape of five short fingers had lain there. Of course, no wonder. The padre had to be roasting in his coarse-textured brown robe. There were beads of perspiration across his forehead.

"Well." Eliot cleared his throat. "I have been blessed to not have to cook for myself. Sheridan and I both have. Eating would be a disagreeable task if we had to depend on her culinary skills or mine." Did he just say *blessed*?

"She has told me she cannot boil water correctly for tea."

Eliot smiled. "She can't."

"The good Lord has given you both other talents, other work to do. Meanwhile He takes care of feeding you."

"And He has fed us well. Mercedes, though, is by far the best chef we have ever known, including those from state dinners at the White House." Goodness! What was with the excessive chatter?

"And to think that she is a simple, uneducated girl. Isn't God amazing? Señor, I know it is difficult for you to come down to Iglesia de San José for Mass. But you know Him, don't you?"

"Uh . . . um . . . I grew up in the church. I believe Jesus is God's Son."

Padre Miguel clapped his hands, pleased as punch at the rote answer. "Then you miss the communal time of adoration. We will get you there when you are ready."

"I'm really fine—"

"Yes, you are."

"Without the church."

The padre shrugged a shoulder. "Oh, what am I thinking? Please forgive me, señor. I forgot why I came. I have messages from señora."

"What?" Eliot all but squeaked. "You have messages from my wife?"

"Yes. Two of them, as a matter of fact. Let me see here." He carefully set the spoon in his bowl of soup and put both hands in his pockets. "We thought it best to write them down." He continued to fumble.

"Padre, please."

"Señora's arrangements to communicate do work, though more slowly than you would like. She called Maria, Mercedes's aunt, two times. Chavez, Maria's second-to-youngest son—or is it third?—who is Mercedes's cousin, hitched a ride with the propane truck driver, Necalli, but he wasn't coming to Topala today. He was going to La Petaca. Well, they got to talking and completely forgot to stop at our turn. So Chavez had to get off further up the road. He began to walk, hoping for a ride. Praise be to God, Xochitl came by. You know her, the pretty one who works at Davy's. She was on her way back from visiting her mother in Borbollones, who has been quite ill for some time now. Anyway, Chavez eventually found me at the church." Padre Miguel moved the knotted rope at his waist to get a better angle to a pocket. "And here I sit, enjoying Mercedes's delicious soup, not thinking."

Eliot removed his glasses and pinched the bridge of his nose.

"Oh. Here it is." He produced a torn piece of wrinkled paper, smoothed it on the table, and read from it. "Señora said, 'Please . . .'" Padre Miguel looked up with a smile. "She is always so polite." He began to read again. "'Please tell my husband that we are fine. We are in Los Angeles.' And the second message, 'Please tell my husband that we are fine. We are in Chicago. It is raining.'"

Never since the shooting had Eliot so badly wanted to run again, and he wanted it every single day. He was a runner. *Had been* a runner. His body was built for running. It released stress and tension and whatever bothered him with sublime perfection.

Had released.

No longer. At the moment he felt like he might crawl right out of his skin.

She was fine? He didn't think so. The thought of Sheridan in a big city, something she had been so fearful of since the shooting, was driving him crazy. And facing her sister and father, the ones responsible for such hurt throughout her life? No, she couldn't be *fine*. And what if light was shed on Harrison's despicable behavior during those years when Sheridan was too young to remember . . . ?

"Padre, I must talk to her."

The man clapped his hands together once, crashing cymbals to announce something. "Let's go."

"What?"

"Finish your soup and then we'll go."

Eliot stared at him, not comprehending.

"Señor, we get in your car and we drive thirty minutes to Mesa Aguamiel and use Maria's phone, and you call señora's number. Simple."

Simple.

Eliot took in a long, slow breath. It felt like a gust of hope in his chest. "We could do that."

Padre Miguel grinned.

CHAPTER 24

WILMETTE

Calissa was going to destroy whatever respect and honor surrounded the name of the honorable Congressman Cole. She was going to lay herself wide open to ridicule, first from her sister and then from the congressional district. Then perhaps even from the state. Maybe the entire country.

It was not a responsibility she chose.

Seated in an upright fetal position, she huddled in a corner of the love seat, her legs folded beneath her. She was wound up tighter than a jack-in-the-box. If the lid did not pop open soon, if she did not speak the truth soon, something inside of her would snap, and she would never move again. They'd have to stick her in the bed next to her dad's.

Rain slashed against the windows. Occasional thunder boomed. Her nerves were not soothed.

Across the coffee table from her, near the marble fireplace with its crackling and hissing fire, Luke stood beside one of the wingback chairs. Like her, he watched Sheridan and Bram.

They stood in the doorway and shared a lengthy, silent bear hug. Moments before, when Sheridan walked down the stairs, Calissa had noted her hair—damp and in desperate need of styling. She noted her knit pants and oversize shirt—eggplant in color and loose fitting but not enough to hide her excess weight. Still, her sister appeared somewhat refreshed, better than she had earlier.

Perhaps she was ready to hear the surprising news?

The hug finally ended. Bram said, "You never write; you never call; you never visit. What am I? Chopped liver?"

An honest-to-goodness grin creased Sheridan's face. "Hello, Abram. If I'd known you were cooking brunch, I'd have come sooner. Please tell me you're fixing dinner too?"

He laughed.

As they teased each other, Calissa twisted one stiff, spiky lock of hair after another. At least she'd had the foresight to assemble exactly the right team for this momentous occasion. What better men to have on hand than Luke and Bram?

When she had introduced them, they immediately sized each other up like a couple of little boys. They'd stopped short of describing how tough their dads were, but she had begun to question her choice. *Men.* When their tone had finally shifted into adult mode, she breathed a sigh of relief.

She knew Luke was an obvious necessity for the meeting. The mysterious figure had proven twice over now that he cared for Sheridan. Now, as he watched her converse with Bram, his face remained inscrutable. His mind probably recorded every word and nuance. What an odd duck. Any other guy would have been fiddling with the fire.

Bram was holding Sher's hands. "How is Eliot?"

The grin faded.

Calissa tuned them out again, grateful that Bram had agreed to be there. Ages ago, when Sheridan was a senior in high school and butting heads on a daily basis with Calissa and their father, Bram had eased into the role of a steady big brother figure as if he'd always been in it. While Calissa's relationship with him remained convoluted—he was married for years—his and Sheridan's was always straightforward.

Calissa suspected that if her sister had had a traditional wedding rather than a private ceremony, Sheridan would have asked Bram and not their father to walk her down the aisle. She had even toyed with the idea that it was Bram who forwarded Sher's mail from Chicago to wherever in the world it was she lived. When she asked him, though, he only smiled and shook his head.

Now Bram said to Sheridan, "We have some difficult news to tell you, honey."

Sheridan nodded. What little color had tinted her cheeks now drained away. How had Luke described her on the phone? She was like a porcelain vase on the edge of a shelf. That wasn't quite it. She looked more like a fragile antique doll, not teetering on the edge but already tumbled from it and badly cracked.

"Shall we sit?" Bram said.

As they sat—Sheridan and Luke in the chairs, Bram beside Calissa on the love seat—Calissa chewed her thumbnail. Bram looked at her, expectant.

But she could not begin. "Sher, do you want some tea? cookies? Are you warm enough? Do you want an afghan? Bram, maybe you ought to add a log. Luke, do you—"

"Liss!" Sheridan's tone did not fit the fragile porcelain doll image. "Can we just get on with it, please?"

"I'm sorry. It's just . . . I've never wanted not to say something like I don't want to say this. It's going to change so many things."

"Just talk to me. What did you mean in your note? You're Ishmael and I'm Isaac, and you have old stories to tell me. Right? That makes you the messenger, not the responsible party." She spread her arms wide, palms up, a clear gesture to get on with it already.

Calissa looked at Bram. "Told you she could figure it out. You didn't think she'd get the Old Testament reference."

"Darling, stop stalling."

She gave a quick nod.

Luke leaned forward, his elbows on his knees. "Calissa, do you want me to leave?"

"No. You need to be part of this. I promised you information, and this is it. Anyway . . ." With a deep breath, she unfolded her legs, bent over, and picked up a box from the floor. It was shirt-size, white, of sturdy cardboard, the name of an Oak Street boutique in discreet blue script. She set the box on her lap and looked at Sheridan.

Some color had returned to her sister's cheeks, a good sign that there was some fight left in her.

"I was in the attic a few weeks ago." Calissa paused. "Wait. Let me back up. For the most part Dad is—was—still sharp as a tack. But he had decided not to run again for office in the next campaign. A wise call given that he's seventy-four and spending more time in Florida than D.C. or here. He even agreed to sell the house and told me to get started on it."

"But why?" Sheridan asked.

"Why what?"

"Why retire? Seventy-four isn't all that old. Until the stroke, wasn't he healthy as ever? And the district loves him. I should say the machine loves him, that group with the money that gets him elected year after year."

Calissa winced.

"What? They don't love him anymore?"

"There's this new guy."

Bram said, "Calissa." A seam between his brows deepened. It was the closest he came to a glower. "Tell her."

She bit back a sigh. "There is a new guy, young and energetic, but the reason they're looking at him is because Dad didn't get an appropriations bill in place, something to do with a Chicago green firm. It doesn't matter. That's not what this is about."

Sheridan shook her head. "It is, Liss. You always have to describe him through rose-colored glasses."

"Only because yours are so blasted dark. Every hint of light is blotted out."

"Ladies," Bram said.

"Sorry. The plain truth is, he's on his way out anyway and it's mostly due to his own fault. All right?"

"Apology accepted." Sheridan exchanged a thumbs-up with Bram. "Why Florida? What's there?"

"An old friend. Specifically, a lady friend. We haven't met." She shrugged. "I signed on with a realty agency and hired a service to do an estate sale. Dad said the things here aren't important to him. I should get rid of it all. I figured you and I already took the few keepsakes we wanted."

"Except Mamá's watercolor of the backyard."

"Yes." Their mother had dabbled in painting but gave away everything she did except for that one.

"He wouldn't let me take it. He always mocked her 'silly hobby,' and yet he refused to give that up."

"I know, hon. You can take it with you this time."

"How thoughtful."

Calissa ignored the uppity tone and straightened her shoulders. "So I met with this woman, Edna, to do an inventory for the estate sale. We went through the whole house, basement to attic. We opened trunks and cedar chests. Grandma Cole's ugly china is still up there." She pointed toward the ceiling. "And our dolls and games and books. Our baby clothes. Nothing really usable or memorable. Remember how Mamá never liked to get rid of anything?"

Sheridan nodded.

"Since we were kids, it's all been shoved into the attic and forgotten about. Dad isn't exactly a housekeeper. Neither am I. Anyway, in one of the cedar chests, Edna and I found linens, a set of encyclopedias, and beneath it all, a locked metal box." She paused.

"And?" Sheridan said.

"Edna told me that I should take care of it, not her. So I did. Later. Used a hacksaw." Again she stopped talking.

"What was in it, Liss?"

"I don't know where to begin." Calissa caught sight of Bram's nod of encouragement and cleared her throat. "The papers I found reveal that Dad made several trips to Caracas. Of course we know he met Mamá there. And that he went for committee work, for the House, through the years when we were growing up. But . . . it turns out . . . the whole time he was involved in diamond smuggling."

"Diamond smuggling?"

Calissa nodded.

"As in carrying them across the border?"

"I'm not sure about that part exactly. He could have. "

"Then what part are you sure of?" Sheridan wouldn't slow down.

Calissa glanced again at Bram. "We can't decipher it all, but it's apparent that he influenced international trade policies."

Sheridan sat back. "Oh, my gosh. You have got to be joking."

Calissa nodded toward the box and whispered, "His notes from meetings are in here. Secret meetings. And there's a ledger."

"He took kickbacks." Sheridan stated it as fact while Calissa kept wondering and hoping. It wouldn't take much to convince Sheridan that their father was a crook.

"Yes, he took kickbacks. Sometimes in diamonds, which he sold. Sometimes cash. He hid the funds through money laundering."

Sheridan's eyes widened. "It's how he bought this house. How he kept up—"

"He bought this house forever ago, back when it wasn't expensive."

"Oh, Calissa, don't do that. Do not stick up for him. He spent his childhood in parking lots waiting for his parents to come out of a bar. They had nothing. Mamá came from nothing. This house was always out-of-sight expensive in their economy. The house in Virginia was the same. There were his cars, his yacht . . . Oh, I feel filthy. So ugly and filthy. We grew up in luxury because poor people mined diamonds that were bought and sold under the radar because our *father* made it possible." She pressed a hand over her mouth as if to stop herself from spouting off more.

Calissa turned to Luke. "Can they arrest him?"

"I'd have to know more to figure that one out."

Sheridan made a noise of disgust. "They should arrest him! Right there on his deathbed. What a despicable life he lived!"

"How recent are we talking about—these activities?" Luke said.

Calissa shook her head. "He's been off the trade committee for over ten years, and he hasn't traveled for ages."

"It's odd," Bram said. "The last entry was in 1983."

"That's a long time ago. He may have kept other books elsewhere. Or computerized them."

"Some trade policies really haven't changed all that significantly over the years. It's as if someone took over where he left off."

"Well, he wouldn't have accomplished such things single-handedly," Luke said. "Others would be in on it. Maybe still are."

Bram took the box from Calissa and stood to hand it to Luke. "This is way beyond us. We figured you'd know what to do with the information."

"I wonder why he chose the attic for these papers?"

"There would have been less people around here than in either of his offices. Calissa said she couldn't remember the last time she was in the attic. I think he simply forgot about it."

"I can't imagine that a man like him would forget something like this. Did you ask him about it, Calissa?"

She began to cry. "Yes. I confronted him. I said, 'Did you do this? Did you lie and cheat and steal? Did you help with diamond smuggling?' He never answered. He just collapsed."

Sheridan stood abruptly. "That's perfect. God can deal with him and save the government some money."

"Sheridan! What a terrible thing to say!"

"Terrible is what he was. My question is, why did I have to come all this way to hear further proof of that? What does it matter now what he did? The man was evil personified. Has that changed in any way? I don't think so." Her voice rose. "Will it change my life? I don't think so. Knowing that he cheated and hurt countless people only affirms what I already knew. What do you want from me, Calissa? Why did you bring me here?"

Hot anger gushed through Calissa. "You mean why would I want you beside me, helping figure out what to do about all this? You mean why would I want you beside me while he dies? You mean why would I ever expect you to be a sister and pull your own weight in this family? Something you've never, ever done?"

"Well." Sheridan exhaled a sharp breath. "You finally said it. Good for you." She strode out of the room.

Calissa moaned and curled back up into a ball. She leaned into Bram and waited for the most interminable moment of her life to pass.

CHAPTER 25

SHERIDAN MARCHED through the old house, blind with anger. Her steps carried her to the back, into the solarium. It had always been her favorite room with its bright southern exposure. When she was small, lush plants and an earthy scent filled it. After her mother's death, different housekeepers would bring in plastic greenery to replace the browning ferns, philodendrons, dieffenbachias, and others.

Rain beat against the many windows now. She turned on a lamp and sank onto a cushioned wicker couch. Such a comfortable, peaceful room . . . paid for by miners who lived in horrible poverty.

By the time Sheridan met Eliot, she had all but disowned her father and Calissa. They did not impact her life except when someone asked her about her family.

"We're estranged," she said to Eliot when he asked. It was on their first official date, two days after they met. "My family and I. When I was seventeen, I left home and have yet to find a reason to go back."

It was her standard explanation of family relationships. Friends she made in college and after knew little about her childhood. She avoided at all costs mentioning her father's position because people invariably wondered what it was like to grow up with such an *important* man. She would dance a two-step around the real answer, that personally he was an *impossible* man. Despite everything, she refused to rat on him. The art of politicking must have been ingrained in her at an early age. The ironic thing was, that probably was what made her a good diplomat's wife.

She remembered Eliot's response to her reply about being estranged. He turned and gazed out the window toward an extraordinary view of Lake Michigan and the Chicago skyline. Of course he'd taken her to The Signature Room atop the John Hancock building. She'd already begun to sense that everything he did was first-class.

A smile crept over his face, a gentle one. No teeth showing, the cheeks rounding, the crow's-feet creasing slightly. Then he turned back to her. His blue eyes twinkled as if a fairy had dusted them. "Ah. You have issues, then. I suppose I should hightail it the other direction."

"Yes, you should. Definitely."

"But you don't know *my* issues."

"Therefore I should hightail it out of here also?"

"Yes." He grinned, a quick show of perfectly straight teeth. "Sher."

She all but swooned. How naturally he tagged her with the nickname that others used occasionally. With him, though, it wasn't so much an abridging of her name as an endearment made extra lovely in his clipped, faintly British inflection.

A tickle danced down her spine. She was doomed. Good grief. It was only their first date. He was old enough to be a big brother on the tail end of the previous generation, and although his blond curls were quirky and his mouth nicely shaped and wide, he was not all that good-looking. But there was . . . something.

He went on. "Who doesn't have issues? Who doesn't have rubbish piled up from the past? It's why Jesus said to those men who wanted to condemn the woman caught in adultery, 'he who is without sin, cast the first stone.'"

His reference to Jesus racked up points for him right then and there.

She could almost feel her deceased mother reach down from heaven and tickle her ear. *"Pay attention to this one,"* she would be saying.

"Jesus?"

Eliot smiled. "As in God's Son. He is all about forgiveness." *Is.* Present tense.

"Yes, I know. I just haven't heard much from Him lately."

"Not to sound preachy, but are you listening?"

"No." She smiled at him. "My mother would like you very much."

"But you're estranged."

"So to speak." She wasn't ready yet to trust him with the loss of her mother.

"I'm sure you've been told this before, Sheridan, but your brown eyes glitter with gold flecks. Truly stunning. I am mesmerized."

More points for being in tune enough to know when to change the subject.

In late April on their third date, the one with the white tie and tails and the United Nations gala, he told her more about his family. He was an only child. His mother had been forty when he was born, his father fifty. Both were now deceased. He still adored and respected them.

She listened in rapt attention. "I am so envious. Your parents obviously loved you beyond measure, didn't they? Completely, totally, unconditionally. Do you know how rare that is?"

His expression turned somber and she knew she'd revealed more about her story than she had intended.

By May they were talking daily, usually by long distance. Through June and July their friendship blossomed into an intense whirlwind of a courtship. He was forty-two, in between overseas assignments, living in D.C. She was thirty and for the first time in forever was not teaching or taking a class. Her volunteer social work all but disappeared from her schedule because he filled it.

That was when she accepted the inconvenient fact that she had fallen in love with Eliot Logan Montgomery III.

And he hadn't even kissed her yet.

The kiss came soon after, though. They had been to an incredible outdoor jazz concert in Grant Park and meandered down to the lake. Their spirits high from the music and the newness of discovering yet another common interest, they strolled along the broad walkway at the lake's edge, under the stars. The summer night air was thick with humid scents of earth and water. In the distance the lights of Navy Pier twinkled.

Eliot reached over and took her hand as if she were an extension of him.

And just like that, she was.

Before that evening there had been the brushing of shoulders, the press of his hand at the small of her back or at her elbow, the physical closeness of lips to ear for a whisper. But not this intimate touch.

He exhaled a solid, manly hum of contentment. "Somehow I knew that holding your hand would give me the sensation of kicking a soccer ball past the goalie and, bam, right into the net."

She laughed. "I was thinking more along the lines of fireworks."

His hearty laugh rang out. Like the rest of him—cute blond curls aside—it was distinguished, deep and rich and full.

He kissed in the same way. And she was awash in something grander than fireworks.

In late July she visited him in Washington. They kissed at the airport, in the limo, in front of the Lincoln Memorial, and on a park bench.

He smiled. "Welcome to Washington."

"Thanks." She giggled like a teenager, thoroughly embarrassing herself.

"You're blushing, dear." His eyes did their fairy dust shimmer again. "Sher, you are a glorious surprise to me."

She knew Noelle hovered in his statement. He had told her that he never imagined himself in a relationship after his wife of ten years was killed in a car accident. Added to his suffering was the regret that she had not wanted children. It was through his pain that he'd found peace and hope in the God of his youth.

He said, "Sorry. I don't want to scare you away."

She shook her head. "You can't, Eliot."

"We've known each other such a short time, and I'm leaving soon for overseas, you know, and—"

She touched his lips. "Shush. You can't scare me away."

"I love you, Sheridan Ysabel Cole."

"And I love you, Eliot Logan Montgomery the Third. And by the way, I think you should hear about my family."

"Ah." A moment passed, his eyes studying hers. "The issues."

"Yes." She had already told him parts of her story, about her mother being from Venezuela and the light of her life until she died. She had told him about her older sister's dominance, her father's emotional absence, her grandparents gone long before her birth, the horrible loneliness of home. She had told him that she had never wanted for physical comforts but ached for heart connections. She had told him how she buried herself in studies and work and found fulfillment in those relationships.

Now she told him the rest. "My father is Harrison Cole, a representative from Illinois. I always hated it when people asked me what it was like to live with such an important man." She shrugged. "I got tired of making up pleasant stories, and so I estranged myself and stopped talking about him."

Eliot gently wiped at the tears streaming down her cheeks and pulled her to himself. "Dearest . . ." He held her for a very long time. . . .

The storm grew loud, drawing Sheridan back to the present moment. Thunder boomed. The wind flung sheets of rain against rattling windowpanes.

Loneliness stabbed at her again, all too familiar in the surroundings of her childhood home.

Maybe it wasn't the house. The ache was familiar because she lived with it in Topala.

How was it that she had married a man who emotionally distanced himself from her exactly as her father had?

CHAPTER 26

TOPALA

Eliot should have quit the moment he saw Padre Miguel behind the steering wheel of the car as it lurched up the hill to where he stood at their front gate. Javier was supposed to be in that seat. Javier was a spacey artist, but at least he was young and coordinated, and although he drove infrequently, he'd driven more times in the past year than the padre had in his entire life.

The priest set the brake and climbed nimbly from the small car, grinning. "Javier is busy." He gestured down the hill. "Look at the crowds."

The town square at the bottom of the hill was indeed full of tourists, the people who paid Javier's bills.

"Padre, we can wait."

"Nonsense." He pried the walker from Eliot's hands, deftly folded it, and popped it into the trunk. "Get in, señor."

Before Eliot could protest, the old man basically folded and popped Eliot into the passenger seat. A moment later Padre Miguel was depressing the clutch at the wrong time and grinding gears. He killed the engine three times before he had the car turned around and pointed downhill.

He chuckled. "Javier only had time to give me one lesson in finding reverse. Now we are set. Do you think this is first here?"

Eliot clutched the dashboard with both hands as they began the descent in free-fall mode, around the square, past shops and homes, past Davy's. Much to his surprise, they made it to the highway without hitting a pedestrian or a donkey. The whole time Padre Miguel laughed and waved.

If the desire to hear Sheridan's voice did not feel like a knife stuck in his chest, he would have ended the trip right then and there.

"Are there four or five gears?" The padre's eyes were glued to the gear stick.

Eliot crossed himself. He couldn't remember the last time he'd done that.

"Good idea." He crossed himself.

"Uh, five."

"Five?"

"Gears."

"Oh. Right." As the car gained speed on the two-lane, he shifted here and there, at last engaging the right spot. "And we are on our way. What exactly is wrong with you?"

"You mean besides my heart pounding in my throat right now?"

Padre Miguel laughed long and hard. "Yes, besides that. Why can't you walk very well without support?"

"I was shot. You probably knew that?"

"Yes, it was all over the papers, in the archives."

"There's nerve damage. It screwed up my balance." He really did not want to talk about this.

"Where exactly is the problem?"

"What?"

"In your back? In your leg?"

"It's in a variety of places."

"Here?" He reached over the console and touched the left side of Eliot's hip.

"Look out!"

The padre jerked the steering wheel and guided the car back into the right lane. A semi barreled past them, the driver laying on the horn and offering a hand signal.

"Bless you!" the padre called as if the other man could hear him.

Eliot's heart hammered in his throat and head and chest. His breathing came in huffs and puffs. He wanted to shut his eyes but dared not. He wanted to tell the priest that he was a meddlesome noodlehead but dared not.

It didn't seem quite proper to bellow demeaning remarks at a man whose mere touch had twice now left a burning sensation on his skin.

❧

MESA AGUAMIEL, MEXICO

"No answer?"

Eliot jumped at the voice of Padre Miguel behind him. He turned from his seat in the kitchen to see him silhouetted in the front doorway.

They had made it to Mesa Aguamiel, to the tiny house that belonged to Mercedes's aunt Maria, the relative with the telephone. He had wanted to use a public pay phone, but again the priest overruled his desires. The priest said Mercedes and her entire extended family would be mortified if he refused their gift.

"No, no answer," Eliot said.

"Well, when it comes to God's clock, there are no accidents of timing. He has a good reason to prevent you two from talking with each other right now."

"Or else there's a sunspot interrupting transmitters. Or she just happens to be between certain skyscrapers on a certain block, in a dead zone. Or traffic noise is too loud for her to hear the ring. Or planets and moons are not aligned just so. There are a dozen reasons she's not answering the phone which she said she would carry with her at all times."

"Exactly!" He smiled. "The good Lord uses all sorts of means to do His business. Did you leave a message?"

"No." What could he possibly say to Sheridan's voice mail? *Greetings from some stranger's house, where I'm sitting, looking like a complete imbecile. First off, I listened to a lunatic whom I've managed to avoid for nine months. Secondly, I trusted in cellular service, of all things. I must be going now. Hopefully I'll get home alive. Don't worry. Ta-ta.*

"She'll want to hear your voice, señor. That you miss her." He looked crestfallen.

Eliot could not form an answer from the sputters in his mind.

"Well." The priest smiled brightly. "Let's do our other errands, and then we can come back and you can try again."

"'Other errands'?"

"Didn't I mention . . . ?"

Eliot stopped listening. What on earth had he gotten himself into?

CHAPTER 27

WILMETTE

Seated on the couch, Calissa drummed her fingers on the coffee table, empty except for the white box. Like a bomb it sat there, loaded with incriminating evidence, ready to explode facts all over their heads, shrapnel that would cut more deeply into her own heart because of her sister's reaction.

Assuming her sister came back into the living room.

There were sounds indicating that Sheridan was in the bathroom now. Bram was in the kitchen, making tea and probably throwing together crumpets. He could be such a mother hen.

After Sheridan had scurried off, Luke had asked questions about their father. It soon became apparent that she and Bram had barely scratched the surface of what Harrison might have done.

Calissa looked at Luke, now at last doing the guy thing with the fire. He added split logs and poked at it. Sparks flew. He shut the screen and backed up, still not looking at her.

Why hadn't he followed Sheridan, talked some sense into her, comforted her? In Houston, he was always at her side, getting her through the rough moments.

"Luke," she said.

He turned. "Hm?"

"Did you and Sheridan ever, you know . . . were you ever . . . you know."

"Did we ever commit adultery?" He shook his head. "No."

"I mean, I wouldn't blame either one of you after what happened. Eliot half-dead, Sheridan vulnerable, you . . ." Her voice trailed off.

"I what?"

"Well, you're a man. There was opportunity. Emotions had to have been crazy off the wall. She needed to be comforted."

"You ever consider writing romance novels?"

"Honestly, Luke, you know most men would have taken advantage of the situation. Most women would have welcomed—"

"Your sister isn't 'most women,' Calissa. I think you might keep that in mind as we go forward here today."

She had no response and grew self-conscious under his gaze. He didn't say it, but he was not like most men, either. Actually he wasn't like *any* man she'd met. She chalked it up to his clandestine type of work. Now she saw something else in him, though, something almost otherworldly.

A shiver went through her. Who was this man? She had the sudden impression that she stood in the presence of someone who trafficked not in the shadows, but in a light. A luminescence.

She shook it off. "But you love her."

He smiled, an enigmatic twist of his thin lips. "And yet that has nothing to do with what you're imagining."

"Whatever." She huffed. "So is she going to make it through this or not?"

"Depends on what you mean by 'this.'"

"This knowledge that our father is a criminal. It's going to reflect on her and Eliot, *The Ambassador*."

"They're not exactly in the diplomatic spotlight anymore."

"Still."

"It's more a family affair, Calissa. It impacts countless details about your life. Things you assumed were true are not. Perhaps what you and she assumed about your relationship as sisters is not true."

Calissa blinked. "What do you mean by that?"

He shrugged. "Maybe there's no reason after all for you two to resent each other."

Now he was getting a little too personal. "But don't you think Eliot will return to public life someday?"

"At this point I'd say it's unlikely. Sheridan and Eliot are expatriates, but they're not simply American citizens living overseas. They've cut themselves off entirely from the government they used to serve and from personal relationships. There isn't even phone service where they live. Mail is not dependable, and so they have a post office box in another town. The shooting and his ill health threw them so far off the track, they don't know what to do except hide away and try to make it on their own, in their own way."

"How are they surviving? Isn't anyone there to help them?"

"There are a few that I observed."

"Locals?"

"It's best that she tell you the details."

Calissa waited a beat and gave up. Even if she prodded, he would not elaborate.

What Luke had said rankled her, but there was truth. These new revelations about Harrison could redefine everything, even her relationship with Sheridan. But still. Why was it she always had to take the lead?

Calissa swore under her breath. "Where do I go to resign from big-sister duty?"

❧

The papers covered the top of the coffee table. The markings on them were varied diagrams, lists, and chicken scratch in everything from pencil to marker to dot-matrix print.

Calissa sat cross-legged on the floor before them and peeked through her lashes at Sheridan sipping Bram's peppermint tea. Her sister had resumed her position in the chair near the fireplace, an afghan around her legs. She'd lived near the equator way too long if she couldn't handle the coolness of a little spring rain.

"Okay." Calissa double-checked the papers, overwhelmed at the hugeness of what they represented. "Basically what we have here falls into four categories: notes, memos, transcripts, and invoices."

Luke leaned forward. "You said the latest reference is from 1983. How long of a period does this cover?"

"From 1975 to 1983."

"And what are these papers exactly?"

"Dad's handwritten notes to himself. Memos between him and a House rep from Kansas. Minutes from meetings of the House subcommittee on trade, specifically about multinational corporations. Those would be classified. And telephone bills showing calls to overseas numbers."

"'Subcommittee on trade' means your father was on the Ways and Means Committee?"

"Yes."

"What's the common thread between these four categories of information?"

Calissa glanced at Bram beside her. She'd been involved in politics since childhood, more or less. She had been her dad's right-hand woman for years. She was preparing to run for the Chicago City Council. In short, she understood the ins and outs of complex issues. But this . . . this she could not begin to explain.

Bram nodded and took over for her. "Diamond trade. Harrison's notes are cryptic, but he makes clear reference to three things: Ysabel's Place, falling stars, and flashers."

"Flashers." Sheridan shook her head. "That's what he called diamonds. He gave Mamá jewelry all the time, usually diamonds, and talked about the 'flashers.' She hated them."

"She didn't hate them," Calissa said.

"Detested, then. Loathed. Whenever she opened one, her face looked like she'd just swallowed a spoonful of cod-liver oil. Except for that gaudy engagement ring, she never wore them, did she?"

Calissa didn't reply. Even as a kid she thought Ysabel's reaction weird. What woman didn't adore extravagant gifts from her husband? What woman didn't love diamonds and gems and jewelry? Apparently she might have had good reason to feel contempt for diamonds and her husband.

Sheridan said, "She must have known what he was up to."

To hear her sister conclude the same thing tore Calissa's last shred of hope to tiny bits. If Ysabel knew, then it was further proof that Harrison was indeed a diamond smuggler, a crook, a lie.

Luke cleared his throat. His bland expression could have been that of a court reporter intently entering information. "What's the reference to Ysabel's Place?"

Bram shook his head. "We haven't figured it out. Ysabel was a native of Venezuela. She and Harrison met there in Caracas, in a restaurant where she worked. Perhaps that's her 'place.' But what it has to do with all this is anybody's guess."

Sheridan stirred. "I know where it is."

Calissa stared at her in disbelief.

"I lived there for five years, remember?"

"You found it?"

"No. Not exactly. I didn't have much information to go on. Mamá had only told me it was a lounge, a popular hangout for travelers. Male travelers. She hinted that more than drinks were served, and it wasn't food. Liss, it wasn't a restaurant. You've got your rose-colored glasses on again."

She bristled. "What does it hurt to clean up the story a bit? Neither Dad's constituents nor our friends needed to know the details of our mother serving drinks in a . . . in a . . . in a lounge."

"Serving drinks and whatever else they offered. Liss, we know she had an awful life before they met. She couldn't bring herself to tell us how bad it was, but as adults I think we can admit that she might have—"

"Does it matter? Does it really matter now what she did for a living?"

"You're the one bringing up their past."

Luke said, "Uh, ladies, let's get back on track, shall we? Sheridan, what were you saying about the place your parents met?"

She twisted her lips into a curlicue, an expression that drove Calissa nuts when they were younger. It meant the verbal argument might be over but Sheridan's mind had not been changed. It meant Sheridan believed she was morally superior to and more intelligent than her sister or their father. Calissa wanted to yell at her, but the sad thing was, those things were true. They always had been.

Sheridan's lips smoothed out. "I wanted to learn more about Mamá's history. The village she grew up in was too remote. It wasn't feasible to visit during the time we had in Venezuela. The next-best thing was to explore Caracas. I got to know much of the city through my work. I thought I might find the place or at least the general vicinity where she worked. To walk where she had walked. . . ." She shrugged. "I don't know. It seemed important to me."

"Of course it did," Bram said. "Just knowing you were where she might have walked would be a link to the mother you didn't have much time with."

"I guess. Anyway, I didn't have much to go on. No name, no address. So I asked Eliot—"

"Eliot?" Calissa exclaimed.

Sheridan rolled her eyes. "He lived there before I met him, remember? It was his first overseas assignment."

"Well, excuse me for the memory lapse."

Bram touched her shoulder. "Darling." There was a reprimand in his quiet voice.

Calissa thrust out her lower lip.

"Anyway, I asked Eliot where government workers might have hung out when he was there."

Luke said, "And when was that? And yes, before you roll your eyes again, I do have this information." He winked at Calissa. "The memory lapsing must be contagious."

Sheridan smiled.

Now Calissa glanced at the ceiling. *Don't tell me there's nothing between you two.*

"Eliot was first assigned to the Caracas embassy long after our parents met," Sheridan said. "Of course he was so straitlaced, I doubted he knew from firsthand experience anything about a lounge frequented by male travelers. But he had heard. I think that was when he started calling me 'naive princess.' He said there were several possibilities, but his news was almost thirty years old, and did I really need to visit one? I pressed him and he gave me information. A driver took me around. Eliot refused to go along."

Calissa said, "It doesn't exactly sound like a walk down Mamá's memory lane."

"No, it wasn't. I guess the point is I don't really know where Ysabel's Place is or was, but I agree that it's probably where Mamá worked, where they met."

Luke nodded. "Okay. What do you all make of the reference to falling stars?"

Bram shook his head. "No clue. Stars twinkle. Sparkle. Maybe it's another word for diamonds, but what does that have to do with falling?"

Calissa said, "I thought of the old song: 'catch a falling star and put it in your pocket.'"

Sheridan hummed. "'Save it for a rainy day.'"

Luke said, "If something falls, that means it's coming down from a higher place. A star can be a person, as in a rising star." He shrugged. "What about the memos and the minutes?"

Bram replied, "They're all about trade with Venezuela during that time period."

"And the telephone invoices?"

"They show calls from a Virginia number that Calissa remembers as theirs at the house, where they lived part-time when the girls were little. The receiving numbers are in Venezuela. We don't know how to trace them, but they'd most likely be disconnected by now."

"All right. So you're surmising what exactly?"

Bram exchanged a glance with Calissa. "We believe that Harrison was in some way involved with smuggling. He used his position on the House subcommittee to cover up, to make it work." Bram sighed. "Sheridan, I think you're on track. It's probably how he paid for his two houses and lavish vacations and everything else. From what I know of Harrison's lifestyle, we know his salary didn't cover it, and I don't think lobbyists could provide quite that much extra." He blew out a breath. "I remember one conversation in particular with him in which he indicated that he was an expert in money laundering. I had no idea it came from personal experience."

"Do you have any proof yet?"

"I did some research into legislation and trade policies. I got a bead on one direct thread from his work on the committee to U.S. policy in Venezuela fifteen years ago. Nothing concrete. But like I said, current policy is so similar it's like his hand has been in it all along."

"You really believe, then, that he may have influenced national policy?"

"Yes, unfortunately, we do. And we're afraid that this business is ongoing. Will you take these papers, Luke? Handle it however you must. I don't know. Maybe it's nothing; maybe it's the tip of an iceberg."

"I only see one problem at this point." Luke reached over and touched the papers on the coffee table. "These are all photocopies. Without originals, it's going to be more difficult to know whether or not they're valid."

"I wondered about that," Bram said. "And I wondered, why would he make copies? Who makes copies of proof of illegal activity?"

"He didn't make them." Luke's brows rose. "Somebody else did. The somebody who hid them in the attic."

Sheridan sighed. "Mamá."

CHAPTER 28

Sheridan had had enough talk about Harrison, his fraudulence, his past, present, and future despicable character.

She needed to talk to Eliot. He would deny that his own reputation still counted, but he was a national public figure. How would this affect him? If even just the autobiography he was working on? His sole dream was to publish his book. Would anyone want to hear from the son-in-law of another national public figure who was a major crook?

Good grief. Probably hordes would want to hear from him. This could be a boon to sales.

She hurried up to her room, ignoring Calissa on her heels, and yanked open the nightstand drawer. She took one look at the cell phone lying beside the crucifix and slammed the drawer shut. The small lamp on top wobbled and bounced onto the carpet.

Calissa picked it up and set it back on the stand. "Swearing helps."

Ignoring the comment, Sheridan plopped onto the bed and sat cross-legged. "I can't call him. He doesn't have a phone. Liss, you *knew* I would need to talk to him about all this business with Dad. Why didn't you warn me before I came?"

"Like I realized you wouldn't be able to call home? Luke never told me you don't have phone service in that godforsaken place you live in. Who can't call home these days?"

"You knew. You don't have a phone number for me."

"So? I figured your *friends* have it."

"And I wouldn't give it to you?"

"No, because you figured I'd give it to Dad, which isn't true. After what he said to you about getting what you deserved when Eliot was shot, I understood why you wouldn't talk to him."

"You knew what he said?"

"He told me. It was awful, but that's his way of dealing with being upset."

"That's a stretch."

"You don't know him like I . . . Oh, never mind. But come on, Sher. How could I imagine that you don't even have a number to begin with? That is the most archaic thing I have ever heard. I cannot believe Eliot has you so completely cut off from the outside world."

"Calissa, the outside world tried to kill him! It was my decision as much as his to be cut off from it. Now how am I supposed to talk to him? He's my husband! This revelation is as much for him as for me."

"Then why isn't he here with you?"

"Don't you dare do that." Sheridan clutched a pillow to her stomach, debating whether to squeeze it against the knot there or to fling it at her sister. "Don't you dare say you told me so."

"Well, I did tell you so. I told you he was too old for you. That you'd be taking care of him someday."

"He got shot, Calissa. It's nothing to do with his age."

"I also said that you hadn't known him long enough. He would let you down someday, and now here we are, in this mess, and he's not with you."

"You just never liked him."

"You never had a sensible bone in your body. You married a guy you only knew for a few months."

"That didn't give you and Dad the right to never accept us."

"For crying out loud, I had dinner with you two once. One time. You wouldn't even introduce him to Dad until after you were married."

"I don't know why I even bothered. He always disapproved of everything I did. And Eliot Montgomery the Third, a diplomat two inches away from becoming an ambassador, was no exception."

Sheridan remembered the events that led to that silly meeting between the men. She and Eliot married in September. It was a private affair in the chapel of her childhood church with the old priest she knew and two friends from her department at the university. Wanting a quiet, romantic spot away from the city, they honeymooned for a week at a yacht club resort in Door County, Wisconsin. Afterward, it was time to move to Tegucigalpa, Honduras, Eliot's new overseas assignment.

Calissa declared that the right thing to do before Sheridan left the country was to introduce her husband to their father. Still trying to gain her sister's approval of her husband, Sheridan set up a meeting at Harrison's office. Eliot tried to talk her out of it but in the end went along with her desire.

Sheridan said now, "What a ridiculous thing that was. They shook hands. Eliot followed the script and said, 'I'll take care of her, sir.' Dad smirked."

"That's his everyday expression."

"No, this one was for me. He might as well have come out and said what he was thinking—that as usual, I was an idiot."

"Again, he was coping. You were married. You were moving out of the country. This was significant. Emotional. But he didn't know what to do with emotions."

"You really think he's ever felt one?"

"Of course he has."

"I don't think so. But, Liss, why you? You were furious when I told you I was getting married."

Calissa sat at the foot of the bed. "You didn't invite me to the wedding."

"Like I wanted you breathing fire down my neck during the ceremony."

"I only would have tsked quietly."

Sheridan eyed her sister like she would a beautiful snake. "Nobody was invited except those people I worked with, and only because we needed two witnesses."

"Yeah." Her voice caught. "The thing is, I loved Bram."

"You loved Bram. This is a news flash? What's that got to do with anything?"

"Just let me get through this."

She blinked at the rare sight of Calissa weeping.

"Before you met Eliot, I loved Bram. For crying out loud, I loved Bram in high school! We were best friends and he married what's-her-face because he thought he should. It was all about ridiculous old-world family ties and expectations. Anyway, I was busy with my career. I had no time to be a wife. Not that he asked me." A tear trickled out of the corner of her eye. "Then you got married, lickety-split. It was too fast. You didn't know him well enough. I certainly didn't, and you were my charge. Still. On top of it all, you threw away your career to follow him. They loved you at the school and the association. And all those women you helped in the programs. You were at the top of your game, and it wasn't volleyball. I just wanted so much more for you."

"Liss, how much more could I ask for? Eliot gave me the world to work in. Things were changing on the campus here. You knew that. There were cutbacks with the programs. Students with a passion for the work didn't exist anymore, at least not in my classes."

"I know." Tears pooled now in her eyes. "Oh, Sher, I was just jealous. That's all. You were in love and the guy married you. I was in love and the guy married someone else."

"Jealous?"

"Yeah. Pretty lame, huh? Instead of being happy for you, I got jealous. I'm more like Dad than I realize: totally dim-witted when it comes to matters of the heart."

If not for Calissa's tears, Sheridan might have wholeheartedly agreed. Instead, she said, "No, Liss. Totally dim-witted is living in a town without phone service." She reached over and squeezed her sister's arm. "You still love him, and he loves you."

Calissa smiled sadly and nodded.

"It's going to be okay, Liss."

CHAPTER 29

MESA AGUAMIEL

Eliot sat again in the kitchen of Mercedes's aunt, at the small dinette table, the black telephone receiver in his hand. Again Padre Miguel and the aunt's family waited outside. Again he listened to Sheridan's recorded voice. "Hi, it's me." Again he hung up.

One of the first things he had noticed about Sheridan was the way her voice lilted, especially when she laughed. What struck him now was that he heard it . . . and the fact that he hadn't heard it in a long, long time.

He imagined her recording the message, perhaps thinking with a smile how absurd to identify herself when the voice mail would most likely not be heard by anyone. Although she said she would carry it just in case Mercedes or her aunt Maria called, or in case he made the trip to Mesa Aguamiel during her short visit. Clearly she did not think it would be used. Was that why her voice did its little singsong?

But wait. Wouldn't she be using the phone now, in the States? to communicate with Traynor? Did that explain the lilt? Or was it because Luke Traynor had been there showing her how to record the greeting?

Eliot removed his glasses and rubbed his eyes. He was not a jealous man. What he and Sheridan had between them was a deep mutual respect and devotion, already ancient, it seemed, on the night they met. His relationship with her was nothing like his with Noelle, his first wife. And Traynor carried no threat. The short man was not even Sheridan's type.

"Good heavens," he muttered to himself. "Now I've been transported back to adolescence."

The problem was that the day had reduced him to a state of agitation. He was not himself.

Movement caught his attention. He replaced his glasses and looked toward the open front door. If that man came inside and asked if he'd left a message . . .

What? What would he do? Burst into frustrated tears?

"Good heavens," he said again. He turned his back to the door, picked up the receiver, and called the overseas operator.

"Hi, it's me," Sheridan's voice trilled once more.

Eliot gritted his teeth. Did she sing because she was away from him? away from the life neither of them wanted?

"Hi," he breathed into the phone. "It's me. At, uh, Tia Maria's. Yes, I am as surprised as you. But it has been a most unpleasant day. Yet here I am, talking to a voice mail. Now that's something I haven't done in over a year."

She was always on him about trying something new, like walking farther or extending physical therapy times. He wondered if this counted.

"Padre Miguel drove us here. You might want to say a prayer for our safe return. He's as scatterbrained behind the wheel as he is in conversation." Eliot paused. "But he always has a point in his speech, doesn't he? It's just not immediately evident.

"About the day. It was a spontaneous decision to drive over here. More like spontaneous combustion with the padre. Are his sermons like that? Well, at any rate, I had no idea there were errands to be done. First off, we went to his friend's hardware shop that carries an assortment of canes. Long story short, not one was long enough for me, but this chap is quite handy. He extended two of them and attached a sort of three-legged prong at the end of each, for stability. They work rather well. So far. Nowhere near as confining as those crutches we investigated.

"Padre Miguel wanted to leave me there while he went about some other business, but I was concerned he might forget about me. You know how scatterbrained he can be. He talks about how he lives according to God's clock, which I do believe in him resembles that attention disorder. What is it? ADD?

"So we went about town and purchased some glazes for Javier and a few things for Mercedes. She was low on flour and sugar. And I found a colorful apron for her. You know how she always tucks a dishtowel in her waistband. I hope she likes it.

"We stopped for tea. Padre wanted a beer, but thankfully I was able to talk him out of that. I said we still have the ride home to think about. He saw my point. Obviously I haven't done a lick of writing today.

"I should apologize for all this nonsensical chatter. I seem to have an attack of logorrhea. It's been going on most of the day. We can safely assume it's the influence of the priest.

"I hope the rain has stopped for you. The dreariness used to bother you. And, Sher, I have been very concerned about you in Chicago. I told him how frightened you've been of crowded city streets since the incident. He's praying for you.

"Well, good-bye. We will see you soon."

Eliot hung up the phone, laid his glasses on the table, and pressed against his eyes. The tears seeped out anyway.

He recalled the lilting way Sheridan had laughed. "Eliot."

It was August, about a month before they married. They sat outdoors at a French café in D.C. He had just delivered to her a scathing review of some newspaper's editorial about the U.S. president visiting in Latin America.

"What?" he said.

She covered his hand with hers on the table. "I adore your monologues."

"Tommyrot."

"No, it's true."

"I apologize."

"Don't."

He studied those dark brown eyes. Gold flecks danced in them. "I can talk a blue streak about folderol, but I stumble over the most important words and even avoid them altogether."

Her expression softened into one of tenderness.

"I do love you, Sher." It was the first time he'd uttered the phrase.

"I know."

He nearly cried for joy.

It was more than male obtuseness. He'd never had a problem telling Noelle how much he loved her.

But then she died.

No. Then she found someone else, wanted out of the marriage, drove off in anger, and died.

That was where his *I love you* went.

Eliot put his glasses back on and folded his hands.

After Sheridan's endearing comment about his monologues, he had told her that tidbit about Noelle. Ten years into their marriage, Noelle no longer wanted to be married. She had decided that she was, after all, a West Coast woman at heart and needed someone of like mind who craved American soil—in particular Sonoma County soil, where the other man owned a vineyard. The overseas adventure was over for her.

Now and then he professed his love to Sheridan. Probably not often enough. Of all times, though, he should have just now, even if it would have been in a silly voice mail.

CHAPTER 30

WILMETTE

Sheridan awoke slowly, not wanting to leave her dream. A sense of deep contentment filled her. She smiled. Eliot had been in the dream, and they'd been making love.

The pleasantness ebbed. She noted the dark room, the plushy blanket that covered her, the chilled air. Her cheeks felt crusted, her eyes all dried out.

She hadn't shared a bed with Eliot in over a year.

How she hated waking up, especially after vivid dreams of Eliot in B.C.E. form like this one. She would see him walking or laughing or hosting a diplomatic event or caressing her. Then, every time, even before her eyes were fully open, reality crept in and she would have to recall that Eliot no longer did any of those things, that she no longer did much of anything beyond seeing that he was kept as comfortable as possible.

And now . . . now there was more to remember upon waking. She was in Chicago. Eliot was not. She was facing a major crisis. Her father had committed crimes, perhaps high treason. She trusted Eliot. She needed him right now.

She jerked upright and turned on the small lamp. She'd fallen asleep and must have slept through the evening. It wasn't yet midnight. She still wore her oversize shirt and stretchy pants.

She wondered if Luke was still awake.

The big old house was cavernous and drafty year-round, like a mausoleum. Sheridan draped the plushy blanket around her shoulders and hurried from her bedroom and down the staircase. Voices came from the direction of the kitchen.

She stepped into the brightly lit room. Three pairs of eyes turned toward her. Not only was Luke awake but so were Bram and Calissa.

Sheridan said, "Tell me it's all a bad dream."

From the table Bram shrugged, and Luke said, "We have no way of figuring that out just yet."

She sighed.

Calissa set a mug on the counter. "Do you want something to eat?"

"I want to go home."

"Sheridan—" without getting up, Luke pulled out a chair—"why don't you sit." He did not intone a question.

She met his gaze.

Mistake.

It was like slipping into a hot bubble bath.

She removed the blanket and folded it, glancing around the familiar room. It was large enough for the oak table that seated six. There was a counter halfway across the center with four stools. Vertical blinds, shut against the night, covered the window over the sink and a sliding-glass door. She took in the country decor and the appliances, white, from the first white era.

"Why didn't he ever remodel this place?" She set the blanket on a stool.

Bram said, "Sit, honey. I made soup and sandwiches. You need to eat."

Sheridan looked at the table, hesitant, trying to get her mind off the man who was there in Chicago with her where Eliot should have been.

Those accusatory papers covered the table. Luke and Bram hunched over them like college kids studying feverishly for an exam. Or like commanders plotting in a war room how best to attack the enemy.

"It's not going away, is it?" she said. "We have to plow through it and figure out what to do about it."

Bram smiled. "Hear, hear! That's the spirit. Do you want chicken noodle or broccoli cheddar?"

Calissa said, "Chicken noodle. She has a tummyache."

Sheridan gave her sister an odd look.

"It's been a long couple days for you. You used to get tummyaches when you got stressed out."

"I'm fine!" She caught Luke's crooked smile. "I am. I am ready and willing to dig through all this junk."

He angled his head toward the chair. "We have a plan. Come listen and tell us what you think."

She sat.

Calissa set a bowl of soup before her. As she ate, Luke pointed out the highlights on some of the papers. There must have been magic in Bram's chicken soup to keep her steady and focused.

Luke said, "I've learned that Bram here is quite the investigative reporter."

"That's how he got started in journalism."

"So I heard. He's going to dig further into Harrison's congressional record and get a detailed history of everything he's been involved with. I'll follow the international trail to see if anything leads to smuggling."

"Smuggling is a fact of life," she said. "It's common knowledge that diamonds are mined in Venezuela and not accounted for and sold somewhere else."

"I didn't know that," Calissa said. "Where do they go?"

"Wherever."

Luke added, "Some information is hearsay; some is documented; some simply points to irregularities. It's true that diamonds are smuggled across the country's borders, which are vast and impossible to control.

The gems are transported into Guyana or Brazil, where they're laundered, and then make it into the legitimate market."

"Who benefits?" Calissa asked.

"Terrorists and the like."

Calissa blanched. "Terrorists?"

Sheridan set down her spoon and swallowed the hot liquid. She'd heard the rumors. She knew all the stuff Luke explained now. But to hear spoken aloud the enormity of the crime her father played a role in was too awful.

Bram blew out a loud breath. "That's pretty big-time. Harrison and others like him—how would they be involved in something so major?"

"I wouldn't want to guess. The complicated answer is he helped put into place certain guidelines that protected smugglers. A simple answer is he and others carried gems into the U.S., knew where to sell them, and pocketed a lot of money. Today you could probably tuck three million dollars' worth of diamonds inside a matchbox."

A wall clock ticked loudly in the silence.

Luke turned over one of the papers and slid it in front of Sheridan. "We found this note." In faint pencil it read, *Hull House, VA*. "What do you make of it?"

"You know Hull House on the campus of the University of Illinois, Chicago. It was a settlement house at the turn of the last century, later made into a museum. Our mother volunteered there and through its association."

"The same as you."

"Right. I don't know what *VA* has to do with it, though."

He shook his head. "Do you think it's your mother's handwriting?"

"I don't remember her handwriting. She didn't write much." It was one of Sheridan's regrets, that she didn't even have a recipe written down by her mother. "Liss?"

"It's her tiny printing."

"Really?"

"Really." Calissa sounded huffy.

Sheridan shrugged at her.

Bram said, "Given that *VA* is the abbreviation for Virginia, we wondered if she did anything connected with Hull House work during her time out east."

"That doesn't ring a bell with me," Calissa said.

"Me neither." Sheridan ate, her mind wandering to the visits with Ysabel to the museum. They were nothing short of glorious. Her mother knew everyone who worked there. She knew the place inside and out. She would take Sheridan by the hand and describe in detail the displays and photos. She knew all the facts about Jane Addams's work with immigrants and all the programs that Hull House provided, from day care to art classes to Mexican potters creating what would eventually inspire Fiesta tableware.

"Sheridan." Luke interrupted her thoughts. "I understand why you want to call Eliot."

Good grief. Her sister must have blabbed about her earlier hissy fit upstairs. "Right, Luke. But you know where we live. You know I can't do that. I can't just pick up the phone and expect him to answer on the other end."

"But you could make arrangements to do that. You could send a message to him to be in Mesa Aguamiel to receive your call at a particular time."

The thought excited her. "I could, couldn't I?" It was possible. Convoluted, but possible. If she got Mercedes to—

"Please," he said, "don't do it."

She stared at him in disbelief. "But why not? He needs to know this stuff. He's Harrison's son-in-law."

"It's not that straightforward. Bram and I need time to research. If we find any indication that Harrison influenced national policy or sold smuggled diamonds, then I'll pass the information on. In the meantime . . ." He closed his mouth.

"In the meantime, what? Finish your sentence."

"Eliot is part of the international scene. He might inadvertently tip off someone who knows someone who, et cetera, et cetera."

She barked a laugh. "You think he talks to people? How? By carrier pigeon?"

"He talks to Mercedes, who talks to Javier, who talks to tourists. Eliot may go into Mesa Aguamiel and write e-mails. Rumors spread like wildfire even from the hinterland."

Anger filled her. "Thanks for reminding me that my cocoon has been obliterated."

"I'm sorry."

"You're saying I'm not allowed to talk to my husband."

"For now." His face closed up.

She looked down, stirred her soup, and muttered, "I really don't like you, Luke Traynor."

"I know."

CHAPTER 31

CHICAGO

The morning after showing Harrison's papers to Sheridan and Luke, Calissa sat in her car with her sister. She turned off the engine and looked out her side window. "Either I'm getting paranoid or that blue hybrid has followed us most of the way from the house."

They were in a parking garage on the U of I campus, near the Hull House Museum, on the trail of an idea Sheridan had had about the *VA* written in their mother's handwriting on the back of one of the papers. The rain had ended in the night, and the sun glinted off the windshield of the vehicle she mentioned.

Sheridan craned her neck to see around Calissa. "Paranoia comes with hanging out with Luke, but so does a sixth sense. Where is it?"

"By the exit, at the curb in front of that SUV."

"The driver is talking on his phone."

"I only noticed because I've been thinking about getting a hybrid, but certainly not that color."

"Let's go ask him how he likes his."

"Sher!"

Her sister was out of the car and almost to the side of the garage before Calissa could unbuckle her seat belt. She caught up with her at the wall, a waist-high concrete structure.

Sheridan waved and yelled through the opening, "Hey, you!"

The guy seemed to turn their direction, his eyes hidden behind sunglasses. Quickly he looked the other way, peeled from the curb into the left-turn lane, and slid through the intersection as the arrow turned red. Someone honked.

"Oh!" The word exploded from Sheridan. "He's doing it again. I cannot believe it."

"What? Who? What are you talking about?" Calissa hurried after Sheridan, back toward the car.

"He's got no right to do this." She talked loudly to herself. "No right. I don't care what's going on. You know there are more of them out there. They're like rats. You see one for every fifty hidden in some black hole. Oh!" She yanked open her car door and got in.

Calissa followed suit. Sheridan was digging through her handbag, muttering incoherently. The name Traynor was spouted once or twice.

Late the previous night, Sheridan had declared her disdain for him and huffed back up to her room. It didn't seem to phase him. He graciously accepted Calissa's offer of the first-floor guest room. By the time she'd gotten down to the kitchen that morning, he had made a pot of coffee and was ready to leave the house. He reiterated what he'd said the night before: *"I need to figure out what's going on. In the meantime, stay close to home. Take her to the hospital; take her to lunch; take her shopping. But do not take her anywhere else or leave her alone."*

Calissa had nearly sprayed a mouthful of coffee across the counter. *In your dreams, mister.*

"Sher, was I really right about that guy in the car? He followed us?"

"Probably." Her face was inside the bag. "This is what Luke did after he left the hospital in Houston."

"He had you followed?"

"Yes."

"Why?"

Sheridan didn't reply.

Calissa thought about Luke's admission that he loved Sheridan but not in a man-woman-eros sort of way. "Sher, he would have just been wanting to make sure you were okay. He'd been protecting you for some time by then, right?"

"Mm." The noncommittal sound was muffled as she still rummaged in the bag.

"How did you know someone was following you?"

"Eliot told me what to watch for."

"Eliot is a spy too?"

"No. That sort of knowledge comes with the territory."

"How to follow someone? Sounds like tradecraft to me, something he'd have to learn from experience."

"Liss, can we stop with the Eliot's-no-good attitude?"

"Sorry." Calissa reprimanded herself. It really was a bad habit she had nurtured through the years. Not liking Eliot was easier than envying her sister.

"You know, Dad's the one on trial here. He's the one we never should have trusted."

Tears stung Calissa's eyes. How could her dad have committed such heinous acts? He was domineering and insufferable at times, but such a personality opened doors to great accomplishments. He had initiated countless positive developments for the state and for Chicago. Perhaps he had not been a great public servant, but he was an above-average one.

At some point while sitting in the hospital's ICU, she had run out of excuses for Harrison Cole. He'd been young, too eager, blind, confused, in love with a Venezuelan. None of them worked. There were no excuses for his behavior. Calissa could not get used to that thought.

"Missed calls?" Sheridan was staring at her cell phone. "Voice mail? When did that happen?" She fumbled with the keypad for a moment. "I can't remember the password Luke told me he set up."

Calissa slumped in her seat. Sheridan was losing it. She'd seen it happen in the hospital in Houston when Eliot was so bad and Luke so attentive. Odd. The situation was similar to the one they were in now. No Eliot, lots of Luke.

She said, "See what number the call came from."

Sheridan couldn't find the right spot quickly. Calissa realized that since there was no phone service where they lived, she probably had not used a cell in a long time. Luke had provided this one. She wouldn't be familiar with it.

"Oh, my gosh." Sheridan looked at her. "It's the number I call in Mesa Aguamiel."

"Mesa Aguamiel? Where's that?" She bit her lip. They'd just slid into a taboo subject: where Sheridan lived.

Calissa met her sister's stare.

At last Sheridan said, "Mexico. Near Topala."

Topala? Calissa did not know Mexico. She had never visited Latin America. She liked Paris. "Oh."

"I have to listen to the message. What if something happened to Eliot?"

"Call Luke for the password."

"I was going to call him anyway." Sheridan fiddled with the phone. "Chew him out for that guy in the hybrid. Look at this. He's put himself as speed dial number one, in case of emergency."

"This qualifies."

"The thing is, Liss, he's the one who creates emergencies." She pressed the phone to her ear.

"What's he done? Why do you treat him like he's a pain in the neck?"

"I met him in Tegucigalpa. Supposedly he was a foreign service officer in public diplomacy. Soon after, there were demonstrations, anti this and that. One became violent. Our Marines put us on lockdown for two days. I thought we might be evacuated. A couple years later I heard of problems in Quito. I learned later that he'd been there at the time. Then he came to Caracas and . . . well, you know what happened there. Hi." Her voice turned steely. "Call them off, Luke."

Calissa watched her sister talk into the phone, glad to hear the chutzpah back in her tone.

"Calissa and I are at the Hull House Museum because I used to work here and I want to visit. If you have a problem with that, you'll just have to deal with it. Not that it's any of your business. And I need the password for my voice mail." She paused. "Yes, I have a message. Why else would I ask for it?"

Calissa smiled to herself.

"Luke, who do you think called? No one else has this number except Calissa and you and Maria in Mesa Aguamiel. Not that it matters, because in about three seconds I'm pitching the phone into a trash can. What?" She listened. "Okay. And call off your watchdogs. We're fine." Again she listened. Suddenly smiling at Calissa, she said, "How did we 'make' the guy? It's a girl thing. His car was the ugliest shade of blue we've ever seen in our lives." She closed the phone.

Calissa chuckled. "So what's the password?"

Sheridan sighed. "Three, five, six, eight. E, L, M, T."

"Eliot Logan Montgomery the Third. Easy enough. It's your nickname for him. Elm, as in tree because of his height."

"That was a long time ago."

"Did Luke know it?"

"I must have told him. After the shooting, when he was around all the time, I probably told him a lot of things I can't remember now. It's such a blur."

Calissa thought about Luke's answers to her questions. *"No, we did not commit adultery."* Most likely, thanks to him. In her clouded state, Sheridan could have gone off the deep end. Calissa would have, even with the likes of Luke Traynor.

"He said it again—that I shouldn't talk to Eliot yet. Do you believe that?"

"I guess I do, under the circumstances."

"What I can't believe is that I'm following his orders. He said I can listen to voice mail. Isn't that kind of him?" Sheridan worked with the keypad. "Okay. Three, five, six, and eight." She entered the password numbers and put the cell to her ear.

A moment later she was crying. Calissa could hear a male voice, but not his words. She handed her sister a tissue. The message went on and on. At last it ended.

"How do I save it?" Sheridan blubbered, into a full cry by now, shoving the phone at Calissa. "You have to listen to it."

Pressing the key to save the voice mail, she said, "Who was it?"

"Eliot. Oh, Lissy." She wiped at the flowing tears. Her voice was almost incoherent. "To make a call he had to get someone to drive him and then he had to ride half an hour each way. We seldom go in the car because it's so hard on him. He's in pain for days afterward. And he went with the priest, who's like a hundred years old. And to a stranger's house. Oh, what he said!"

Calissa mentally moved their plan to visit the museum to the bottom of their agenda. It wasn't going to happen that morning.

❧

The sisters sat in Grant Park, on a bench in a quiet area. Sunlight through budding tree branches warmed their heads. In the distance before them Lake Michigan melded with the sky, lovely shades of blue. Behind them the Chicago skyline hovered like the arms of a gentle giant watching over them.

Calissa figured it beat the guy in the blue car. She loved her city.

They drank bottled water and talked nonstop. Calissa had listened to Eliot's voice mail and knew she could not begin to comprehend the relationship he and Sheridan shared. It was true; she had never liked or trusted the man. His breezy tone did not link up with Sheridan's totally stressed-out demeanor.

"Liss, he hasn't talked like that since the shooting. So why now?

Huh? That's what I want to know! Why now, when I am thousands of miles away, why does he *notice* me?"

"Absence makes the heart grow fonder?"

"And he buys a gift for Mercedes! The last time he bought a gift for me was two weeks before the shooting. Not that I've expected him to. I mean, life is not normal. But this." She flung her hands in the air, at a loss for words.

"What was the gift that he gave you?"

"A tote bag. Colorful, for fun. I don't even know what happened to it." She rubbed her forehead. "Every now and then I think of things the staff packed up, things sent to the storage unit in Virginia. I hadn't remembered the bag because it was so new. It wasn't part of my life yet."

"Sher, I'm sorry. I can't imagine what your life has been this past year and a half."

"And I'm sorry I haven't told you."

Calissa felt something shift between them. It was like a crevice opened in a rock. She wanted to peer inside. "What's Topala like?"

Sheridan gazed at her, sadness written all over her face, her mouth turned down. Then she began to speak. The words tumbled out, words she had not shared, she said, with anyone because they had been compelled to keep their life hidden from the world.

Sheridan described the small village where she lived, Mercedes and her boyfriend, the sculptor Javier, the priest, the locals, the cobblestones. She talked about what it was like to need propane, drinking water, and food delivered, to get along without Internet or telephone, to watch the sun rise over the magnificent Sierra Madres.

And to have her loquacious husband slip into a wide-awake coma, lost in a world of physical and emotional pain, not present enough to interact with his wife on a heart-to-heart level. Eliot sounded like a bona fide hermit or like a drowning person clinging to the nearest body and dragging her down with him.

Except for that message he left on Sheridan's voice mail. Mr. Congeniality now.

"Liss, Topala feels safe. It's home, and I'm was okay with that. But now . . . I don't know."

"You don't know what?"

She met Calissa's gaze. "Now Eliot's acting so weird, I don't recognize him. I don't know if I can go back there and start all over again with a stranger."

Calissa scooted nearer her sister and draped an arm around her shoulders.

CHAPTER 32

TOPALA

"She calls me Elm Tree." Eliot smiled at Mercedes across the desk. "For my initials."

The girl nodded, head down, writing quickly on a yellow legal pad.

"Mercedes, you don't have to wear the apron all the time."

She looked up, grinning. "But it is so pretty, señor." She fingered the ruffles at her shoulders. "So special. Sunflowers are my favorite, and you didn't even know."

Her giddiness over his simple gift touched him. She'd donned it the moment she pulled it from the bag the previous evening. When she served him his tea this morning, she wore it with a clashing multicolored print skirt, making for a bit of a gaudy outfit.

"Señor, we should work while you have the energy."

"I feel great. I plan to work all day."

"Let's do it, then."

"Señorita, you are such a *taskmaster*. Do you know that word?" They conversed in Spanish, but he sprinkled in English with the intention of expanding her vocabulary.

"Sí. *Taskmaster* means señora. She *es epítome* of *taskmaster*." Mercedes switched to her tangle of the two languages, no doubt to rile him because it often did. "I learn from the best. Now, *por favor, manos a la obra!* Chop-chop!"

"'Let's get to work please, chop-chop'?" Eliot laughed heartily. What a pleasant companion! And what a lovely day!

The sentiments surprised him. But he had slept well and suffered no ill effects from the strenuous jaunt to Mesa Aguamiel the previous day. This morning he had used only the new canes for support and maneuvered his way through the ground floor of the house and around the backyard without incident.

"Señor Elm, you were saying?"

"I was saying that I was named after my grandfather and father."

"Elm One and Two?"

He smiled. "Yes. But Sheridan and I already covered that part of my history. I was talking about how we first met."

"But, señor, you are jumping too far ahead. We have information about your childhood." She flipped through a short stack of paper, Sheridan's latest printout, skimming as she spoke. "What growing up in foreign embassies was like. Your university years. How you followed in your father's footsteps in a diplomatic career. How that was both a help and a hindrance."

Her literacy impressed him. He had not expected such a high level from her. When she had first come to work for them, she knew how to read and write. He recognized that she was a quick learner, but it amazed him how much she had blossomed under Sheridan's tutelage.

"Yes," he said. "And your question is . . . ?"

Mercedes looked at him. "I do want to hear how you and señora met and fell instantly in love. But, señor, you said that happened when you had been working in Latin America for several years. Shouldn't we go in chronological order and begin with your first overseas assignment, before you met her?"

"I think it best to spice up the story at this point by inserting more current affairs. The role of an ambassador is much more intriguing than the ones that preceded it. Sheridan was my wife when I became ambassador, so we'll need to introduce our marriage. Mercedes, what is it?"

The girl whipped her head back and forth, a vehement no. "It sounds confusing. We should go in order, just to organize everything, and then you can rewrite it afterward."

"That's not how I am doing it."

"But señora said my job is to listen to you talk about your life and write what you say. She said my job is to begin from where she left off with the internships during your time at the university. We are ready to record about your very own first assignment and then about your first wife."

"Mercedes." He heard annoyance in his tone. "Your job is to do it my way. Now, wouldn't you rather hear about señora and me visiting with the president of the United States when he appointed me as ambassador to Venezuela than about me writing memos to some undersecretary?" He reached for his drink and clipped the corner of a book. It knocked over the full glass, and water spilled across the desktop. "Ah!"

He fumbled to right the glass. Mercedes untied her apron and pressed it into the spill.

"See why I wear the apron all the time?" She mopped efficiently and rolled the cloth into a ball. "There, all done. I will get you some more and then you can tell me about the la-di-da affair with the president of the United States."

Eliot watched her leave the room, drained of the energy to remark on her humorous English phrase. Sheridan would have taught her that. It was a favorite of Sheridan's when she felt like pinching herself because embassy life seemed like a fairy tale to her.

And she the daughter of a well-known politician.

Eliot had noted the smile on Mercedes's face that did not reach her eyes. He heard the forced cheer, the resigned tone . . . the insinuation that he was insufferable and it was best for everyone's sake to simply go along with him.

He recognized those things in Mercedes because they mirrored Sheridan to a T.

Sheridan had made a similar argument. *Let's go through things chronologically. Later we'll play with the style, rearrange where and how it works, hire a professional editor.*

Chronological meant to cover the time period after the Harvard master's degree, after the rigorous tests, acceptance into the foreign service, and commissioning as a foreign service officer. They would start with the story of his first overseas appointment in Caracas.

It had been everything he had hoped it would be. He was back in a U.S. embassy on Latin American soil, much like the ones he'd grown up in. He was working with an amazing diplomat, much like the kind his father had been before retirement. But now Eliot was an adult, officially representing his country, giving his all in service, carrying out policy, making an impact.

And meeting a vulgar congressman who undermined the whole thing.

Eliot wondered if the man was dead yet.

CHAPTER 33

CHICAGO

Sheridan stood on the sidewalk, chilled to the bone in spite of warmish spring temperatures and her sister's long black wool coat. With Calissa beside her, she gazed at Hull House, a lovely two-story redbrick structure with a wraparound porch and numerous tall, narrow windows. Built in 1856, it became a settlement house in 1889 through the efforts of two women, Jane Addams and Ellen Gates Starr. They served the surrounding neighborhood of immigrants, providing whatever was needed to combat ignorance and poverty.

Sheridan turned to her sister. "Remember why Mamá found her way here?"

Calissa chuckled, obviously catching the reference to their mother's rendition of why she connected with the outreach programs still in effect when she first came to the U.S. As if on cue, Calissa followed the script. "Mamá was drawn to Hull House because she was an immigrant."

"No." Sheridan smiled. "Although she was an immigrant."

"She needed help with her thickly accented, nearly unintelligible English."

"No. It was still English, you know."

"Then it was because she needed help finding a job."

"A job?" Sheridan rolled her eyes. "Good heavens, she was married to a United States congressman. Which, by the way, gave her a direct link to the deceased Jane Addams, whose father had been in politics as well and a friend of Abraham Lincoln. Well, maybe *friend* is an exaggeration."

"But, oh, my!" Calissa made a wide O with her mouth and cupped her face in her hands the way Ysabel would. "What a famous, honorable person to be associated with!"

They laughed.

Calissa said, "I swear, she told everyone she met about her 'Lincoln link.' She never did get around to answering her own question."

"Sure she did."

Calissa turned somber. "Yeah, yeah. Something about Jesus."

Sheridan mimicked Ysabel's lilting tone. "Jesús—He call me here so I find the association. Then I volunteer and help all the women in Chicago."

"Saved countless numbers."

"Liss, why are you so sarcastic about her work?"

"It's not her work. I respected her work. It was the syrupy religion that bugged me."

"It wasn't religion. It was her relationship with God."

"I know. I just never understood it." She shrugged. "But it also explains why you found your way here."

"Yeah, right." Sheridan chuckled. "From Abe to Jane to Ysabel, with some Jesús mixed in."

"The point is, you are very much like her. You have the same faith and the same dreams, neither of which I understand, but that's it."

It had taken Sheridan some years to realize that her mother's dream was indeed her own. All through high school she had ignored an ever-present tug to serve. She wasted years pursuing one phase after another, from volleyball to piano to art to arguing with her sister.

"Liss, was I an awful pain in the neck for you?"

"That's putting it mildly. But looking back, I can see now how hard it was on you to lose our mom. You were only thirteen."

"But it had to be hard on you, too."

"It's over. Though I do remember being especially happy when you 'found yourself' here and settled down. Mamá's work was reignited in you, and you blossomed in it."

"Did I ever tell you . . . ?" Sheridan's throat tightened, and she had to wait a moment before going on. "In Caracas, I wanted to do what Addams did here. I wanted to live in the neighborhood, not just open a center and go home at night and pretend the women Reina and I were helping had homes to go to that were warm and cheery with stocked pantries."

"You always were such a dreamer, Sher. Like Mamá. I remember one particularly horrid argument she and Dad had. She wanted to do the same thing—get an apartment near the center where she worked on the west side."

"I don't remember that."

"I wouldn't want you to remember the fight. Actually, you weren't home at the time." She paused. "It happened not long before she died."

"Why would she get an apartment? Was it for herself? What did she mean?"

"Um, I'm not really sure." Calissa was stuttering again.

"But what did she say?"

"It doesn't matter now."

"Did she want a divorce?"

Calissa sighed a few times before replying. "She wanted distance from him."

Kind of like me. Sheridan wondered if she ever would be free of Harrison Cole. She suspected not even his death could accomplish that.

⁂

Sheridan and Calissa stepped into the museum. Instantly Sheridan felt at home. The tall ceilings gave an airy feel to the first floor that contained an information desk, a counter where books were sold, and three large interconnecting rooms with artifacts and historical photographs.

A group of elementary-age children filled a room on their left, the hardwood floors creaking with every movement. A docent, a young woman who most likely was a student at the university, spoke to them much like Ysabel had to Sheridan when she was young.

Another memory—the one that had struck her early that morning—hit again, this time sharp and vivid. It was of Mrs. Van Auken, a dear friend of their mother's, a docent at Hull House all those years ago, the "VA" in the note. She talked to her in this place about doing good works.

The woman behind the desk smiled now. "May I help you, ladies?"

While Calissa went over to talk with her, Sheridan roamed the rooms, familiar to her even after a long absence. She paused in front of an early photograph of Addams. Her round, almost childlike face; the unsmiling lips; the high-necked silky dress—all spoke of another era. And yet, decades later the woman's dream-come-true at the turn of the twentieth century had captured Ysabel Cole's heart.

Decades after that, Sheridan caught it herself.

As a teacher at the college, she had urged her students to dream big and to work hard to make their dreams become reality. She would quote from Addams: *"What after all, has maintained the human race on this old globe despite all the calamities of nature and all the tragic failings of mankind, if not faith in new possibilities, and courage to advocate them?"*

Words she lived by in the B.C.E. years.

Sheridan missed her fellow dreamer and coworker Reina so much, she ached inside. She missed her work. Both had been torn from her in the blink of an eye.

There were holes in her heart. Gone was the beauty that graced it whenever she held the hand of a poor woman and talked to her about gaining skills necessary for her to make a living. Gone was the beauty of hilarity when she and Reina laughed as, one after another, obstacles disintegrated when teachers, employers, and babysitters volunteered their services. When landlords offered space free of charge. Gone was the beauty of joyful tears she and Reina wept as they watched needy women gather, learn, and find jobs. Gone was the beauty of hope that their own center would open. She had even lost the vision of her and Reina dancing a silly jig as soon as Eliot cut the ribbon at the grand opening ceremony.

Sheridan inhaled the museum's musty air and wondered if she would ever be able to work in that way again, totally consumed with helping others. Somehow being consumed with helping just one named Eliot didn't seem the same. Why just one when God had given her a heart for women and the abilities to serve many?

"Sher."

She jumped at Calissa's voice beside her.

"Sorry. I got it."

"Okay."

They exchanged determined looks, their brows raised and mouths set. That morning, they'd greeted each other with the same questions: What about Mamá? What had she known about her husband's activities? What was she doing thirty years ago while he flitted down to Caracas, a place she never cared to visit? Who were her friends?

Sheridan recalled only one woman in particular, Helena Van Auken, who worked at the museum and through the association too. Calissa vaguely remembered her. It seemed she had a daughter her age and they had interacted eons ago. Sheridan, as an adult on the campus, had bumped into Ysabel's old friend now and then at Hull House.

Calissa said, "Armed with your reputation, Professor Cole, and the exalted congressman's, learning about Helena was not a problem. She still volunteers here. Can you believe it? I'll go outside and give her a call now."

"I'd like a few more minutes in here."

"Are you all right? I mean, I know you're not. The city and all. The memories here. That message from Eliot. But . . ." She cocked her head, empathy on her pouted lips.

"Thanks for the concern, but I am fine. Really."

"Okay, then. I'll meet you out front."

Sheridan watched her leave, surprised at the empathy she had voiced.

Funny how different she and her sister were. While Sheridan embraced their mother's passion to help underprivileged women, Calissa had caught their father's passion for politics. In politics they served others too, but Harrison's ego was always obvious. He liked the power and prestige that came from his work, not the people.

Calissa liked those things as well. She had never pretended otherwise. But her new plan to run for city council had altruism written all over it. She had a heart for people's welfare.

Sheridan wondered now, surrounded in the museum by all the evidence of dreams being fulfilled for over a century, how one person's work went on and on.

Like her mother, she had worked in the association's outreach programs. She had even helped create a few. It was at a fund-raiser to launch one of those where she and Eliot met. In Chicago on some business, he visited his father's friend, Malcolm. Knowing Eliot's interest in such things, the man invited him to the event.

Of course the rest was history. Their instant heart connection was rooted in the similarities of their work. It was what began their never-ending song of conversation.

The one that ended on a sidewalk in Caracas. . . .

Both were gone now, their conversation and their work. Now all they did was get through every day the best they could in a tiny village forgotten by time.

Sheridan bit her lip and blinked rapidly. *Dear God, I just want our life back the way it used to be. We were living out our dreams. What was so wrong with that? Huh? I'd really, really like to know.*

CHAPTER 34

TOPALA

Working with Mercedes on his autobiography, Eliot summoned forth reserves of stamina he thought were nonexistent.

Then again, perhaps they were nonexistent. Perhaps he was running on adrenaline, the natural response to several fearful questions roiling inside of him.

Had Sheridan listened to his voice mail yet? What effect did it have on her? Did she think him an even bigger fool than she had already considered him? Had she returned the call? Was a message waiting for him in Mesa Aguamiel? Would she return the call? Was Traynor still with her? Why would he be? Where was he sleeping?

Was she all right? Did she remember the counselor's caution—that even years after a traumatic event, certain sights or sounds or smells could trigger unhealthy responses? Why hadn't Eliot reminded her to be attuned to such things?

Would anyone in the world give a flying fig about what he had accomplished as an ambassador? Would the agent still be interested in trying to sell the story six months from now?

And beneath it all rumbled the question that threatened like an earthquake's tremors. The answer to it could completely shake apart his world. Had the old man talked?

Adrenaline, fear, and stress surged through him. Regardless of his exhaustion, he would not be able to rest as he did most afternoons at this time. At least the agonizingly slow process of dispensing personal information to Mercedes diverted his attention.

"Señor," she said, "what do you mean when you say that you and señora 'connected' at the fund-raiser when you met?"

He sighed. The language two-step wore on him. "Sheridan describes *connected* as our hearts communing. It was as if we knew each other already."

"Oh!" Mercedes smiled. "Love at first sight! Women will like to read about this."

"It wasn't love at first sight! It was a deep knowing that we were alike. That our goals and passions were the same. That we shared worldviews."

"Sí. Love at first sight. You must have thought she was beautiful."

Struck wordless, Eliot stared at the girl.

"Oh, I talk too much. I am sorry, señor. Javier says I should just listen and take notes. That's what señora said you needed. I am supposed to help you outline what you will write later." Her eyes widened, and she leaned forward over the desk. "But I have an idea! I can write this part. I can describe love at first sight. How beautiful she was. How handsome you were. How butterflies fluttered inside you both. It was the same for me and Javier. What do you think?"

"I think that you were not there and that you are only eighteen. Sheridan was thirty years old when we met. I was forty-two."

"Sudden, head-over-heels love is the same for everyone, no matter what the age. You married almost right away. Señor, it was love at first sight. Women will swoon over this part of your story."

Eliot gripped the edge of the desk with both hands. "Mercedes."

"All right, I will stop." She sat upright and looked at her pad. "Back to business. We need to put this in order. Why did you go to this event where it was love at first sight?" She winked. "I mean where you *connected.* I think God must have led you there."

The window to his left spun to where Mercedes sat. Mercedes melded into the bookcase on his right. The wall behind him rounded his left side, into his peripheral vision.

Vertigo was one of Eliot's new realities since the shooting. Its cause had not been determined. Some inner ear reaction to the bullet? Some medication's side effect? He had not isolated a trigger. It came unexpectedly. Like now.

Unlike previous times, though, it hit him quickly and hard, as if an on-off switch had just been thrown.

Mercedes's voice came from behind him. "Señor!" Or was it from his left? "Señor!"

Why had he gone to the fund-raiser?

It wasn't love at first sight.

Curiosity had propelled him to the fund-raiser. If curiosity killed the cat, it slaughtered Eliot. Meeting her decimated his preconceptions, prejudices, expectations, bitterness, blindness, self-defenses, disdain, hatred, fears.

It was as if she had called forth a new Eliot.

No, it wasn't love at first sight, but rather forgiveness at first sight—forgiveness for what he had been.

But that went beyond words. Even if he had words, they would not be included in any outline, note, or essay.

The room spun viciously. He shut his eyes. The carousel still pulled at him; his head swirled round and round and round in blackness.

Eliot screamed. He shouted. He swore. He verbally attacked Mercedes and her family and the entire village of Topala.

With a yell, he swept his arms across the wide desktop, one side to the other, clearing it in one swoop. Laptop, papers, pens, clock, and books clattered to the floor.

The pain hit him then. The one that seared like fire under his left shoulder blade.

The workday was over. The night's rest was over. But those were the least of his fears.

His life was over. Sheridan was in Chicago, with Calissa, with Harrison, and with a history he had kept hidden from her since the day they met.

CHAPTER 35

CHICAGO

"I wondered when you two would find me." Helena Van Auken's unabashed smile sent folds up her face, puckering her eyes until only the twinkle showed. "Come in, come in."

Sheridan stepped into the apartment first and into the woman's open arms. "Hello." After a long moment with no indication the hug would end anytime soon, Sheridan melted into the compassion that oozed from her mother's old friend.

At last the woman let go and then gave Calissa the same hug.

"Hello, Mrs. Van Auken."

"It's Helena." A spry seventysomething in blue jeans and a wild purple shirt, she wore some of her white hair in a bun. The rest sprung out every which way. "Now tell me, when did your father pass away? I must have missed the announcement in the newspaper."

"Pass away? He hasn't."

"Oh. Well then, you are ahead of schedule. Please, have a seat."

Sheridan and Calissa shrugged at each other and followed Helena. The apartment was small and sparsely furnished. A few steps past a kitchenette, they sat on a couch. There was only one door off of the room, presumably to a single bedroom and bath.

Chatting the whole time about the beautiful sunshine and impossible neighborhood parking, Helena served them iced tea and dainty homemade sugar cookies.

She sat in the armchair by the sole window, its sill full of potted plants. "Calissa, running for city council. Sheridan, former ambassador's wife. What lovely women you've become. Ysabel must be busting at the seams with happiness."

Sheridan glanced at her sister.

Helena chuckled. "Oh, don't go making faces at each other like I've lost my marbles. I know she's passed on, but she could very well be able to see you if the good Lord wants her to."

A wave of warmth flowed through Sheridan. "I know a priest who talks like that, about the departed saints joining us at the Eucharist."

"Yes, exactly, my dear."

Calissa's pained expression deepened. "Sounds a little weird to me."

"Mystery always does." Helena's green eyes sparkled. "I am so glad that you've come at last. Now, where shall we begin?"

"Did you expect us?" Calissa asked.

"Oh yes, for years. Ysabel said, 'When they come, tell them everything.'"

Sheridan exchanged another surprised glance with Calissa. "She knew we'd find you?"

"Daughters can always find their mother's best friend. I think it's another mystery."

"But," Calissa said, "we never knew you. I remember seeing you at the museum once in a while. I thought Mamá's best friend was the neighbor."

"Lorraine 'Snoot' Boots?"

Calissa laughed. "How did you know?"

"Dears, your mother confided in me about many things. Her neighbor Lorraine was snooty, but then it was difficult not to be so in that neighborhood where you lived. Life was all about keeping up with the Joneses. You can't do that for long and not lose the essence of yourself."

Sheridan said, "Why didn't we know you, Helena? I even saw you at the museum when I worked on campus, but we never really spoke."

"Well, that's all part of the story. Now, ladies, it is not my intent to disparage your father. But the man frightened me for years. Even after your mother's death, I never dared approach his daughters."

"What did he do to make you feel that way?"

"He did not approve of Ysabel's activities through the association. That included me. He made that very plain, to my face one time in your kitchen. I was not welcome under any circumstances in your home ever again. He told me I would deeply regret contacting his wife. He was a powerful man, perfectly capable of wreaking havoc in my world. I truly feared he would somehow hurt my family."

"Did you stop seeing our mother?"

"She continued working with the association. Naturally our paths crossed there, but we minimized our personal outings to coffee now and then in out-of-the-way places. It was nothing like before, and that hurt. I missed her tremendously, and I think she felt the same."

"When did all this happen?"

"You girls were quite small. Sheridan was just a toddler—two years old, three at the most. So, Calissa, you would have been around nine."

"Why was he so against your friendship?"

"My husband—how do they say it?—screwed him over. That was ages ago. Gil didn't do it intentionally, of course. It was a business deal that went crosswise. Harrison lost money in the deal."

"Gil Van Auken?" Calissa sounded surprised. "That's who you are? I mean, his wife?"

"Widow now." Helena smiled. "God blessed us financially quite a bit."

"'Quite a bit'?" Calissa turned to Sheridan. "Real estate. As in skyscrapers."

Helena chuckled. "Oh, Gil was a smart man."

"If I may ask, why do you live here in this neighborhood? I imagine you could afford otherwise?"

"Perhaps financially, but not personally. It just wouldn't be 'me.' About thirty years ago, Gil and I finally did what Ysabel wanted to do. We left a north suburb, an opulent house and lifestyle, and moved to a poor area in the city. This will sound like we smoked a funny pipe, but the truth is we wanted to emulate what Jane Addams and her friends did. We wanted to live in a seedy, indigent neighborhood and serve. Unfortunately Gil passed on only two years after we moved. The stress of business had already taken such a toll on his poor heart." She set her glass on the end table. "Tell me about Harrison."

"He had a stroke and isn't expected to live much longer," Calissa answered.

"Then you found the papers while he was still alive."

"The papers! You know about the papers?"

"Yes, of course. Ysabel showed them to me, and then she hid them. At least she told me she planned to bury them deeply in the attic. She always sensed that he would outlive her. You know how she battled respiratory problems. So she said to me, 'After he's dead, the girls will find the papers and then they will find you. Tell them everything you know.'"

"I found them." Calissa's voice cracked. "I confronted him and he couldn't say a word. He just had a stroke right then and there. Collapsed in a heap."

"Oh, my dear." Helena moved quickly to sit on the couch between them. "It's not your fault." She pulled Calissa to herself and reached over to grasp Sheridan's hand.

Calissa sobbed.

At the uncharacteristic sound from her strong, independent sister and the feel of her mother's friend's hand in hers, Sheridan began to cry.

Tears dried, iced teas and cookies replenished, they returned to their seats. Helena began to tell them about their mother.

"I loved her dearly. She was quite a bit younger, but we were both new mothers when we met. New mothers in dire need of a break from mommy duty. This was before you were born, Sheridan. Calissa was a tyke. I imagine what solidified our friendship right off the bat was that instead of shopping or planning galas like most of our peers, we were either serving at a soup kitchen or teaching English to adults at some community center. And don't you two make fun of that. Her language skills were excellent."

Overcome with the realization that Helena represented a direct personal link to her mother, Sheridan melted into the cushy sofa, her head against a doily. "Seeing" her mother through this woman's eyes slathered a balm on a hurting spot that had never been touched, the one she had tried to soothe by exploring the streets of Caracas.

"What do you girls remember about her history?"

"She grew up in dire poverty," Calissa said, "in a remote, rural area in Venezuela. Her father was a farmer. He and her mother died before she was twelve. She had no other family and eventually moved to the capital city and found work in a restaurant—" she glanced at Sheridan—"bar, or something, where she met our father."

"I'll fill in the gaps because she asked me to. I'm afraid it's not a pretty picture."

"I think we suspected that."

Sheridan gave Calissa a half nod, glad to hear her sister admit the truth.

"Yes." Helena smiled sadly. "She was so ashamed, but she never made excuses for her choices. She would have told you herself, when the time was right. To begin, you know she was a godly woman."

They nodded.

"Harrison accused her of trying to win God's favor by volunteering herself to the whole world except him. But that wasn't it at all. Ysabel was filled to the brim with God's love and forgiveness. She knew no one can earn that gift. She worked to help others because of her love for Him. If she'd been a nun without a husband and children, we would be talking about Mother Ysabel today like we do about Mother Teresa."

Calissa leaned forward. "But she did have a husband and children, and she was gone all the time."

Helena studied her for a moment. "Is that what you remember, or is that what Harrison told you?"

Calissa bristled.

"Dear, you had twenty years with her. Is that what life was like? Was she not there when you got home from school? Did she miss your dance or piano recitals? In an average week, how many meals were takeout? Did she not help you move into the dorm, going all the way to Stanford with you?"

Sheridan figured the answers were negative, but she was younger. She only recalled her mother always being around. If Ysabel did volunteer while Sheridan was not in school, Sheridan went with her.

Calissa shook her head sharply. "It was what they always argued about—that she was gone too much. He wanted us to spend more time with him in Washington."

"I appreciate your seeing things with your own perspective. Yes, he wanted that. She disliked uprooting you. When it came to you girls, she knew how to hold her own." Helena sighed. "Ysabel was born, as you said, in a remote area. Her parents were both sickly and died early. Diamond mines were located there. Smuggling was a common thing in their border town. It provided a way for your mother to support herself. There were always men around." Helena paused. "She became a prostitute. She was fourteen."

Calissa inhaled sharply.

Sheridan felt like she'd been punched. Although she had considered the possibility, hearing it stated aloud as fact wrenched her emotions. How she ached for her mother! Fourteen? She never imagined.

Helena went on. "She moved to the city, where so-called businessmen arranged for her to go and work. It was what we might call a gentlemen's club geared toward foreigners. Her employers would target certain vulnerable men. Many were foreign government employees who traveled back home without the hassle of customs inspections. The 'ladies of the evening' would lead them into compromising situations that paved the way for blackmailing them into smuggling. In the early days, it was all sorts of contraband. Later they specialized in diamonds.

"Harrison Cole heard rumors about what went on at this place. When he first went there, he was a brand-new representative, but he knew what was up. The opportunity to make money by carrying diamonds back home appealed to his greed, his sense of adventure. He signed on. An odd thing happened, though: he fell in love with Ysabel."

"In love?" The words burst from Sheridan. "In love? No way. I can't see that."

"See what, dear? That he was capable of loving?" Helena nodded. "He was a horse's behind, meaner than a bear, wilier than a fox. But he recognized beauty when he saw it. And I don't mean just physical beauty. Your mother carried a light inside of her that could not be extinguished. Keep in mind, Harrison wears many faces. Obviously people respect him; they keep voting him into office. Along life's path he lost contact with the conscience the good Lord gave him."

"Did Mamá love him?" Calissa said.

"She said she did. I think she wanted to see herself as being a faithful wife because in a very real sense, he saved her life by removing her from that situation. She was only eighteen when they met. Barely nineteen when he scooped her off to the States. Of course she would be indebted to him forever. Perhaps it grew into some sort of love and respect on her part."

Déjà vu pricked Sheridan. Forever indebted for being saved? It described her relationship with Luke.

"It wasn't a simple love story, however," Helena said. "Her employers did not like losing a beauty like Ysabel. Harrison had to buy her freedom. Stuffing his pockets with diamonds now and then wasn't going to be enough. He agreed to recruit others. And most significantly, he agreed to use his political career to help keep them in business. He promised to weigh in on national dialogue, apply pressure to slant things in any way possible in their favor."

"Like . . ." Calissa frowned. "Like promoting policy that doesn't pressure certain gem-producing countries to follow trade rules."

"Yes," Helena whispered.

Calissa kneaded her forehead.

Helena cleared her throat. "Politics is complex. He influenced, but he certainly wasn't powerful enough to make policy all by himself. The bad guys in Venezuela who could have ruined him were taken care of. Life went on. You were born, Calissa, within the first year of their marriage."

Calissa lowered her hand and looked at Helena. "You tell us our mother was a prostitute, and now you're sugarcoating?"

"It's the Puritan in me. Creeps in once in a while."

Calissa gave her a half smile. "Helena, I did the math when I was eight. I was born five months after they married."

"Right. Well. The pregnancy wasn't the reason he married her. He wasn't exactly a moral man. Which is why I believe he did love her." Two bright red spots flushed her cheeks. "Most of this Ysabel did not share until we had known each other for years. She carried around that burden of what Harrison was doing all by herself for a long time. Naturally she feared what might happen if she told the truth. It wasn't just that it would destroy his career. She understood firsthand the ruthlessness of the people he worked for."

"How awful," Calissa said.

Helena nodded. "I am sorry, girls. There is one happy ending, however. That's you two. She gave birth to two wonderful women who have made an incredible impact for good in this world."

Sheridan's earlier cozy feeling diminished. The happy ending wasn't the end. "About those papers . . ."

Helena visibly tensed.

"Did Mamá make the copies and hide them?"

"Yes, she did."

"Why?"

"Oh, my." The old woman sighed and stood. "This may take a while. I'll get us some more tea."

CHAPTER 36

LUKE CAME IMMEDIATELY.

Sheridan knew he would.

Like a newborn foal, she had left Topala on wobbly legs. With every step since, she had gained strength and stamina. But that afternoon, an old woman's tales undermined her progress. Once again she was struggling to get on her feet, slipping and sliding and calling Luke.

She and Calissa had left Helena's apartment a short while before, their hearts too full of sadness for Ysabel and Harrison and their own pathetic childhoods. Helena had given them more details about their parents, many more than Sheridan could carry by herself.

She spotted Luke down the hospital corridor, weaving his way between others. Sight of his familiar, confident strides propelled her out of her seat.

He caught her in his arms and, without a word, held her close.

Face against his wool sport coat, she hid herself from the world and soaked in his presence, in the very "is-ness" of Luke Traynor. Tears she had kept at bay since leaving Helena Van Auken's apartment flowed.

She despised herself for calling him and saying, "I can't do this; I just can't do this." She despised Luke for rushing to her side and intuiting how to meet her needs.

"Like it's his fault," she muttered.

He leaned back to look at her. "Who?"

His guard was down; she could see that. The proof was in his eyes. They weren't all gray, the color of his anger. Neither were they the prevailing gray-green, all charming but impersonal. Instead, green shone, the color of his true self, the one with a heart.

"You. I meant, 'Like it's your fault.'" She wiped at her tears. "I don't like that I owe you gratitude."

"Sheridan, don't think that. Don't think that at all. You do not owe me a thing."

"But—"

"Shh. I mean it. I was in the right place at the right time."

"You really think you're an angel, don't you?"

He chuckled, gave her arms a quick squeeze, and let go. "What's happening with your dad?"

"Nothing. There's no change."

Earlier, after listening to Helena's bombshells, Sheridan and Calissa had been speechless. They drove off, admitting to each other they needed time to process the disturbing information. Sheridan voted for home and a hot bubble bath. Calissa insisted they stop at the hospital first. Since Calissa was the one behind the wheel and the bossy one, that was where they went.

Sheridan refused to go to his room with Calissa. Instead, she phoned Luke, the only one who could help her process.

She said to him, "Calissa said we had to visit Harrison."

Luke gave her a curious look, of course deducing there was more. "Something happen at the museum? After the guy in the ugly blue car left?"

"You could say that."

His jaw clenched, but he spoke evenly. "Have you had dinner?"

She shook her head.

"You need to eat."

There he went, figuring out exactly what she needed.

And there she went, letting him do it.

✱

Sheridan and Luke sat in a booth in an obscure little place, a quiet neighborhood restaurant-bar with lots of oak wood, muted ball games on television screens, and dim lights. They had invited Calissa, but she chose in her martyrlike attitude to remain at the hospital.

Sheridan savored a french fry, no ketchup, just enough salt, a hint of garlic. "I've missed these. They are the ultimate comfort food, in my opinion. Almost as good as ice cream. Any flavor."

He smiled.

"Go ahead and ask."

"Ask what?" he said, biting into a thick hamburger.

"Is eating high-carb, high-fat comfort foods one of my post-trauma coping mechanisms? Actually you don't have to ask, because I am obviously twenty pounds heavier than the last time you saw me, so the answer is yes."

"You were too thin before, and you lost weight that first month."

"Whatever." She felt a rush of well-being, no doubt thanks to blood-sugar levels getting a hit of food. "What did you and Bram do today?"

"Research. We're going to have to travel before we can nail things down. We'll start in D.C. I'll most likely visit Caracas, too."

Sheridan set her hamburger on the plate. Sometimes even gluttony didn't help.

"Sher, you need to eat more. I mean, *Sheridan*."

"What's in Caracas?"

"The beginnings." He sipped his soft drink. "So the blue was ugly, huh? As in garish?"

"Offensive."

"Tacky?"

"Yucky." She gave him a quick smile. "We got a phone number at the museum. You really don't know where we went after?"

He shook his head.

And so she told him.

At some point in the retelling of Helena Van Auken's story, she noticed that Luke quit eating. When she got to the part where Helena said that the happy ending lay in Ysabel's daughters, she quit talking.

"And?" Luke prompted. "What about the papers?" He echoed her own question to Helena. "She'd seen them before?"

Sheridan twisted the linen napkin on her lap. "Mamá showed them to her."

"Then your mother knew what your father was doing?"

"Oh, Luke. She worked as a prostitute at that bar. They would take compromising photographs and blackmail guys. It was a way to recruit unsuspecting foreigners and force them to smuggle contraband."

"Photos wouldn't necessarily be that big of a deal, even back then . . . unless the guy was a big deal."

"They targeted diplomats and politicians."

"Big deals. Like Harrison, a newbie congressman."

She nodded. "But he was one conniving step ahead of them. He'd heard rumors and wanted in on things. He played them like they were the dupes. He pretended to be drunk and went off with my mother. They never got to the photo. He demanded to see her employers. They reached some sick agreement."

"That took some nerve for him to go into a group like that and make demands."

"Nerve or something. I'm really not impressed. Anyway, he became a smuggler. He recruited others. He got paid for it. And according to Helena, he fell in love with Ysabel Ortiz."

Luke's eyebrows rose slightly.

"I know. It doesn't compute, does it?"

"I've seen her photograph. She was a beautiful woman."

"Besides that, I'm sure he had ulterior motives. She was gentle. She would go along with whatever he coerced her into doing. She would look good next to him on the campaign trail. And most of all, she would provide reasons for him to visit Venezuela more often than his work might dictate. So why not marry her?"

"I've heard of odder arrangements. Ysabel's Place, then, most likely referred to this bar, as we thought. Flashers were diamonds. Falling stars were rising stars, such as diplomats, who were compromised, brought down, and caught in a blackmail trap."

"Catch a falling star."

"Yep." He paused, his eyes unfocused. "As of thirty-five years ago, according to those papers, diamonds were the thing. One question is, how widespread was it? One-time visitors got caught, carried a few million dollars' worth of diamonds to their home country, handed them off. All for free. Others—perhaps those assigned to Venezuela and living there—may have been used differently. They may have literally smuggled or simply kept their mouths shut. Harrison and others like him—"

"Others like him?"

"Sheridan, you know he wasn't the only crooked politician involved with this. It would have taken a team effort to keep such an operation going. He may have created it or simply joined a crew already in place. The main concern now is the possibility that such a team still exists or, at the least, their influence continues via a younger team."

"That's just way too much to think about."

"You don't have to. It's not your job." He paused. "You said that Helena saw the papers?"

"My mother showed them to her right after she photocopied them at the library. She told Helena that she had found them lying out on his desk at the house."

"Seems odd that he'd be so carefree about such things."

"I think he underestimated Mamá. She was uneducated but streetwise. She understood the gist of his notes, that he was still personally involved in Caracas. She wanted Helena to see the papers before she hid them in the attic and confronted him. She said it was the last straw.

She was leaving him and taking me with her. Calissa was already away at college."

"What exactly did the notes indicate to your mother?"

"Helena said they were convoluted, but one thing was evident." Sheridan took a deep breath. "Through the years my mother was aware that Harrison influenced policy to favor the illegal diamond trade."

"Ysabel actually said as much to Helena?"

"Yes. They couldn't prove anything, though. They couldn't do anything about it. My mother's main concern was more personal. Harrison had promised her that he was no longer involved in the day-to-day business the way he was in the early years of their marriage. But these papers showed that he *was*. That he still helped those people who had . . ." Words failed her. Those people who had what? What verb described what they had done to young Ysabel Maria Ortiz and countless others in her situation? Persecuted, raped, imprisoned, coerced, controlled? The list seemed endless.

Luke reached across the table, gently drew her hand up from her lap, and took hold of it. "The notes showed that he was still involved with the likes of those men who had hurt your mother."

"It was still going on! Girls were still being used. I can't imagine how that must have devastated her."

He nodded. "What happened when she confronted him?"

"Helena never talked to her again. Mamá died two days later."

"I'm so sorry." Compassion filled his expression. "How?"

"She was home alone and had an asthma attack. Until today, that was all I'd ever heard." Sheridan gritted her teeth and tried to put order to jumbled thoughts.

"What did you hear today?" Luke asked softly.

"That either she committed suicide or he killed her."

"Those are strong statements."

"How do you kill yourself with an asthma attack? Her meds were right next to her on the nightstand." Sheridan shook her head. "I've often wondered if she was allergic to him. Sometimes stress triggered her attacks, especially after they argued. If she confronted him as she told Helena she planned to do, she could have become that upset. He could have provoked her to the point of being ill and hidden her medication until he found her later that day."

"Nothing provable, huh?"

"There . . . there was a note. Harrison showed it to Calissa after the funeral, and then he burned it. She believes it was Mamá's handwriting but can't swear to it. She only saw it for a moment before he held a match to it. It said she loved us but she couldn't go on. I can't buy it. She was gentle but strong-willed. She would have followed through on her decision to leave him."

"Sheridan, no one wants to believe their loved one chose to leave them by suicide."

"I know. It just doesn't seem . . ." Sheridan felt resigned. Ysabel very well could have given up in the face of Harrison's anger and, most likely, threats that she would never be free of him. She knew too much about him for him to allow her to go.

"Why didn't Calissa ever tell you about this before?"

"He made her promise not to. In case you haven't picked up on it, Calissa and Mamá didn't relate very well. I think he used this as another way to show Liss what a poor mother she was."

"Why didn't he tell you? Because you were only thirteen?"

"I doubt my age mattered. I never really counted for much in my father's eyes. I argued with him all the time. If I'd heard this wild tale about suicide, I probably would have caused him even more grief."

"Why didn't you two get along?"

"I often wished it were because I wasn't really his daughter. But I have his ears and his chin. I also have no doubt that if I wasn't, he would have disinherited me long ago and enjoyed telling me why." She shook her head. "The thing he despised about me was that I was too much like my mother, whom he may have loved in a selfish way but certainly did not like. He despised her faith and her interest in volunteer work with the underprivileged, the two interests that I inherited as if such things were genetic. One of my earliest memories is telling him that Jesus loved him. I was four, and he slapped my face."

Luke studied her. "Did he do that often?"

Often? If her mother was not in the room and she said the words *God, Jesus, church, faith, cross, catechism* . . . She shrugged. "Depends on how you define *often*. I eventually figured out I could argue about anything, but I better not talk about God if he was within hearing. The last time I slipped up, I was seventeen."

"What happened?"

"It doesn't matter."

"It does matter. The more I know about him, the better the investigation goes."

She noted his green eyes and the warmth of his hand around hers. The sting of his cold words about the investigation lessened. "Well, so long as you're prying for impersonal reasons, I don't mind introducing you to all my skeletons."

He let go of her hand, glanced away, and pressed his lips together for a moment. "I apologize."

For what? she almost asked but didn't need to. She understood *for what* as well as he did. For blurring the line between business and personal. For holding her hand longer than necessary. For being an unmitigated knight in shining armor with eyes that went green.

Now it was her turn to glance away and weigh her words. Perhaps the pang of loneliness stemmed from Eliot's voice message or perhaps the emotional time with Helena. Whatever. She only knew that she welcomed Luke's straying over the line into personal and wished he'd take her hand again.

She looked at him. "About a year or so after my mother died, Harrison began going on drinking binges once or twice a year. He seemed to time them around House sessions. One night, right after high school graduation, my boyfriend brought me home. We were on the front porch, kissing good night as teenagers do, and my father opened the door. He called me every name in the book, beginning with *slut*. He said I was exactly like my mother, the whore. I told him he was going to rot in hell. He smacked me. *Hell* was a religious word, you know, the thing that always pushed him over the edge." Sheridan paused, shame hot in her chest, the sight of her black eye vivid in her memory. "The guy took me to my best friend's house, whose mother was a jewel. They let me live with them until I moved into a dorm that fall."

Luke clasped his hands in a tight fist atop the table. "Did he abuse Calissa or your mother?"

"He never touched Calissa. I don't think he hit my mom, but if the sounds coming from their bedroom were any indication, he abused her physically in other ways."

He exhaled an angry noise. "A real peach of a guy."

"Yeah. His dark side remained hidden from the public. But for me, diamond smuggling and dishonest political dealings do not take much stretch of the imagination to believe."

"You said you were like your mother, but it certainly doesn't sound as if you had one ounce of her gentle nature."

"No, I didn't. And I'm sure my independent streak exacerbated the situation for him."

"I'm sorry, Sheridan. I'm so sorry."

"Thanks."

They sat for a while, not speaking. She listened to the compassion in his silence, felt the strength in his presence.

Luke Traynor, aka Gabe the angel, carried her once again to a safe haven. There wasn't a whole lot she could do about that except stay in it as long as possible.

CHAPTER 37

Seated beside her father's hospital bed, well into her third acrylic nail, Calissa chewed, gnawed, and picked away.

It was an idiotic way to sublimate, to trade an emotional pain for a physical one. Stopping the behavior didn't seem to be an option, however.

She watched her father breathe, or rather she watched the machine breathe for him, cajoling him onward and upward. *Hang in there. I might let you off the hook yet. Sheridan might show up yet. I doubt, I seriously doubt, she'll let you off the hook, but showing up will be something at least. You know?*

Sheridan. She had it worse. They'd all wanted to protect her. Calissa, Ysabel, even Harrison. But now, learning what they'd kept from her, it wouldn't sound like concern. It must sound like betrayal. From their mother, too, with her suicide.

Maybe it wasn't suicide. Maybe that was only Harrison talking out of another side of his mouth, getting in one last cruel joke on his wife.

Helena said he loved Ysabel. He sure had a funny way of showing it.

On a scale of one to ten with ten being *Little House on the Prairie*,

Calissa rated her childhood as a seven. Everybody's parents argued, at times loudly, right? Every parent kept secrets, especially about the past. Her parents and several others she knew disguised their love as buying everything the kids needed and keeping the peace when necessary, say at piano recitals. Some parents, like Harrison and Ysabel, added one last note: they continued to live together. Increasingly frequent times apart notwithstanding, they kept up that facade.

Face it, she thought. Childhood trauma was a given. So she should just get over it. Even if it crept into her life when she was forty-seven years old. Right?

Calissa heard movement at the doorway and turned.

Sheridan entered, a Styrofoam container in her hand. "Fries." She gave it to her and sat next to her in the other chair. "Garlic."

"No way." The distinct aroma floated out as she opened the lid. "Oh, yes way. Thank you. This beats fingernails."

Sheridan touched Calissa's left ring finger with its bloody nub of natural nail. "Ouch."

"You get used to it." Calissa ate, stealing glances at her sister gazing at Harrison.

Something had changed, something intangible but real. First off, Sheridan gazed rather than glowered. And she was calm, but not like a stoic. What had happened? She'd left an hour ago, pale, eyes swollen, arm entwined through Luke's. Calissa didn't think it was the garlic fries. Had she opened a can of worms by forcing her sister and Luke together?

She popped another fry into her mouth. She really didn't need to take on one more load of big-sister guilt. Who knew? Maybe Sher and Luke had been in touch all along. Maybe Luke didn't have to use his super-duper spy powers to track her down.

Sheridan said, "Liss, do you remember that mean kid who lived down the street when we were young?"

"Mean kid? Oh yeah. Ty 'roly-poly' Foley."

Sheridan smiled.

"I still owe him one," Calissa said. "The day I got my first car, he put a tack strip under the back tire."

"Big deal. What about ruining my ninth birthday party? He smashed his hand right through that beautiful cake shaped like Wonder Woman."

"I plan to hunt him down. I figure as a city council member, the police will do me a favor and scare the living daylights out of him—what?"

Sheridan was shaking her head, her eyes wide.

"I'm kidding." Calissa pointed a french fry at their dad. "I am not that conniving."

Sheridan seemed to be concentrating on taking deep breaths.

If Calissa had learned anything in those disastrous years trying to mother her rebellious teenage sister, it was when to keep her mouth shut. She closed it around another fry. Despite the calm exterior, Sheridan was still in bad shape.

Sheridan moved her head as if stretching out kinks. "My point is, Mamá always said Ty's life experiences were not mine and I should forgive him."

"He was a mean, destructive little monster."

"She didn't say to be his best friend and allow him to do whatever. She just said don't look at him like he's a pile of dung."

"Be nice to him, in other words."

"Deeper than that. Like Jesús. Love him in spite of everything."

"The kid should've been locked up."

Sheridan grinned. "Probably."

Sheridan, Mamá, and Jesús. Calissa felt a stab of annoyance. The three of them had always left her out of their tight little loop.

"Liss, she would say forgive him." Sheridan wasn't talking about the neighbor boy. She was looking at their dad.

"But he doesn't deserve it."

"No. Neither did the neighbors or the store clerks or the D.C. socialites. Remember?"

Calissa cringed. Racial prejudice was up close and personal when it came to going out in public with a Latina mother.

Sheridan said, "No matter how people treated her, she treated them with love. We watched her do it, day in and day out. You or I would be upset or embarrassed. But she'd say, without a trace of sarcasm, 'Let's pray for her. Poor thing, she must not like herself very much. She must not know how much Jesús loves her. If we forgive her, she might start to believe that He does too.'"

"You were like that too. I swear, you had more friends than anybody as a kid. Even in high school you never had an enemy."

"Except him. He was the one person I could not forgive. Remember how Mamá did, though?"

"How?"

"You really didn't notice?"

Calissa shook her head.

"She smiled at him. Every single day she smiled at him. Her face lit up. Actually, I don't think it was *her* smiling. God smiled through her at him."

"Weird."

"Mysterious." Sheridan sighed. "I'm tired, Liss. Tired of holding on to the junk."

Calissa closed the empty take-out container and stared at their dad, helpless and hopeless. "Bram tells me it takes too much energy to carry all the garbage of past hurts. It's hurting us, Sher."

"Yeah. I think it hurts him, too. Maybe that's why he doesn't go."

"Maybe he would apologize if he could right now."

"Maybe. Maybe he is." Sheridan met her eyes. "I want to forgive my dad."

"I don't know how."

"Do you want to?"

Calissa nodded.

"Just tell God, then." Sheridan turned toward Harrison. Her eyes were open and her lips moved, but she made no sound. Their mother used to pray like that, in silence so that her husband and eldest daughter wouldn't make fun of her.

God, I'm sorry. I'm sorry. I don't know how to tell You. Calissa watched her sister and nearly panicked. "Sher! Do it for me too? Out loud?"

Sheridan nodded and then she began to pray audibly. In Spanish, fluent and flowing.

Calissa shut her eyes and felt another stab of annoyance. No, not annoyance. Envy. She might as well admit it. She'd been jealous of Sheridan her entire life. There was the role of the cute little baby, born when the older sister was in the seven-year-old, not-so-cute stage. There was the knack for languages by age two, the unabashed compassionate heart, the athletic prowess, the PhD, the marriage. The special connection with Mamá in all things churchy. The special connection with God Himself.

Lord, forgive me.

Calissa reached out and grasped Sheridan's hand. *"En inglés, por favor."*

"Holy God—" there was a smile in Sheridan's voice—"I miss You." The sound of a smile faded, and she whispered. "Mamá would tell us that You are here, though. That You hear me. Us. I quit. I don't want to carry the garbage anymore. I don't want to look at my father as if he were a pile of dung. Please forgive me. Please forgive him. And for Jesus' sake, help me to forgive him."

Calissa cleared her throat. "Ditto."

"Amen."

"Amen."

CHAPTER 38

WILMETTE

In spite of the long day that had begun with an ugly blue car and ended with a prayer at the hospital, Sheridan felt too keyed up to sleep. Calissa and Luke appeared to be in the same condition. Late that night they lingered with her in the living room in front of the fire he'd built and drank peppermint tea.

"So. Lucas." Calissa's eyes twinkled. "Did Sher ever tell you about our ancestor?"

Sheridan groaned. "Liss, I told you he wanted skeletons, not childhood fantasies."

"But this goes to your motive for marrying Eliot."

"You're saying that's a skeleton?"

"No. I'm saying it's interesting background material."

"Well, you're skating on thin ice, Sister."

Calissa smiled.

Sheridan couldn't help but grin. Something had broken loose between them. Undoubtedly it was related to that prayer at their father's bedside, to their willingness to let go of Harrison and all the hurt he had caused in their lives.

Calissa nearly flounced in her seat as she turned to face Luke. "Sheridan was convinced our mother was descended from royalty."

His brows rose slightly. He was in noncommittal mode.

"You're not impressed," Calissa said. "It could very well be true. Our great-grandmother Ysabel told our mother Ysabel that her great-great-great-something-grandmother, also named Ysabel, had sailed over from Spain and settled in what became Venezuela. All the firstborn daughters from that point on were named Ysabel. Our mother, her mother, her grandmother."

"But not you," he said.

"Why is it people always point that out? Obviously not. The story goes that Harrison was not keen on the idea of ancestral tradition. Eventually he did agree to give Sheridan *Ysabel* for her middle name. Anyway, this grandma Ysabel showed our mother a shawl." She leaned forward as if to emphasize her next words. "Made of purple silk. Purple. The color of royalty. Ysabel, as in Isabella, as in queen."

Sheridan said, "As in, it was fun to pretend some great-great-ancestor of ours was a cousin to the queen of Spain. It made us feel special."

Calissa snickered. "You felt so special, you married an ambassador so you could live like royalty."

"I can't believe you said that."

She shrugged. "Just another of my zany notions to explain why on earth you left the life you had here in Chicago. Your work was a dream come true. Ask her what her favorite game was growing up." She nodded at Luke. "Ask her."

He looked the question at Sheridan.

"School," she said.

Calissa shook her head. "Nah. It was benevolent professor."

Luke chuckled. "Benevolent professor?"

"I swear, that was what she called it. She was an odd little four-year-old. She'd say, 'Let's play benevolent professor.' Mamá and I laughed, but we'd play along. We'd mess up our hair, smear mascara on our cheeks, and wear mismatched clothes. Sher put on a fancy dress and a tiara. Why the tiara? We didn't know. Next she lined up her dolls, picked up a heavy dictionary, and gave them a lesson on kindness. Then we'd sit and beg for food. She'd give us apples and candy bars and hugs." Calissa's eyes glistened.

Sheridan felt her own sting at the sight. Was it possible her sister hadn't always seen her as a burden?

"Remember, Sher?"

"Mm-hmm."

Calissa turned back to Luke. "Fast-forward several years. Professor and social worker, dream come true. Except for that curious tiara. Hm. Fast-forward some more. Eliot enters the picture and offers Dr. Cole a chance to live in an embassy and be benevolent. Ta-da."

"Ta-da?" Luke said.

Sheridan grinned. "Well, yes, ta-da. Embassy life is as close as an American can get to living like a princess short of marrying a prince. I had huge staffs and lived in enormous, beautiful homes. I entertained heads of state and wore gorgeous gowns."

"And," Calissa added, "you kept up your benevolent work like all good princesses. I think maybe your dream was less about classroom teaching and more about being related to Queen Isabella."

She sighed dramatically. "I only wish there'd been a crown."

Calissa laughed loudly.

Luke cleared his throat. "Excuse me, ladies."

Calissa said, "Oh, buzz off, Traynor. We don't want to talk shop anymore tonight."

Sheridan grinned. "Yeah, Traynor, buzz off."

"Sorry, but I'm leaving in a day or so and I'm wondering—"

"A day or so?" Her rare sense of lightheartedness drained. "What do you mean?"

"Bram and I have to leave as soon as possible."

"But you can't." She heard the anxiety in her voice. She didn't know where it came from, but she couldn't stop it. "It's not over yet."

He stared at her for a long moment. "It is, Sher. It's over."

Calissa glanced between them. "What's over?"

He waited another long moment before he broke his gaze and looked at Calissa. "When I found Sheridan and Eliot in Mexico, I destroyed their sanctuary. I dragged her out into the world that still frightened her because of what happened in Caracas. What's over is her need for a crutch while she's in it."

How could he say that? Not many hours ago she was a basket case phoning him to come be her crutch.

"You are okay," he said to her. "Here you are in Chicago, giving me grief about a tail, visiting your mother's old friend, laughing with Calissa. You're not the same woman I picked up in Topala."

Sheridan stared into her mug. Her earlier panic hadn't been because city sights and sounds bombarded her with Caracas flashbacks. No, it was because she faced an emotional abyss and she was so very tired of facing emotional abysses by herself.

Calissa said, "You were saying you wondered what?"

"I wondered if Helena would talk to me. I may hear something helpful."

"I don't think she'd mind. I'll call her and ask if you can come with us tomorrow. We planned to meet after she goes to the bank."

"The bank?"

"I didn't tell him that part yet," Sheridan said.

"Our mother mailed something to her for us," Calissa explained. "She's kept it in a safe-deposit box all these years." Her forehead creased. "It arrived after Mamá died. She must have sent it just the day before."

"Did Helena say what it was?"

"It's a padded envelope that she never opened. Mamá wrote on the outside of it, asking her to save it for us in case she . . ."

Sheridan filled in the blanks. *In case she died.*

Luke said, "For your sakes, I hope it's simply a memento of a mother's love. But I'd appreciate if you invited me along."

"Because," Sheridan said, "it could be more."

He nodded.

With that curt gesture, Sheridan felt dismissed. Gabriel the angel had finished his work. She was where she needed to be, literally and figuratively. She was with her sister, and she could navigate her own way back home. He could get on with his work, no longer entangled with her needs.

With every ounce of willpower she squashed a growing desire to sit beside him on the couch, snuggle in his arms, and lay her head on his shoulder.

CHAPTER 39

THE BUZZING AND CHIMING of the cell phone startled Sheridan awake. She grabbed it from the top of the nightstand where she had left it last night, turned on, volume set to high and vibrate. She wasn't going to miss another call from Eliot.

"Hello?"

"Señora!" Mercedes nearly shrieked the word and launched pell-mell, in Spanish, into a description of Eliot's night.

"Slow down, honey. I'm not quite awake." Sunlight filtered through the blinds already. The clock read 7:10. And she was still in bed? Odd. In all the upheaval, she was sleeping better than she had in a long time.

In over eighteen months?

"Oh, señora. His night was so bad. Javier massaged his shoulders. I rubbed his feet. We gave him medicine. Padre came and prayed. And still, he moaned and cried for hours and hours."

Sheridan sat up, her stomach twisted in a knot. Poor Eliot. If she were there, things would have been different. He depended on her so much.

Too much. Too much. She simply could not carry him long-distance this week.

"Mercedes, I'm sorry. Is he sleeping now?"

"Yes. I left when he went to sleep. I had to come to my aunt's and call you right away. I got a ride with a deliveryman down at Davy's."

"But you should be at home, sleeping while he does."

"No, no. Javier must go to work and padre has things to do. We promised not to leave him alone, señora, so I had to come now to call you."

Sheridan rubbed her forehead. What was she supposed to do from Chicago? "I am so sorry," she said again. "Did you say it started yesterday afternoon?"

"Yes. That is why I am calling. His worst never happens then, does it?"

Eliot's pain varied in intensity. The nurses at the hospital would ask him to give it a number from one to ten. When he stopped replying "Twelve" every time, they let him check out. Nowadays, she had to ask—much as they both disliked the question—in order to gauge his medication. The number moved up and down, unpredictably but usually between six and eight. She knew it hit ten and above when he refused to reply.

One constant remained, however. What Mercedes described was a twelve. As she said, those did not happen in the afternoon.

Something must have triggered it.

"Mercedes, what was he doing when it started?"

"Before he cleared off the desk with one swoop of his arm?"

Sheridan shut her eyes. "Yes."

"We were working. He was jumping ahead in his story, not going in order, telling me about meeting you. I said—oh, I talk too much—I said we should write about his first embassy assignment and his first wife. I think that was when he knocked over his water glass. Then he only wanted to talk about you, about your hearts *communing*."

A pang of nostalgia hit her. Eliot had always liked the way she described their first meeting.

"Finally I gave up. I said to myself, *I should just do it his way.* So I said we need to put this in order. Why did you go to this event where it was love at first sight? I said I think God must have led you there. And then . . ." Her voice caught.

Sheridan drew her knees up, laid her forehead on them, and held her breath.

"And then he went kind of crazy. With the pain and vertigo, too. But, oh, señora, it scared me. It scared me so much. He pushed everything off the desk and he swore. I ran outside and rang the bell."

Mercedes and Javier had devised the signal. When she needed him, she would swing a cowbell as hard as she could until he stepped out of his shop and waved up the hill.

"He came right up and we got señor into bed. I straightened the study. Padre checked out the computer. He says it's all right."

Sheridan tuned her out. Eliot never really minded talking about his first wife, Noelle. There was always regret and hurt in his voice, but nowhere near what would set off an incident like this. Conversation about his and Sheridan's first meeting always made him smile. It had been innocuous on the surface, but underneath was that heart communion that led rather quickly to their marriage. It was a happy moment to remember.

What was his problem, then? Why would he go crazy when Mercedes mentioned the idea of God bringing them together? Eliot believed. Until the shooting, he'd been more faithful than she about attending church. It reminded her of her father's reaction to God talk.

A shudder went through her. Eliot was nothing like Harrison.

Sheridan finished the conversation with Mercedes, unsuccessfully ordering her to hire a nurse or a housekeeper to help. Evidently the girl had just wanted Sheridan's assurance that she had not done anything wrong.

Still scrunched into a tight curl, she noticed the crucifix on the nightstand. She'd left it out with the phone the night before. Looking for comfort? Trying to hear His voice again?

"I'm listening, Jesús. What do you want from me? He's sick. And I can't fix him."

Exactly.

Exactly.

"Sher!" Calissa called out, and then she opened the door. "Sher!"

A first glance at her wide eyes and Sheridan knew. She hurried over to her. "When did it happen?"

"A few minutes ago." Calissa put a hand over her mouth. Tears formed. Sheridan had no words for the passing of their father. She didn't have any tears, either.

So she just hugged her sister tightly.

CHAPTER 40

TOPALA

"Padre Miguel." Eliot shifted his weight gingerly on the padded lounge chair. "I'm quite fine now. You needn't sit with me. Javier is right inside the house."

A wide grin creased Padre Miguel's cherubic face.

The old codger was indefatigable.

"Eliot, it's no problem." Sometime during the middle of the night he had lost his formal address of señor.

The familiarity did not ruffle Eliot's feathers in the least. Which should have surprised him, but he seemed incapable of surprise this morning.

Seated at the table nearby, the area dappled by sunlight through tree leaves, the padre tore off a piece of hard roll and slathered it with jam. "Javier is resting. We'll let him be for a bit. And Mercedes may be delayed in town."

"But I do feel absolutely fine, and I'm sure you have other things to do."

Padre Miguel chewed, and his deep brown eyes danced.

Painwise, the night had been Eliot's worst since moving to Topala. Unlike past experience, the off-the-scale torment struck quickly and early in the day. It made no sense and frightened him. Was it yet another new development he would have to learn to live with?

Then he remembered the events leading up to it.

"Why did you go to this event?" Mercedes had asked. *"God must have led you."*

The enormity of what he'd done hit him like a walloping box to the ears.

There were things Sheridan didn't know, things she didn't need to know, things no one needed to know now.

The year before, while lying in the hospital in Houston, he had begun to consider what he would do with his time. Given his physical limitations, it seemed that writing his memoirs might be a good choice for occupation. He calculated the risks of revisiting certain times of his life. Old difficulties would be stirred up, no question about it.

But it was his story. He would choreograph the entire thing, present what he deemed significant. There was no reason for it to be exhaustive. Who would care to read every detail of some minor official's existence anyway?

He would write biographical vignettes, from his childhood overseas to his diplomatic service as an adult. Recent American history would be included. His whole purpose would be to inspire readers. Far too few young people aspired to such a goal anymore, to serve in the capacity he and his father and grandfather had. He wanted to encourage the next generation.

The detail of his encounter with one malevolent man would simply not be addressed.

End of story.

"Why did you go to this event? God must have led you."

Padre Miguel brushed crumbs from his hands. "May I get you something more to eat?"

"No. No thank you."

"So." He folded his hands on his small paunch. "You feel absolutely fine. Isn't that marvelous?"

Eliot nodded.

"Is it odd? I mean, after such a night?"

He stared at the priest, not sure whether to be appalled or amused at his ability to snooker him into the core of a matter with such innocuous observations.

The priest went on. "In spite of my faith and prayers, I feared we would be driving you to the hospital in Mesa Aguamiel."

"Good heavens. Promise me you'll get an ambulance if ever the need arises."

"Ah, but that involves so much time and expense."

"Padre, I can hold on for days by a thread, and I have the money. Please."

He smiled. "It is odd, isn't it, that you're up and about?"

Eliot figured there was no escape. "Yes. It was odd first of all not to hurt the night after our trip by car. It is extremely odd that after last night I am now awake, not the least bit foggy-brained, and relatively pain-free."

"What do you suppose is going on?"

"I don't know."

"*Odd* often points to God's hand tipping the scale."

God's hand. In for a penny, in for a pound. "Speaking of hands . . . the day we went to Mesa Aguamiel, you touched my arm and hip. I felt a distinct impression of intense heat."

"That happens sometimes." Padre Miguel smiled. "Odd, isn't it?"

"Indeed."

"Tell me, Eliot, where are you on the scale this morning?"

"You know about the scale?"

"I am nosy, and señora sometimes obliges. Once when we talked of your pain, she explained this measurement. I suppose it is helpful, although inadequate. In reality none of us is able to put a number on our hurts, are we?"

Eliot felt like an insect splayed on a board. Straight pins held wings, head, and legs in place. He couldn't move; he couldn't speak. All he could do was lie there, totally exposed and vulnerable to an old Mexican who had the power to touch him with God's hand.

"Hurt encompasses whole worlds beyond the physical." Padre Miguel pulled on his lower lip as if in deep thought. "I'm talking about when other people hurt us. Our psyches are wounded as surely as if a bullet could strike them. Scar tissue forms. Things look healed on the outside, but underneath, the pain goes on and on." He paused a beat. "We feel it at various levels throughout life. Sometimes it reaches a two on the scale; sometimes it soars up to a twelve."

Eliot blinked.

"If we truly want to be free of the pain, then we must forgive the offender. Of course. That's a given, don't you think? 'How many times shall I forgive,' Peter asked. 'Seven?' 'No,' Jesús said. 'Seventy times seven.'"

Eliot could only blink again and wait for the punch line he knew was imminent.

"Our Lord told His disciples that if they did not forgive someone, then that person's sins would be retained." He bolted upright, palms against the chair arms, his eyes bright and focused on his captive insect. "Now where do you suppose those sins might be retained?"

Eliot didn't think the man really wanted a reply.

Padre Miguel slapped a hand to his own chest with a thump. "Right here. Right here inside of me. If I do not forgive someone who has hurt me, then I am holding on to sin in my heart. In *my heart*. It gouges me deeply. It puts down roots, and after a time it even bears fruit."

"Fruit?"

"Yes! Anger and fear and pride and . . . well, you get the picture." He settled back in his chair, hands folded once more across his midsection. "Don't you?"

All energy drained from Eliot. Virtually pinned down, he'd been slit open, his inner self exposed. He rasped, "The man wreaked havoc in my life and countless others."

"And retaining that fact in your heart helps you how?"

A warming sensation flowed through Eliot, as if the exposure was not to shame but to a radiant light.

Padre Miguel said softly, "When we simply let the offense go, Eliot, when we simply hand it over to our Lord, the fruit withers up. And we realize how rotten it tasted."

Eliot formed his lips around the sound of *b*, the word *but* on the tip of his tongue. But . . . there were no other words to defend, explain, or argue. In essence the padre had delivered an ultimatum: continue to wallow in anger, fear, and pride or let go their cause. *Let go the wrongs committed against you by Harrison Cole.*

Padre Miguel smiled. "Don't try to analyze it. God will show you how."

The kitchen door banged open and Mercedes rushed out onto the patio. She reached Eliot's chair and knelt, red-faced and perspiring. "Oh, señor! It's señora's father. He is dead. I am so sorry."

Eliot had waited nearly thirty years to hear such news, such rattling good news.

But . . . His stomach clenched. How was Sheridan taking it? How was he supposed to take it? And now what? Now what was he supposed to do about forgiving that piteous excuse of a man for wreaking havoc in his life? Was it now a nonissue? Did he even need to address it anymore? It didn't feel like it was over for him.

He looked at Padre Miguel, who did not need to hear a question before answering it.

The priest shook his head, a small smile on his lips. "No, Eliot, you're not off the hook."

❧

Eliot did not understand how to let it go.

In the kitchen, he watched Mercedes prepare his medication, deftly collecting pills from various containers and placing them in a yellow bowl.

Padre Miguel's words resonated. Eliot had no quarrel with them. But how was he to implement them? On his way out, the old priest had pointed heavenward and tossed him an enigmatic smile, reminiscent of Eliot's father.

Eliot Montgomery II had been a wise and tender man. When correcting his son, he often said, "You'll figure it out," and then he'd smile in the way Padre Miguel just had.

Mercedes's hand stilled on one of the bottles. "Señor?" Her weary face questioned. "You seem almost agile."

"Almost." He almost smiled as well. His body communicated clearly that it was damaged. It ached, no question about it. His hands grasping the canes, what he had dubbed his mini walkers, proclaimed that his movement was restricted.

But it all added up to a two on the scale. A *two.*

"I believe," he said, "that we can eliminate that pill this time around."

"We want to stay ahead of it, you know. On top of it."

"You're lecturing me." He chuckled at the sound of his wife's words coming at him in Spanish in a young girl's voice. "We will skip that pill."

She gazed at him for a long moment and then returned to her task.

"I appreciate you, Mercedes. You are doing a top-notch job, and I'm glad that you refused señora's suggestion to hire a nurse."

She smiled shyly. "Thank you."

Had he been aware of Mercedes's early-morning trip to Mesa Aguamiel to phone Sheridan, he would have forbidden it. "Tell me again about your conversations with señora. She wasn't too upset?"

"No." Mercedes summarized the exchanges that she had already given to him. "She wasn't too upset about her father's death, either. Of course he was old and sick. Maybe she was in shock. We had just said good-bye and I hung up when she called right back. I was hugging my aunt farewell and the telephone rang. Señora." The girl's face fell and she began to talk in a monotone, which was totally out of character, especially for the information she delivered. "Señora said, 'My father died a few minutes ago. Please tell señor. I will call again when we know the funeral schedule.'"

Eliot suspected that her tone echoed Sheridan's. Of course his own response had been the same when Mercedes had blubbered out the news to him in the courtyard. How did one express sadness that simply wasn't there?

But he could see that the naive child before him could not fathom a lack of sorrow. The woman she loved and admired confused her with what looked like stoicism.

"Mercedes, you've told me that your father was a happy man. He always made you laugh and feel safe. Then he passed away when you were only nine. Your life was extremely difficult after that."

Her chin quivered.

"Señora's life would have been happier and safer if her father had not been part of it when she was little."

Mercedes gasped. "How awful!"

"Yes. It makes her sadness different. Do you understand?"

"I think so. It's hard to cry for a nightmare that's over."

Eliot rethought his use of *naive* and *Mercedes* in the same sentence.

"I am sorry for her." She gave him the yellow dish of pills.

He looked at it and suddenly felt a tidal wave of sadness. He missed his wife beyond words. "Uh, next time, may I have the brown pottery, please?"

"The brown—señor!" She smiled. "I did not know you had a preference."

"That's because I never said."

There were many things he had never said. Perhaps it was time to speak.

God, I don't know how to let it go. But I do know that I desperately want to.

CHAPTER 41

CHICAGO

Calissa exploded at the funeral home.

Evidently the director's kind attentions and the soft music did not have their intended effect on her. She flounced about on the cushy armchair as if it had tacks on the seat.

Sheridan sat back and watched the conniption fit without comment, but with plenty of distress. What was it she had considered earlier? Something about Calissa having a heart for people? Hogwash. Only her vocabulary had changed. She'd become much more creative with four-letter words, adding prefixes and suffixes, using them as different parts of a sentence.

"Mr. Ford!" Calissa resembled a barking terrier with frosted, spiked hair. "Do you have any idea who my father was?"

Sheridan certainly hoped not. The distinguished gentleman may not want the body of a criminal lying about, fouling his lovely home.

Mr. Ford bowed his head slightly, not bothering to reply to the ridiculous question. They'd already covered Harrison's career, which of course he knew about because he had voted for the man time and again.

Calissa went on. "Then why in the world would we hold a visitation here? Thousands of people will be paying their respects to my father. There is no way this place could accommodate such a crowd."

Sheridan stopped listening. Calissa had always referred to *my* father, never *our* father. She wondered, not for the first time, if it was significant. Was she Harrison's daughter? Maybe it would come out now. No, she wasn't. Their mother had had a torrid affair with a very nice man. That would be welcome news. What if this imaginary man were still alive?

Mr. Ford stood. "I'll give you sisters some time alone to discuss these matters. Just give a shout when you're ready to view the coffins."

Sheridan could have sworn his eyes twinkled at her when he said *shout*. She gave him a little nod as he left the room. *Shouting will not be a problem.*

"Well," Calissa said. "What do you think?"

Sheridan realized every muscle in her body was tight, as if prepared for a blow that was to come. She couldn't speak.

"You sit there, Sher, and you don't say a word. I'm a little tired of always making the decisions. At least you managed to get here in time from the other side of civilization. The least you could do now is help figure out the funeral."

"Is he my father?" She interrupted the blow.

"What? Who? Him?" Calissa wiggled her thumb toward the door.

"Harrison. Is he my dad too?"

"Sheridan! What an awful thing to say!"

"You always say 'my father' like he's only yours."

"Maybe because you never claim him."

"Why would I?" Sheridan's voice rose. "You know what my most vivid memory is growing up? You talking at me like I'm a moron because I don't see life the same way you do. And then there was Dad." She nearly spat the word. "He disapproved of everything I ever did. I was never good enough to be called his daughter. He treated Mamá the same way. It's no mystery why she checked out."

"You checked out too, just not as permanently. And don't you dare blame him for her death. As despicable as he was, he never would have stood by and watched her die from an asthma attack. Whether she chose that way out by deliberately not taking the meds, we'll never know."

Much as she wanted to blame Harrison, Sheridan had to agree. They'd have to resign themselves to not knowing exactly what happened.

Calissa's tirade wasn't over. "She was unhealthy and physically weak. You were too young to know how much he didn't do because he had to take care of her needs."

"Well, excuse me for being born seven years after you. Or ever."

"Well, excuse me for being the oldest and knowing more than you."

"You are such a shrew, Calissa."

"Shrew? Mamá left us, Sheridan! She chose to leave us. Who did she think was going to take care of her precious little girl, hm? Dad had no clue. He planned to ship you off to . . . Oh, my gosh, I did not say that."

Sheridan stared at her in disbelief. "He planned to ship me off where?"

"A boarding school." She muttered one of her favorite four-letter words. "Maybe you would have liked it better than having a shrew for a stand-in mom. But somehow it just didn't seem right to me. I couldn't let him do it."

"He really didn't like me, did he?"

"You reminded him too much of Mamá." Her voice grew quieter. "The parts he loved about her and couldn't control."

They sat for a few moments. Sheridan felt her muscles relax.

"Liss, you were always on my case. It seemed like you went out of your way to make my life difficult."

"I was twenty years old. I quit Stanford. I moved back home from California to take care of you. I didn't have any warm fuzzies to give you. On some level I'm sure I resented you, blamed you for ruining my life. Instead of dating I was driving you to volleyball practice. Instead of hanging out with friends I was making sure you kept curfew, making sure no one took advantage of you, making sure you kept up your grades. You had your master's before I finished my undergrad degree."

"I'm sorry."

"Oh, Sher, it's not your fault. It just was."

Sheridan imagined herself as a thirteen-year-old going off to a boarding school somewhere, wallowing alone in the grief of her mother's death, trying to fit in with a whole group of strangers. Not living under her dad's or Calissa's thumbs did not make that scenario as attractive as she would have guessed.

"Liss, thank you."

She waved a hand in dismissal. "I should thank you for being born, especially seven years later. When I moved back home to torture you, I started working with Dad, really working, grown-up style. That was the true beginning of my career. I couldn't have done it any other way."

"God worked it out."

Calissa shrugged.

"Mamá would have prayed before . . ." Sheridan ached at the thought of her mother's last minutes. She could not comprehend the anguish that she would have experienced. "Liss, I know she would have asked Him to take care of us. She may have given up, but she knew He wouldn't."

"You're starting to channel her with all this God talk."

"That's the nicest thing you've ever said to me."

"It is not."

"Okay, it's not. So what do you need from me? Honestly, I figured you and Dad would have had the arrangements all made in advance. Obit written, casket chosen. Invitations sent to distinguished guests. Buffet lunch at the club with his staff." She smiled.

Calissa gave her a small one in return. "He was egotistical to the point of not believing he would die. Sorry to burst your bubble, but this is going to take a while."

Sheridan went over to her big sister and gave her a hug. "I'm here for as long as you need me."

❧

WILMETTE

Seated on a bench in the backyard, Sheridan made the requisite phone call to Mercedes's aunt with funeral details. She told her there was no rush to deliver the message to her husband.

Sighing, she closed the phone. Eliot might have his own meltdown when he heard that the funeral was scheduled for her tenth day away. That was the date she had told him she would return.

"Sheridan."

She turned and saw Luke walking across the lawn. "Hi."

"Hi." He sat down beside her and looked out toward the lake. "This is an amazing backyard."

"Apparently paid for by money laundering."

"It's still amazing."

"I suppose."

It *was* amazing, and especially beautiful on a sunny afternoon. A small, sandy beach lay only a few yards from them. Lake Michigan reflected the blue sky and its whitecaps were few. The breeze carried birdsong and scents of spring. Some leaves had opened, flecks of celery green on dark branches.

"What will you do with it?" he asked.

"Sell it as soon as possible. We would have needed the money for his attorney fees and spin doctors, but he took care of that nicely, didn't he? Now that he's gone, he can't be prosecuted for what he did."

"Nope."

"I would love to give the money back to the people hurt by the whole operation, but where would we begin? Maybe with those poor women like my mother in Caracas, working for criminals."

"I think you already helped some of them in similar situations, didn't you? With Reina and the job-training courses you two had going, I'm sure you impacted women who could have been involved with the drug trade in some way. Women who didn't have a choice but to work for the underworld."

She nodded. "If Reina were still there, I could . . ." She let her voice drift away. *If, if, if.*

"How did things go at the funeral home?"

For once she was glad for his change of subject. "There was a catfight." She gave him a silly rendition of her and Calissa's squabble and filled him in on the schedule details.

"Will there be a memorial in D.C.?"

"Yes, at some point." She didn't even want to consider attending such an event, where she'd have to listen to his name extolled. "Calls have been pouring into his office. Calissa got a list of names. I always was surprised at the people he knew, people with big names. My sister actually talked personally to the president."

"Impressive. Will Eliot come for the funeral?"

"It's not possible. Just riding into Mesa Aguamiel is too hard on him. He's incapacitated for at least a day." She thought of Eliot's voice mail. It bothered her to remember his animated voice, his description of buying a gift for Mercedes, his errand running with Padre Miguel, his new canes.

"What did you say?" Luke asked.

She turned to him. "Hm?"

"You said something."

"I did? Oh, I must be talking to myself again. Calissa's been accusing me of it." She paused. "Eliot left a voice mail the other day."

"That's why you needed the password."

"Yes, it wasn't Mercedes or her aunt. Do you remember telling me that if you were in Eliot's shoes, you'd want your wife right beside you?"

He nodded.

"In his voice mail he sounded happy. He sounded great. He wasn't faking it. He just was fine. He was even interacting with people. Mercedes drives him up the wall at times and he bought her a gift. He avoids Padre Miguel, but he was out doing errands with him in Mesa Aguamiel."

"That's good news."

"But why now, when I'm not there? Have I been in his way all this time?"

"I can't say, Sher. I mean, Sheridan. It could be that with you not there to take care of him, he's had to push himself harder. I can tell it bothers you." His eyes shimmered green.

"I guess my feelings are easily hurt these days. Anyway, Mercedes called this morning. He had a bad afternoon that went on into the night, the worst she has ever seen. I don't think he'll be traveling to Chicago."

"I'm sorry."

"Thanks. I called Helena. She doesn't mind talking to a spy."

His left brow went up.

"Does tomorrow morning work for you?"

"Sure."

They sat in silence.

At last he said, "The funeral is going to be tough on you. The crowds, the commotion, the stress. In spite of what I said last night, this might be a time to pull out the old crutch. Do you want me to stay?"

She turned to him. "You can't stop what you're doing."

"I can rearrange some things. Right now, you're more important."

She shook her head. "Don't do that." *Don't make me important. Don't make me care for you.*

He touched the edge of her eye with his little finger and wiped the errant tear. "Hey, I'm Gabe the angel. Remember?" He shifted his position subtly until he was on the far corner of the bench, his arms crossed, offering distance instead of a hug.

He understood. She wanted to slip into his arms and snuggle against him as she'd done countless times before. But that was when he was Gabe the angel, the guardian, the comforter, the bad guy–slash–good guy who inexplicably kept her sane when her world crashed.

Now he was Luke the man, the one who cared for her in ways her husband did not. And now she was Sheridan the woman, who could once again stand on her own two feet, who could once again long for the response of a healthy man to her femininity.

It would be best not to be hugged by Luke Traynor.

CHAPTER 42

CHICAGO

The following morning Sheridan sat with Luke across the table from Helena Van Auken in a coffee shop. They had been there for at least an hour, Luke listening to Helena's story. At last he was finished with his questions.

"Dear." Helena patted Sheridan's hand on the table. Her hair, or some of it, was again in a bun. She wore a floral print skirt with a bright top, this one royal blue. "I am sorry for your loss. Not his death, particularly, but the loss of a relationship. The man created a hole in your life by not being a loving father."

Sheridan couldn't have spoken even if she knew what to say. The woman had a knack for touching heartstrings.

"I am sorry Calissa didn't come, but I understand she is preoccupied today."

That was putting it mildly. Her sister had spewed harsh words at Sheridan for not postponing the meeting with Helena. She said Sheridan truly was all "princess." Where was her benevolence now? What happened to her "I'm here for as long as you need me" promise?

As usual the little sister had let down the big one, thinking of her own wants.

Sheridan responded to Helena, saying, "Yes. She's inundated with calls and visitors. But friends and the housekeeper are there helping out. I'll get back as soon as I can. This business here is time sensitive."

"I agree. I mean, how long can we . . ." Helena glanced over one shoulder, then the other. Leaning forward, she whispered, "How long can we keep the CIA at our beck and call?"

Luke winked at her. His charm had immediately won her over, of course. "Where would you get that idea?"

Helena shrugged, the picture of innocence. "When Sheridan referred to you as a government official, I just assumed." She smiled.

He smiled back.

Sheridan put a hand over her mouth to hide a grin. The two of them had been flirting since the first hello.

Helena sighed and pulled an eight-by-ten padded manila envelope from her large handbag. "Well, whoever you are, Luke, it is kind of you to help. I am so grateful that at last the officials are stepping into this mess."

"I'm not sure I can guarantee any justice, Mrs. Van Auken, but we will do our best to get to the bottom of things."

"The act of unburdening this information releases me. I hadn't realized I felt guilt until the girls visited the other day. I've known about his shenanigans for years. I should have done something to put a stop to him."

"Oh, Helena," Sheridan said. "Don't take on any guilt. There was absolutely nothing you could have done."

"Perhaps not while your mother was alive, but later. I could have told someone in Washington what I knew."

Luke shook his head. "Without proof, it would have gone nowhere. Harrison was an important man."

"I suppose so." She smiled coyly. "But if I'd found a confidant as cute as you, it might have been worth my trouble. Now—" she slid the envelope across the table and tapped it—"this arrived in a box addressed to me. The mailman brought it my door. There was nothing else in it. See here where your mother wrote, 'H, please keep this for my girls, just in case. Thank you. Y.' It doesn't say anything about not opening it, but I never did. I always felt it was too private. It was between you girls and her. I have no idea what is inside, although I am sure, given Ysabel's personality, that she wrote you a love note."

Sheridan felt a tickle of excitement. A note from her mother? "Thank you for keeping it safe all these years."

"You are most welcome, dear. I'll leave you to open it." She slid to the end of the booth. Her eyes twinkled as she smiled. "Call me if there's any good stuff, all right?"

"I promise."

A few moments later, after good-byes were said, Luke moved to the other side of the table. "What do you want to do?"

"I should wait and open it with Calissa."

"But she told you to do whatever you wanted with it."

"But she was mad when she said that."

"*But* I think she meant it. She won't be ready for this for some time. She's dealing with too much else." He smiled. "And besides, you're ready to burst at the seams."

"I can't imagine. A note from my mom! She must have written it when I was thirteen."

"Go ahead. Open it."

She began to work at the seal. "I suppose we could go to the car. People probably cry in coffee shops all the time, though. It might be there isn't even anything meaningful in here. I don't want to get my hopes too—Oh." She was looking inside the envelope now.

"What?"

"There's a black velvet bag." She met his gaze.

"Oh. Hm. We might not want to open that in a coffee shop."

Sheridan's hands shook. She gave the envelope to Luke. "See what it is."

After a slight hesitation, he reached inside and removed a business-size envelope. "Here's the note." He smiled.

She took it with a sigh. Her mother had written a note! In her fine print on the outside was: *To my daughters, Calissa and Sheridan*. "She always printed. Cursive was a struggle for her."

"I'm untying the bag now." His hand was inside the envelope. "Mm."

"What?"

"Um . . ." He angled the envelope to get a better look. "Mm-hmm."

"Luke!"

"Well, I'd say it's a good thing Helena kept this locked up in the bank."

"It isn't . . ."

"Yeah, it is. A pouch full of flashers." His jaw hung open. "Your mother mailed this. She *mailed* it. Through the postal system."

Sheridan shrugged. "She loved the United States. She always talked about how wonderful everything was. She truly adored its systems. The post office alone never ceased to amaze her."

"Okay." He folded the envelope flap back into place. "We'll save this for later."

"How much is there?"

"Enough to fill my palm. They're large. I have no clue what they're worth."

She blew out a breath. "Why would she?"

"Read the note."

"Yeah." Sheridan carefully unsealed the smaller envelope and withdrew folded papers. "It looks like two separate letters. This one is just a page." She scanned the short one, holding it out where Luke could see it too.

Dear Girls,

My heart is too heavy. I took these diamonds from your father's coat pocket. He just returned once again from Caracas.

They are proof of what he is doing there. Later today, he will miss them. And then I will tell him I know. He will laugh, and then he will be furious. They are illegal and would pay for his new boat. I do not understand what you are allowed to do with them. Maybe you can sell them to thieves and give the money to the poor instead of the boat seller. I am sorry to trouble you with this problem. But when you read this, you will be grown.

Love, Mamá

Sheridan looked at Luke. "Huh?"

He shrugged. "Beats me. Know any thieves?"

"No."

"Why don't you read the other note?"

She studied it but the words blurred. She skimmed through it. "It looks like the whole story that Helena told us about my mom and dad meeting. How guys were set up at the place she worked. His involvement with the smuggling trade. His influence on foreign policy. She says, 'He rescued me. I love him for that. I love him for helping the United States. But he does wrong things sometimes. This upsets me.'"

"Read the good parts."

"What do you mean?"

"The good parts." Luke smiled gently. "The parts where she says how much she loves you."

She shook her head and handed it to him. "I can't."

He glanced over the pages. "Like this, Sher. Listen. 'Sweet Sheri, I see the woman you will become and I am so proud. Your heart is the most giving one I have ever known. You are intelligent and independent. You are a graceful athlete, so beautiful to watch. My prayer is that God will plant His dreams in your heart, that you will see them as gifts He wants to fulfill. I trust they will involve your smart brain and your altruism. See? I remember the word you teach me last week.'"

Sheridan pressed a napkin to her face.

"And later she writes, 'Girls, I am not well. I fear my health will quit before I am old. And my heart. It is so weary. I love you both more than I can say. You have always been the lights in my life. I am so sorry if I cannot be a mother to you long enough. I know how it hurts not to have a mamá. But God is with you, calling your name. Never forget that. Keep listening for Him.'"

She felt Luke's hand on her elbow.

"Let's go."

He murmured more, his voice near, but the words were indecipherable. She heard only the comfort in his tone and the sound of her mother's love echoing down from when she was thirteen.

❧

WILMETTE

That afternoon, alone in her bedroom, Sheridan procrastinated going downstairs to receive casseroles and condolences from an endless stream of visitors. It wasn't that she feared Calissa's wrath or even playing the role of dutiful daughter.

No, she could handle those things. For now, she just wasn't finished listening to her mother's voice.

Seated at her old desk, sunlight pouring across it, the sound of cars on the drive below coming through the open window, she fingered the note. What a precious gift it was! Despite the troubling information, it soothed her like a caress on her soul.

Ysabel had been ashamed of her writing skills. There were no letters or cards or even recipes among the few photographs Sheridan had of her. Even the memory of her mother's expressive words of love had faded over the years. To hold papers that she had held and to read her handwriting and the affirmations of a mother to her daughters almost overwhelmed Sheridan. To think she was only thirteen when her mom wrote it. Sheridan was forty now, a year older than her mother had been when she died.

She smiled sadly. When she turned thirty-nine in Caracas, they had a wonderful dinner party. Reina and everyone they worked with and Sheridan's staff all came. Later that night, Eliot suggested they do something wild and crazy for her fortieth, something like climb Machu Picchu in the Andes.

The day he was shot, there was still leftover birthday cake in the kitchen. She turned forty in Topala. A week after, Eliot asked her if she'd like to shop in Mesa Aguamiel by herself to celebrate.

Not that she'd really thought much about the so-called big event. In their cocoon situation, what did age matter?

Sheridan scanned the pages yet again. Their mother's long letter had included personal notes to Calissa, too. Like in Sheridan's, she spoke of Calissa's abilities. Her prayers were for God to use the speaking gifts He had given Calissa, perhaps leading her to become a good politician. She had underlined the word *good.* Sheridan took it to mean one that was honest.

Calissa remembered more about their mother than Sheridan could. Twenty years old when Ysabel died, she was already a young woman, on her own in college far away.

Sheridan looked again at the date her mother had printed at the top of the letter, a day in May 1983.

She reread the date. Why did it feel so familiar? Probably because it was the month and year of her mother's death. Probably because she'd been reading it for the past several hours.

The month of March.

March?

The same year.

Sheridan's breath caught.

March 1983. Caracas.

May 1983. Caracas. *He just returned. . . . I took these diamonds from your father's coat pocket.*

"Dear God."

Sheridan reached into her handbag, pulled out the cell phone, and called Luke.

He answered on the second ring. "Hey."

She shut her eyes. They'd said good-bye on the driveway earlier. He had brought her home from the coffee shop after they put the diamonds in a safe-deposit box at a bank and made copies of the letters for him to take with him to D.C. He'd taken a cab from the house to the airport.

"Sheridan, you there? I'm on board and a flight attendant is glaring at my phone."

The good-bye had been a good one. She was upbeat, ready to take on whatever Harrison's funeral might throw at her. Ugly memories, praises from politicians for his accomplishments, Calissa's barbs, Eliot's absence, the chaos of a big city.

She was ready for it all because her mother had written her a love note. She had not written of suicide, only of ill health and giving up. She had tried as hard as she could. Given her asthma and perspective, though, life with Harrison had become unbearable. She entrusted her daughters to God's care and foresaw their personal strengths, those gifts that would serve them well as women.

Luke had returned her hug in like manner. Intense. Conveying a depth of feeling.

"Sheridan?"

"Luke. He was there. Eliot was there when Harrison went to Caracas!"

Silence filled the earpiece.

"Luke!"

"I know. 1983."

"You already figured it out."

Silence again.

"What if—"

"Don't. Just don't do the what-ifs. They were in the same city at the same time. I'll get more information in D.C."

"I'm calling him, Luke."

"I gotta go. I seem to have this problem with flight attendants. All done, sir!" he called out obviously to someone on the plane. "Turning it off right now. Bye, Sher."

Silence.

She closed her phone.

What if Eliot had met Harrison? What if Eliot went to that lounge or wherever her father did his dirty work at that time? What if Eliot . . .

No. Eliot would never. He wasn't like that. He'd been a straight arrow since he could talk. No, he'd never . . .

They could have met. Their paths could have crossed. They both worked for the government. Why not?

Why not? Because Eliot never mentioned it to her.

So then . . . they never met. It was simply a weird, bizarre, ironic timing thing.

There was no reason to call and try to set up a time they could talk. None whatsoever.

CHAPTER 43

TOPALA

Eliot awoke. The bedroom was dark. He glanced at the clock. It was 6:20. He really needed to get rid of those sun-blocking shutters. He liked the early morning light.

The night had been a restful one with no incidents of torturous pain.

Except for a mental one that had accompanied a dream. He couldn't recall it now, only the remnants of anguish and fleeting images of Caracas almost thirty years ago.

Which added up to his history with Harrison Cole, that segment he was going to leave out of the memoirs. . . .

As a young man, Eliot arrived in Venezuela, a bucking mustang fresh out of the chute. *Watch how high I can jump.*

It was his first overseas assignment as a foreign service officer. Or rather, it was his first official assignment as an official diplomat. Unofficially he had already been serving simply because he happened to have lived most of his childhood in foreign embassies.

Of course location wasn't the only advantage that blessed him. There were his parents, diplomatic role models extraordinaire.

He idolized his father and even as a tyke—or so his mother's story went—mimicked the demeanor and skill of Eliot Montgomery II. By the time Eliot III was eight, he possessed—or so his mother proclaimed—amazing poise. A French statesman said—again, according to his mother—that the boy's *savoir-vivre*, his enjoyment of life, the ability to meet it with civility, was enviable.

He felt a sense of destiny being first assigned to Venezuela, where he had lived a short while as a young teen when his father was ambassador there. Now the Montgomery baton of statesmanship had been handed off to him. It didn't matter that his duties would be mundane, probably for years to come. He didn't mind paying his dues because the country and the position of foreign service officer was where he belonged.

Then he'd met Mr. Cole.

The House representative from Illinois arrived with a splash. Eliot should have known immediately that the man was made of sludge.

Despite Eliot's heritage, he was still wet behind the ears. Hobnobbing with a member of the subcommittee on trade impressed him. And hobnob he did. His job description included showing the man around the city, accompanied of course by a security detail.

Except Mr. Harrison Cole knew the city already, and he knew when and how to travel about it with the detail.

Eliot and Harrison were on their own when the older man took him to a bar. Obviously Harrison had been there before. Obviously he slipped something into the beer he put in front of Eliot. Obviously the girl was ready and waiting.

But first they had talked about opportunity available right in Eliot's backyard.

Harrison spoke in nuance. By the time Eliot caught on, he realized the man helped in the smuggling of diamonds and that he needed the new guy on the block to look the other way.

When Eliot awoke from a drugged stupor, the honorable Mr. Cole greeted him with a list of two addresses: Noelle's and his parents'. He also showed him two eight-by-ten glossies, one with the girl and the other with Eliot receiving a handful of uncut diamonds.

The message was loud and clear. Eliot could look the other way or he could lose his lifelong dream-come-true in a heartbeat.

The passage of twenty-seven years had done little to diminish the horror of that moment.

Eliot gazed at the ceiling, his hands behind his head on the pillow—

Hands behind his head? Arms raised?

Well, that was odd. His shoulders weren't screaming at him.

How much of the painkillers had he taken? He hadn't had more since eleven last night, had he?

He hated the regimen of taking pills to mask the pain, but it worked. He was mobile—at least semimobile, anyway. He didn't have much of a choice whether or not to take them.

He'd made it through the previous day with very little of the pain medication. Did he dare view that as a hopeful sign? He wasn't sure. It was such an odd day all the way around.

Wouldn't that be grand, though? To wake up without that drugged stupor . . .

The fading dream slammed back into his imagination, an instant replay in vibrant technicolor.

He was sitting in a courtyard, not in Caracas but right there in Topala behind the house. Harrison Cole was spoon-feeding him pills, an ugly sneer on his face.

Eliot cringed at the vivid image. His stomach turned.

That was exactly what had happened those many years ago.

Exactly?

Were his arms tied? his feet glued to the floor? his brain checked at the door?

"God." Eliot listened to the sound of his own voice addressing the Almighty. "I was doing my job. He took advantage of me."

He sighed. Whining! At his age!

"All that aside, I made idiotic choices. I was pompous, full of myself.

Please forgive me. And I've been angry at him. Please forgive me. I've been fearful. Please forgive me. I've cheated on Sheridan by not revealing everything to her. Please forgive me."

He shut his eyes. Tears seeped out.

Help me to . . .

He swallowed. His ears needed to hear what was in his heart.

"I want to forgive Harrison. Please help me."

As Eliot wept, he did not analyze. He did not debate. He did not negotiate.

He just let it happen.

CHAPTER 44

CHICAGO

Clearing the air with Sheridan at the funeral home had been a good thing, Calissa thought. Fussing at her about meeting Helena and picking up that stupid note from their mother and letting Calissa greet visitors half the day all by herself had been a good thing. That Sheridan had poured out her fears that Eliot and Harrison might have met in Caracas and neither one had told her was a good thing.

It was always good to talk straight to each other and not avoid the tough subjects.

Calissa reminded herself of all this now as she sat in the back of the hired car and watched pedestrians along Michigan Avenue travel faster than the vehicles.

She wanted to tell the driver which route to take to get them out of there faster.

She wanted to tell Sheridan, seated beside her, to take a hike.

Instead she bit her tongue and reminded herself about the hug at the funeral home and the shared tears at Ysabel's sweet words. This day, too, would all work out. It would.

"Lissy, I'm sorry."

Calissa sighed.

Sheridan said, "You may as well say it out loud rather than just keep exhaling like a locomotive."

She looked at Sheridan and wrinkled her nose. "That was a sigh, not a huff, and it meant, 'Oh, nuts, my heart just turned to mush.' You play me like a harp, Sher. You always have."

"I have not."

"Have too."

Sheridan frowned. "All I said was 'Lissy, I'm sorry.'"

"Exactly." She shook her head in dismissal. "Go on with the apology. You're sorry because you huffed your way through Saks and Neiman Marcus. Because you whined as if the hairdresser and manicurist were torturing you. And that disdainful lip twist says it all—that hiring this car is the biggest waste of money when we could have driven ourselves downtown."

Sheridan laughed and laughed. "Actually, no, that's not what I wanted to apologize about. Those things are just me, right? I've always been like that."

Calissa narrowed her eyes. "Yeah, I guess so."

"I appreciate it all, Liss, really. I needed new clothes for the funeral. I didn't want to look like I just got off a cruise ship wearing all my good finds from Mexico."

Calissa had been appalled at what Sheridan had brought with her from home. Brightly colored tops and skirts. One sweater and a lightweight jacket. *That* was for a funeral in Chicago in the spring? Then Calissa had been informed that Sheridan didn't even have most of her clothes at the house in Topala. They were packed away in a storage unit out east with their other possessions. Why on earth, she said, would she need pearls and black cocktail dresses and business suits in a village tucked away in Podunk, Mexico?

Well, *Podunk* was Calissa's term. That sure was what the place sounded like.

"And," Sheridan said, "I did need a haircut. I like it." She touched the new, shorter style. Layers had loosened the natural curl, reviving its old bounce. "And the car is not a big deal. Factor in gas and parking and the chiro adjustments we'd need after hauling sixteen bags around, the cost is not that much more." She stopped talking.

Calissa watched her forehead furrow and her lips crease, pulling her mouth downward. If it didn't resonate with guilt, she didn't know what would. It was probably a Luke thing. The two of them had begun to exchange looks, the kind that hinted at something below the surface. At dinner the one night, Sheridan had outright flirted with him.

"Sher, you can tell me. What is it?"

"This." She pointed to her face and burst into tears.

"Oh, hon." Calissa dug through her bag for a pack of tissues and handed them to her. "These things happen, and after what you've been through, it's totally understandable."

Sheridan dabbed at her eyes. "I didn't think you'd understand. It sounds like such a fabricated excuse. Post-traumatic stress disorder. How do you measure that? And honestly, eighteen months later? But I'm a mess again. The city unnerves me."

Post-traumatic? Not sleeping with Luke? "You—you seem okay."

"You didn't notice. I kept dodging people on the sidewalk. I almost jumped out of my skin every time I heard a siren. Those first days here I slept well, but not anymore. I'm eating like a horse. I want to go home. I don't want to go home. What am I going to hear about Eliot now? What if he did meet Harrison? He almost would have had to. A young diplomat, wet behind the ears. A visiting politician on the prowl for young diplomats wet behind the ears. What if Eliot is involved with all of that business? I would know, right? But we didn't know about Harrison."

"What does all this have to do with Luke?"

"Luke? Nothing. Unless maybe with him and Bram in D.C., I've lost a sense of security. Though I'd hate to admit that. I was making progress. I really was."

"Oh." Calissa adjusted her impression of Sheridan's turmoil. It wasn't

Luke and romance, just leftover stress cropping up again. "Do you need to talk to someone? clergy or counselor?"

Sheridan thought for a moment. "I need to go to church. Actually, I'd like to visit the church where Mamá used to take us."

"You got it. We'll swing by there on the way to the house." She unclipped her seat belt and leaned over the front seat to give the driver directions. Seizing the natural opportunity, she also suggested a turn coming up that might get them to Lake Shore more quickly.

He smiled like a father indulging his child. "Yes, ma'am."

She smiled back. "I am a pushy prig at times."

He chuckled, and she slid back next to Sheridan.

"Liss, I'm sorry. You're still taking care of me, like you've done your whole life."

She gave Sheridan a one-armed hug. "That's what big sisters are for, hon."

❧

The quiet, empty church seemed to calm Sheridan immediately. Calissa sat in a rear pew while her sister went to one nearer the front and knelt.

Things had not changed inside Sacred Heart. The wood still shone; the stained glass still glistened; the scent of incense still lingered in the air. The large crucifix above the altar still wrung her heart.

Calissa's memories were good ones. Ysabel had loved the place and the people. She made going to church a fun adventure. Harrison even accompanied them to services when Calissa was small, before Sheridan was born, before life seemed to get complicated.

Through the years, Calissa went her own way, different from her mother's. She believed in God but never thought she needed to be in a pew on a regular basis in order to talk to Him. When she attended church, she preferred the larger and livelier group not far from her condo downtown. They made a big deal about Jesus, but He too was larger and livelier there, not always hanging on the cross.

Networking-wise, the people she met were better connected. But in all honesty, some of them, most especially the pastor and his wife, reminded her of her mother. Ysabel would have enjoyed them.

Harrison would not have. Nor would he have cared for the congregation at his wife's former church. Calissa still wasn't sure about her decision to have the viewing at the funeral home, but the choice for funeral location was an easy one. It would be at a nondescript church where he had sometimes put in an appearance. He figured most of his voters liked at least a passing nod to tradition.

Funny, she thought, how he got by without really mentioning the name of God.

Eventually Sheridan made her way back down the aisle, her face serene, almost luminescent.

Calissa nearly jumped at the sight. She was looking at their mother, at an inner light that radiated from her at times.

It was obvious that Sheridan was like that, like Ysabel. She possessed the same faith, that same huge heart for others. Also like Ysabel, she was in a marriage that defined despair, yet she continued to give herself away.

Calissa prayed that the resemblance to their mother ended there, that Sheridan would not abandon all hope.

WILMETTE

Calissa waved at the neighbors heading across the drive to their house. She shut the front door, locked it, and pushed at Sheridan's shoulder. "Quick, turn off the lights before somebody else drops by with food and condolences."

"It's after nine."

"Wagners came at 8:52 last night. Not that I noticed the time."

Sheridan smiled. "Yeah, you're right. Let's turn off the lights."

A short while later, the house dark except for one small lamp in the kitchen, they sat down at the table with cups of tea.

"Sher, are you okay? There's been a lot of commotion since we got home."

"I am eyeing that cherry pie over there." She took a deep breath and let it out slowly.

Calissa smiled. During the string of visitors that evening, her sister hadn't ducked out once. "So you really like the hair and the clothes?"

"I do. Thank you for getting me out there."

"I'm sorry, hon. I cannot begin to comprehend what you've been through. To think that you didn't even have a nice black dress to pack."

"Liss." She chuckled. "That was the least of my worries."

"I know, but I can almost imagine not having a dress. I can't imagine not having my home or career or friends. You lost it all in the blink of an eye. If I had to start over in a new city, without knowing a soul, I'd crack up for sure."

"It's more than that," Sheridan murmured softly.

Calissa waited, unsure if her sister wanted to speak or not.

Sheridan sipped her tea. "Imagine being married to Bram. By the way, when was the last time he proposed?"

"A week or so ago." She rolled her eyes. "Okay, I'm imagining we're married. It's not that difficult anymore."

"Hm."

"*Hm* yourself. Now what?"

"Now take away his personality."

"Huh?"

"Bram has stopped calling you 'darling.' He's not interested in his business. He never laughs. Never. Nuances in conversation go over his head. Not that there are many nuances, because conversations revolve around how much he hurts and what he can't do and when he takes his next dose of meds. He's short-tempered. He never initiates a hug or a kiss." She paused. "He doesn't want you in his bed."

Calissa stared at her and felt a tightness in her chest.

"It's just the way it is. Kind of like you pulling big-sister duty. It's not my fault. This isn't his fault. It's not what I signed up for, but . . ." She shrugged.

"Whew."

"Yeah."

"Can I do anything for you?"

Sheridan smiled softly, her eyes sad. "Make him well?"

Calissa reached over and squeezed her hand. "I'll see what I can do."

CHAPTER 45

CHICAGO

Sheridan held the crisscrossed shoulder strap of her new black bag tightly between both hands and stared straight ahead. The upholstered seat rumbled beneath her as the train began to roll. In her peripheral vision, through the window, the platform blurred.

Breathe.

"That helps," she murmured to herself and tried it again. "Okay. That's good."

Maybe she should have heeded Calissa's concern. What was she doing heading off on the el, the day of their father's viewing, to wander around downtown by herself? Her sister had protested vehemently. "You said you're a mess being in the city. That it unnerves you. And you were with me! Why would you do this alone? Are you nuts or just a masochist?"

Sheridan had replied that God told her it was time to push past her fears.

Calissa went ballistic on that one. "God told you? God?"

Sheridan wondered now if she'd heard wrong.

"Breathe, Sher. Breathe." She was glad not to have a seatmate listening in on her monologue.

She and Calissa had finally reached a compromise. She swore to go straight downtown and not to her old stomping grounds at the university campus. Calissa would drive her to a Red Line stop, thereby eliminating a train change, a complication that might, according to Calissa, upset her. Sheridan agreed to take a cab to the funeral home no later than three o'clock.

She gave up trying to explain to Calissa what had happened. It wouldn't have helped her case.

The thing was, she had prayed in the church the other day. She had prayed Niebuhr's words, that God would grant her serenity in the things she could not change. Such as Eliot's condition. And she asked for courage to change what she could. Such as the ostrichlike existence. Self-imposed limitations based on her fears needed to go.

So there she was, zipping along on the train, all by herself, because apparently God had heard. That morning she'd awakened with an undeniable, unshakable determination to find a missing piece of herself, the one that had gotten lost over the past year, the one that was buried on an October morning in Caracas at twelve minutes, thirty-five seconds past ten.

Breathe, Sher; breathe.

She loosened her grip on the strap and smoothed her skirt. It was a pretty floral print, muted grays and whites and blacks with a few splashes of red. The gray jacket, white blouse, and pearls were too somber, but she wore them rather than debate over one more fashion matter with Calissa.

She forced herself to look around the train car. It wasn't rush hour, which explained the sparse crowd. There were two teenage girls in tight jeans and T-shirts, chattering excitedly. Perhaps it was spring break for them and they were going into the city to play. One young man slept hard, a uniform jacket on his lap. Perhaps he had worked all night at a hotel. Another guy looked like a college student, his head buried in a book. There were a handful of business-type men and women, young and middle-aged. A spry elderly lady fiddled with her cell phone.

Sheridan took it in, the microcosm of the city she had loved.

Loved.

Could she love it again?

She wasn't sure.

She relaxed, let go of the strap altogether, and watched the neighborhoods go by.

❧

Breathe.

Sheridan smiled to herself. The city was a glut of aromas.

It was the scents that at last released emotions buried for over eighteen months in the deep recesses of Sheridan's heart. As she emerged from the underground stop at Lake and State streets, the stuffy air tight in her nostrils with metal and oil gave way. She inhaled acridness, that every-city concoction of fuel, smoke, concrete, and warmth held captive between skyscrapers. Putrid garbage, cloying designer perfume, fried food, Asian spices, and unbathed bodies added their odors in passing waves.

Sheridan smiled, stood still, and shut her eyes. If she concentrated hard enough, she could pick up a hint of river water.

In the past, friends teased about her fondness for offensive smells. But to her the odors represented the fragrance of humanity, life in all its messiness. And it was in the messiness that she came alive.

She had caught her mother's dream to help poor women. With her own gifts, the ones her mother recognized so long ago, she had forged the dream into a work. She was at her best creating programs and teaching, mingling with humanity.

Those things she had not engaged in for over eighteen months.

"Let's not go there."

She inhaled the sour bouquet and smiled. Something loosened inside of her. It felt a little bit like hope.

Over the sounds of traffic and passersby, she heard her phone ring and remembered she had promised to call Calissa the moment she landed.

She pulled the cell from her bag and answered it. "I made it, Liss. I'm fine."

"Uh, Sher?" It was a male voice. "Is that you?"

"Eliot?"

"Yes, yes, it's me. Hello."

"H-hi."

"At last we meet up. How are you?"

"O-okay."

A mishmash of feelings bombarded her. She couldn't sort through them fast enough to respond coherently. How she had wanted to talk to him! Now she didn't know where or how to begin.

Eliot said, "I am so glad I reached you. Did I understand correctly? Today is the visitation?"

"Uh, yeah. This afternoon and evening."

"And the funeral is tomorrow, right?"

"Yes."

"Well, you know you have my condolences. How are you holding up?"

"O-okay." She was okay. As a matter of fact, she was good. Quite good. Why couldn't she tell him that?

Because she was also mad. Furious about that voice message he had left, so upbeat in her absence. Furious at his absence in the midst of all the good and terrible that was happening. Furious at the question about 1983 that coiled at her heel like a snake ready to strike.

"Where are you now?" he asked.

"Um . . ." Sheridan blinked, needing to get her bearings all over again, shoving down an anger she could not adequately express on a cell phone, thousands of miles between them. "Look, Eliot, I can't think straight. There's too much to talk about. I don't know where to begin."

He didn't reply.

She listened to his silence. It angered and frightened her all the more. He didn't know where to begin either. How did they start a dialogue that required speaking a truth that might tear them apart?

"Sheridan, let's begin with I'm sorry I'm not there."

"I know. It can't be helped."

"Still." He paused. "Did you talk to him before he died?"

"Eliot, he was in a coma." Was he fishing for information? Oh, she didn't want to second-guess him. Anger coursed through her. It pumped her legs into long strides between people on the crowded sidewalk. "I really, really can't talk now."

"Where are you?"

"I'm downtown in the Loop."

"By yourself?"

"Yes."

"Should you be—?"

"Yes, I should! This is long past due. It's been eighteen months. I refuse to allow big-city demons to scare me any longer. I rode the el. Now I'm heading toward Marshall Field's or whatever it's called these days. I'm going inside to stand under the Tiffany ceiling where I worked when I was a teenager. Then I'll check out all my other favorite places."

"The Picasso sculpture. The Art Institute. That Italian restaurant on Madison."

He remembered all that?

Reaching an intersection, she glanced both ways and stepped off the curb, joining the flow of others walking against the light. A horn blared. A shoulder jostled hers.

"You belong in a city, Sher."

She reached the other side of the street and went to the department store's corner entrance. It reminded her of the row of glass doors on the front of a women's center in Caracas, Venezuela. She stopped and stared.

And waited.

No crowds ran helter-skelter. No guns popped. No blood spattered the sidewalk. No bodies sprawled on it. No shattered glass. No pain in her arm. She turned a slow circle and carefully noted everything. Skyscrapers, stores, buses, construction, theaters, stoplights, blue sky. All in place.

All right. The city was hers again. Did she belong in a big city?

No, she belonged with her husband.

If she still had one.

She took a deep breath. "Eliot, did you know Harrison visited Caracas when you were there in 1983?"

"Yes." His voice was scarcely a whisper.

Her head spun. She'd asked wrongly. But he didn't pick up on it. He didn't clarify. Maybe it was nothing.

But she had to keep going.

"Did you meet him?"

Only the sound of his ragged breathing filled the earpiece.

Dear God, please no. Please no.

"Sher, we need to talk face-to-face. We'll talk when you get home."

The anger loosened her tongue now. She stepped over to a large display window and spoke against the plate glass in a low tone. "When I get home. Eliot, my mother left me a letter. My father committed despicable acts I can't even hint at over the phone. Your path crossed his the year my mother died. I do not know what to do with this information. I have no intention of coming home anytime soon."

"But we must talk!"

"Good grief. We've had eleven years to talk. Tell Mercedes if she doesn't want to hire a nurse, she can hire one of her cousins to help out. I need to help my sister for once in my life. Our father left a mess."

"I'm sorry."

"I heard you the first time."

"I love you, Sher."

The reply, normally automatic and heartfelt, got stuck in her throat.

The line went dead. He'd hung up, not on her, but on his tears.

Perhaps her husband was no longer a deaf-mute after all. Too little too late?

She didn't know.

❧

Had Eliot called her *Sher*? More than once?

Seated in the back of a cab after hours of walking the city, Sheridan finally replayed their conversation in full. She had avoided thinking about it. She'd filled her mind with visiting all her favorite places, accumulating distance between Eliot's deception and her emotions, riding out the storm before pondering what to do about it.

Yes, he had called her by her nickname. When was the last time he had done that? An eternity, it seemed. He seldom even called her Sheridan.

Over the past year and a half she had watched Eliot disappear somewhere inside himself. She blamed the excruciating pain, physical and mental, the great losses he had suffered. It swallowed his personality whole.

It also swallowed *them*. It swallowed *her*. Everything had changed, even the one constant that should not have ever changed: the heart connection they had known since day one.

Maybe now, in light of the past, Eliot realized what he had put in jeopardy. Naturally he would make nice. Well, he'd been absent eighteen months and dishonest long before that. She had some catching up to do.

❧

Sheridan made it to the funeral home with time to spare.

Calissa hugged her. "Two minutes to spare. I could strangle you."

"I talked with Eliot." She gazed into her sister's eyes.

Calissa winced. "No."

"Yeah. I asked. And he said we would talk when I got home."

"He didn't answer you?"

"That was an answer, Liss. It's a yes. He and Harrison met. Tell me again you had no clue."

"Oh, hon. Dad never breathed a hint of it. When I told him you were marrying Eliot Montgomery, an ambassador-to-be, he said that life would suit you."

"I'm having a little crisis of trust."

"I would guess so. But you look fairly perky."

She flashed a smile. "Thanks. I had a good day of killing dragons. I asked myself, what is it I'm afraid of? My husband is in about the worst shape he could be in. He has probably kept secrets from me. My father never was a dad to me and was a crook. My mother had stronger faith than anyone I've ever known and yet apparently lost all hope. I've suffered from PTSD, and it will probably always be there in some form. I don't work in my field and have no hopes of ever doing so again. I live so far off the map you had to hire a spy to find me. I mean, how much worse can it get?"

Calissa blinked as if in surprise.

Sheridan smiled. "I just fell in love with the city all over again."

"Chicago?"

"Chicago. Caracas. The city. Any big city."

"You're talking lifestyle."

Sheridan cocked her head. "I guess so."

Calissa smiled. "Welcome home, Sis."

The afternoon faded into evening, the hours a whirl of visitors come to pay their respects to the departed and his daughters. To her surprise, the whole thing energized Sheridan.

Hours into it, Bram appeared at her elbow and waited for a break in her conversation. "Got a minute?" They stepped away from the long line. "Do you think," he whispered, "that some of these people have come to make sure it's him in the casket?" He winked. "You look great. New do. New duds."

She grinned. "Thanks to Liss."

"Yeah, she told me she dragged you out shopping like old times."

"Not exactly like old times. I swear, I did not pout. At least not as much. So what happened in D.C.?" Bram had followed Luke there once Calissa got through those first days after the death.

"Not much to tell yet. The investigation is moving forward. Luke talked with his friends, so it's official now. Government resources are at our disposal. This is big-time."

She felt a shiver go through her. There was such a mix of positive and negative in that statement. "Is it wrong to honor a man today who might be the center of a scandal tomorrow?"

"Harrison accomplished a lot of good for this city, this state. Let's not forget that. People are grateful for it and are here to pay respect to his role in their lives. It was no secret that he was a difficult person."

"No one has greeted me with 'He was such a lovely man.'"

Bram smiled.

"Is Luke back?"

"He's here somewhere." He smiled and stroked his thick beard. "You actually look as if you're having a good time."

"Well, actually I am. I haven't talked with people in forever. I mean, not like this. This is like the good old embassy days. One of our favorite duties was entertaining so we could mingle with locals and foreigners from all over the world."

"You're sounding wistful now. I hope you and Eliot find that place again where you can participate in the world." He gave her cheek a brotherly kiss. "I better let you get back to this duty at hand."

As he strolled away, she watched her sister in the receiving line. Calissa held court like a queen, more elegant and efficient than ever. She would have to tease her about her tendency toward royalty.

Hopefully Calissa could move out from under the shadow of their father. She had her own career goals, but what would happen when the truth about him came out?

Sheridan looked around the spacious, crowded room, eager to see Luke.

Too eager?

Probably.

A moment later he stepped into view, about ten yards away, dozens of people between them. Dressed for the occasion, he wore a black sports coat and slacks, a pale green shirt unbuttoned at the collar.

Their eyes met. His, she knew, would be all green.

For a long moment they gazed at each other. Then she raised her eyebrows in question, indicating she was ready to hear the truth about Eliot. What had he learned in Washington?

Luke shrugged and shook his head. He hadn't learned anything more.

Or at least not anything he wanted to tell her. But maybe there was nothing more to learn. Eliot's and Harrison's paths crossed. They met twenty-seven years ago, an innocuous event. Maybe. And neither her father nor Eliot had mentioned it because it was innocuous. No big deal. But it all came down to the fact that, innocuous or not, Eliot knew who Harrison was years before he met Sheridan Cole. Which raised the question, then, did he already know who she was when they met?

Stop, she told herself. *Stop, stop, stop!* No way could she possibly figure that one out. No way was an explanation going to be found in a government file. She would simply have to ask her husband at some future point, whenever it was she might feel up to hearing if there was any reason on the face of the earth they should stay married.

Luke came into view again. "You okay?" he mouthed.

Her skin tingled. Her angel still watched over her.

Except he wasn't a heavenly being. He was a man, and she tingled for two reasons. Because one, she was a woman. And two, she knew that if she asked, he would postpone the flight he'd booked for that night to Caracas. He would walk across the room and wrap her in his strong arms and hold her for as long as it took to forget they didn't belong together. This time, he would stay.

But it wouldn't make things right with Eliot or Harrison or Sheridan's sad childhood or the current messy situations.

She took a deep breath, released it, and nodded. Yes, she was okay. She mouthed, "Thank you, Gabe."

The corner of his mouth twitched, his virtual smile. He gave a thumbs-up.

People moved, blocking him from view again. When they parted, Luke was gone.

Sheridan understood that he was gone because he knew it was time. At a deep level where words were unnecessary, he knew that she no longer needed him.

And he knew that granting her desire for him was not an option.

PART two

CHAPTER 46

TOPALA

A very interesting three weeks and two days after burying their father, Calissa sat in the passenger seat of a rented car.

Her sister braked and turned off the engine. "Welcome to Topala."

"That's what I was afraid you were going to say. You are, without a doubt, utterly nuts." Calissa had spotted the town sign a ways back at some point, at some curve in the hill, about the time the asphalt ended and the road became dirt.

Dirt. Her sister lived in a village at the end of a dirt road. *Podunk* didn't exactly fit Topala in the flesh. *Dark Side of the Moon, Mexico,* on the other hand, was perfect.

Sheridan pointed ahead to their right. "This is Davy's restaurant."

"*Davy* sounds American."

"It is. Davy came here decades ago from California and stayed. His son-in-law still runs the restaurant. We'll come for lunch tomorrow. Their specialty is banana cream pie."

Calissa eyed her with suspicion. Was she joking?

"Let's go." Sheridan got out of the car.

Calissa followed, immediately struck with the abundance of plants and the humming cacophony of insects. "We're parked in the restaurant's lot."

"Can't get a thing by you, Liss. You are one of the sharpest knives in the drawer." She grinned.

If not for that grin, Calissa might have wrestled the keys from Sheridan and hightailed it back to the Mazatlán airport. Well, perhaps it was the grin and the vision of driving by herself along a lonely Mexican highway in the dark.

She had watched her sister's smile emerge a little more each day, except when the subject was Eliot. Just twenty-four hours ago she and Sheridan realized that all the loose ends they could tie up in three weeks were tied and knotted. Crazy exhausted, they brainstormed crazy plans.

Sheridan declared it was time her sister saw Topala. "And," she had said, "it's time I talked to Eliot. I . . . I need you for that, Lissy, and I don't think I'm going to get him to Chicago."

It was the first time her sister had said she needed her. How could Calissa say no? And so they crazy brainstormed a spontaneous trip south of the border. They found cheap seats online for the next day and booked them. Sheridan said God was watching over them. Calissa thought it remarkable that their mother could speak through Sheridan without an accent.

Since Harrison's funeral, they had worked around the clock with attorneys, real estate agents, and the estate sale people. They had packed up a few mementos and stored them at Calissa's condo. There was no word from Luke Traynor. No media hinted at a possible scandal involving the late Harrison Cole.

His office went chaotic. Calissa did what she could to help but lost the emotional battle. She had been easing out for the past year and easing into her own campaign to run for city council. None of it appealed to her now. Recognizing the need for a break, she delegated what she could and put other duties and plans on hold.

And with her eyes, her tone, and her body language, she put Bram on hold as well.

He was such a patient man.

"Liss." Sheridan smiled now across the car roof in the evening dusk. "Are you ready to go back in time?"

"Then we haven't landed on the moon?"

"No. The time machine dropped us off here."

"Okay, let's do it. Are you ready?"

"Sure." Sheridan's smile faded. "Maybe."

Calissa groaned to herself and hauled out Big Sister. "Listen up. Last night you invited me to your secret hideaway. Last night you swore that if you didn't air things with Eliot in person, you would pop. Last night you said you felt confident and like your old self. I'll be a monkey's uncle if you think I'm letting you toss out all that progress."

"I should have called him." She had left messages for Eliot every few days or so with whoever her phone contact was, letting him know about the post-funeral progress. They had not personally talked, though, and she had not informed him of their plans to arrive in Topala that night.

Calissa said, "Yes, you should have called him."

"Not that he would've necessarily gotten the message before we arrived."

Calissa rolled her eyes. "Procrastination will not change things."

"The cell phone doesn't work here."

"It doesn't work anywhere, Sher. I'm not paying for it any longer. The mission was accomplished."

"You just came because you want to hide from Bram."

What did that have to do with anything? Calissa glowered at her. "Hey, you promised me food and music in the town square if we got here by now. News flash: we are here!"

Sheridan pursed her lips. "Are you sure you don't want to put on one of my skirts? You're going to stick out like a sore thumb in black."

She looked down at her black travel dress. All she owned was black.

Sheridan snickered. "But then you are five-nine and have blonde hair—short and spiky at that." She giggled. "You'll be sticking out like a sore thumb no matter what."

"Ha, ha. Back to my original, brilliant observation. We're parked in a lot. Where's your house?"

"Life is complicated here, Liss. There is no parking space at the house. It's not very far, though. Maybe three city blocks. We hike from here."

"With all this luggage?" She nearly shouted. "Are you kidding?"

"No. We'll drive to the house and drop it off later and—well, you'll see." She paused and squared her shoulders. "Eliot and I have never been to this weekly fiesta. He's not interested and usually in bed by the time it gets going. And I . . . Well, I've just stayed home with him."

Calissa walked around the car and looped her arm with Sheridan's. "That was B.C.E."

"Huh?"

"Before the *Chicago* Episode." She winked. "Before you got your big-girl boots back on."

Sheridan smiled.

"Okay. Let's get this show on the road."

"It's uphill. On cobblestones."

"Sheridan." She sighed. "I'm wearing heels."

"You're always wearing heels. And you think *I'm* utterly nuts."

Calissa laughed with her and clung more tightly to her sister's arm, not eager to start her vacation with a sprained ankle.

❧

"You weren't kidding. We did just go through a time warp." Calissa stood at the top of an impossibly steep cobblestone hill and tried to catch her breath, neither a simple feat. Her ankles wobbled, reduced to jelly in the heeled shoes. Her lungs felt like they'd been rubbed with sandpaper.

"That's what I said the first time I climbed that hill. Do you believe I agreed to stay? Now you have proof of how scared and confused I was."

"I'll say." Calissa pointed toward the town square, about a block away at the end of a slight incline. "That scene is sort of enchanting, though.

Lights strung all around and crisscrossing over the square. Mariachis in a band shell." She swung her hips to the upbeat music. "Everyone in bright colors, dancing and laughing. Shops and covered walkways. Kids playing in the street. No traffic except for those parked donkeys. Enchanting and unbelievable."

"It's a lovely village, and the people are wonderful."

"I hear the *but* in your voice. But you'd rather live in the twenty-first century?"

"I think so. I think I'm ready to return to it."

Calissa heard more in her sister's tone than hesitation. Sheridan was afraid to learn Eliot's side of the story. It would determine whether she stayed or she went. It would determine whether she wanted him to be a part of either of those scenarios.

"Hey," Calissa said, "I smell food. What was that sweet thing you promised?"

"Honestly!" Sheridan huffed in mock disdain. "Are you sure we grew up with the same mom in the kitchen? Mamá made them all the time. *Sopapillas.*"

"It's my lack of ear for Spanish. I remember fried pastry and honey."

"Eat enough while you're here and you too will switch to elastic waistbands."

Chuckling, they continued the hike into the center of town, toward a party in full swing.

The scene mesmerized Calissa. Her Spanish heritage had often been a source of embarrassment for her. As a youngster, she cringed whenever her mother visited school. Grateful for her own blonde hair and blue eyes, she told friends that her mother tanned easily year-round and talked weird because a dentist had bungled work in her mouth.

No wonder her mother didn't seem to like her much.

Calissa was convinced that Sheridan emerged from the womb speaking fluent Spanish. As an eight-year-old she did Calissa's high school Spanish homework for her.

Calissa should probably see a therapist.

Sheridan said, "I see Mercedes and Javier. There, to the right. She's wearing . . . she's wearing . . ."

"What all the women are wearing? Flouncy tops and skirts—oh, my gosh." The crowd had parted briefly and now Calissa saw what Sheridan saw: Eliot, seated on a bench, a walker in front of him, the festive lights glinting off the lenses of his glasses.

Eliot. The guy who never cared about going to this thing. The guy who was usually in bed by now.

The guy her sister really did not want to talk to until morning.

CHAPTER 47

Sheridan watched Eliot grasp his walker and stand. The surprised O of his mouth settled into a grin.

A grin?

Calissa squeezed her elbow and whispered, "Remember who you are, Sheri."

The phrase hit her like another bucket of cold water thrown over her. Sheridan shivered. Now her sister was quoting their mother? *"Remember who you are, Sheri."*

"You are," Calissa said softly, "God's daughter. He expects you to be kind and courteous to everyone. Else you'll give Him a bad rep."

Sheridan looked at her.

She winked. "So I ad-libbed a little."

"I'm leaving."

"No no no. That's not allowed."

"God's daughter? Right. Liss, did you realize we're daughters of a prostitute and a smuggler who pimped on the side? And we thought we were la-di-da hot stuff from the north burbs."

"Name-calling is not allowed either. Come, now." She held Sheridan's arm, subtly pushing and pulling, inching her forward. "This is way too public a place for a tongue-lashing. You can lay into him tomorrow. Just fake the bit about kind, courteous, and God's daughter, okay?"

Sheridan went with her, reluctant, angry, fed up, confused, afraid, and tired. How was she supposed to greet this man given what she now suspected about him?

The music was loud and fast. They stayed along the edge of the square where there were fewer people. Eliot stood, head and shoulders above the crowd, waiting, smiling at her. Beside him, Padre Miguel grinned and bobbed his head.

"Sheridan!" Eliot let go of the walker and held out his arms. "What a delightful surprise! Welcome home."

Just out of reach, Sheridan stopped. When was the last time he had smiled and offered a hug? It wasn't just the questions about three decades ago. It was the past eighteen months of his muteness. It was the sudden, inexplicable nice-guy act. Her head spun.

Calissa pressed at the small of her back, shoving her forward. "Well, this is awkward," she said out of the side of her mouth. Then, louder, "Hey there, Eliot!"

"Calissa. You're actually in Mexico! Welcome."

Sheridan got close enough to let him hug her, the walker between them, her hands at her sides.

He leaned down and kissed her temple. "I'm sorry."

"Save it." She felt his cheek, smooth against her forehead. He'd shaved for the event. At his neck she smelled the American soap he still preferred. He wore a freshly laundered guayabera.

He was all skin and bones.

She felt like she did not know the man at all.

"I'm sorry," he whispered again.

Me too, she thought. *Me too.*

"Calissa." He turned to her sister. "I can't believe you're here."

Calissa hugged him better than Sheridan had. "I can't believe *you're* here. This is a movie set, right? And the monk here speaks English, right?" She nodded toward Padre Miguel, who wore his brown cowl tonight. "Like the majority of the townspeople do, right?"

Eliot chuckled. "No on all counts."

"Yikes. That's what I was afraid of."

Padre Miguel touched Sheridan's elbow. "Welcome home, my child."

She bent to hug him. "Bless me, father," she whispered, "for I have sinned." She sighed again, overcome with guilt. Thirty seconds ago she blatantly disrespected her husband. Beneath the surface she harbored anger. Then there was that brief consideration in a Chicago funeral home to run away with another man.

"Shh, señora. This is not the time or place."

She blinked rapidly.

His eyes twinkled with compassion. "Señora, our Lord hears your heart's confession and forgives."

She knew that. She just needed to hear it out loud right now before she raced back down the hill and away in the car to Mazatlán. Funny. Not many weeks ago she was heading the opposite direction, thinking only of hurrying back to Topala and Eliot and ignoring the rest of the world.

"Eliot." Calissa smiled, kindness and courtesy personified again. "It is so good to see you out of the hospital. Now tell me, where are the sopies?"

"The what?" he said.

"Sopies. You know, fried pastry."

Sheridan shook her head. It was going to be a long, long night.

⁂

It was not the homecoming Sheridan had envisioned. She had planned to introduce Calissa to all the colorful quirks of Topala, from its layout to inhabitants to burros to tourists' favorite spots to her adobe house with the perfect balcony. Eliot was to have been asleep through that entire first part.

But at the sight of him on that bench she had lost her enthusiasm. The village was a backward little place that made her feel safe. It had taught her how to extract oxygen from sand in order to live with her head buried and take care of her invalid husband.

Now, she spread a blanket on the sofa in the study and wondered for the first time ever if there was a pill in Eliot's bag of goodies that would knock her out.

"Sheridan." Eliot appeared in the doorway.

She plopped down on the sofa, more exhausted from her attempts to be nice than from the long day itself.

With one hand he held a new cane and with the other, the doorframe. She was unaccustomed to such a sight. Once in a while he would inch a short distance down the hallway or across a room, balancing himself against the wall, but this . . . this was different.

Uneasy confusion riffled through her again. Or still.

"Uh," he said and left it at that.

She waited. She really had nothing to say. Except . . . "Eliot, look. I'm sorry, but I've used up all my good graces for tonight. I'm exhausted."

"I understand. And I understand that you're angry and confused."

In the past such insight from him would give her goose bumps. Now she wanted to say *whoop-de-do*. She didn't, though, and chalked up her politeness to childhood training that refused to go away.

Eliot sighed. "Evidently we didn't count on overnight guests when we bought this house, did we? We figured there were plenty of bedrooms, even with Mercedes living with us. After all, no one even knew where we were. Who would visit? And now Calissa has come. I am very glad she did, by the way."

"Yes, you said that. Once or twice."

He tried to smile, but it fell short. "And you've given up your room to her. Well, the thing is, the couch can't be comfortable for you. I've been sleeping better, but I'm afraid I'm not quite ready yet for the couch. Anyway, uh, what I want to say is that you're welcome to share my bed."

At first she did not comprehend his words. They'd left his mouth like a distant lightning bolt and split the air. The clap of thunder would follow; its boom would rattle her from head to toe.

More than eighteen months had passed since they had slept together. After his injury, he was overly sensitive to sound and space. At first he could hardly bear to be touched, let alone share the confines of a bed. She kneaded his back and exercised his legs but gave up offering the hugs and kisses that he recoiled from.

The doctors and counselor said it was to be expected. They said give him time. They said don't take it personally; it was not a rejection of her but rather of the situation.

It hadn't felt that way. It felt very, very personal. For over a year and a half he had pushed her away both physically and emotionally. At some level that must be his own choice.

Just like not telling her about his past was his choice.

Sheridan reached up and switched off the lamp on the end table. "Good night." In the semidarkness she crawled under the blanket and lay on her side.

A moment later he shuffled away. Another moment and the hall light switched off. Another moment and the thunder crashed over her, reverberating all around her.

She cried herself to sleep. It took some time.

CHAPTER 48

MIDMORNING THE DAY AFTER Sheridan and Calissa's arrival, Eliot sat in the study, drank tea, and waited. How bizarre life was! As it fell apart around him and Sheridan, they still attended to the everyday. They ate, drank, slept, showered, and talked to those with them. Earlier he had chatted with her and Calissa about Harrison's funeral and their spontaneous decision to come to Topala.

All the while he longed to hold his wife and beg forgiveness.

Even now she continued with the everyday, showing her sister the courtyards, putting things in order around the house, catching up on household details with Mercedes. Earlier Sheridan had helped him with his medication, her eyes red and ringed in deep purple hues. She used the brown bowl and nodded when he said the pain was at about a seven.

"Expected," she said. "After last night, going down to the square. You probably overdid it."

"Padre Miguel has a way about him. Like Calissa. He could talk a zebra into giving up its stripes."

She hadn't smiled. But neither had she cried or stared at him with fear, which was what she'd done last evening while Calissa flitted around the square, meeting the locals, making them laugh with her silly Spanglish, and dancing with them.

At last now Sheridan came into the study. "Okay." Her voice was low and hoarse. "Are you feeling all right enough to talk?"

"Yes."

She paced twice across the room and finally sat on the edge of an armchair near his.

He said, "Do you want to tell me what you learned in Chicago? Then I'll fill in the gaps or—"

"One thing. I need one thing. Before you went to the fund-raiser, did you know who I was? Did you know I was Harrison Cole's daughter?"

That was it, then. With his answer, he would be finished before he'd even begun.

He gazed at her beautiful brown eyes. The dark lashes. Noted the absence of gold flecks. "Yes. I knew you were Harrison Cole's daughter."

She blinked. "When? When did you find out?"

"When?" He swallowed. "When you were thirteen."

Sheridan sprang from her chair and rushed out of the room.

Eliot sank back against his chair, a heavy mantle of despair pressing him into the cushions.

❧

Twenty minutes passed. Eliot could hear the sisters in another part of the house, their voices raised, arguing. He tried to calm himself with thoughts of Padre Miguel.

When Sheridan had delayed her return home from the States, the old priest intuited problems in their marriage. Never probing, he talked about it without really talking about it. Fascinating how the man could do that.

However, last night he ventured close to the heart of the matter. "I will pray for fruitful conversation and reconciliation with señora," he had said before leaving the town square. "May I suggest you do likewise?"

The man was wise. Two weeks prior and Eliot would have lambasted him without remorse.

Which was far too telling about Eliot's state of mind. How had he gotten to such a low point? Could he really blame the shooting, the medication, the situation?

"May I suggest you do likewise?"

"God," Eliot whispered now, "please give me a chance. Give us a chance. Please."

Finally Sheridan entered the room, Calissa right behind her.

He had expected as much, but that didn't prevent his hackles from rising. His sister-in-law resembled his father-in-law. Eliot had never been able to get completely past her cloned personality.

But without Calissa, he doubted his wife would have returned to Topala so soon. No matter how much or how little Sheridan knew, she was devastated. He vowed to accept Calissa's intrusion if it killed him.

The women sat at opposite ends of the couch. He nodded at them from his recliner.

Calissa said, "Eliot—"

"I'm sorry. I humbly apologize for deceiving both of you. There is absolutely no excuse for my despicable behavior. I never intended to hurt you, Sheridan. It's easy to say those words, but my motive was always . . ."

Was always to protect you. That was what he'd always told himself. Why couldn't he say it?

Because it wasn't true. That was not his motive.

"Eliot?" Sheridan spoke softly. "What is it?"

He removed his glasses and covered his eyes with a hand. His fingers were soon soaking wet. His chest heaved. He gasped for each breath.

"Eliot." Sheridan took the glasses from him and held his hand.

He looked at her through his tears.

Seated now on the ottoman beside his chair, she gazed back at him, her face gentle with compassion and resolve. "Talk to me. What was your motive?"

"Pride." He steadied his voice. "I told myself I was protecting you, but I was only protecting myself. If my past mistakes became public knowledge, I would never be appointed an ambassador. I would never keep such a position. I would shame the Montgomery family."

Sheridan stiffened, her entire body rigid, her hand cold as ice on his. "They were all dead by then."

He nodded. How could pride have had such a stranglehold on him? How could he have been such an idiot? To not tell the love of his life the truth because he might lose prestige?

Sheridan let go of his hand. "You're saying that your dead parents and grandparents and your career were more important to you than being honest with me."

Again he nodded.

"You smuggled for my father."

"Yes," he whispered.

Sheridan handed him his glasses and stood. "You had it all wrong, Mr. Montgomery. I wouldn't have bothered to tell a soul."

Eliot watched her pace the room in jerky strides, praying that she not decide to do what she would have done years ago. No, she would not have told a soul. But neither would she have stayed with him.

CHAPTER 49

After Eliot's confession that he smuggled for Harrison, Sheridan paced the room in silence, letting the truth she had suspected settle into her heart.

At last she plopped onto the couch next to Calissa. Her sister gazed silently into midair as if shell-shocked at the information.

Why was it Sheridan did not feel the same?

Because she had spent the last three weeks fearing it. There simply was no other reason Eliot would not have told her that he had met her father. For three weeks she had pondered her mother's letter. It had become clear how someone in Eliot's position might be caught. Young and foolish, he went to the bar like the other cool foreign guys. On the fast track to a lofty position, an incriminating photo would carry a threatening wallop.

She looked at him. He'd gotten his emotions under legendary Montgomery control, a finger over his lips.

She had to ask. "Was there a photograph?"

He started.

She said, "Did you know that twenty years before you fell for that trap, our mother worked as a prostitute and lured diplomats into similar setups?"

"No. Oh, dear God."

Calissa leaned forward. "Eliot, tell me it's not still going on."

"It's not." He cleared his throat. "When we lived there—Sher and I—I made inquiries. Discreetly, not through our people. According to the local authorities, diamond smuggling has grown more sophisticated."

Sheridan closed her eyes briefly. She thought he had shared everything with her. She had no idea what he had done as ambassador, the connections he maintained.

Eliot said, "How did you know about me?"

"We didn't," Calissa answered.

"So no one knows?"

"Eliot!" Sheridan nearly spat his name. "Are you kidding me? You're still concerned about who knows what you did almost thirty years ago?"

Calissa laid a hand on her arm. "Hey, give him a little space until we explain everything."

Sheridan seethed. She may as well let Calissa do it her way. Eliot had known her identity when she was thirteen. When she was thirty, he met her, knowing full well she was Harrison Cole's daughter and not saying a thing. What else mattered?

Calissa said, "Eliot, we put two and two together and guessed the answer had to be four. We found out what Harrison was up to. We learned he was in Caracas when you were there the first time."

Eliot nodded. "All right. Can you start at the beginning?"

Calissa began to talk about the incriminating papers she found in the attic. She explained Bram and Luke's hunches about his past relationship with Harrison. She described the meeting with their mother's friend, Helena Van Auken.

Sheridan listened with one ear.

Of course Eliot needed to hear from them. He was still in the dark about what happened when she was in Chicago, although she assumed he had guessed at much of it. Once she left Topala, he would have pondered the unusual scenario. Calissa, a dying Harrison, and Luke Traynor? A note Sheridan would not discuss and a sudden departure? His reaction to Mercedes's probing of the fund-raiser revealed that he was worried.

The day she spoke with Eliot, when she was by herself downtown in the city, she heard the hints. Had she talked to her father? Yes, before she asked him if he'd met Harrison, Eliot had figured out that his past had been unveiled.

Eliot remained quiet during Calissa's story. He did not jump in to defend himself or explain. But it ravaged his face. The seams and pallor were worse even than the first time Sheridan saw him in the hospital after the shooting.

When Calissa finished, she leaned forward and her demeanor softened. "Eliot, I have to tell you that my father's actions make me want to throw up. I idolized him. He was my mentor."

He nodded.

"Bram and Luke have been investigating. They went to D.C. Luke is in Caracas right now. The government is in on it. I don't know what this means for him. I don't know what this means for you."

He nodded again.

Sheridan saw it coming then. The physical pain was digging into him, taking over, replacing his ability to focus on anything else.

"Oh, don't you dare," she said, although he could not comprehend her words. "Don't you dare check out on me now."

He looked her direction, but she knew he was gone.

❧

Sheridan and Calissa had no choice but to let Eliot be. They walked down the hill that afternoon to join tourists and explore the village.

"At least he can sleep," Calissa said. "How long will the nap last?"

"No clue. Let's buy you a flouncy top and skirt."

"Do I look like the flouncy type?"

"All women are the flouncy type. It's very feminine. Bram will like it on you."

"I just want some sandals. Yours are a little tight on me."

"They're better on the cobblestones than your heels, I hope."

"Yes. You know, it doesn't sound like revenge."

"You'll want a sculpture too. Javier has some nice pieces that would fit your decor."

"Javier is cute. I said, it doesn't sound like revenge. Eliot did not go to the fund-raiser to seek revenge against Dad by harassing his daughter. He was just curious to meet you. Then—I can't believe I'm saying this—then I think he fell head over heels in love with you. He didn't give a rip who you were after that. He was just nuts over you."

"You heard him. It was about pride. He wasn't going to jeopardize his future or his family name."

"It went beyond that. The man just doesn't know how to express his heart."

"You're taking his side again."

"It's nothing to do with taking sides. It's about collecting all the facts, and those are not in yet. Yes, he deceived you. Yes, you two married way too fast. But he gave you your dream life, Sher. From what I've heard, he's been your best friend all these years. If that's not love, I don't know what is."

"He knew who I was when we met. He would have known you, too. Have you thought of that? He would have known that our mother died."

"Sher." Calissa halted and grabbed Sheridan's arm to stop her babble. "You lied to him first. Remember? You told him hardly anything about me and Dad and Mamá when you met. You didn't tell him about your father's career for months."

"That was different."

"How? Neither one of you wanted to acknowledge that Harrison Cole existed. It's exactly the same thing."

Sheridan shook her arm free and continued walking, not wanting to think about anything except putting one foot in front of the other.

Eliot did love her. He couldn't express it easily, but she knew it. Now he cried, something she'd never, ever seen him do. And Calissa defended him.

It was way too much to tuck away into her aching heart.

CHAPTER 50

SHERIDAN SPENT THE REMAINDER of the day with Calissa, filling the hours with mundane activity, waiting for Eliot to wake up. With each passing hour, a straitjacket of fear laced itself tighter and tighter around her until she could scarcely move.

Later that evening, Calissa and Mercedes went down to watch Javier sculpt.

Alone in the kitchen, Sheridan puttered about, wishing and yet dreading that he would wake up. She wanted to hear all the facts. She did not want to hear all the facts.

At last she heard him stir in his bedroom. She headed down the hall, wondering which version would greet her. The B.C.E. Eliot who'd been gone for over a year? The deaf-mute she'd lived with all that time? Or the strange man who thanked God and cried?

"Eliot?" She pushed open his door.

His gaunt frame reclined against a stack of pillows on the bed. His glasses were on the nightstand, its lamp lit. The window shutters were open and cool air wafted in with a bird's evensong.

"Hi." He smiled.

Open shutters and a smile. The strange man took shape.

He said, "I can't quite make it farther than the bathroom. Thought I'd stay put." He shifted and the smile slid into a grimace.

"Are you hungry?"

"No."

"You should have something. Maybe some soup. I'll get it."

"Do you mind just sitting for a few minutes?"

Yes. No. She sat in a bedside stuffed chair, one comfortable enough to rest in throughout long night hours.

"Tell me," he said, "what did I miss?"

She waited for him to continue, a habit she'd formed over the past year. He no longer chitchatted with her, no longer conversed in a give-and-take manner without going off on some tangent that had nothing to do with her or the subject at hand. It had become less frustrating for her to just stay quiet.

He looked at her, apparently waiting for her to reply.

The strange man had indeed taken up residence in him.

"Um," she said, "Mercedes and Javier invited Calissa to watch him work and then to go out for a taste of village nightlife."

"The sidewalks are probably rolled up by now."

"They didn't want to tell her that. She was hoping for coffee and maybe another 'sopie' at the inn."

He smiled.

Again.

"Sher, can I tell you my side?"

She nodded.

He shifted again, turning slightly in order to face her directly. "Calissa and Bram did an impressive job of putting together the puzzle pieces. It happened pretty much as she presented it."

"Mamá's letter confirmed most of what they figured out from Harrison's notes. How . . . Never mind."

"I was enamored by Harrison Cole. His credentials were impressive. When he invited me to see the real Caracas, I jumped at the chance.

He ditched his security detail and we went to a bar. We had drinks. He hinted that there was serious money to be made if one knew where to look. Easy cash, he said."

Sheridan almost laughed. Like Eliot would care about money. Her father could be so stupid.

"Naturally money didn't interest me, but a young woman flirting with me did. Obviously in the aftermath I realized my drink was drugged. Compromising photos were snapped. I have no memory of the evening after a certain point. I don't know how I got home. The next day Harrison showed me the pictures. I was a perfect candidate for blackmail. Who would believe my word over that of a representative who had 'proof'?"

Sheridan heard his cut-and-dried tone, the one that did not make excuses for actions but only listed the facts. It was how he got opposing parties to sit down together in the same room and talk.

She said, "You were a low-level government employee who committed an indiscretion like countless others and happened to get caught. It's not like you were running for president."

"The photos were not with the woman. They were of me accepting diamonds and shaking hands with some faceless man as if I'd made a deal with him." He paused. "I was a Montgomery; my father was still alive; my goal had always been to follow in his footsteps; I was engaged to Noelle."

Sheridan swallowed, her throat suddenly parched. "Your future would have gone away."

"Every last bit of it. You understand I'm not making excuses. I don't want to be excused. I am guilty of smuggling and, worse, of turning a deaf ear to policy discussions that clearly favored the practice."

She stared at him, hoping against hope that he was not talking about himself.

His forehead furrowed. "No photos were found, then? in the attic or from Helena? of myself or others?"

"No. Nothing like that."

"Thanks be to God." The uncharacteristic phrase floated from him like the sound of a breath. "I imagine if Harrison still had them, they would have turned up by now. I assume you and Calissa received all of his private documents?"

"Yes."

"All right." His forehead smoothed out.

Straining against the impulse to bolt from the chair, Sheridan waited. Her heart hammered, muffling the volume of his voice.

A pained expression filled Eliot's eyes, as if he saw into dark corners of his mind. "Harrison laid it all out for me. The diamonds were in my sock drawer in my apartment. I would be sent to Washington the following month, hotel reservations made for me. I was to leave them in a drawer in my hotel room. It all happened as he said. I was unexpectedly sent stateside. After a day of pointless meetings, I returned to the hotel room to find the diamonds gone and the photos in the drawer."

Sheridan's stomach turned. "Did you destroy them?"

"No. I gave them to Malcolm."

Malcolm, the loyal bulldog, old Montgomery family friend.

Eliot went on. "I was a wreck. I realized, of course, it wasn't over just because I had the pictures. Harrison would have copies or negatives. Obviously others worked with him, people able to pull strings that affected my agenda. More would be expected of me. So I made a last-minute change at the airport and stopped off in Florida, where Malcolm was."

Sheridan clutched the chair arms.

"Eventually Malcolm informed me that he'd taken care of it. Harrison never asked anything of me again, but I worried. I watched and stayed mute on trade policies that were slanted in ways I could not fully support. It was vague, no monumental matters, nothing specific to which I could point a finger. But I could have—I should have—raised questions in certain circles. Instead, I minded my own business and married Noelle, who never saw the photos."

"But what about Malcolm?"

"He visited Harrison."

"And so in essence, Malcolm blackmailed *him*."

"I never asked what was said between them. Malcolm is a powerful man, not violent, but not faultless, either. I assume he approached Harrison as he did others. They had a civil chat. Malcolm described his vast network of resources. Harrison understood. This stranger could ruin him with one phone call."

"Oh, Eliot. It's all so slimy."

"It comes with the territory, as we've talked about in the past. I tried not to wallow in the slime, but there were situations when I had no choice. I had to take the low road because it was the only route to get to the higher one."

It was convoluted reasoning, but true. Eliot was right. He had told her about such situations. Despite circumstances, he had a goodness about himself that was obvious to most. Even in the midst of negotiating with people who did not have a shred of integrity, he exhibited it in abundance.

"However it went down, Harrison met his match and our paths never crossed again."

"Until you met me."

He inhaled deeply. "I was an idiot. I put myself into the situation at the bar with Harrison. Then I didn't have the nerve to tell my father, and so I went to Malcolm. I was a ninny but an angry one. I began a file of my own. I harbored no motive beyond wanting to know my enemy."

"A file?"

"About Harrison Cole. Public record stuff. Newspapers, magazine articles. He and his wife had two daughters. They lived near Chicago. The year I started my file, the year I met him, the year your mother passed away, you were thirteen."

She shivered.

"Dearest—" he reached over and touched her hand—"it wasn't a literal file. I simply read whatever I could find. There was nothing sinister in what I did. The fact that Harrison had a family was a small part of the profile I studied, a minor fact that exited my mind as soon as it entered. I was more concerned about his politics."

"Did you keep track of us?"

"No. My curiosity was satisfied. A few years later Harrison was in the media. It was reported that his older daughter worked as his assistant and his younger was seventeen, off to college in Chicago. That's it. End of story."

"Until the fund-raiser?"

"Years and years later."

She met his gaze. "Malcolm brought you."

"Yes. As you know, he was an anonymous donor to the association, long before you were involved with it. There was no early connection in that way. All right? He did not sign on to follow your activities."

"You're sure?"

"Yes. I'm not holding anything back."

She nodded.

"You know this part too. I was in the States. In Chicago on business. I planned dinner with Malcolm. It happened to be the week of your fund-raiser. Sheer serendipity. No, not that. Padre Miguel would say God arranged it."

God could arrange all sorts of things, even return trips to Topala, but she wasn't buying this one. "You told me that Malcolm invited you to the party because he thought you might want to donate. It was a cause he knew you cared about."

"Right." He paused. "It truly was happenstance that I was in town for two days, one of which was the date of your event."

"Okay." *Happenstance* left God out of the equation.

"That night on our way into the hotel where it was being held, Malcolm said to me, 'Oh, by the way, I never did shut the file on a certain House rep. His daughter will be here. Sheridan Cole does amazing work through the association.'"

Sheridan gasped. This was worse than she had imagined. "Eliot! I don't want to hear it!"

"Please, Sher. Let me finish."

"I liked Malcolm! I trusted him with our mail! He's the only one I told about moving to Mexico! He knew who I was all along?"

"Yes."

"How could you? How could you stay there and actually meet me and not say a word?"

"Plain old curiosity again. I deeply despised Harrison. I could not grasp the thought that such a contemptible person could have a family. What in the world would his grown daughter be like? And good heavens, she was involved in good works? How could that be?"

"I don't believe this."

"When Malcolm first told me, I was appalled. I chewed him out for keeping his file open. He reminded me that he was covering my back. Why would he quit? My father had saved his son. He owed it to me."

Sheridan shook her head.

"He pointed you out through the crowd. I avoided you for a long time that evening. Then somehow we were in proximity and I overheard you, and then you said something and I couldn't help but agree and someone next to you overheard me."

She remembered. Oh, she remembered the exact moment. "I looked over at you."

"I looked into your eyes."

"You made me laugh." She had been such a somber person back then, much like she was now. Eliot had entered her life, a burst of fresh air into a locked-up room, and made her life. "We started talking."

"And we kept on talking."

Yes, they kept on talking. Until . . .

"You didn't tell me. My father didn't tell me. You two met in his office as if you'd never . . . Oh, Eliot. How could you pretend like that?"

"By then he was out of the international game. Why bring it all up and jeopardize everything you and I had?"

"You and I had? You were the one with the family name and the high-profile career."

"It was all yours, too, Sheridan. I sometimes feared you married me for those reasons alone. Embassy life appealed to you, as did my heritage. If they were gone, you might be too." He paused. "Like now."

Suddenly overwhelmed with it all, she stood. "I can't listen to any more."

She hurried through the house, ran upstairs to her room, and lay down on the bed. Within moments, her head too full and her heart shut down, she sank into a deep sleep.

CHAPTER 51

MESA AGUAMIEL

Calissa snagged her cell phone from her skirt pocket and flipped it open. "Unbelievable!"

Sheridan smiled. "Told you so."

"I thought you were joking."

"Liss, you've been in Topala for a week and you haven't figured out yet that when it comes to modern-day technology, I am probably not joking?"

"But we're in Mesa Aguamiel. The *city*." Calissa glanced around from where they stood by the car. Compared to Topala, the place bustled.

There was traffic. The town square was a true square, not a spot to walk across in order to save a few steps. There were vendors on the sidewalks. People filled the area—real people, not the cruise ship folk. It was too early in the day for them.

It was a far cry from a city.

"Come on," Sheridan said. "I'll take you to the coffee shop."

"Dial-up Internet and public phones?"

"All the conveniences of home."

"Ooh." Calissa smirked and followed her into the street. "And look at this. Pavement and curbs. Wow."

"You better behave or I will leave you all alone to order coffee."

"Don't you dare."

Sheridan chuckled.

Calissa sighed to herself. The chuckles had been few and far between in the Montgomery household. Most of them came from that darling girl Mercedes and her cute artist friend Javier.

Despite the fact that the cell phone did not work even in the nearest city, it was good to get out of town. Town? Topala was a burp in the desert air.

Calissa felt worn down after seven straight days of watching Sheridan and Eliot dance some sort of weird tango. They aired all the dirty laundry, in a dignified manner, naturally. No knockdown drag-outs with them. Eliot appeared genuinely contrite. She believed what he said. They both slept a lot. Separately.

Calissa considered moving to the little inn down by the church, until she thought of the language barrier and the hike up the hill to the house that always made her sweat.

They reached the coffee shop. Sheridan helped her place a call on one of the public phones. With a promise not to leave her stranded, her sister went off to use a computer.

"Darling, is it you?" Bram said once the operator got out of the way.

"Bram." Calissa melted. Even if it hadn't been ninety degrees, she would have. "Hello."

"Hello."

They cooed for a bit. Seven days without speaking to each other was a record she did not care to repeat. She listened to the news of Chicago and then gave him the highlights of her week.

Bram said, "When are you coming home?"

"I don't know. And I can't believe I said that." She sighed.

"Do I hear Big Sister putting in overtime?"

"I suppose. Sher is so fragile. I told her she's taken off her big-girl boots. She said she was knocked right out of them."

"I'm sorry."

"I've seen him do what she calls his deaf-mute act. It's like he checks out. He's in the room, he talks, he hears, but not really."

"What sets it off?"

"Pain, I guess, but not just physical pain. It was triggered when we told him about the papers and Mamá's letter."

"What's Sheridan's take on it all?"

"To tell you the truth, she's so confused she can't decide what to eat or wear. I know I never cared much for Eliot in the past, but he is a good man and she is married to him. This lifestyle in the middle of nowhere, though, could pulverize even Pollyanna. I don't know how either one of them keeps it up."

"What's your advice, then?"

"For once I don't have an opinion about what my sister should do. I'm just the referee."

"So you'll be staying."

"Yeah."

"Then I better come."

"Really?" She smiled. "Really?"

"A few days at a resort on the beach in Mazatlán sounds awfully inviting. Then you can show me Topala. I'd like to see Eliot, if he's up for it. What do you think?"

Calissa grinned. "I think Mexico just got a whole lot brighter."

MAZATLÁN

Less than forty-eight hours after their conversation via pay phone, Bram arrived at the Mazatlán airport, wearing shorts, a flowered shirt, and a sun visor. The man was not prone to frittering his money away on last-minute plane seats. Either God was directing ticket purchasing again or Calissa was worth every nickel it took for Bram to zip down from Chicago so quickly.

Whatever. Both made her tingle with delight, and so she did not ask him. All that mattered was that she had missed him more than she thought possible, and now he was sitting beside her in Mexico on low-to-the-sand beach chairs, watching an awesome pink and purple sunset.

On second thought, it must have been God.

"Calissa, are you sure you can relax for a couple of days away from Sher and Eliot?"

"I'm not sure. They both thank me daily for being there."

"You know it's understandable if you want to bow out of the campaign for city council. There's always next time."

"What does that have to do with the price of beans? We were talking about my wacko sister and brother-in-law."

He smiled. "Look at that sailboat out there. The ocean looks like lapis lazuli. What a gorgeous scene."

"Bram."

"Darling, your world has been turned upside down. Generally speaking, people give themselves time off after a parent's death, losing a job, learning the worst possible things about a dad they idolized or sordid secrets about their brother-in-law. When all those things occur at the same time, polls show that a whopping 95 percent of people take an extended leave of absence."

"I still have my job. I mean, not for long, but it's not over."

Instead of saying duh, he simply looked at her.

"Anyway, I am totally taking time off. I've been here a week with no plans to leave yet."

"My point exactly. You're here by default. Not in a million years would you choose to hang out in Mexico, most especially in a tiny village where people do not speak English and there are no cappuccinos. And how restful can it be in the Montgomery household these days?"

She sighed and went to the source of the problem. "He never took a day off."

"You are not your father. And you will never please him."

"So I should quit trying?"

He reached over and touched her cheek. "Yes. Forty-seven years is long enough."

"I do have my own goals, you know. It's not all about my father. I love politics and . . . and . . ."

Bram slid the short distance from his chair down onto the sand.

On his knees.

Right in front of her.

Until that moment she never truly believed that hearts could do cartwheels. "What are you doing besides getting sand all over yourself and missing the sunset?"

"I'll watch its reflection in your eyes." He smiled. The last rays behind him formed a halo of white hair. "Do you want to hear my suggestions for what you might do if you postpone the campaign?"

She pointed to her throat and shrugged. The last cartwheel had sent the heart right up into it and she couldn't talk.

"We could take a long vacation together and see all those states that we've talked about wanting to see but never do. It'd be sort of like a honeymoon." He reached into the pocket of his shorts. "Or it could be a true honeymoon." A ring box was in his hand now. "Calissa, I love you. I will always love you, and whether you say yes or no, I will never leave you. Will you marry me, darling?"

She smiled. "This is your most intriguing proposal yet. What's in the box?"

"A bribe. I thought I'd add it this time round."

She laughed and leaned forward to hug his neck. "I love you, Bram. And yes, I will marry you." She kissed him.

He sighed deeply. "I can't tell you how happy that makes me."

"I thought you'd never ask."

"You mean, *again*."

"Yeah, again." She began to cry. "Am I only saying yes now because he's gone?"

"Maybe." He kissed her eyelids while she wept. "But that's okay. It's over. We're here now. And if you ever get around to opening this box, we can declare on the record that we are engaged."

Calissa only cried harder and buried her face in his neck, hoping he wouldn't change his mind before she released about twenty years' worth of pent-up regrets.

CHAPTER 52

TOPALA

"Do you know what I adore about this old church?" Padre Miguel glanced at Sheridan seated in a pew beside him.

She eyed his profile as he gazed toward the altar. "I imagine your answer could take all day."

He chuckled.

They were alone in the church. It was the middle of the week, late afternoon, the village clear of the daily tourists. Since returning to Topala ten days before, she had gotten into the habit of sitting quietly on a pew for a short while as often as possible. If nothing else, it was a surefire way to take a break from the tensions of home.

But she hoped for more than respite. She hoped to be rid of the guilt that clung to her.

Why had she married Eliot?

Why did she consider leaving him?

In her consternation she had even begun reading the Bible, too, her mother's red one. Surely there was a passage that hinted that leaving a husband was acceptable in the sight of the Lord if the marriage was a mistake in the first place? Surely He would give her a sense of release as she sat in His house?

So far she'd only gotten the respite. Nothing so far indicated a free pass on separation or divorce. He hadn't revealed everything about himself. The relationship had turned sour. She was denied her life's work. He was physically and—as far as she was concerned—emotionally handicapped. He was not interested in intimacy. She was not sure she loved him.

Nothing fit. Nada. Maybe she could find a nonbeliever to convince her that guilt was a figment of her imagination.

Instead she got the priest.

Every now and then while she sat in the church, he slipped in and out, sometimes speaking, sometimes not. Today he had sat right down with her.

She turned her attention back to him. "Tell me, Padre Miguel, what do you adore about this old church?"

"That the faithful have not abandoned her. Not once in over five hundred years. They have taken care of her needs, cleaning her and clothing her. They've filled her with their prayers and tears. They've blessed her with their presence, just like you sitting here today."

"It's a building."

"Ah yes, you are right. Mere walls. Stone and mortar. However, the idea reminds me that we ourselves are mere bodies. Bones and skin. Unless the faithful attend to us, unless we are cared for, we wither up inside and die, even if we continue to breathe."

Okay, she would ask. "Who are the faithful?"

"The ones placed with us, the ones expected to care for us. Mothers, fathers, sisters, spouses. When they don't—when God's order is not maintained—then we are abandoned. And the thing is, in this imperfect world, His order is never maintained. We are always, every one of us, abandoned."

She shut her eyes. Was this little homily personalized just for her? Was he saying it was a wife's duty not to leave her husband? that her duty was to stay put and take care of Eliot no matter what?

"Señora, sometimes the faithful leave us because they do not know how to stay. Either literally or figuratively. A mother dies. A father ignores. A sister dominates." He paused. "A husband copes with inconceivable pain. He keeps old secrets."

He wasn't preaching wifely duty.

Eyes still closed, she felt the air shift as Padre Miguel stood.

"Tell Him, señora. Tell your Lord how much it hurts. He understands. Everyone abandoned Him, too." The priest's footfalls grew softer as he walked away.

Sheridan slid to her knees and bowed her head.

CHAPTER 53

ELIOT TALKED LONG and deeply with Bram Carter in the study. Sheridan wasn't home yet from what had become her daily visit to church. Calissa was in the kitchen with Mercedes, preparing dinner.

Over the past ten years, on the rare occasion he had visited with Bram, Eliot enjoyed his company. He respected the accomplishments of the newspaper magnate who was a bit younger than himself and already white haired. Unlike Sheridan, Eliot never pondered the man's longtime love for Calissa. What better way for him to sharpen his wits than against her abrasive personality?

"Bram," he said, "you haven't mentioned the elephant in the room."

"Leaking Harrison's story to the press." His dark eyes twinkled. "Pulitzer material, eh? I can't say I haven't thought about it. I've even considered which journalist I'd want to interview you; which angle we'd take; how many sidebars between Harrison, you, and other young diplomats; the history of smuggling worldwide. But, Eliot, I'd never impose upon our relationship and expect you to talk to us on the record."

"As far as I'm concerned, you can have exclusive rights to an interview with me. If you personally do it yourself."

Bram studied his face for a moment. "All right. You've got a deal. Not that it's imminent. Working with Traynor has given me some new insight into national security. I'm not about to leak what I know. They'd lock me up in a heartbeat."

"The story may never be allowed for public consumption. There could easily be repercussions still in motion from Cole's work. And it does seem a little late to expose him. What would be the benefit now?"

"Only one: I'd sell a few papers. That's it. Calissa and Sheridan would suffer. Politicians would get yet another black eye. And Harrison Cole's positive work would be forgotten."

"Not worth the Pulitzer?"

"Not when I'm married to the guy's daughter." Bram rubbed his beard in a nervous gesture.

"Is that an engagement announcement?"

"Uh. Sorry. Nuts. Whoops. I wasn't supposed to tell."

"Congratulations."

"Oh, we're not engaged." He smiled sheepishly. "We're married."

Eliot grinned. "Married! That's even better. Congratulations."

"Thanks. Act surprised, okay? Calissa wants to tell you and Sheridan together."

Sheridan and him. Together.

Now wouldn't that be an answer to prayer?

❧

Already privy to Calissa and Bram's surprise, Eliot sat back and watched Sheridan receive their news.

She smiled. She giggled. She laughed. She clapped her hands. And then she fiercely hugged them both, tears streaming down her face.

How he loved her. How he missed her.

True to the beautiful character she was, in the week and a half since she returned home, Sheridan still treated him with respect, still saw to his needs, still spoke in her forthright manner with grace.

But she altered their daily routine. That was partially due to giving Mercedes a lot of time off and partially due to Calissa's presence. He suspected, though, that it was only the beginning of change.

Although she administered his physical therapy, she refused to work with him on his writing. She left the house often and without telling him what she was doing or how long she expected to be gone. Sometimes she took her paints with her. Sometimes a handbag. He knew about the daily church visits only because Padre Miguel mentioned it as a way of encouraging Eliot. A wife who turned to God in her hour of need, he said, would turn back to her repentant husband.

Eliot doubted it.

More often than not that peculiar expression was on her face, the one that pinched her mouth, her eyes, her forehead, and that snarled his insides. The one that filled him with fear. The one that obliterated the sparkle.

The sparkle that Calissa and Bram now shared.

How he loved her. How he missed her.

"Eliot." Sheridan approached his desk, pinched expression in place, with a shade of hesitancy that now laced her tone whenever she wanted to talk. She cocked her head, a new habit, as if reading his face for clues before speaking.

Clues to what, he didn't know.

"Can we talk?" Her eyes still danced, most likely from her sister's news.

"Of course."

She sat across the desk from him. "Liss and Bram have gone down to invite Javier and Padre Miguel to dinner."

He smiled.

"Are you okay with that?"

"Why wouldn't I be?"

The gold flecks in her eyes went dark, as surely as if a candle had been snuffed out. "Let me count the ways." She shook her head. "I'm sorry."

"No, Sher. We're all about trying to be open these days. What did you mean?"

"Eliot, for over a year we've avoided people like they all carry the plague."

"True, I haven't felt up to company, but this is your sister."

"We moved here so neither she nor anyone else could bother us."

He slumped back in his chair. "I'm sorry."

"It's just the way it is. I understand. We were in agreement on our living situation a year and a half ago. I felt the need for anonymity and safety as much as you did."

"We were recoiling, in recovery."

"Yes." She leaned forward. "But is that time over?"

Images flashed through his mind. Reina, Sheridan's friend and coworker, grinning over her shoulder at them, reaching for the door handle of their newly opened center. Her body arching, jerking backward. Himself, reaching out and shifting violently sideways, intuitively, before Reina hit the ground. White jagged streaks. Total darkness.

"Eliot!"

In the time it took to refocus on Sheridan seated before him, he felt himself travel a million miles.

"Eliot, where are you?"

"What?"

"Where are you when you do that?"

He stared at her, not comprehending.

"It's like you go somewhere far away, like you check out. The lights are on but nobody's home. What were you thinking just now?"

He shook his head, trying to clear it. "I don't have words—"

"Eliot! Stop avoiding it. I asked if that time is over and you went into your deaf-mute act." Sheridan was near tears, her voice strained.

"Deaf-mute?"

"I'm sorry. It's not an act, but that's what you resemble. You can't hear or speak."

He tuned her out and then realized what he was doing. "Sher, I don't want to share my horrors with you."

"You were thinking about Caracas."

He nodded.

"You went through all this with the counselor. Remember? He said flashbacks would come. He said let them out, talk about them. Don't bottle them all up inside."

"I talked with Padre Miguel. He said to let the light shine on them. Tell God because God has the power to heal my memory—"

"You told Padre Miguel about them?" There was hurt in her tone. "I'm here with you day in and day out and you don't tell me. Instead you just go inside yourself."

"I burden you with enough."

"I am not a hothouse orchid."

"No, you're not." Eliot studied his wife's face and saw the delicate hothouse orchid he'd always seen. "But in a sense you are to me. I've always wanted to protect you from harm. It's one reason why I didn't tell you about my past."

"You were protecting yourself on that one. If I'd known that you knew who I was, or if I'd had to go through this mess about my father's extracurricular activities back then, our relationship never would have gotten off the ground."

"Yes, I protected myself. But I also protected you. I could not bear to see you hurt. Perhaps I overcompensate trying to keep you safe emotionally because I can't protect you physically anymore. I can't tell you how devastated I was when you went to Chicago with Traynor, a man who could do what I can no longer do."

Compassion softened her face as if she understood. "Eliot, it's not your fault you were shot."

"You know that's beside the point."

"Yeah. Why is it that when I left town, you came alive? You started talking to the priest, whom you avoided all those previous months. You made an unscheduled trip to Mesa Aguamiel and even shopped for a gift for Mercedes. You went to the weekly dance."

"I—I don't know, Sher. I can't explain it."

"It's as if I've been in your way, holding you back."

"Perhaps I put you there, in the way. In all my trying to protect you, I shut down."

"But by that you stopped letting me inside, Eliot. That's what hurts so much."

"I'm sorry."

"I know you are. You can stop saying it." She sighed. "So you still have flashbacks. Are they less frequent as time goes on?"

"Yes, thanks be to God."

"And I see progress in that you don't mind visiting with locals and you don't mind having company for dinner tonight."

"Correct."

"I'm okay with those things too."

He didn't point out that she was obviously okay with much more than those things. She had traveled to Chicago and back.

She went on. "I'd say we are beyond the season of recoiling. We no longer have to make every decision based on fear. It's time to move forward, to make decisions based on hope. Don't you think?"

He met the real question in her eyes. It threw him into the struggle again. Should he protect her heart by not speaking his own?

No, she wanted him to let her inside, all the way through to his inner heart.

He had to admit that fear was still very much a part of his daily life. Fear that pain would overtake him. Fear that he might fall. Fear that he could not finish writing his book. Fear that his work in any capacity was over, that his life from here on out was shuffling across the floor and taking the next pill. Fear that God found him unworthy. Fear that he would let his wife down time and time again. And still, fear that there would come a physical situation in which he would be unable to keep her safe.

Debilitating fears, each and every one. They formed the answer to her real question.

"Sheridan," he said, "I'm sorry. I can't leave Topala."

She closed her eyes for a long moment, and then she looked at him, her expression unreadable. "I'll go help with dinner."

CHAPTER 54

Sheridan frowned. "Liss, I am not ready for you to leave."

"I bet you never thought you'd ever say such a thing in this lifetime." Calissa laughed.

"Well, now that you mention it—" she snickered and bumped her shoulder against Calissa's—"no."

They sat on a bench in the deserted town square in front of the inn, drinking coffee from travel mugs that Sheridan had carried down from the house not long after sunrise. Her sister and brand-new brother-in-law planned to leave soon, after only three nights in Topala.

Calissa sighed. "I'm going to miss Mercedes's coffee. And sopies."

"'Sopies.' You are hopeless."

"So is Bram. Shouldn't you go inside and help him check out?"

"He'll be fine. José, the inn owner, speaks excellent English."

"Excellent to you is 'Huh, what'd he say?' to us."

"Does this mean you're never coming back?"

Calissa looked at her. "Oh, Sher, we will. I promise. And you'll come visit us." She paused. "Now that we like each other."

Sheridan couldn't return her sister's giggle. Loneliness crept in. Long tendrils of it wove their way through her and spread the ache that had lain dormant since Luke first showed up to take her back out into the world, the world where she belonged.

"You know, Liss, I really don't think I could travel to the States alone. I've only taken one major step: I rode the el downtown. Whoop-de-do."

"It *is* a whoop-de-do—a big one."

"I don't even think I'm ready to be by myself again here in Topala."

"Now that's a different kettle of squid. Think of what's changed here. You and Eliot talked through the tough things."

"Nothing's exactly settled except that it's all out in the open."

"Aside from that, it's a good, solid start. And you've set new boundaries, like giving yourself a break from his needs and letting Mercedes or someone else take over. Then the crème de la crème happened when you hosted your first dinner party. Trust me, you are going to be just fine."

"If you put this pep talk in writing, I could pull it out whenever I needed it." Sheridan's smile faltered. "The bottom line is that this situation is not what I signed up for. Alone in the middle of nowhere. Not working in my field. Not working in any field. Nursing an invalid."

"And Eliot *did* sign up for those things?"

"You've been defending him a lot."

"I'm tired of being angry at him." Calissa inhaled deeply and exhaled slowly. "Tell me, Sher, how does being in a situation that you didn't sign up for nullify your marriage vows?"

Sheridan wasn't sure she heard correctly.

"Yeah, yeah. I'm an expert now since I just said them myself."

"Liss, there can be all sorts of extenuating circumstances that nullify them. For one, he hasn't been up-front with me since the day we met. I'd call that an abuse. Emotional, psychological, whatever. I'm supposed to forget it and go back to life the way it was? I don't think so. It's time we made some major changes. First and foremost we need to find some normalcy in life again. That won't happen in Topala, but he says he can't leave. Can't . . . or won't."

"Nothing is going to happen if you don't forgive him, Sher."

"I've forgiven him."

"No, you haven't. And that's okay. It's too soon. But if you take off now, leave here without him, then . . . well, then you'll cheat yourself out of the best that life can offer." She rolled her eyes. "Okay. I mean, you'll cheat yourself out of the best that God can offer. And wants to offer."

"Now you're channeling Mamá?"

"Oh, get over it. What I'm saying is that Bram never gave up on me. Even when I pushed him away, he was on my side. He's always been my biggest fan. His love is what's kept me going all these years."

"You're saying Eliot is on my side."

"No. I'm saying Eliot needs you on *his* side. He needs a cheerleader. He needs to know you're not going to give up on him. And now I'll tape Big Sister's mouth shut." She pursed her lips and then opened them right back up. "Except to say that Bram is God's best. He is the most beautiful person I know. The more he gives, the more God fills him up with extra goodness so he can give even more to me and everybody else. Sher, don't you see? You're like Bram. I'm the whiny, needy one like Eliot."

"That's not true. You gave up everything to take care of me."

Calissa shook her head. "Not willingly. Now I'm a forty-seven-and-a-half-year-old pushy dame who sets people's teeth on edge."

They looked at each other for a silent moment.

Sheridan sighed. "But you're a pushy dame with a gorgeous new ring and a beautiful husband."

"True." She wiggled her hand until the sunlight bounced off the diamond in a myriad of dancing colors. "Unlike you and Mamá, I've always liked diamonds. But I am glad that Bram bought one he could trace to its origin."

"Hopefully no one was hurt along the way." Mining, trading, smuggling . . . Sheridan didn't want to think about it, not any of it. The world was overwhelmingly full of pain. She might after all welcome back the off-the-map gig in Topala for the remainder of her life.

Calissa grinned and stood. "Here comes that beautiful husband of mine now."

Smiling, Bram walked to them from the inn. Sheridan could tell he was happy to be leaving, eager to begin his new season of life with Calissa. They planned to regroup. He would step down from his CEO role; she would put her campaign on hold.

Sheridan tried not to envy their freedom. At the moment, it was a losing battle.

The dreaded good-byes began.

Bram held her tightly. "It's a fun place to visit, hon. Don't stay too long."

Calissa blubbered and held Sheridan's face between her hands. "Don't forget what I said. And one more thing: remember who you are."

As they drove away, Sheridan comforted herself with the changes they'd put in place. Calissa and Bram now had her and Eliot's real mailing address. They had Mercedes's aunt's phone number, the one Sheridan called from Chicago. They even knew their way from the Mazatlán airport to her house.

Another whoop-de-do. The fact was they still lived thousands of miles away and could not speak directly with her at the drop of a hat.

She thought about their conflicting advice. Bram more or less said to set a deadline for leaving Topala. Calissa said stay because her place was with Eliot.

"Jesús, what do You say?"

❧

Sheridan took a long walk around the village, swinging three empty travel mugs in her hands, listening, listening, listening. She went up and down the steep inclines, past Davy's restaurant, partway down to the highway, beyond whistling distance.

Not a word came to her.

At least she worked off the compulsion that had nearly propelled her into the backseat of Calissa and Bram's car. If she didn't get home soon, Eliot might imagine she'd done just that. Surely he sensed her ambivalence about staying.

It was the one thing they hadn't talked openly about yet.

Hot and sweaty, she entered the kitchen, set down the mugs, and filled a glass from the bottled water dispenser. She drank it and filled it again, hydrating and procrastinating.

Dabbing her face with a hand towel, she finally went into the study.

Eliot looked up from the sofa where he was reading. Except for the sight of the nearby walker, he appeared healthy. Why was he on the sofa and not in the recliner? He never sat on the sofa. Upright, he looked almost chipper.

Suddenly her marriage vows came to mind. She and Eliot had promised the traditional ones about never leaving or forsaking, about staying together in health and in sickness.

She wanted to spit.

Instead she said, too brightly, "Alone at last."

"You must feel awful, Sher. What can I do for you?"

She stared at him, rooted to the floor. His words knocked every defensive, angry, hurt wind from her sails.

"It must be God's timing." He smiled gently and removed his glasses. "I'm at a two on the scale and experiencing a rare sense of clarity. It won't make up for the year and a half I've missed of being there when you needed me, but I'm here now. For you."

She couldn't move or speak.

"You'll notice I did not dash across the room to embrace you and dry your tears. Evidently I'm 'here' in a limited capacity."

"I'm not crying."

"I thought you might, once it sinks in that you're all alone again with the deaf-mute."

"Oh, Eliot."

He gestured, putting his hand out as if offering her a gift. "Sher, I won't push you away this time."

What had Calissa said about herself and Bram? *"Even when I pushed him away, he was on my side."*

With Eliot, his physical avoidance of her was related to his injury. In the hospital she could hardly find a place to touch him that was not bandaged or hooked up to some tube or wire. Later his body cried out in pain when she hugged him, and so she had stopped. Even hand-holding caused discomfort, and so she had stopped.

He'd curled up inside himself, perhaps because of those things he could no longer do, and avoided even her kisses, never returning or initiating them. Their physical contact began and ended with her massaging his back and exercising his legs.

She hesitated. Did she want a hug from him? It wasn't going to change his deception. It wasn't going to change the situation of living in the middle of nowhere.

Then reality crashed all around her. Calissa and Bram were gone. A void yawned inside her. Her first inclination was to run upstairs to her room. She could lie down on her bed, one pillow against her aching stomach and one at her cheek to catch the flow. It was a familiar scene established the day they'd moved into the house.

The thought of reenacting it hurt worse than her sister's absence.

Sheridan walked over to Eliot and put her hand in his. He drew her nearer, onto the sofa beside him.

Turning toward her, he embraced her. His movements were stiff. "Sorry. I'm a little out of practice." He sighed. "Well, that and the fact that things just don't work quite the same as they used to."

She sank against his frame, lankier than ever, her head at his shoulder, near enough to feel the echo of his heartbeat. Words she had held in for months and months tumbled out.

"I've missed you, Eliot. I've missed you so much."

CHAPTER 55

THANK YOU, GOD. Thank You, God. Eliot held Sheridan, his cheek against the top of her head, as she sobbed uncontrollably.

How often had she cried by herself? In the beginning, right after the shooting, friends could not get to her. Perhaps strangers held her, security and medical people. Luke Traynor. Later, in Houston, others came. Calissa. Malcolm. Friends in the foreign service who were in the States at the time.

He smoothed her hair. She was warm from walking up the hill. In the past, when she played volleyball or ran with him, he loved the rosy glow on her face. Sometimes she would tease, announcing no hugs until a shower. And then she would lead him into the shower.

Well . . . best not to go there.

He felt her tears on his neck. Sheridan did not often succumb to weeping such as this. Not before Caracas, anyway.

He had listened to her stories about students who questioned her apparent hard-heartedness. She would teach them about the need to separate themselves from the utter despair they would encounter in social work. If they wanted to just sit on the floor and bawl with an

HIV-positive, pregnant fifteen-year-old bruised from a boyfriend's beating, then they should consider changing majors.

The first time she had needed Eliot in this way was when they lost the first baby. It was in Honduras, two years or so after they married. Sher was only a few weeks along.

The second time was two years after that. They were in D.C., in between overseas assignments, an extended stay that meant a stateside birth. The pregnancy was going well until her fifth month. There were complications—too many. A hysterectomy followed the miscarriage. She was only thirty-five. They buried a daughter. For a while after that, Eliot knew she had stopped trying to hear the voice of Jesus.

He felt her grow still now.

Wiping at her face with a kitchen towel, she looked up at him with a wobbly smile. "So what's going on? Where's Eliot?"

"You mean the deaf-mute. He's taking a break."

She searched his eyes. "He'll be coming back then?"

"I—I can't say." He wanted to kiss her. Her face was mere inches from his, rosy and wounded. The distrust in her voice, though, paralyzed him.

"Why did he go away?"

"I don't know."

"Who are you?"

"I hope the real Eliot."

She let that sink in for a moment. "I hope so too. I like being noticed as a flesh-and-blood woman for a change."

Eliot never had a problem understanding why his wife's former students asked about her apparent hard-heartedness. She did not shy away from speaking hard truths.

He said, "I'm sorry for the long wait."

"You didn't have a choice, did you?"

He shook his head. "But I do right now, in this clearheaded moment. A part of me wants to kiss you. A part of me believes you won't let me. I'm a cripple who's deceived you and I do not deserve your affection."

Her forehead creased. "Oh, Eliot. Is that why you avoid me?"

"Most often it's because of the pain. Oh, blazes. Yes, it is why I avoid you. I admit it. At first it was the intense pain. However, in recent weeks, when I've had less pain, my focus has been on myself. I don't deserve you, so I should back off. Padre Miguel says that's pride. It puts all the attention on me, myself, and I."

She stared at him as if at a loss for words.

He smiled. "Padre Miguel is a treasure, isn't he?"

A short laugh burst from her. "And to think you always ducked when you saw him coming."

"Maybe change is in the wind, Sher. I know the deaf-mute is on hiatus because Padre Miguel prayed for me to have strength for you today."

"The man has been praying like that for months."

"But that was before. Once I confessed my sin of deceiving you and my sin of pride, the wall was removed between me and God."

"And now you can receive from Him." Her eyes softened and she tilted her head. "So simple."

"Faith 101. We both learned it at our mothers' knees."

"Calissa says I haven't forgiven you yet."

"You don't need to for my sake."

"No. It's for my sake. Strange how it was easier to forgive my dad."

"Well, you don't have to live with him or wonder if you can ever trust him again."

She nodded. "I do forgive you, Eliot."

"Faith 102. Forgiveness is a choice, and love is a verb. No feelings involved."

"Eliot the erudite."

"But it takes time to work out such choices. I mean, the words are easy to say, but they come with emotional tails. My pressing question is, will you . . . ?" A shadow shifted inside of him, quick as a flash. It was the curtain. It floated downward. He lost the thread of his thoughts.

"Will I what?"

Eliot clawed his mental way to the front side of the curtain. He had to hear. No, he had to ask her. Ask her what? *God, help me.* What was it?

Sheridan held his hand on his lap. He must have lowered his arm from around her. She had felt so good against him.

"Eliot, you're wondering if I'll stay. You're thinking that if I've forgiven you, then why wouldn't I stay?"

That was an easy one. "Because you have better things to do than tend to an invalid. And you do, Sher. I understand."

"You've always understood. It's one of the things I most appreciate about you." Her smile faltered. "Thank you. I . . . I do love you."

She wasn't answering the question.

He moved his lips. The smile to coax more from her twisted into a grimace. He dove under the curtain, swimming toward his shoulder blade where the bullet had entered. The area needed his entire attention.

"Eliot? Eliot!"

CHAPTER 56

MAZATLÁN

Two weeks after the breakthrough with Eliot, Sheridan whined into a pay phone in a Mazatlán cafe. "Liss, everyone is looking at me as if I'm the ultimate ugly American."

"You sound like one, Sher. Buck up, wouldja? Get a grip."

She rubbed her forehead. Calissa and Bram had begun their honeymoon across the States and that week were visiting a Texas ranch. Her sister kept talking like a cowpoke.

Calissa said, "You were saying the deaf-mute has returned with a vengeance."

"No. I said Eliot hasn't been doing well at all."

"Same thing. He hugged you two weeks ago. He was his old self for about twenty minutes. Then life went kaput again."

"Yes."

"James, chapter one, verses two, et cetera, et cetera. It says, 'Yippee-ki-yay! More trials! Am I glad or what? Ain't no way I'd ever learn to live by faith without them big challenges, so bring 'em on; I say, bring 'em on, Lord.' Or something to that effect. It's like our mantra here.

It has to do with not giving up when a cow doesn't do what I want it to do."

"Huh?"

Calissa laughed. "The ranch owners are Christians. Do you believe it? Bibles in the bunkhouse."

"And you stayed."

"Darn tootin' I stayed. Bram's here." She giggled. "Oh, Sher, I feel like I did when we were in high school. He was a senior and I was a sophomore. Total infatuation."

"That's—that's great, Liss. I'm happy for you."

"And I'm happy for you and your challenges. You are so far ahead of me in the mature faith department; I am jealous."

"That's not funny."

"I'm sorry. I was just trying to lighten the conversation. You have to apply the James verse for yourself."

She had been telling her sister about life in Topala. Eliot's efforts to reconnect with her were evident. They had even begun to work together again on his memoirs, jumping ahead on the timeline like he wanted, zeroing in on his career as ambassador's assistant and ambassador. Reminiscing on their nine years together in the foreign service was a good exercise.

He tired so easily, though. When the pain was tolerable, he only checked out emotionally while still engaged mentally. Sometimes, though, the pain took over and he had unbearable nights and fuzzy, medicated days.

Sheridan said, "It's just the way life is. I suppose the sooner I accept that fact, the sooner I'll . . ." She let her voice trail off.

"You'll what? Tell me, Sher."

"The sooner I'll stop greeting each sunrise with a hopeless sigh and my own mantra: 'All right. I'll stay for today.'"

"Do you say that out loud?"

"Yes, but I'm the only one on the balcony. I get through most evenings with a silent 'All right. I'll stay until I can't stay any longer.'"

Silence filled the air between them.

"Liss, I do have some great news. Mercedes and—"

"Sher, he can sense it." Calissa's voice was low. "He can sense the *if* inside of you. Does he know you're in Mazatlán?"

"He knows I was going to Mesa Aguamiel. I decided on the highway to keep on going. I needed the ocean. I needed distance just for a few hours."

"You should call Mercedes's aunt. Maybe somebody can get a message to him."

"Liss, it doesn't make a difference. I'm only sixty minutes farther away."

"Are you leaving him today?"

"What? No! I wouldn't do that. I wouldn't just take off."

"Okay. He probably needs to hear that."

"Next time he checks in, I'll tell him."

Calissa waited a beat. "So what's Mercedes's good news?"

Sheridan noted a customer's glare. She returned it with one of her own. The woman huffed and swiveled to face the wall.

"It's great news, Liss, and it's all your influence. Javier asked her to marry him."

"Really?"

"Mercedes said you told her how you regretted not saying yes to Bram when you were eighteen and he ended up marrying his parents' choice."

"Yikes. Does this mean if it doesn't work out, I'll be blamed?"

"Yes. But it will work out, so you'll get all the good credit. They're perfect together."

"They're a sweet couple. How they put each other's interests ahead of their own is amazingly mature and poignant. Is that true love or what?"

"I think the cattle are calling you."

Calissa laughed. "Yep. Time to go knot up my lariat."

They said their good-byes and Sheridan hung up. A moment later she realized she was frowning. She massaged the crease from between her eyes and counted her blessings.

First off, she was able to drive to the ocean. Second, she could call her sister's cell phone, not from home but less than two hours from home. What else? Today was open for her to spend it however she chose. Alone, yes, but free from schedule restrictions. She could find some way to reenergize herself, like walk the beach, shop for an engagement gift for Mercedes, browse bookstores. She had money to buy as many books as she wanted.

She had money to buy a one-way airline ticket.

Sighing, she gathered her things. On the way out, she apologized to the woman for being rude.

It wasn't her fault that Sheridan lived in Topala and spent every other day struggling to put her husband's interests ahead of her own sanity.

TOPALA

Traffic had delayed Sheridan's exit from the city longer than she anticipated. She arrived home after dark.

Eliot was a mess.

Padre Miguel sat with him in the study, on the ottoman next to him in the recliner. "Señora!" He flew to his feet. "Señor, she's here; she's here. See? Just as I said she would be. Women take longer than I do with their business in town. Sit, señora; sit, please."

"Eliot." She slid onto the ottoman and placed a hand on his forehead. He felt as he appeared—feverish. His eyes were unfocused and he was restless.

"You came back." His voice rasped.

"With books!" She reached into the bag still in her hand and pulled out book after book. "I spent hours in bookstores. Here, Padre Miguel. This one is for you."

His eyes lit up as he took it from her. "Deep-sea fishing!"

She smiled. The man had lived his entire life in the mountains. "And, Eliot, look at this. Honduras. I figured the photos will help jog our memories. I have one about Chile because we've never been there. We can all travel by books. I got cookbooks for Mercedes. One is Italian dishes. I even bought her a pasta maker. It'll be fun. I think I'll ask her for cooking lessons. Look at this—"

"Sheridan." He still fidgeted, his face contorted in pain.

She bit her lip, holding in her sister's phrase—buck up. "Let's get a cool washcloth for your head. Did you eat anything?"

Padre moved toward the doorway. "I'll go get Mercedes."

"Thank you. Eliot, you'll be fine. Here, have some water." She picked up his glass from the end table next to her.

He gestured, bumping it from her hand. Water splattered everywhere. "I'm sorry."

Sheridan watched the glass roll away while anger built up inside of her. "Eliot." She grasped his hands and gazed into his eyes. "Look at me. Look at me!"

He responded as if slapped. His eyes found hers. "I'm sorry, Sher. I panicked. I thought you were gone."

"I'm going to say this just once. I am not Noelle. Okay? I am not Noelle. I will not go out and find a boyfriend. I will not drive like a crazy woman and spin out of control on a rain-slick highway and over a cliff." Her throat constricted, choking off the words, those words she had spoken to herself last night. They echoed through her head. *I'll stay until I can't stay any longer.* Until she couldn't stay any longer. What did that mean exactly? Until things got—until they got what? Unbearable? How did one measure unbearable?

Was she keeping score? Did this situation in front of her right now deserve extra points because it was out of the ordinary? because he had given in to a fear that shouldn't be there? because it was more irrational than a simple physical response to his condition? because it upset her more?

"Sher." Eliot reached over and clumsily brushed his fingers over her damp cheek.

They came now, the words. "I am staying, Eliot. I will stay." She couldn't add the postscript. She couldn't say *"until I can't stay any longer."*

Because it wasn't true.

He cupped the side of her face in his large hand.

She leaned toward him. "Do you hear me? I am staying."

The corners of his mouth lifted, almost imperceptibly.

Her anger at him and life and the world in general fizzled out. "And another thing. I'm tired of not kissing you right here." She lowered her head and gently kissed his lips.

He didn't flinch.

She did it again.

"Does this mean you're staying?"

She frowned at him and then saw the laughter in his eyes. "Eliot Montgomery, you are teasing."

"Maybe full-blown anxiety attacks are good for me."

They chuckled softly.

It was a new sound in their house in Topala.

CHAPTER 57

ONE PROPER HUG. One heartfelt kiss. One visit to church for Sunday Mass. Three trips together to Mesa Aguamiel. Four shared moments of near hilarity. Semiregular dinner guests in the form of Padre Miguel and Javier. A daily touch, the brushing of fingertips or a cheek caressed. A nightly kiss between best friends.

All that within four weeks.

"But who's counting?" She scrunched her nose. "Way to be chipper, Sher. You can do it."

Actually she *was* feeling chipper. She and Eliot planned to spend the day in Mesa Aguamiel. Besides their usual errands, they hoped to call Calissa and, if Eliot was up for it, visit Mercedes's aunt. They owed that woman a thank-you gift for the use of her telephone during Sheridan's trip.

She sipped her tea on the wet balcony and waited for a sunrise that would be another no-show. The summer rains had started a little early, the end of June instead of the first of July. Low, thick clouds hid the mountaintops, but for now the torrential downpours were halted.

She had kept up her daily routine of rising early, but new things permeated the alone time.

For one, she refused to linger in past memories. It did no good to recount life with Eliot B.C.E.

Her prayers had changed too. She focused more and more on thanking God for His beauty revealed in nature and for Eliot's life rather than her old demands that God change their situation. The pronouncement "I will stay today" became a prayer: "Lord, give me the strength to stay in this marriage today, physically and emotionally. I choose to forgive him." The stabs of loneliness were turned to a whimpered "Let me love him like You do."

Daily, though, she fought the battles. She still wanted to leave, still wanted a different life. On particularly bad days she still cried and mourned the death of her life's work.

There was progress, the kind that came with three steps forward and two steps back.

"Chipper, chipper!" Grinning, she turned to go inside, but the sound of footfalls against the cobblestones pulled her back to the railing. She saw shadowy movement, and then a figure appeared in the mist.

Luke Traynor.

She laughed and hurried indoors and through the house. Flipping off her shawl, not slowing for shoes, she flung open the front door and rushed down the walkway. She went through the gate and nearly fell as her feet hit the wet stones at a fast clip.

"Luke!" she cried out, almost upon him, and laughed again. "Am I desperate for company or what?"

Smiling, he caught her in his arms, lifted her off the ground, and hugged her tightly.

If Mercedes had seen them, the girl would have once more questioned their relationship. Sheridan knew because at the moment she wondered the same thing herself. Most days she wondered it. On particularly bad days, she longed for his presence.

He lowered her to the street and held her at arm's length. "Yeah, I'd say you were desperate for company to welcome me like that, but I'll accept the greeting anyway."

She smiled. "You're not just passing through?"

He laughed. "No."

"Coffee?"

"Mercedes's?"

"Yes."

"Love some."

❧

Mercedes made coffee and put together pastries for them. Despite the damp, Sheridan preferred the outdoors. They wiped down the back patio table and brought out chair cushions from the house to sit on.

At last they sat. The courtyard's ambience resembled a cozy greenhouse. Its humid air was thick with an overpowering floral scent. Low clouds hid the palm treetops from view.

Luke said, "How is Eliot?"

"Fine."

He angled his head, questioning.

"Really. I mean it this time, at least relatively speaking. He's not his old self by any means, but we see improvements almost daily, not just with the pain but his mental health. We've made progress on his book. We plan to spend the day in Mesa Aguamiel—or maybe not." She pulled apart a bun. "I suppose you have news for us?"

He nodded.

She imagined that Luke had been halfway around the world and talked with numerous people since she last saw him. That had been at her father's funeral visitation eleven weeks and two days ago.

But who was counting?

"It's not over, is it?" she said.

He touched her hand, busy with bread shredding, and stilled it. "Don't worry. I'm not Gabriel this time. I'm not here to make some huge announcement and turn your world upside down. There are just a few loose ends to tie up. Okay? You look great, by the way. Much healthier than the last time I saw you. Tell me how you are, Sher. Sheridan."

She searched his face—the green eyes, the thin lips, the attractive shape of his jaw. "I'm fairly good. Our life is so much better than it was even three weeks ago. It's hard, though. It's unbelievably hard. The day in and day out of being nursemaid, chauffeur, and secretary in Topala after I've pulled my head out of the sand is . . . is . . ." She shrugged, unwilling to fill in the blank. It didn't help to say *tedious, excruciatingly nerve-racking, disappointing, desperate, bleaker than bleak . . .*

Luke gave her hand a brief squeeze and let go. "But overall you're fairly good?"

"Mm-hmm." She smiled. "Learning and growing."

"Everything out in the open with Eliot?"

She nodded.

"Did he know who you were when he met you?" He maintained eye contact.

She nodded again.

"And you've stayed."

"Topala is not where I want to be. But . . . it's the right thing to do."

"That's marriage."

"According to the vows."

"I'm glad for him." Luke looked away.

She studied his profile. She knew she wanted to memorize it in order to hold it close after he was gone.

He spoke, still gazing toward the back wall. "I think we get tagged for things. This isn't where you want to be, and yet here you are. No doubt you're touching the lives of these villagers. Certainly you're making all the difference in Eliot's life. You are fulfilling some purpose even if you don't know what it is."

"I've stopped saying I didn't sign up for this. That attitude doesn't exactly help matters."

He smiled at her. "Doesn't change a thing, does it?"

"No. Are you doing what you signed up for?"

His smile faded. "Got tagged. Just like you."

"What would you rather have done with your life?"

He gave his head a slight shake as if he didn't want to answer.

It saddened her that he would leave once more and this time not return. In all their forced togetherness, she had been too busy rejecting him and the situations to discover much about him. Now she yearned for information about the man who saved her life.

And so she pressed him. "Tell me. I really want to know. What would you have signed up for?"

He rubbed his chin, glanced away, came back to her. "I'd have signed up for a white picket fence, amateur baseball, and marrying you."

She returned his gaze, a world of questions, regrets, and dreams passing between them.

His brows rose and he smiled his little smile. "'Nuf said."

They drank their coffee, sitting in a silence now grown comfortable.

CHAPTER 58

WHILE GETTING DRESSED, Eliot heard voices and looked between the curtains on the French doors in his bedroom. He saw Sheridan sitting in the back courtyard with Luke Traynor.

He heaved a sigh, part relief, part anxiety. Evidently it was time to finish things with the government.

Something captured his attention in the outdoor scene. Was something said? He couldn't hear their words.

Because they weren't speaking now.

But he sensed, though, that they were speaking. He felt it deep in his bones.

He let the curtain fall into place and sat on the chair to button his shirt.

What was the relationship between his wife and the agent? Eliot had complete confidence in Sheridan's faithfulness. As she proclaimed the day she was late and he feared her gone, she was not Noelle. No. She was nothing like Noelle in appearance or demeanor or character. There was a solid core to Sheridan that nothing could shake.

Not even the agony of watching her husband almost die? How about nearly two years and counting of life with a deaf-mute who failed to meet any need or desire she might possibly have?

Traynor had rescued her, for heaven's sake. The very nature of that event created a bond nothing could nullify. Eliot imagined it was a lifelong bond that neither Luke nor Sheridan could deny.

He had heard the details from Sheridan. Traynor wasn't security, but he had been present that day for some obscure reason. He had intuitively covered Sheridan with himself. Once the shooting stopped, he extracted her from the volatile scene. He saw to her immediate medical needs for a broken arm and ribs. He accompanied her through the maze of hospitals and travel and accommodations.

Sheridan described it all in her usual candid, sensible manner. She wasn't hiding anything.

But the bond was undeniable.

So what did that mean for Eliot?

He shut his eyes and leaned back in the chair.

It meant he better do some praying before he went outside and took a mortifyingly feeble swing at the guy.

❧

"Mr. Ambassador." Luke stood at the patio table as Eliot approached.

He waved a hand in dismissal. "Traynor, I told you before, enough of that nonsense."

Sheridan walked to meet him, her eyes overly bright, and kissed his cheek. "Good morning. You're up and about early. And just one cane?"

He smiled, the gossamer touch of her lips still tingling on his face. "I was a bit eager to start our special day." Frowning, he made a show of peering around her shoulder at Luke. "Shall we take Traynor with us?"

"I don't know if he'd be interested." She walked to the table with him. "We could ask. Apparently he already knows our routine."

"Spies." He tsked. "Can't live with them. Can't live without them." He stretched his hand toward Luke and smiled. "Hello, Luke."

"Eliot. You are looking well."

"Thank you. Sit; sit. It takes me a moment to get myself lowered." As he bent stiffly to sit on the padded wrought-iron chair, he noticed Luke the charmer wait politely before he himself sat. Eliot tried not to resent the man's youth, vigor, jaunty air, sporty blue jeans, ball cap, and white T-shirt tucked neatly at the trim waist—generally everything about him.

The table was set for three. Sheridan poured tea for him. "Luke has news. Or rather a few loose ends to tie up. May I leave this time, Mr. Traynor?" Her voice went up. "I've heard all I care to about my father. Whatever the government wants to do with his legacy is fine with me. Not that they're likely to ask my opinion."

Eliot knew she was more concerned about him than Harrison. They had argued about whether or not he should admit to smuggling. Could they arrest him?

"Sher," he said, "take a deep breath. We'll get through this together, all right?"

She shook her head, clearly not wanting to stay and listen.

"You're free to go," Luke said. "Eliot can tell you later what he thinks you should know."

Now Eliot shook his head. "She needs to hear everything directly. I want no misunderstandings between us later. We're done with middlemen and holding back information. Sheridan?" He gazed at her until she met his eyes. "Except for Calissa and Bram, the people who love you most are here with you right now. You're not alone. Okay?"

"Okay," she whispered and cleared her throat. "Okay."

If he had any remaining ability to read her eyes, he would say that the gold flecks glittered just for him now. She loved him.

Well, he thought, *that exchange went better than throwing a punch.*

CHAPTER 59

THE MOMENT LUKE began to speak, Sheridan scooted her chair nearer Eliot's. Wrapping her shawl tightly around her shoulders, she tucked her legs beneath herself and leaned against him.

Her self-defensive posture didn't help much. Even tuning out the details of international trade didn't help much. She followed Luke's story down shadowy paths that frightened and appalled her.

"Harrison's ties to the smuggling world go back forty-plus years." Luke spoke in a whispery voice, as if trying to cushion the blows. "As far as we can tell, he engaged in everything. What started out as small-time when he met Ysabel grew into big business. He literally carried diamonds into the U.S. He laundered them and money. He recruited and blackmailed. He influenced national policy with lies and bribes and old-fashioned politicking."

Eliot asked him about specifics, and Luke provided them.

Eliot said, "My word! You're describing current international conditions."

Luke nodded. "There are lingering effects. He didn't work alone. There are still people out there who may have been involved."

"Which is the problem."

"Which is the problem, yes. His trail is murky. The man was quite crafty." Luke winced slightly in Sheridan's direction.

"Like I don't know how despicable he was." She frowned. The facial expression was less messy than crying over a heritage she couldn't change. "Can you tell us anything about the trail?"

"It's being followed."

"Are you arresting people?"

"There's more following involved. Tracing. Collecting proof. Trying to get to the sources."

"And so," Eliot said, "we can't disclose this information to the world, can we? The repercussions would be too far-reaching, too damaging. International relations and the market would just be the tip of the iceberg."

"Even disclosing what Harrison was up to decades ago would be like setting off an earthquake."

"So he gets off scot-free," Sheridan said.

"If there is a God, I would think not exactly scot-free." Luke shrugged. "Years from now, it may be in the nation's best interest to expose him. Tarnishing his legacy at this time would only hurt you and Calissa and his constituency."

"It's not fair."

"No, it's not. Neither is it fair to ask any more of you two."

Eliot smiled. "But you will because I may be of some help. Where and when?"

Sheridan said, "Wait. What's going on?"

"They need to talk to me, Sher. They know Harrison was in Caracas when I was. That he was by that time entrenched with an underworld that included the shaping of foreign policy. Just over eighteen months ago I was there again. As ambassador I discussed policy, influenced by him, with government leaders." He turned to Luke. "How much do you know about me?"

"We suspect that you met Harrison Cole in 1983 because you were in the same place at the same time." He shrugged.

"That's it?"

"Yeah, that's it."

Eliot glanced at Sheridan. She bit the inside of her lip. *Don't tell him. Do not say a word. We'll get a lawyer!*

Eliot gave his head a slight shake. "Well, there's a bit more to the story." He proceeded to tell Luke everything.

Every little detail.

Luke listened, expressionless. After Eliot finished, Luke let out a low whistle. "Okay, thanks, sir."

"I need to make restitution."

"Then talk to us. There is no evidence of your ever breaking the law. I think your wife may be hyperventilating."

She shook her head. "I-I'm fine."

"He's not going to prison."

She nodded. *Thank You, God.*

Eliot said, "Just to clear the air, Traynor, are you quite sure you overturned every stone in my past?"

"Yes, sir, every single one. And if I had found evidence, I would have considered it planted."

The two men stared at each other, odd little smiles on their faces.

"What was the name of my first golden retriever?" Eliot asked.

"You never had one. But the name of your first English sheepdog was Tennyson. You were six."

Eliot grinned.

Luke turned to her. "Your husband is so clean he squeaks when he walks." He smiled. "And I'm not referring to canes and walkers."

Eliot chuckled. "Back to the question at hand: where and when?"

"Are you up for Mazatlán? Say in two weeks?"

"Yes."

"Eliot," she said, "that's too much for you. Why can't whoever 'they' are just come here to the house and question you?"

He raised his brows. "I call her 'naive princess.'"

"It suits," Luke said. "Sheridan, it won't work here. The meeting needs to be under the radar. Topala is out of the way, but a large group of American government types might draw attention." He said to Eliot, "You'll stay in a safe house. Our guess is two days, three at the most, largely depending on your stamina."

Anxiety tightened Sheridan's throat, pushing her voice up. "By himself?"

"Yes. We hope that you agree to drive him to the city. Once you arrive, security will be assigned to you both. A room at a resort has been reserved for you, Sheridan, but you're welcome to choose wherever you'd like to stay. Think of it as a retreat for yourself. Lounge at the beach, read, and shop until it's over."

"Oh, that sounds just like my kind of vacation." Except for the beach lounging, which she never enjoyed, it described her life for the past year, shopping and reading alone. "Eliot?"

"I'll be just fine, Sher."

That wasn't the protest she expected to hear from him.

"We'll get through this, and then we'll be done." He laid his hand, palm up, on the arm of his chair between them.

She placed her hand in his.

"It'll be like the old days," he said. "We'll go our separate ways, complete our business, and meet up later." He grinned. "And not talk about most of what we did. Life in the diplomatic lane, remember?"

Eliot almost resembled his old self. His B.C.E. self.

When he crashed again, it would be all the more difficult for her to deal with his shell.

Abruptly, she excused herself and carried the carafe into the house to get more coffee.

❧

Sheridan returned to the courtyard. Eliot and Luke were heavy into details of foreign policy.

Clearly energized, Eliot described how the United States might add nuances to trade agreements. Luke leaned forward, his eyes narrowed, listening intently, asking a question now and then. Sheridan imagined his brain recording everything Eliot said so that he could pass it on back at the office.

It was a bittersweet scene. Her husband engaged in his work made her want to cry. That very passion was what had been stolen from him.

She poured coffee, rearranged the pastry basket, laid a napkin over the fruit plate, and saw the note. Printed in Luke's hand, it was an itinerary, the where and when in Mazatlán.

She set the carafe on top of it, sat, and pointedly studied the low cloud ceiling. The thought of four or five straight months of rain was a concern. First came the floods whooshing down the roads. Some years mudslides followed. She had already worked with villagers, placing sandbags where needed, including her own back wall and down at Javier's shop. Tourism would fall off for a time, another burden on the locals.

At last the men's conversation slowed.

Luke said, "Eliot, you know once you're up for it, your services would be welcome in any capacity."

"Thank you, Luke, but I've about hit my limit for serving this morning. Most likely I'll sleep the rest of the day away. Can't imagine engaging formally again."

"I am sorry for the added stress of today and the upcoming ordeal."

"No need to be. Overall it is a good challenge for me." Eliot smiled. "The doctors say there cannot possibly be a full recovery in the damaged nerves. Padre Miguel says not to listen to them but be hopeful that God will prove them wrong. I don't know."

"The Bible says nothing is impossible for God."

"Amen."

Sheridan said, "Can I tell Calissa?"

"About your father?" Luke said. "Tell her she's a sharp cookie."

"She already knows that."

He laughed. "I bet she does. Then tell her that she and Bram correctly connected the dots. You can share what I told you today about

Harrison, but please emphasize that the information cannot be leaked. Bram will be disappointed. You can cite 'national security' for not discussing the whys."

"You mean I can parse my words like any good amby's wife?"

He smiled. "Exactly. I'm sure you can still do it."

"Of course I can."

Eliot said, "Luke, I've been wondering. Why were you there the day of the shooting?"

Luke blinked, his eyes turning all gray with a slow sweep of lashes. It seemed every muscle went taut, as if he summoned up the robotic guy. "You figured it out, didn't you?"

"I think so. I wish not, but I think so." He took a deep breath. "Let's get it all out, shall we?"

"Due respect, Sheridan doesn't have to hear."

"My wife lost one of her best friends that day. She should be privy to the information."

"What are you two talking about?"

Eliot's face was full of compassion. "After you told me about your mother's background, I realized how cut off I've been from Caracas news. So I've begun asking Malcolm to send me the old articles, coverage about the shooting and what came after."

She cringed. "I've never looked at those."

"In hindsight, it's revealing. Think about that day, about the events that led up to everything."

Sheridan thought of the group that accompanied her and Reina. The center was already open and running, but this was to be their grand opening, the time for officials to visit, ribbons to be cut, cake to be eaten. They had invited the mayor's assistant, a flamboyant man who enjoyed the limelight.

She had teased Eliot, inviting him too, never really expecting him to make time for such a small, local event, even for her. His schedule was a juggler's nightmare. Much to her surprise, he joined her in the limo at the last minute.

Of course he traveled with an entourage. Security was necessary at all times, and hers wouldn't be enough. Then there was his personal assistant, an indispensable aide. Other staff members, kind people who supported his wife's work, trailed along.

And Luke trailed along as well, an out-of-place character within that group.

"Neither of you were scheduled to go," she said. "Why did you go, Luke?"

"I went because we knew something was going down. We had no clue what it was or even what it was related to. Naturally I assumed it was related to the ambassador, so where he went, I went."

Eliot nodded. "It seems that for a while there you attended other events, ones you wouldn't normally be involved with."

"Right. And what about you? Why did you go? You canceled a meeting with the French ambassador that morning, at the last minute."

Sheridan said, "He went because I'm his wife?"

"Yes, Sher, but there was more," Eliot said. "You know that I had sources. Like Luke, I always needed information. My staff needed information. People talked to us through various channels."

She nodded. "I know all that. It came with the territory."

"One thing we had been hearing was that your women's center was not being kindly received in certain quarters. Even before you opened it, your work was noticed." Eliot stumbled over his words. "Your influence on the community was a threat."

"A threat?"

He reached over and took hold of her hand. "Dearest, you took women off the streets. Women who made their living by prostitution connected to drug trafficking. Women that some people could not afford to lose."

She stared at him, his words bouncing in her head, unable to meld into a coherent thought. "What are you saying?"

"That I went that day to publicly declare my support for the work you were doing. From what I'd heard, I knew that you and Reina might be intimidated. I wanted 'them' to know that the United States would not tolerate such a thing. I never imagined they would . . . Oh, dear God." He shut his eyes. "Luke. I can't do it."

"Do what?" she cried. "Eliot!"

Luke touched her arm. He was on the other side of her chair, kneeling, forcing her by the sheer power of his presence to meet his eyes. "The assassin had no idea Eliot was going to be there. His job was to shut down your center. Sher, you and Reina were his targets."

CHAPTER 60

REINA AND I were the assassin's targets?

Sheridan rested on the couch in the study, processing what Eliot and Luke had told her a short while ago. Her head pounded, but she noticed Mercedes tiptoe into the room.

"I'm awake, Mercedes."

"Okay." The girl tiptoed all the way to the couch. "I have a cold cloth," she whispered and laid it on Sheridan's forehead.

"Thank you. Sit with me for a minute?"

"Are you all right, señora?" She sat gingerly on the edge of the cushions, her voice still hushed.

"I'll be fine. What are the men doing?"

"They're eating lunch in the kitchen and talking. They talk a lot. They talk too much." She put a hand to her lips. "I talk too much."

Sheridan's head protested when she tried to smile. She pulled Mercedes's hand down and held it. "I'm fine. They told me some disturbing news. That's all."

"Oh, señora, do you have to go away again?"

"No, I don't." As a matter of fact, she might never go away again. The world was far darker and slimier than she had imagined.

"What does it mean?"

She had no idea where to begin to answer that question. It meant if not for Eliot figuring things out about the center, Luke would not have gone, and she would be dead and Eliot would be alive and well and whole.

Worse, it meant her father had been right. The last time they spoke, by phone when she was in Houston, he said she had gotten exactly what she deserved. If she had not insisted on doing her own thing in Caracas working with locals, if she had just stayed put and stuck to the wifely script, then Eliot never would have been shot.

It was as if he reached out from the grave and slapped her one more time.

As if in response to it, her head had begun to pound, and she made a beeline indoors. She wanted no more information, only sand in her lungs.

She groaned a strangled noise, part chuckle, part cry. Caring for her dear husband in the charming village of Topala certainly fit the ostrich existence.

Sheridan covered her eyes with the damp cloth, but the haunting images remained, once again vivid and larger than life.

❧

Later that afternoon Sheridan stood with the men at the front gate. Her head still ached. Her heart still ached. Luke had misspoken. His visit had *Gabriel* written all over it and left her reeling like a top.

Eliot placed both hands on his cane. "Traynor, promise me we will never see you here again."

Luke smiled. "I'll do my best, sir."

"Seriously, though, I would welcome a familiar face in Mazatlán. Will you be part of the crew?"

"No, sorry. I have another assignment."

"I understand. Well, have a safe trip." He shook Luke's hand.

"Thank you, Mr. Ambassador, for everything. Take care."

Sheridan said, "I'll walk you to your car." She kissed Eliot's cheek. "Be right back."

"No hurry." His blue eyes shone. "It's time for a nap. Maybe the pew is beckoning you?"

Who was this unneedy man? "It might be."

"I shall see you when you get home."

She joined Luke in the street. A fine mist fell as they walked slowly down the wet cobblestones. At the bottom of the hill, they turned onto the short, flat walk alongside the square where only a small herd of tourists roamed.

"I'm sorry about today," Luke said. "Are you all right?"

"Sure. I've concluded beyond a shadow of a doubt that hiding out in Topala is the life for me. So far I haven't gotten into any trouble here. Maybe though I should stop giving English lessons to the kids. They might pick up on some crazy ideas about having a future and a hope. And that will upset somebody's apple cart."

"Caracas wasn't your fault."

"Yes, it was. Eliot and Reina were directly my fault. Telling women they could change their circumstances was mean and cruel. I meddle too much. I always have. I should have just let things be."

Luke tugged at the bill of his cap and hooked his thumbs in his back pockets. His shoulders moved with a loud exhale. "I don't think God wants you hidden. He does not want you to stop meddling."

"Ha. He's telling me exactly the opposite."

"So you've heard His voice again?"

Again? She frowned at him.

"One night in Houston you told me about your mother, how she heard His voice everywhere. You said you used to hear it too."

She watched the cobblestones under her feet, vaguely recalling the conversation. During those long hours with Luke, bewildered and uncertain about Eliot's future, she had poured out her heart at times.

Was she hearing God's voice again? Was He speaking in the stillness as she sat in a pew? Was that His voice in the birdsong reminding her of His beauty?

"A little," she said. "In snippets, maybe. Whispers."

"Good. You know He talks through you. If Jesus is God with skin on, He even looks like you. In Caracas I'd watch you inspire those women. You breathed new life into them. You pulled together that center against all odds. Yes, it got blown away along with your best friend and your husband. That's the world we live in. But lives were changed for the better, and that can't be taken away. Then later I'd watch you cry in hospital chapels and come out fighting like you had an army of angels at your side."

All she could do was stare at him. God spoke through her? Through all that time she couldn't hear His voice? Through all that nightmare when she didn't know which way was up or down and she couldn't even pray?

"Sheridan, don't give in to the fear again. Just don't." He grasped her elbow and halted their walk, turning her to face him. "I didn't want you in on any of that briefing, but I respected Eliot's decision. The thing is, you're a woman and your feelings get in the way. Reina's death and Eliot's disability are not your fault."

She rubbed her forehead, still tender from the headache. "Reina and I were the targets. You said it yourself, that there was proof."

"That's true, but listen." He leaned forward until they were almost nose to nose. "Their mission was accomplished. Your center closed. You and Reina are gone. But you, Sheridan Montgomery, are not in any danger. No one is after you. No one. The world needs your meddling, and someday you will leave Topala in order to do it again."

She heard the assurance in his words and saw the promise in his gray-green eyes. The challenge was to hide them in her heart for the next time it became necessary to engage with the world outside the village.

Because one thing was certain. Luke would not be there beside her to repeat them.

❧

They reached his car parked in the lot at Davy's restaurant. Sheridan felt the passage of time as if it were a solid thing slipping from her grasp.

How did one say good-bye to Gabriel, a rescuing angel?

"Gabe," she said as they stopped next to his rental, "thank you for saving my life."

Luke hit the automatic unlock and opened the driver's side door. Resting his arm on top of it, he looked at her with a puzzled expression.

"Whew." She raised her eyebrows. "I never came out and said that to you, did I?"

"You yammered something along those lines after the doctor gave you a sedative."

"I'm sorry. I was always so angry at you, blaming you for the whole thing."

"Now that sentiment you have stated clearly once or twice. Not a problem." He paused. "Sher—Sheridan—"

"The nickname is okay."

"About time." He smiled briefly. "You know I didn't really save your life, right?"

"What do you mean? Of course you saved my life. What else would you call shoving me out of the way of flying bullets?"

"Eliot shoved you out of the way."

"Eliot? But you . . . He was . . . Oh my gosh."

"You didn't know? Eliot never said anything?"

She shook her head.

"He probably just assumed you knew."

"He thanked you, though."

"For rescuing you, as in getting you out of there. Tell me, what do you remember?"

"Lying on the sidewalk. You were holding me down, yelling. I heard shouts and cries." She glanced at her wrist. "My watch was smashed. You pulled me up."

"It happened so quickly. You were probably down before it registered that someone pushed you. That was Eliot. It was instantaneous. His reflex was to reach out and protect the one he loved."

Eliot had saved her life. Hers. The one he loved.

Luke said, "You and Reina were at the front. Eliot was at your side, a little behind. Reina was hit before the shot was heard. He threw himself directly behind you and pushed. Even as he was doing that, he was struck." He stopped talking.

"What happened after that?" She was reliving the scene in her mind, this time from a different angle.

"Then I covered you."

"Why?"

"Training. The ambassador was down. Others were assigned to him. Next in line was his wife. I was there."

"But you weren't security."

"Comes with the package."

She saw it now—the layout of the group. Reina was a bit ahead, reaching into her bag for the scissors Eliot would use to cut the fuchsia ribbon from the front door. The storefront was small, not conducive to a major ribbon-stringing. They had laughed about how it had to be tied around the door handle.

"You weren't next to me."

He shook his head and turned toward a thick grove of plants. Replaying the scene too or parsing his words?

At last he looked back at her and smiled. "Reflex."

She heard his unspoken words, the ones he'd used to describe Eliot's "reflex." *"His reflex was to reach out and protect the one he loved."*

"Thank you."

"You're welcome."

She stepped into his outstretched arms. For a long moment she lingered in an embrace that would need to last a lifetime.

CHAPTER 61

ELIOT AWOKE SLOWLY, moved tentatively, assessed the pain level, and saw despair like a cloud billow to the forefront of his mind.

"Blazes."

He smiled. Was that what Padre Miguel suggested the other day? to get in the face of despair and curse it off?

In a sense, yes.

The priest had come Sunday afternoon to serve him Communion. It was a new development, a weekly occurrence, that somehow Padre Miguel in his inimitable way had inserted into their lives with ease without asking permission. On Sundays he wore his black cassock and collar and appeared quite hot.

"Eliot," he had said as they sat in the study, "I'm just curious. What do you do first thing when you awaken in the morning?"

"I list everything I can't do. Most often I begin with not being able to spring from the bed, pull on my running shoes, and take off." He heard an undertone from Padre Miguel. "Are you tut-tutting me?"

"Apparently hearing is one thing you can still do." He smiled blissfully, one of the most annoying men who walked the face of the earth.

"Need I remind you that you have never been in my situation?"

"I believe you just did. What do you do when you're finished with this 'woe is me, can't-do' list?"

"Go back to sleep."

"I would too. Who could face the day with such a terrible attitude?"

"It's not attitude. It's facts."

"And where do you think attitude comes from?"

"I never thought about it."

"My, my. For such an intelligent man, you missed the boat on this one."

Eliot frowned.

"Try this. You have your list of disheartening facts. You also have a list of facts not so disheartening. For example, you have two legs and you can walk. You have food. You have a beautiful wife." His eyes lit up like they always did whenever he mentioned Sheridan. "You live in God's backyard. Now, which list do you choose to focus on?" He shrugged. "There's your attitude. If it's one of gratitude, you can hardly wait to get on with the day to see what other gifts He has in store for you. Now, might I suggest you give it a try?"

"I think you just did."

Padre Miguel smiled again and leaned in close. "You might even get out of bed early enough to get your rump down to Mass on time."

Now, in the quiet of his bedroom, Eliot laughed out loud.

A moment later, the door opened and Sheridan came in. "Hey. Good morning."

"Good morning, dear."

"Whoa. 'Good morning, dear'?" She smiled and sat gingerly on the edge of the bed. "Thank you."

"You're welcome." With his elbow against the mattress, he tried to hoist himself to a sitting position.

"Let me help."

He fell back against the pillow and looked up at her. "I just wanted to kiss you good morning. Do you mind coming to get it?"

She smiled and lowered her face to his.

"Do you mind giving me my glasses first so I can see you better?"

She sighed dramatically. "*High maintenance* does not begin to describe you." She handed him the glasses and resumed her position, her face a few inches from his. "Better?"

He straightened the glasses on his nose and smiled.

"Since you're obviously feeling chipper, I have a complaint to file. You, Eliot Logan Montgomery the Third, broke my arm."

"Yes, and I already apologized. Didn't I?"

"You knew and you apologized?"

"I thought so."

"I don't remember it."

"The first time I saw your cast, I apologized. Were we still in Caracas, or had we arrived in Houston? At any rate, it was in a hospital. The first one is hazier than the second, but I distinctly remember your thick white arm next to a thick doctor in a white coat. The sheets were all white too."

"And you were too drugged to make coherent conversation. Eliot, you saved my life!"

"Well. Yes. But you knew that."

"No, I didn't. You pushed me down and saved my life."

"You didn't know?"

"Not until Luke told me yesterday. He assumed I knew."

"Hm. Imagine that. Actually I only accomplished the first part. If he and the others hadn't done their part . . . I am sorry about the arm."

"Don't forget the ribs."

"Ribs?"

"Two were cracked."

"Well, I'm sorry about those, too."

"If I still had the cast on, I'd whack you with it."

He saw the twinkle in her eyes, but also the dark half-moons, the pronounced fine lines. They hadn't really spoken since the previous day when he had told Luke good-bye. His last clear thought was a sweet parting with Sheridan as she walked away with Luke.

After that Eliot's afternoon and evening hours were spent napping and drifting in a fog of mental absenteeism. That state was still Sheridan's main despair. The fact that they could not dialogue like the old days intensified her loneliness.

Evidently they hadn't dialogued over the past year and a half even a trace as much as he remembered, or thought he remembered. She hadn't known who pushed her down? It baffled him.

"My word, Sher, you truly did not know?"

"No. I was down so fast and then Luke was dragging me away. I saw you and Reina." She winced.

"I'm so sorry." He smoothed a strand of her hair from her cheek. "It was so awful for you. Have you had nightmares lately? You haven't mentioned them in a long time. At least not that I can remember."

"Eliot, you're my hero."

"Aw shucks, ma'am. 'Tweren't nuttin'." He smiled.

"Thank you, O knight." She touched his chin. "Seriously, Eliot, you sacrificed yourself for me."

"You don't need to say anything."

"I can't help but remember what you said about wanting only to protect yourself, your image and career. But when it came down to a matter of life and death . . ." She shrugged.

"I love you."

"I know. You proved it in the ultimate way. You chose me over your own well-being." Her brows slid up and down; lines creased her forehead; her lips pursed and smoothed. "I have forgiven you, but as you said, there have been emotional tails."

He gazed at her and held his breath.

"I haven't been able to let it go. Now, though, it's like something is washing over me, like God is flooding it from me. Why would I hold it over you? Why would I want to see you through a lens clouded with mistakes you've asked me to forgive? Because it makes me feel better or safer from hurt? Those are emotional tails that I'm cutting off. They have no place in our marriage."

He breathed again.

"Does that make sense, Eliot?"

"No." He grinned. "But then forgiveness doesn't make sense. How you can forgive and forget is a mystery. And I'm fine with mystery."

She smiled, her expression at last one of peace.

It was an awkward angle, Sheridan leaning sideways over him, he unable to raise his head. But he slid his fingers up through her hair and pulled her closer. Silently, briefly, he thanked God for his beautiful wife who thought he was her knight.

And then he kissed her.

CHAPTER 62

ON THE HIGHWAY TO MAZATLÁN

As requested by Luke and his cohorts, a debriefing was planned for Eliot in Mazatlán.

Sheridan tried not to bemoan the necessary trip. It was an interruption to the plateau they had reached since her discovery of Eliot's heroic effort in saving her life. On one level, nothing had changed; and yet in an abstract sense, everything had changed.

Eliot's needs still dictated most of their routine. Pain scale numbers, medications, physical therapy, naps, and work on his manuscript consumed the hours.

But a new sense of peace filled Sheridan's heart. She rode the lonely, unbearable times more gently, consciously turning her thoughts to the One who tagged her as Eliot's helpmate. If that was where she belonged, then God was going to have to give her the ability to stay there.

"Sheridan." Eliot turned to her now from the passenger seat as they drove toward Mazatlán. "I have something to confess."

Her stomach did a quick double flip. The phrase unsettled her. Had he been more involved with diamond smuggling after all?

Ridiculous.

Eyes dead ahead on the highway, she took a hand off the wheel and pressed it against her stomach. "We should have brought Padre Miguel with us."

"Maybe." He exchanged a smile with her. "What do you think the feds would do with our wise man?"

"Shake their heads and ask him how he *knows*."

He chuckled, a good sign for this trip. It promised that he was determined to make it through the coming difficult days with the agents.

He said, "I think if I say this out loud, it might defuse its hold on me. I'm scared, Sher. I am scared witless."

"But why? With your service to the country, they're not going to arrest you for something they can't prove. And they're certainly not going to lock you up for talking to Harrison Cole eons ago and getting blackmailed by him." She glanced at him. "And you've already fallen flat on your face, so it can't be that."

He chuckled. The sound gained strength, and soon his deep laugh filled the car. "That wasn't funny," he declared and laughed some more.

Sheridan giggled with him. "It was, Eliot; it was."

His fall had happened three days before, on a Sunday. His decision to attend his first church service in Topala had surprised both her and Mercedes. They scurried about, helping him get ready. Sheridan fetched the car, drove him the approximate block and a half down to the church, and then parked the car back at Davy's. Meanwhile, he waited out front of Iglesia de San José with Mercedes because he wanted to enter the church with his wife.

With the iffiness of the rainy season, tourist numbers had slackened, but there were at least a few busloads present that morning. The visitors had gathered in the square and in front of the church, milling about.

One of them bumped into Eliot's cane.

Still several yards from him, Sheridan watched in horror as he fell. To fall in public and not be able to get up was his greatest fear.

One cane flipped some feet away; the other wobbled. He went down in slow motion. Mercedes reached out too late. He tumbled to the stone walk, one section of his body at a time, in a sort of roll onto his back.

Sheridan almost laughed.

She reached him, words ready to soothe his mortification, but he burst into laughter. She knelt beside him. "Are you all right?"

"I tried to call out 'timber.'"

She grinned. "Oh no! There goes the elm tree!"

They both laughed until tears ran down their faces.

Now in the car he smiled again. "I need not fear the embarrassment of falling in public ever again. Been there, done that. Could do it again. No more pride left to hurt."

She only hoped he wouldn't hurt his body. "Then what are you afraid of, hon?"

He took a moment to reply. "The city."

She reached over, squeezed his arm. "No big deal. Been there, done that. Can do it again, right beside you."

❧

MAZATLÁN

"It's the utter despair that undoes me." Sheridan looked at the woman beside her.

Annie Wilson swept the street with professional eyes hidden behind designer sunglasses. The woman had been assigned as Sheridan's babysitter while Eliot was off at some secluded spot answering questions. Sheridan wondered if Luke had any input in suggesting a certain personality type to keep her company, because Annie was a perfect match for her.

When they first met and Sheridan announced she would be avoiding the beach, pool, and trinket shopping, Annie said, "Cool." The young woman didn't bat an eye as Sheridan led her through a maze of blocks, far from the tourist hot spots, to an obviously seedy part of the city.

Aside from her toned biceps, the firearm most likely stuffed in her fanny pack, and her fluent Spanish, Annie was a nondescript American. Thirtysomething, short medium brown hair styled in a blunt cut, hazel eyes, and dressed like any tourist in a colorful summer skirt and sleeveless top, she fit in with the crowd.

Except for the one they stood with now.

Annie said, "I am watching every vice known to man being committed before my very eyes, in public, in the middle of the afternoon. This is when I say, ma'am, we don't want to be here."

"We'll be fine. Just don't make eye contact."

Annie chuckled under her breath. "How do you know this place?"

"It's Mexico. It's Venezuela. It's Chicago, L.A., New York. I have a nose for finding the neighborhoods. Let's go this way."

"What are we looking for?"

They rounded a corner and Sheridan nodded toward a church. "That."

"Mrs. Montgomery, what are we doing here?"

"The name is Sheridan, and I guess you're here to protect me. I'm here to find myself."

Without comment, Annie walked beside her down the street, to a back door of the church, and into a community room full of the poor and needy.

⁂

Later that evening the women ate dinner at the resort, outdoors on a patio overlooking the ocean. It was a beautiful setting, complete with twinkle lights and a classical guitarist in a far corner.

Sheridan wished Eliot sat across the table from her, but she was grateful for Annie's company. Technically the woman was off duty for the night, but she had accepted Sheridan's invitation while her nighttime replacement took up his spot in the room adjacent to Sheridan's.

Annie gestured at the elaborate surroundings. "How do you make the leap from that room at the church to this?"

"I just leap. There is only a chasm in between, no connecting bridge." She forked a bite of salad. "The world is an unfair, unequal place. As I said, the utter despair undoes me. To combat that, I jump in and do what I can, reminding myself I can't begin to do it all."

"Would you have gone there without me?" Annie's voice was incredulous, a departure from the even-keeled tone she had used all day.

Sheridan smiled. "Two years ago, yes. Today, no way." They had already covered the Caracas incident. "Thank you for giving me today. It was a huge gift."

"My pleasure. By talking with those needy women, you were jumping in. Is it what you meant when you said you wanted to find yourself?"

"Yes. That was my life, working with impoverished women in centers like that one. I needed to reconnect with that woman I used to be, the one that has been buried for so long."

"What do you think? Is she still alive and well?"

"Would you like to hear the idea I came up with today to teach computer skills? I'd incorporate it into the program they've already got going. Yeah, she's alive and well." *Masquerading as an invalid's nurse, but still breathing.*

"I'm sorry for your life being turned upside down." Annie seemed to read her thoughts.

"Thanks, I appreciate that. But as my sister would say, yippee."

She cocked an eyebrow. "Must be a family joke."

Sheridan smiled.

"Yippee-ki-yay! More trials! Am I glad or what? Ain't no way I'd ever learn to live by faith without them big challenges, so bring 'em on; I say, bring 'em on, Lord."

Calissa's paraphrase of the Bible verses both delighted and disconcerted Sheridan. Welcome more trials? No. But trust that somehow they served a purpose? that they would teach her how to more completely live by God's grace? Little by little she was getting the hang of that.

❧

Three days after arriving in Mazatlán, they headed home. As Sheridan drove them toward the city outskirts, she reached for Eliot's hand and gave it a quick squeeze.

He squeezed back. "We did it, Sher. We reentered civilization with aplomb, and we survived, aplomb intact."

"You did it."

"Only because you were with me."

"Only because when we got to the city, you did not barf. I told you I would pretend I didn't know you if you barfed in the parking lot or the lobby."

"You've acquired some interesting vocabulary. Annie's influence?"

Sheridan chuckled.

When they first arrived, Eliot had been obviously nervous. She encouraged him with exaggerated tales of herself being sick at the airport before leaving for Chicago. She made him laugh with her intricate plan to elude Luke, rent a car, and escape back to Topala. In hindsight, she laughed at herself.

By the time they reached the resort, where the agents met them and she kissed him good-bye, Eliot was calm. He walked steadily with his two canes, his back less hunched than it had been.

"Sher," he said now, "are you horribly disappointed not to stay at the resort another day?"

She considered how to reply without hurting his feelings.

"Parsing your words, are you?" He adjusted his seat to its fully reclined position. His body resembled one long, slender, limp rag. "I am sorry to disappoint you."

"The ocean breezes might have refreshed you, but the noise and the people might have canceled it all out."

"What would you have done while I sat on the balcony soaking up the ocean breezes?"

"Well, let me tell you." She had imagined the scenario.

The agents had driven Eliot back to the resort, exchanged pleasant farewells, and left. He seemed tired but content. The interview must have gone well. And so she took the plunge and said that her room was available for a longer stay. He wasn't interested.

Life with Eliot.

Not that she really expected a different response. Still, though, she had allowed herself a tiny sliver of hope. The place was incredibly romantic. It reminded her of the old days, the B.C.E. days. Dates had been precious and few for them, but their favorite was twenty-four hours away, in unfamiliar surroundings. Dinner under the stars, fresh seafood, classical guitar music, and invisible security were the icing on the cake. The Mazatlán resort had the icing on the cake complete with rosebuds and sprinkles.

She imagined how, away from the daily routine in Topala, they could rekindle that romantic side of their relationship. Wasn't it time to try?

But now, just a few miles from the highway, she saw no reason to share that part of the scenario with him. So she told him the other part.

"I would have soaked up the ocean breezes, too, and worked on a new project." She described her and Annie's visit to the poor church and how she had talked with people there, learning about their needs. "I actually had an idea for a program to teach computer skills. I thought while we sat on the balcony, I could write the plan."

He chuckled. "That's wonderful."

"Oh." She waved her hand in dismissal. "It's totally frivolous."

"Why do you say frivolous? Think of the possibilities. You can still write the plan. Mazatlán is only an hour and a half from home. You could visit, perhaps twice a month or so. Anything you offered, even informally, would be helpful. You know how the simple sharing of ideas makes a difference."

She concentrated on traffic and making a turn.

"What are you thinking?"

She sighed. "First off, I couldn't step foot in that neighborhood alone. I know I always complained in Caracas and elsewhere about not being able to go anywhere without security, but now I'm too scared to try it."

"We could hire a bodyguard, Sher."

She shook her head. "The other thing is I can't get involved again. I can't meddle again. Who knows what some of those women might be up to? I might step on somebody's toes. Annie pointed out obvious clues. Drug trafficking was happening right outside the church door."

Eliot didn't reply. They rode in silence through several more turns. Finally they reached the highway, and the city fell away behind them.

The visit had rejuvenated her. Annie was a likable companion, Besides giving her a sense of safety in the dangerous neighborhood, she helped her shop for linens, an engagement gift for Mercedes and Javier. The whole business of finding her old self encouraged her more than she realized. Even the pipe dream of imagining a new work reminded her of what she was capable of, not of what she could no longer do.

"Sher."

"You're awake?" She glanced at Eliot. "I don't mind if you nap. You must be exhausted."

"Dearest, I truly want to hear about your ideas."

"I'm okay, Eliot. Really. They were just for the moment. A mental exercise that proved to me I am not brain-dead after all."

"Where would you get the computers?"

She smiled, and then she smiled some more. A bubbly sensation tickled her from the inside out.

"Well, Eliot, for your information I would let someone else get the computers."

"Now how in the world would you do that?"

She proceeded to answer that question and many more, all the while fizzing inside like a dozen uncorked champagne bottles.

The point didn't seem to be about her pie-in-the-sky plan. It seemed to be about the fact that Eliot asked.

Evidently the dreaded interruption to their plateau had catapulted them onto yet another one.

And to think she still doubted God knew what He was doing.

CHAPTER 63

TOPALA

In the days since Sheridan and Eliot had returned from Mazatlán, the heavy rains had begun. With each drop, Sheridan's discontent grew. Why hadn't she insisted they stay on the coast? Why had she given in yet again to his need to hide away? At the resort they could have at least enjoyed ocean views, restaurants, movies, bookstores. His recovery time from the debriefing might have been lessened. They might even have gotten around to that romantic dinner.

Not in Topala. In Topala he slept and slept. In Topala he didn't ask her about how she planned to save the world. In Topala he ate breakfast and balked at going to Mesa Aguamiel.

Sheridan looked at him across the kitchen table. "Why don't you want to go?"

"The rain, of course. Properties are in danger."

"I told you, Javier helped Mercedes and me. We finished the sandbagging around the house and retaining wall. They'll be done with his shop soon. I don't know of anything else to do here." She listened to the steady patter on the roof. "It's not that bad."

"Driving in it, though, is not wise."

"It's not snow."

He sighed. "Sher, I'm not comfortable with the thought. Remember last year's mudslide on the road into town?"

She stood and grabbed her dish half-filled with scrambled eggs. "Would it be so bad to get stuck in a city?" She stomped over to the counter and slammed the plate so hard against the tile it broke. She swirled around to face him. "I love you, Eliot. I choose to hang in there with you. But this—this I cannot take. I can't." She shook her head vehemently.

"What can't you take? The rain?"

"No, not the rain. Life is just so hard."

"I know."

"How do you know? You are incapacitated with chronic pain and you're disabled, and none of that is your fault, but you are. It's just the way it is. You're absent three-fourths of the time. What am I supposed to do? I came home from Mazatlán absolutely ecstatic because we *talked*. We talked about possibilities. About new things, for the first time in over a year." She spread her arms wide. "But now what? It's all forgotten. You don't even want to go to Mesa Aguamiel."

"I'm sorry, Sher. We can talk about whatever you like. Let's not work today. We'll explore possibilities."

"That's too little, too late." She pulled her slicker from a hook. "We can talk. Yeah, right."

Without a backward glance, she bolted outside and slammed the door shut behind her.

❧

Sheridan's anger burned as if fueled by rain. Water sloshed up her legs and pelted her face. It drenched the hooded raincoat and began to seep through to her shoulders and back.

She walked and walked, down to the square, around the church, around the square, past the inn and shops, down to Davy's, back up, following side streets with inclines steeper than hers, down and up again.

She argued aloud. "I'm talking to You, God. I am not talking to myself anymore, and I am certainly not waiting around anymore for You to talk. You're going to have to shout over my voice. What is it You want? For me to love Eliot? I got it. I got that part. *Love* is a verb. I'm not going anywhere. I'm there for him. Whether he's present or checked out and only a shell of the man I married."

Like an oyster shell.

It wasn't a shout, but a new thought.

"Okay. He's still a pearl inside his shell, but most days he is so tightly shut I cannot see it, and yes, I forget it's even in there. I forget he hurts as much as I do. But it's different, Lord. You know it is. He has me to feed and clothe him. On some days literally. Figuratively I carry him, day in and day out. Emotionally, I fill him up."

She stopped in the middle of the deserted cobblestone street, spread her arms wide, and turned her face upward until the rain beat full on it. "Who carries me? Who fills me up? And don't say You do, because I do not *feel* that. I was not cut out to be a cloistered nun!"

She lowered her face, hugged herself, and whispered, "And I still want to call Luke." It was still, weeks after the fact, Luke's visit that weighed on her. His virile presence revealed Eliot's stark absence.

Look for Me. I am a pearl, a treasure often hidden from sight, but I will never leave you nor forsake you.

"God, it is too hard."

Nothing is impossible for Me, My daughter.

Sheridan wept quietly. She was His. No matter what. No matter what.

"Oh, Mamá, He talks in the raindrops, too."

❧

"Señora! Señora!"

Making yet another round of the empty square, Sheridan meditated on God's love. She plowed through her memory for Bible verses and stories, stuffing them into her emotional corners, rousting the anger and loneliness that had filled them for so long.

It was an all-consuming exercise. The calling voice scarcely registered.

"Señora!"

She heard Mercedes's shout and turned toward it.

From the steps that led to the covered walkway in front of the shops, the girl gestured frantically for Sheridan to join her.

Sheridan waved and then felt water swirling at her ankles.

"Señora!" Behind her the innkeeper and others yelled and gestured for her to move.

She looked back to Mercedes. At the bottom of the set of four steps where the girl stood, a stream flowed.

It was fed by a river gushing down the incline of what had been her street.

"Eliot!" She had to get home.

The water flowed freely, filling the width of the narrow streets, banking off of walls, racing across earth sunbaked for months and solid as concrete.

Sheridan didn't have a choice of direction. She slogged her way to the nearest end of the elevated walkway, leaped up the steps, and hurried down to Mercedes. Javier and Padre Miguel now stood with her.

For a moment the four of them exchanged glances, the disturbing realization sinking in.

Mercedes said, "Who is with señor?"

Sheridan got down two steps before Padre Miguel and Javier grabbed her arms.

She struggled. "He's alone! I have to get to him!" She had left him, rushed out into the rain without a word. She'd broken the cardinal rule the four standing with her had agreed upon months ago: Eliot would always be covered. One of them would be with him at all times.

There were few exceptions. If he was not well on a Sunday morning, Sheridan stayed home from church. If he was well and he promised to be very careful if he had to get out of his chair, then she went with Mercedes, after asking the neighbor to check in on him.

"Señora, it's not possible to go." Padre Miguel spoke in a soft voice. "But God is with him. He will be fine."

"It's not deep!" she cried. "I can make it."

"But see how fast it moves. You would be washed up against a wall and be injured. No, no. You must stay here. Come, señora. We will wait together inside."

Sheridan knew he was right and reluctantly went with them into Javier's shop.

Lord, please take care of him. Please take care of him. Please take care of him.

What was it she had just been spouting off about to God a short while ago? That *she* took care of Eliot? Apparently that wasn't true.

Mercedes prepared tea for all of them in the back of the shop, the area that served as Javier's living quarters. Chairs from his courtyard had been brought indoors. While the others sat in them just inside the open door at the rear of the display room, Sheridan paced nervously.

How long would the flood last? Was Eliot all right? Would he remember which pills to take? And when? How could she have left him alone? How could she?

Because she couldn't think straight. She had been so angry, she couldn't think straight. Noelle's behavior made absolute sense to her now.

His first wife would have felt that same level of anger. In essence she had found a lover because Eliot did not meet her needs. Noelle had thought she signed up for one lifestyle and then learned that the wife of a diplomat was not it. She had seen only the honor and special privileges, not the adjustments of living in a foreign land and being the face of America, sometimes welcome, often not. When Eliot refused to give Noelle a divorce, refused to let her go, was she so angry that she couldn't think straight?

Sheridan shivered. The air was warm and humid but her thoughts frightened her. How close had she come to repeating Noelle's scene?

Javier's shop was sparse, furnished with only the necessities of a studio. There were a few shelves and tables to showcase his work, another artist's silver and bead jewelry, and her own small paintings. He added new items almost daily, from wooden carvings to clay sculptures to pottery, in the form of flowers, animals, and tableware.

"Señora." Javier looked up from the palm-size chunk of wood he was carving. "Señor Montgomery is fine. Relax."

She stopped to listen. The artist's low voice soothed better than the priest's. He was handsome and quiet with dark, soul-searching eyes and a quick smile. No puzzle why Mercedes and female tour guides adored him or why visitors flocked to his wares.

Javier whittled as he spoke. "He will play chess against himself and know that you are safe with friends."

"It's true." Mercedes handed her a mug too beautiful, in Sheridan's opinion, for everyday use. The boy could be a wealthy man in some major city.

Sheridan sat beside Padre Miguel and leaned close to him.

He held up a hand. "Whatever you did, it is forgiven."

"I left him all alone."

"You know he is not alone."

"He has memories."

"Noelle."

Her brows rose.

"Your husband shares freely." He smiled. "You are not like her in any way. He told me. You are much more beautiful."

"I left him angry and ran out into the rain."

"Did you take the car keys?"

She sat back, dumbfounded. "No."

Padre Miguel shrugged. "Sometimes we have to get out of the way so another may hear the Father's voice better. Now rest, my child. Have some tea. It's what you brought us from Chicago." He raised his own mug and sipped.

❧

Sheridan realized she had been stranded with the three most serene people she could ever hope to meet. Eventually she stopped checking the flowing river, sat still, and watched Javier work. The flick of his carving knife and the falling wood chips mesmerized her.

Other shopkeepers and their families came and went, those who lived on the same side of the square as Javier. Food was passed around, guitars strummed, games played. Two young girls asked Sheridan for English words. A sweet-faced three-year-old boy dozed on her lap. Time passed.

Javier handed her his carving. "A gift for you."

"Thank you." It was a tiny, fat bird. Unlike his others on the shelf, this one had smooth sides. "Javier, it doesn't have any wings."

His smile was as enigmatic as one of Luke's. "They're tucked away. You can't see them. She'll use them when it's time."

Sheridan clutched the figurine to her breast. Were her wings tucked away or clipped off for good?

"Señora, listen." Mercedes's eyes were wide, and she walked to the front door.

Sheridan followed her. "It's the cowbell!"

They went outdoors. Rain still splatted on the walkway's overhang, but the sound of the bell was loud and clear. The river still flowed, though not quite as deep as before.

The overhang, the trees, and a slight bend in the street hid her house a block uphill from view. She stepped gingerly down the set of stairs, Mercedes at her elbow. Clasping the girl's hand, Sheridan stuck one sandaled foot into the stream. It covered her ankle. She plunged in the other one and looked up the hill.

Eliot was on the balcony, swinging the bell with all his might.

"Eliot!" She waved frantically.

He spotted her and stuck his thumb in the air.

Eliot Logan Montgomery III had never in his entire life given a thumbs-up sign.

Sheridan laughed.

Mercedes was next to her now. "He's upstairs!"

"Yes. Isn't that wonderful?"

"He shouldn't climb the stairs by himself. Lord have mercy if he goes down them."

"Oh, honey, you worry too much. He's fine. He is just fine."

CHAPTER 64

THEY TALKED NONSTOP.

Sheridan and Eliot's conversation began when the rain ended, first from a distance without words. Then, when she was able to get back up the hill to their house, it continued with hugs and kisses. At last it moved to words.

"You really are all right?" she asked. "You've been alone for six hours!"

"I am absolutely fine." His grin stretched from ear to ear. "You didn't take the car keys."

Their dialogue went on through dinner, a simple salad affair Sheridan threw together because Mercedes was busy helping other villagers return to their homes. It went on through the dispensing of Eliot's medication and kitchen cleanup. It continued halfway up the staircase to the second floor.

They halted and stopped talking, side by side on the same step.

"Hm." Eliot glanced about as if perplexed at his one hand on the rail, the other on a cane. "It seems I've taken a wrong turn."

Smiling, she held her hand out to him.

"Or perhaps not?"

"I think not. It's just another little detour from routine."

"Sher." He winced. "I'm not sure."

"Well, I am." She took the cane from him and entwined her arm with his. "Come on, Eliot. Sunrises are better from up here."

❦

Like everything about the small village tucked into the foothills of the Sierra Madres in west central Mexico, sunrise was a leisurely event.

Sheridan waited for it, tea mug in hand, shawl over her cotton night-gown, bare feet chilled against the tile floor of the second-story balcony. Alone, she listened in the dark to the squawk of roosters.

And she smiled.

There were no clouds. There was no rain in the middle of the rainy season. There was only a sunbeam winking at the top of a mountain and the soft tap of her husband's cane against the tile.

She turned. "You're awake! Good morning."

"Good morning." He crossed the balcony to her. "Yes, I am awake and actually moving about." His glasses were askew, his curls mussed, his face in a half grimace. "I didn't want to miss the sunrise."

She stood on tiptoe, straightened his glasses, and met his kiss. "I was counting on that. I have your tea."

They sat at the table and in silence watched the slow motion of dawn breaking over Topala.

He sighed and looked at her. "That was beautiful. Thank you."

"This is your first at this house."

"Yes." His eyebrows went up and he smiled.

"I was talking about the sunrise."

"Ah, the sunrise. That was beautiful too."

She laughed. Evidently conversation after a flood could rekindle romance as well as dinner under the stars at a resort.

"Sher, I've been thinking about how you care so passionately for the work you're not engaged in. It breaks my heart. It's not right for me to keep you from living out that dream."

"*You* don't, Eliot. It's the situation."

"They're one and the same."

"It breaks my heart too that you can't live out your dream either. I think how if I hadn't worked on that center and if you hadn't come . . ." She shook her head.

"We can't waste energy trying to undo the past. It's over. And you were right; it's time to stop living from the center of the fear it created." He paused. "It's not only the fear of living in a big-city environment, Sher. It's my fear of losing you that must end as well."

"Eliot, I don't know how else to communicate that I am not leaving. I may well lose it again as I did yesterday, but it's a simple blowing off of frustration. It doesn't mean I want to hightail it out of here."

"But I've thrived on my fear for over a year. Whenever I sensed a restlessness in you, I was afraid you would leave. I was not consciously aware of it, but I welcomed the pain because it kept you close by."

She stared at him in disbelief.

"I can see how I manipulated you. The pain is chronic and it is unbearable, but there were times I chose to make it my focus instead of you. Will you please forgive me?"

She nodded. "I do."

"When you left with Traynor, I was more frightened than ever that once you got out there again, you'd stay. Then came the realization of what you might learn about your father and me. That nearly drove me insane. If not for Padre Miguel, I don't know how or if I could have survived. And if not for your choosing to stay with me after everything I'd done . . ." He shook his head.

She laid her hand on his arm. "If not for God, I wouldn't have."

"Yes. It all comes down to Him, doesn't it? Would you mind if I prayed right now?"

Talk about a detour from routine. She whispered, "Of course not."

He smiled and placed his hand over hers. "I'm new at this vocal, unwritten version."

"I think I know that."

"Dear Lord." He closed his eyes. "Thank You for my precious wife. I release her now to You. I gave her my dream to live overseas and work. I gave her my demented dream to live like a recluse. I humbly ask You, the Dream Maker, to fulfill the dreams You place in her heart."

Tears seeped through Sheridan's eyelashes. By the time he said amen, she couldn't speak.

"Padre Miguel says there's no right or wrong way to pray."

She chuckled.

"All right, on to the business at hand. You said that Mazatlán scares you. Does Chicago? You told me how you fell in love with the city again, how you rode the el and visited familiar places. It sounded as if you would be able to go there and work again."

She was back to staring in disbelief.

"Does it scare you?"

"A little."

"Have you thought about it?"

She whispered, "Every single day since I got back here."

"That settles it, then."

She found her voice. "What settles what?"

"You can go to Chicago."

"Are you coming?"

"No. I thought perhaps you could go for the school year. Spend holidays and summers here."

"Whoa. Back up, mister. Didn't you just ask God to give me my dream?"

"Yes, and—"

"Then why are you filling in the blanks?"

"Because I'm not going to hold you back any longer. Of course it will be a different lifestyle, but not that different. Aside from the past year, we are accustomed to going separate ways for long periods of time."

She tuned out as he elaborated on details of their new arrangement.

Her husband had once again handed her dream life to her on a silver-plated platter. She thrilled to the image of herself in her home city, involved, in the thick of it like the old days. Excitement took hold of her.

She thought of the tiny carved bird on her dresser. Did her senses tingle because her wings were beginning to unfurl?

She watched Eliot speak, more animated than he'd been since the shooting. The pain was there, in the way he held himself, in his forehead creases. He was fighting it, but it would win again. And he would be lost to her for who knew how long. The beloved conversation and the sweetness of rediscovering intimacy would fade away, for days or weeks or more at a time.

But . . .

"Eliot."

He stopped midsentence. "What?"

"I didn't marry you because of what you offered me. You made me laugh again. You were heart-stopping handsome in a tuxedo. And whenever we talked, I heard music. I married you because I loved you."

"Oh."

"This dream you're proposing, it's not my dream."

"I believe it will be, though, once you think about it."

"No. My dream is to be God's best at what He puts before me. Right now what's before me is being your helpmate. A friend who pops in for holidays doesn't quite cut it."

"But I can't ask anything more of you."

"You don't have to ask."

"But I will not accept the sacrifice of your life for my comfort."

"I give it freely."

"But I'm an invalid."

"And that does not negate our vows, does it?"

"But I release you of those vows. That's my choice."

"I think only God can do that."

"Sheridan—" he blew out an exasperated breath—"think about it. Unless God zaps me with a miracle, I won't be changing. I'll never be in the physical shape I was in before. I will never 'be there' for you 100 percent of the time or even 50 percent."

"You never know about the zap or another year under the Mexican sun and eating Mercedes's meals. Eliot, you've gone from a walker to two canes to sometimes only one." She shrugged.

"And meanwhile, waiting for the zap, what are you doing? Painting trinkets or teaching kids English so they can out-bargain the tourists. Those are not exactly the best uses of your time and talents."

"Oh, hush, Eliot, and go back to releasing me."

He just stared at her.

She smiled. "We didn't choose this season of living in fear and hiding out in Topala. It's a bumpy side road that events in Caracas forced us onto. Somewhere along the way, though, it turned into our main highway. And, Eliot, we are traveling it together, not separately."

He gazed at her some more, his eyes alert.

"Mr. Ambassador, are you redesigning your strategy?"

A slow smile spread across his face. "Yes, I am. I like yours better. It has much more potential, don't you think?"

"New dreams are like that."

He raised her hand to his lips and kissed it.

Epilogue

CHICAGO
A YEAR LATER

"So, Liss—" Sheridan put her elbows on the countertop and smiled at her sister—"do you think Isaac and Ishmael became friends after they buried their father?"

Calissa looked up from the three-layered red cake she was icing. "Let's see. I married Bram. I gave up last year's campaign. I've been to Topala twice, once for a wedding where only the bride and groom spoke English. My husband the landlubber took Padre Miguel deep-sea fishing. You and I arranged to have every last cent of our inheritance donated to the Hull House Association. You and Eliot are in Chicago, staying in our condo. And I have baked a birthday cake for him. At this point I'd say anything is possible."

"Not to mention that you like your brother-in-law now."

"I thought the Betty Crocker routine made that evident." She smiled and spread another scoop of buttercream frosting on the top layer. "I can't wait to hear about Eliot's lecture today."

"It was great."

"The gigs were a success?"

"Definitely."

The "gigs" had been Eliot's idea. Not long after their first shared sunrise in Topala, he suggested a shared trip to Chicago. They made it a goal and worked toward it for almost a year.

They offered their services to Sheridan's former university and were quickly signed on to teach. He opted to give a lecture on foreign affairs, which he had done that morning. She had already given one seminar and was scheduled for two more.

"I almost feel guilty for having so much fun," she said.

Eliot's voice reached them from the hallway. "What's so much fun?"

"Being married to you." She met him in the kitchen doorway with a kiss. The scent of cool autumn air clung to his tweed sport jacket and turtleneck. "Where have you been?"

His blue eyes twinkled behind the glasses. "Shopping with Bram."

Calissa groaned. "Let me guess. My nonshopping husband is now jogging down to the lake in his dress shoes and tie."

Eliot chuckled and set one of his canes in a corner. "He said twenty minutes tops. It's my fault. I asked him to go with me. Not only was he required to go into stores, he had to open doors, get cabs, catch me once—"

"Eliot!"

"I'm fine, Sher. No harm. Just a crack in the sidewalk I missed. Or rather found. Escorting me about the city is unnerving. Bram did remarkably well, all things considered."

"Why were you shopping?" Calissa said. "It's *your* birthday, big guy."

"But in the past couple years I've missed Sher's birthday and our wedding anniversary, and we really should have celebrated the A.C.E. anniversaries."

A shiver of anticipation tickled Sheridan's spine. Gifts meant less and less to her as time went on, but she loved Eliot's attention. "What is it? What did you get me?"

"Not an apron."

"I can live with the disappointment."

Smiling, he reached into his inside pocket and pulled out a small square box wrapped in silver and tied with an exquisite orchid bow. "Happy birthday, happy anniversary, and happy A.C.E., Sheridan."

Like a little kid, she snapped off the bow without a second thought and ripped apart the paper. Inside the box was another box, and inside that was a watch.

"Oh, Eliot."

It resembled her broken one. Sapphires ringed its face. The bracelet band shone like twenty-four-carat gold and silver. A second hand swept gracefully past large numerals, reminding her to savor life's moments.

"It's so elegant."

He laughed. "With numbers big enough for Big Ben?"

"Still," she said. "Sapphires?"

"Small ones. For a touch of sparkle."

She hugged him. "Thank you."

"Thank you for still being the sparkle of my life."

A Note from the Author

Dear Reader,

Thank you for choosing to read this book. I hope that it entertained as well as encouraged you in your own faith journey.

Sometimes a story idea presents itself like a whisper in my ear. "Psst. Pay attention. There is a story here." Such was the case with *Ransomed Dreams* as I stood on a cobblestone street in Copala, Mexico, falling in love with a time-forgotten village. When I spotted an adobe house for sale, I was truly smitten. What sort of American would move here? To want to live so far off the map, she would have to be carrying a heavy burden indeed. She would most likely have lost something dear and desperately want to hide away and nurse her wounds.

Although the characters (and some of the towns) in this story are fictitious, my goal was for the characters to mirror reality. Sheridan and Eliot experienced an event that instantaneously split their lives into a "before" and "after." It forced them onto a path of lost dreams, a side road of pain they would never have chosen to travel. Ultimately, they recognized God's healing touch and the ways in which He was continually speaking love, forgiveness, and hope into their hearts.

May our hearts always be open to such mercy.

Peace be with you.
Sally

E-mail: sallyjohnbook@aol.com
Web site: www.sally-john.com

Discussion Questions

LIFE SOMETIMES THROWS us for a loop. People who love us hurt us. Illness wreaks havoc. Disaster—natural or otherwise—strikes. As when we must follow a detour off a highway, we are forced onto a side road of life, one we had not planned on taking.

1. The shooting changes everything for Sheridan and Eliot. What are some of the short-term effects on them? long-term effects? physically, emotionally, spiritually?
2. Have you ever experienced an event that upset your life in a profound way? What happened? What was your response to it? How did it impact relationships?
3. Discuss the relationship between Sheridan and Calissa. If you have siblings, how is your relationship with them similar to these two? How is it different?
4. Putting aside for a moment the mutual attraction between Sheridan and Luke, how might his love for her reflect the way Christ loves us?
5. What do you think of Sheridan's response to the attraction between her and Luke? Luke's response? How should people react

when they find themselves drawn to individuals other than their spouses? What can a person do to prepare for or prevent this?

6. In what ways did you identify with Sheridan? What did you admire about her? What did you disagree with? You may not want to share details with others, but have you been faced with forgiving someone for deeply wounding you? How was your experience similar to or different from Sheridan's?

7. Forgiveness occurs in several relationships in this novel: husband-wife, siblings, daughter-father. What was its effect on the different characters and relationships?

8. Sheridan's detour brings her to the realization that her marriage is not what she signed up for. She must choose whether or not to stay in it. At first it is a decision of her will: she will stay because that is what she promised and what she believes God wants her to do. At what point does her decision become heartfelt as well as intellectual?

9. Many marriages reach a similar point at some time: "My marriage is not what I signed up for." How does this happen? Is it a normal "season" of marriage? What are some possible ways to get through such a season?

10. Sheridan wants what she has lost: her marriage as it once was and the work she found so meaningful. Discuss the balance between clinging to a dream and letting it go and trusting God with it. Have you faced a similar situation at some point in your life? How can we tell if our dreams have become more important to us than the God who inspired them?

About the Author

When the going gets tough—or weird or wonderful—the daydreamer gets going on a new story. Sally John has been tweaking life's moments into fiction since she read her first Trixie Belden mystery as a child.

Now an author of more than fifteen novels, Sally writes stories that reflect contemporary life. Her passion is to create a family, turn their world inside out, and then portray how their relationships change with each other and with God. Her goal is to offer hope to readers in their own relational and faith journeys.

Sally grew up in Moline, Illinois, graduated from Illinois State University, married Tim in 1973, and taught in middle schools. She is a mother, mother-in-law, and grandmother. A three-time finalist for the Christy Award, she also teaches writing workshops. Her books include the Safe Harbor series (coauthored with Gary Smalley), The Other Way Home series, The Beach House series, and In a Heartbeat series. Many of her stories are set in her favorite places of San Diego, Chicago, and small-town Illinois.

She and her husband currently live in Southern California. Visit her Web site at www.sally-john.com.

ALSO BY SALLY JOHN:

- **The Other Way Home series**
  - *A Journey by Chance*
  - *After All These Years*
  - *Just to See You Smile*
  - *The Winding Road Home*

- **In a Heartbeat series**
  - *In a Heartbeat*
  - *Flash Point*
  - *Moment of Truth*

- **The Beach House series**
  - *The Beach House*
  - *Castles in the Sand*

- **Safe Harbor series (coauthored with Gary Smalley)**
  - *A Time to Mend*
  - *A Time to Gather*
  - *A Time to Surrender*

www.sally-john.com

CP0388